PRAISE FO..
DAUGHTERS OF THE DRAGON

"William Andrews has taken a nearly-buried historical fact and used it to create a masterpiece of fictional encounters cemented by a strong central character in Jae-hee . . . Readers who look for authentic historical meaning, strong protagonists, believable and involving dialogue, and a gripping saga will find *Daughters of the Dragon* just the ticket. Anticipate brutal scenes, revelations, and struggles for survival and post-traumatic stress that follow the realistic paths of life in a powerful story of dignity, atrocities, and roads to recovery . . . It's a shame this story hasn't been fully explored before. It's a revelation that's long needed exposure, and it's outstanding that Andrews has seen fit to research and bring it to public attention now, in a format accessible to more than just history buffs and scholars."

—D. Donovan, Midwest Book Review

"*Daughters of the Dragon* is an inspirational and insightful tale of a former sex slave (euphemistically known as a "comfort woman")—her life, loss, survival, and triumph. Author William Andrews weaves a narrative that honors the 200,000 sex slaves of the Japanese Imperial Army in WWII, and brings to light this historical, systematic atrocity. As the author of House Resolution 121, which called on the government of Japan to acknowledge and apologize for its systematic enslavement of young women throughout Asia and the Pacific, and as a lifelong educator, I firmly believe these atrocities must be taught and preserved accurately and faithfully, so that such crimes never repeat. For the memory and souls of the thousands of young women whose youth and dignities were stripped away, may they find peace in knowing their story lives on in each of us."

—US Representative Mike Honda

DAUGHTERS
OF THE
DRAGON

ALSO BY WILLIAM ANDREWS

The Essential Truth

The Dirty Truth

DAUGHTERS

OF THE

DRAGON

A COMFORT WOMAN'S STORY

WILLIAM ANDREWS

LAKE UNION

PUBLISHING

Published by Lake Union Publishing, Seattle

www.apub.com

Amazon, the Amazon logo, and Lake Union Publishing are trademarks of Amazon.com, Inc., or its affiliates.

ISBN-13: 9781503936263
ISBN-10: 1503936260

Cover design by Suzanne Pfutzenreuter

Printed in the United States of America

For all the women forced to be comfort women

ONE

My first name is a palindrome. When Mother was alive and I was in one of my moods, she would say, "I see we have the backward Anna today. I hope the forward Anna will come back soon." I often wrote my name with the capital *A* at the end so when someone said I spelled it backward, I could say, "No, I didn't. It's a palindrome."

Since my name is the same backward as forward, I used to make fun of everyone else's backward name. Mother was Nasus and Dad was Htennek, even though everyone called him Ken. My dog was Ydnas, and we were the Noslrac family. I always had to write the names backward so I could pronounce them, but Dad could do them in his head. It was truly amazing. You could give him any name and he'd immediately say it backward. Even long ones like Aunt Elizabeth. "Thebazile Tnua," he'd say without missing a beat.

I was born in Korea twenty years ago and adopted by Htennek and Nasus when I was five months old. All I've ever known is life with my adoptive parents. But people constantly reminded me that I wasn't their birth child. We didn't look alike, of course—I didn't have Mother's wavy auburn hair or Dad's Nordic eyes. We had different personalities, too. Mother was fiery and impulsive, Dad was a stoic Scandinavian, and I was somewhere in between.

Sometimes people would look at me with my Caucasian parents and ask dumb questions or say stupid things. It would upset my mother royally. Most times, she'd just ignore them and complain later about "insensitive, stupid people." But once, when a waiter said I was "gourmet Asian takeout," she went postal on him right there in the restaurant. She actually called him insensitive and stupid to his face. I was so embarrassed. I mean, he didn't mean anything by it, although it really was a lame thing for him to say.

I didn't think much about the fact that I was adopted while I was growing up, and I didn't think much about my birth mother, either. Most people think adopted kids like me have this need to connect with our biological roots so we can discover who we really are. They think being "takeout" is totally different than being "homemade." But we're not different at all. I mean, my birth parents were just my gene donors. My *real* parents were the ones who raised me, the ones who were there when I needed them, the ones who actually *wanted* me. And why should I have cared about my birth mother anyway? I had this perfect life—awesome parents, my studies at Northwestern, Chad Jenkins and his adorable smile. My Korean birth mother was a million miles away, probably raising the kids she'd decided to keep. I'm sorry, I didn't care.

But everything changed when Mother died. Dad was devastated. I had to drop out of Northwestern and move back home. Dad said I should stay in school, but I really didn't see the point. My heart wasn't in it. I was going to be a senior and still didn't know what I wanted to major in. And Mother's death shook me. For the first time in my life, I was lost and afraid of becoming like so many other kids I knew—young adults with dead-end jobs forced to live in their parents' basements. You know, what the rich kids at Northwestern called "losers."

Back home, everything was so different. It was sad, of course, for Dad and me, but it was more than that. It was tragic, if you know what I mean. Every day Dad sat alone in the living room with the drapes closed and the lights off. When I got home from the grocery store or a jog, he'd ask how I was doing from inside his darkness. I'd lean against the kitchen door and we'd exchange some small talk. Then he'd make dinner wearing the grilling apron Mom gave him for Christmas one year. I'd head upstairs past my parents' bedroom, and sometimes I'd expect to see Mother inside doing her hair or getting dressed for a night out. There were times when I thought I could smell her perfume. It was all so weird, and I realized that someday I'd have to come to grips with the fact that I didn't have a mother anymore.

Except that I did—a million miles away. In Korea, raising the kids she'd decided to keep.

Adopted kids call our gene donors "birth parents" instead of "natural parents" or, God forbid, "real parents" so we don't imply that our adoptive parents are somehow unnatural or not real. Growing up, people told me that my birth mother made the adoption decision because she loved me. That's why we say "adoption decision" rather than "give up for adoption." The former supports the love theory—a thoughtful decision to do what's best for the baby.

Who knows? It might be true. But honestly, I don't know for sure. And that's why I decided to come to Korea and meet my birth mother.

So here I am, sitting in the lobby of this orphanage in the middle of Seoul waiting to meet her. It's the place they brought me when I was three days old. It's in a seedy section of Seoul, which they somehow managed to avoid on the first ten days of our tour. The building is crumbling and sad, and the paint on the walls is something between gray and green. Every little sound echoes. The furniture is tattered and unmatched, and the entire place smells musty. The fifteen other American families with Korean adoptees on our tour finished meeting with their birth families an hour ago, and now they want out of this depressing place. I'm the only one who hasn't had my meeting, so they all have to sit around and wait for me.

There are the Smiths with their sugar-addicted ten-year-old twins, Elsa and Elizabeth, who are literally running in circles in the hallway.

There's Mrs. Dahl sitting on a bench with her thirty-year-old Korean-born daughter. She has a full-size box of Kleenex in her purse because she cries at every little thing. There's Max Klein, who, as always, is playing some inane game on his phone. Then there's Katherine Austin sitting in a straight-backed chair with her knees properly together and her hands folded in her lap. She's my age and is as taut as a piano string. Standing behind her, her poor parents don't have a clue how to reach her. Everyone keeps shooting looks at me as if it's my fault they have to stay. Sorry, people, but I don't know what's taking so long, either. I want to get on with it way more than you do.

In my lap is this photo album I made for my birth mother. I spent a ton of time on it. It's the story of my life—from when I arrived from Korea in front of dozens of my family and friends at gate 33 of the red concourse of the Minneapolis-Saint Paul airport, to the photo of me and Mother together in the hospital the day before she died. She looks horrible in it, but I had to include it. I mean, it's the last picture I took of her. I pasted each photo into the album just so and added captions in my very best handwriting.

I must say, it's perfect. It has to be. I mean, think about it. If my birth mother really made the adoption decision out of love, then I want her to see that I turned out all right and she did the right thing. On the other hand, if she gave me up because I was just some inconvenience, well then, I want her to see that she made a huge mistake. After all, I'm going to graduate from college someday and maybe even go on to grad school. I want her to believe that her little inconvenience grew up and is having an awesome life without her. Okay, so maybe I'm exaggerating, but it'd be true if I could get my act together. Of course, she doesn't need to know that.

My stomach is churning sitting here waiting. I absolutely hate that the other families are staring at me. Dad says we should ask someone why it's taking so long, but before we can, an American social worker comes and tells us to follow her. From the pinched smile on her face,

I can tell this isn't going to be good. I take my photo album, and we follow her into a small meeting room with bad lighting. We sit at a rickety table.

The social worker shakes her head. She isn't smiling anymore. "Anna," she says, "I'm sorry to have to tell you this. You can't meet your birth mother. You see, she died."

I stare at her for what seems like forever. I'm not sure I heard her right. In fact, I'm not entirely sure if any of this is actually happening to me. "She's dead?" I say.

The social worker nods. "I'm afraid so. I'm sorry."

After I take a few seconds to process this tidbit, I ask how my birth mother died. The social worker, a large woman with straight gray hair, tells me she died twenty years ago, in labor—with me. *With me.* Perfect. I ask about my birth father.

The social worker opens a manila folder. She thumbs through papers and stops at a page. She tells me my birth mother wasn't married when I was born and that they don't know who my birth father is. I ask if I have any birth brothers or sisters. She says they don't know. "Given the circumstances of your adoption," she says, "it would be impossible to find out."

Wonderful. The churning in my stomach turns into a knot. I feel like I did when my mother died, like this thing was somehow my fault, but I didn't have a clue why. I want to scream at these people for not knowing about my birth mother. Instead, I look down at my photo album and run a finger along the words "My Life" written in my very best handwriting.

"How could this happen?" Dad asks, trying to help. "Why weren't we told? Before we came here?"

"Mr. Carlson, they're poorly funded here," the social worker says. "They're understaffed, and they can't always check the facts."

"Anna's been looking forward to this meeting for months," Dad says.

The social worker does something between a nod and a shake of her head. "I know. We just found out. I'm so sorry."

Dad looks at me. "Maybe I should talk to the orphanage director."

I just want out of here before this train wreck gets any worse. "Let's just go," I say. I grab my photo album and leave.

I walk into the orphanage lobby and head for the exit. When they see me, the Smith twins stop running around to stare. Mrs. Dahl grabs a handful of Kleenex from her purse. Max looks up from his game, and Katherine turns her head and studies me. Everyone wants to know what happened to me, why they postponed my meeting for so long, and why it lasted only a few minutes. I don't look at them. It's none of their business. I clutch my photo album to my chest and realize it shows that I didn't get to meet my birth mother. I see a wastebasket in a corner and go for it. But when I get there, I can't throw it in. I spent so much time on it.

I walk out the front door. Seoul's heat and humidity closes in on me. The bright haze hurts my eyes. Off to the side, our tour bus is idling, and the diesel fumes invade my nose. I turn away and close my eyes. I can't believe this is happening. What a disaster. I feel so incredibly stupid for coming here.

After a few minutes, I turn toward the bus. There, standing in front of me, is an old woman with a thick braid of gray hair. She's pressing a package into my hand. She leans in close and whispers, "This is for you. Do not show it to anyone. It is important that you hear my story so you know what it means. There is an address inside. Come alone."

I look at the package, then back at the woman who's hurrying away. "Wait!" I shout. She doesn't stop and disappears inside the orphanage.

I look again at the package in my hand. It's a little larger than a billfold, wrapped in a faded brown cloth and tied with twine. As I pull on the string to open it, Dad comes out of the orphanage looking for me. Behind him, the other families are heading to the bus, doing a bad job of trying not to stare at me. Dad puts a hand on my shoulder and tries to reassure me with a smile. I slip the package in my purse, and we follow the other families onto the bus.

As we head back to our hotel, I can only think about my birth mother. I wanted to talk to her, make a connection, you know? I wanted to see what I'll look like in thirty years. Well, at least I got one of my questions answered. There was no adoption decision—not out of love and not for convenience, either. No. They put me up for adoption because I killed my birth mother. How nice.

I look out the window at Seoul. It's rush hour, and everyone's heading home. I wonder what it would've been like if my birth mother had lived. I'd be one of them—a homemade Korean instead of gourmet Asian takeout living in America. I'd speak their language, listen to their music, and think like a Korean.

Maybe I wouldn't be so cursed.

TWO

The bus enters the busy Myeong-dong district where our hotel is. Dad is leaning back against the headrest with his eyes closed. Poor guy. My little ordeal here was probably hard on him, too. Since Mother died, he's tried to be there for me. He thinks it's his duty to be both my father and mother. Every day he asks if I'm okay, and every day I say that I am. But who am I kidding? I mean, I was the one who pushed us to go on this trip so I could connect with my biological roots. I was the one who was so eager to meet my birth mother. That had to hurt him, but he never said a thing.

I remember the package the elderly woman gave me. *Don't show it to anyone,* she said. *You must hear my story,* she said. Just what I need, more drama. I reach inside my purse and take it out. I turn it over and open the cloth. Inside there's a piece of paper with an address in Seoul written in beautiful cursive handwriting. I pull back one more fold of cloth, and there is a comb with an inlay of a dragon.

It's the size of a woman's hand, made of dark green tortoiseshell, gently bowed, with long tines. In the handle, in tiny pieces of what looks like ivory, is a dragon. Solid gold curves along the spine. Its size and shape make it look delicate, but in my hand, it feels sturdy.

I wonder why the old woman wants me to have this. Whatever the reason, I can't cope with it now. Not after what happened today. But before I wrap it up, I take a closer look. The comb is amazing. It absolutely gleams in my hand. The dragon has two heads, with curled tongues and claws that seem to reach for me. I run a finger over the gold spine. It's smooth and cool, and I realize I've never held anything so valuable in my entire life. Suddenly I don't feel so wiped out.

I look around to see if anyone's watching me. They're all looking out the windows at the buildings and streets of Seoul or quietly talking to each other. Even the Smith twins have finally settled down. I quickly wrap the comb in the cloth and slip it back into my purse.

We get to the Sejong Hotel in the middle of Seoul's financial district. We all drag ourselves from the bus to the hotel. Inside the marble and glass lobby, our tour director, Dr. Kim, comes up to Dad and me. He asks if he can have a word with me alone. I just want to get back to our room and crash and cry a little. But Dr. Kim, a small, energetic man, has been just great on our trip. Maybe he knows something about my birth mother. I tell Dad I'll catch up with him and follow Dr. Kim to a corner of the lobby. He tells me he saw me looking at something on the bus. "Something valuable," he says. He wants to know what it is.

I tell him it's nothing, but that doesn't satisfy him. "Anna, if you were given something, we must know, we must know. The government requires that we record everything given to American children placed through our agency."

"It's just a comb, Dr. Kim," I say.

He stares at me as if I'm a child. "It's against the law, against the law for heirlooms to leave our country," he says firmly. "Anyway, if it's just a comb, you should be willing to show it to me."

It's a law? I don't need an even bigger mess than I already have, so I take out the package and show him the comb. He leans in, and his eyes grow wide behind his thick glasses.

"This is not nothing," he whispers. "I should take it and give it to the right people."

"The right people?"

He slowly shakes his head. "You cannot have this, Anna."

"Why not?" I ask.

He doesn't answer. Instead, he tells me again that I should give the comb to him. "It's important," he says. "You must do the right thing. Give it to me. I take care of it, I take care of it."

Standing there in the lobby of the Sejong Hotel, I almost give it to him. Then I remember the woman saying the comb means something. I think it might actually mean something to me, and based on Dr. Kim's reaction, I suddenly want to know what it is. I fold the cloth around the comb and put it back in my purse. I tell Dr. Kim that I don't want to break any laws but that I want to show it to my dad first. I manage a polite smile.

I walk through the lobby to the elevator and push the button. As the doors open, I turn to see if Dr. Kim is still there. He's following me. "Trust me, trust me, Anna," he says, looking straight at me. "You do not want that comb."

I step into the elevator and let the doors close.

◆ ◆ ◆

When I get to our room, small and modern with light-colored wood furniture, Dad's crashed out on his bed. He's on his back and has his hands folded across his stomach like a corpse. I toss my backpack and purse on the desk and look in the mirror over the dresser. An Asian woman stares back at me. She's the backward Anna, and I don't know her. She's pretty, I suppose. She has dark hair, smooth skin, and she's slender and straight. I want to know who she is, but I'm not getting any answers.

From the bed, Dad asks what Dr. Kim wanted. The woman in the mirror says that he wanted to see something someone gave her at the orphanage.

"Someone gave you something at the orphanage?" he asks.

"Yes. Outside, after our non-meeting meeting."

Dad raises his head off the pillow. "What is it?"

I turn from the mirror and show him the comb. He climbs off the bed for a closer look.

"Good lord," he says. "It's magnificent."

"The woman said I should go to this address to hear her story." I hand him the note.

He reads it and shakes his head. "I don't know about this, Anna. Seoul's a big city, and you don't know who the woman is. What did she look like?"

"She was older, but . . . I don't know. I didn't get a good look at her."

"What did Dr. Kim say?"

I take the note from him and wrap the comb in the cloth. "He said I shouldn't take it. He said I should give it to him so he can give it to the right people, whatever that means."

"Maybe you should."

"Yeah, I guess, but I want to find out about it first. I want to go to this address."

"When?" Dad asks. "We leave tomorrow."

"Not until seven o'clock at night."

"Yeah," Dad says, "but the bus to the airport leaves at four thirty. We're supposed to go to Itaewon during the day to shop. I have to pick up my new suit."

"And I wanted to buy that celadon pot I saw there," I say. "It doesn't matter, though. I want to do this instead."

He thinks it over for a second and then says, "Maybe I should go with you."

"The woman said I should come alone," I reply.

He blows out a sigh and slumps on the end of the bed. He looks defeated, the way he has since Mother died. I sit next to him. I promise him I'll be careful.

He nods. I give him a quick hug and go to the bathroom to get ready for dinner.

That night after we settle in our room, Dad is in his pajamas when he finally asks if I want to talk about my birth mother. Yeah, I do. I want to talk about a lot of things. I want to figure everything out and get on the right track again. But for some reason, I say I don't want to talk. Not now. He looks both hurt and relieved and drags himself to bed.

It breaks my heart to look at him. I thought this trip might help him, but it hasn't. He hasn't said more than a few dozen words since we came here. He doesn't study the tour books or embarrass me by asking endless questions of the guides like he always did when we traveled with Mother. I think being here reminds both of us of her. She would have loved it.

I lie on my bed staring at the ceiling and try to remember the highlights of our tour—the palaces, the museums, a disturbing trip to the demilitarized zone between North and South Korea. And today, the visit to the orphanage and the awful news that I killed my birth mother. I try to pull everything into a complete picture, but I can't. It's all too raw. So I crawl under the sheets and wonder what I'll find tomorrow at the address that came with the comb.

THREE

Weird dreams haunt me all night. Mother used to say that dreams are who you are when you're too tired to be yourself. When I was young, I tried to remember my dreams. But they were totally bizarre and left me afraid of who I really was. So today when I wake up, I push my dreams away. I'm still tired and realize it's one of those days when I'll need a supreme effort to cope. I pull the covers to my chin and wish I could stay in bed. Then I remember the comb with the two-headed dragon and my plan to go to the address that came with it. I force myself to get up.

Dr. Kim told us we'd leave for Itaewon at 9:30 a.m. Dad's already showered and mostly dressed. He's got his face in the mirror, shaving. I say good morning, and he grunts a greeting back at me. I hope he'll agree to help me. When he comes out of the bathroom, I tell him I want to go to the address to see about the comb. I ask him to tell Dr. Kim that I'm sick and have to skip going to Itaewon.

"Are you sure you want to do this?" he asks, pulling on his shirt. "Maybe you should give the comb to Dr. Kim like he said and come with me today."

"Dad, please," I say in a way to remind him that I'm not a child anymore.

He sighs and agrees to tell my fib. "Promise you'll be careful," he says.

I tell him not to worry and that I'll be here at the hotel when he gets back from Itaewon. He hands me two hundred dollars from his billfold and gives me a sad smile. He heads out the door.

◆ ◆ ◆

After Dad and the rest of the families leave, I sneak out of the hotel and hail one of Seoul's ubiquitous tiny white taxicabs. I give the driver the address that came with the comb. "You sure, lady?" he asks. From the *x*'s and *o*'s in his name on his cab license, I can tell he's Chinese. He's anorexic thin, and stringy hair hangs over his ears. I read the address to him again. "Okay," he says. "Thirty-five dolla' American. Or thirty-five thousand Korean won."

The fare seems high, but I really don't care, so I say okay. We pull onto the main boulevard and head south toward the Han River. The sky has a brown haze, and it looks like it'll be another sweltering day. We drive through Seoul's financial district and past big department stores like Kosney and Hyundai and dozens of high-end boutiques like Bulgari, Gucci, and Jimmy Choo. There are hundreds of smaller shops with neon signs in Hangul, English, Japanese, Chinese, and a few languages I don't even recognize. Trendy cafés compete with high-end restaurants. Street vendors push their merchandise at passersby. People fill the sidewalks, and cars cram the streets. We drive across the Han River over the Mapo Bridge. In every direction, city skyscrapers stand like soldiers at attention.

We cross another bridge and turn a corner into yet another shopping area. I can tell the driver is taking the long way, probably to justify his bogus fare. Okay, whatever. I'm feeling better and actually enjoying his little tour. I push myself to the edge of the seat and roll down the window. Smells fill the taxi—street food, automobile exhaust, and big city grit. There are neon lights, and signs in Hangul, and people dressed in all different styles, and tiny cars, and taxis with blue tops, and noisy trucks with more Hangul lettering on the side. Everywhere, apartment buildings tower over the city. Car horns honk, truck engines roar, street vendors shout, and energy fills the air.

So this is Korea. Now that I'm finally free from the tour, I'm seeing what it's truly all about. It isn't just the palaces, museums, and tourist traps we've seen on our trip. It's here, on these streets. This is where I was born. I share DNA with these people. I believe my answers are here.

And now I have this comb. It has to be something important. I haven't had a chance to study it carefully, so I take the package from my purse and open it. I hold the comb close and look for something I might've missed. The almost black tortoiseshell is a perfect match to the white ivory of the two-headed dragon. The elegant tines and gentle bow of it are amazing. The gold spine gives the comb a perfect balance. I wonder how an elderly woman got hold of such a magnificent thing. I wonder why she thinks I should have it.

"What you got there?"

I snap my head up. We're at a stoplight. My driver has an arm over his seat, and he's pointing at the comb.

"Just a . . . ah . . . gift," I say.

"A gift?" he asks. "You kidding? It real deal! Who you give it to?"

"No, no. It was given to me." I quickly fold the cloth around the comb and shove it inside my pocket.

The driver grins, revealing bad teeth. "You lucky! Very, very lucky. It real deal. Real deal!"

I sit back and ask how much farther we have to go. He tells me we're almost there and turns back to his steering wheel. The light changes, and we drive on.

Soon the neighborhoods become dirty, and the colors change from bright to drab. We're in what looks like Seoul's version of a ghetto. There are only a few people on the street, and there's something I haven't seen in Korea before, litter. I roll up my window and slouch in my seat. We turn down a narrow street lined with slummy apartment buildings. We pull to the curb. The driver tells me we're at my address.

We've stopped in front of a nasty, eight-story building. Rusty air conditioners hang from half the windows. From an open one, a woman is staring vacantly at the street below. An old man shuffles along the walkway. Above a crumbling entry are letters in Hangul and the number 315. I ask the driver if he's got the right address. He assures me he does. "You want I wait?" he asks.

I scan the filthy street and realize that if my driver doesn't wait, I'll have to walk for blocks in this creepy neighborhood to find another cab. "Yeah, that's a good idea," I say.

"I wait," he says, turning off the engine. "Fifteen dolla' American every fifteen minute. First, you pay thirty-five for here."

I take thirty-five dollars from my purse and hand them to him. I climb out of the cab and look at the building. I tell him I don't know how long I'll be. He tells me he'll wait as long as I need. "Fifteen dolla' every fifteen minute," he repeats.

I walk to the entrance. There are rows of buttons on an antique intercom system that's practically falling off the wall. I take the note from my pocket and read the apartment number, 627. I scan the buttons until I see it. I don't press it.

This doesn't feel right at all. It's way too intense. And Dad was right—it isn't safe. I turn to go back to the cab. The driver is watching me. *Real deal,* he said. I put my hand in my pocket and run my finger over the comb. I remember how the dragon almost seemed real. I turn back to the intercom and take a deep breath. I push the button. Several seconds later, a woman's voice comes on the speaker and says something in Korean.

I say my name. There's an uncomfortable pause, and I wonder if I have the right address. Then the voice says in perfect English, "Welcome. I am so glad you came." She tells me to go through the security door and take the elevator to the sixth floor. She says her apartment is three doors on the left.

The security door buzzes, and I walk through. It's gross inside. The lights are harsh and overexpose the stained carpeting and smeared walls. There's a pay phone alcove in the hall with a bare wire where a phone once was. I step inside the elevator and push the button for the sixth floor. The elevator jerks up, and a few seconds later, it jerks again to a stop. I get off, walk down a dark hallway, and find apartment 627. I swallow hard and knock.

The door opens, and the old woman greets me.

FOUR

She's wearing dark blue slacks frayed at the hem and a thin cotton sweater over a clean white blouse. Her thick gray hair falls down her back. Her eyes are intense but kind. Her skin is amazing. The only flaws I see are a small scar on her upper lip and another one over her eye.

"Good morning, ma'am," I say with a half bow.

She examines me with an odd smile. She steps aside and says, "You may come in."

I remember to take off my shoes, then step inside a small, clean apartment not much bigger than our den back home. I smell the sweet, spicy scent of kimchi. There's a low dresser, a rust-stained sink, a ceramic double-burner stove, and a miniature refrigerator. On a cheap low table below the apartment's only window are two photographs in a plain wooden frame. A purple flower blossom in a glass bowl rests on the windowsill.

She points at the table and tells me to sit. Her posture is perfect, like I've seen in upper-class Korean women on our tour. She doesn't take her eyes off me, and I feel that she's sizing me up. I wish I'd spent more time on my hair and worn a dress instead of jeans.

"You must have been disappointed you couldn't meet your birth mother," she says. Her English is flawless. She has no accent at all.

"Yes." I nod. "How did you know about that?"

"I volunteer at the orphanage," she says. "I have for twenty years now."

I do the math in my head. It was a little over twenty years ago that I was brought to the orphanage. Okay, this is starting to feel creepy. I'm already regretting coming here. Maybe I can make this quick. I tell her I don't think I should have the comb and that I came to return it.

"You might change your mind when you hear my story," she says. She continues to stare at me. I fidget in my chair. I realize I don't know her name. I ask her what it is.

"My name is Hong Jae-hee. And I am your maternal grandmother."

"Seriously?" I gasp. I take a long look at her, and here's the thing. When a birth child looks into her parents' faces, she sees herself. She has her mother's eyes or her father's chin. But for twenty years, I never had that connection to anyone. Until now. Even though she's sixty years older than me, the resemblance is clear. She's petite like me and has my high cheekbones. I'm thrilled that for the first time in my life, I see myself in someone else. Suddenly I'm not so anxious to leave.

I try to remember the right way to behave toward a Korean grandparent. "I'm glad to meet you, ma'am," I say with my eyes low like I remember being taught during our tour orientation. "What would be the right way to address you?"

"Since we have just met," she says, "perhaps you will feel most comfortable calling me Mrs. Hong."

"Yes, of course, Mrs. Hong," I say.

"I understand your adoptive mother died last year."

The image of my dying mother comes rushing in, and I feel guilty for the selfish joy I had just seconds earlier at meeting someone from my birth family. I look at my hands and nod.

"It is difficult to lose loved ones. Isn't it?" she says.

"She loved me," I reply. "And I loved her, too. It was an awful loss. I guess that's why I came here, to Korea, to meet my birth mother.

They told me she died giving birth to me. What happened? What was she like? Do I have any brothers and sisters? Who is my birth father?"

Mrs. Hong turns to the window. She keeps her chin high, but her eyes are soft. "You have many questions, Ja-young."

"Ja-young? Oh, that's my birth name. My parents named me Anna."

"Very well, Anna. You say you have the comb. You can give it to me now."

I take the package containing the comb from my pocket and set it on the table. She stares at the lump of cloth but doesn't reach for it. She waits a minute, then two. Finally she carefully unfolds the cloth. When she sees the comb, she brings her other hand to her mouth, and the lines around her eyes deepen. I think she might cry. "I don't take it out much anymore," she says. "It brings back too many painful memories."

I push myself to the front of my chair. "Excuse me for asking, Mrs. Hong, but if you don't want it, why don't you just sell it? You could probably get a lot for it and move to somewhere . . . you know, more appropriate."

"I was tempted many times," she says without looking up. "But I could not. It is too important to sell, Ja-young . . . Anna. And you must have it."

"But Dr. Kim—he's our tour director—he said I shouldn't take it. He said there's a law or something against heirlooms leaving the country."

Her eyes snap to me. "Did you show this to him?"

"I—I had to," I say. "He saw I had it."

"What did he say? Tell me exactly."

"He said I should give it to him so he could give it to the right people."

Mrs. Hong clucks. "That is a problem. He might know what it is." She wraps the comb in the cloth and sets it on the table.

"Anna," she says, "I asked you to come here because I want you to do two things. First, you must hear my story and that of the comb with the two-headed dragon. You will know what the second thing is after you have heard my story."

"Of course," I say. "I want to hear your story, but I don't want to get in trouble."

"Listen to my story, and you will know what is right."

I let out a sigh. I wonder what I've gotten myself into. But why not stay? She's my birth grandmother, after all, and the tour won't be back from Itaewon until midafternoon. Maybe she has some answers for me. And what trouble could I possibly get into? I mean, if it gets too intense, I could just walk away and leave the comb with her. Right?

Outside, a breeze kicks up dirt on the street. The cab. I forgot about the cab. *Fifteen dolla' American every fifteen minute.* I grab my purse and tell Mrs. Hong I have a cab outside and should let it go. I have to give him a time to come back. "How long will your story take?" I ask.

"It's a long story," she says, picking up the photographs from the table. "A very long story."

I say I'll tell the cabbie to come back at three o'clock. I wait for her to say okay, but she just stares at her photos and says nothing. I tell her I'll be right back.

I go to the door, pull on my shoes, and run out to the cab. The driver rolls down the window when I get there.

He tells me he's been waiting twenty minutes and that I owe him thirty dollars. "Fifteen dolla' American every fifteen minute," he says.

I take thirty dollars from my purse and give them to him. I tell him I need to stay and ask if he can come back to pick me up. He says okay and asks for a time.

"Three o'clock," I answer.

"Okay, three o'clock," he says. "If I wait, fifteen dolla' Amer—"

"Yeah, yeah. I know," I say. "Fifteen dolla' American every fifteen minute." The driver flashes his bad teeth in an amused grin and drives off.

Mrs. Hong's apartment door is open when I get back. She is standing next to the table framed by the light from the window. She has changed her blouse and slacks for a yellow hanbok made from what looks like silk. It has long, loose sleeves, and the flowing skirt ends a few inches above the floor. She has braided her hair and pinned it up with an ornate binyeo. She invites me in. "Granddaughter, *unlinahyi*. Are you ready to hear my story?"

I nod and say yes. I feel like I'm in a dream.

"Come," she says. "Sit, listen, and learn."

I sit at the low table again. She moves the flower blossom and the photographs to the center of the table, next to the package containing the comb. She sits straight with her hands in her lap. She takes a long breath and starts in a voice clear and strong.

"A young soldier on a rusty motorcycle delivered the orders from the Japanese military command in Sinuiju . . ."

FIVE

September 1943. North P'yŏngan Province, Northern Korea

A young soldier on a rusty motorcycle delivered the orders from the Japanese military command in Sinuiju. I was the first to see him motoring up the hill toward our house. The motorcycle trailed a plume of dust, like a long snake's tail that curled and twisted all the way across the sea back to Japan. As the snake came near, I wanted to run outside and throw a rock at it. I wished I was strong like a boy or older—I was only fourteen—so I could throw a big rock and kill it once and for all.

I had seen the snake before. The soldier had come the previous fall to deliver orders for my father. The orders said Father was to report the next day to the military headquarters in Sinuiju so he could work in Pyongyang in the steel mill there. The next morning, the sun had not yet climbed over the aspen trees and the air was cold when Father said good-bye to me, my older sister Soo-hee, and our mother. I think Mother cried a little as Father walked past our persimmon tree with his head high and his orders in his pocket.

I loved my *appa*. He let me get away with things my mother never would. But after that day, I never saw him again.

As the soldier came near, I quickly gathered the nappa cabbage I had been washing. I wrapped it in a large cloth and stuffed it under the sink. I ran to the back door.

"Soo-hee!" I said to my sister, who was digging up clay onggis of rice and vegetables we had hidden behind our house. "The soldier on the motorcycle is coming!"

Soo-hee stood and looked down the road. When she saw him, she gave me a look that told me we had to be careful. "Stall him," she said. She dropped to the ground and quickly pushed the onggis back into their holes.

I ran inside the house and watched the snake from the kitchen window. I hoped the soldier would drive past to another house up the road, but he stopped and leaned his motorcycle against our persimmon tree. The afternoon breeze caught the tail of the snake and played with it, stretching it thin until it disappeared, leaving only the soldier standing next to his motorcycle. He took off his gloves and slapped them across his legs, sending puffs of dust into the air. He reached into his leather satchel and pulled out a yellow envelope. He came up to the front of our house.

"Hello!" he called out in Japanese. "I have orders from military command. Come out! Come out!"

I pushed aside the gray tarp where our beautiful carved oak door had once hung. I folded my arms across my chest. "Go away," I said in Japanese.

The soldier's uniform was brown with dust. His face was brown, too, except for two clean circles around his eyes where his goggles had been. His goggles hung around his neck and were as dirty as his uniform. I thought he looked silly standing there covered with dirt and raccoon dog eyes. But he must not have felt silly, because he looked at me in a most authoritative way. "Is that any way to treat me?" he asked. "I've come all this way to deliver your orders." He held out the envelope. "Here, take them."

"You should throw them into the Yalu River instead of bothering us with them," I said, not moving an inch. "Why do we always have to do what you say?"

The soldier grinned, turning his raccoon dog eyes into narrow slits. He leaned against our house. "Because you are Japanese subjects. If you don't follow our orders, you will be shot."

"It would be better to be shot," I said.

The soldier's grin dropped to a scowl, and he didn't look silly anymore. "Soon you will learn how to serve Japan."

I was about to tell him how I felt about serving Japan when Soo-hee came from the back, wiping her hands on her dress. "Yes? What is it?" she asked in Korean. She couldn't speak Japanese like I could.

"*Konnichiwa,*" the soldier said. "I see you haven't learned to speak Japanese yet," he added, switching to Korean. "Perhaps you should take lessons from your disrespectful little sister."

Soo-hee bowed her head. "I'm sorry for my sister. She is young."

"She is not so young," the soldier replied, eyeing me.

He straightened and lifted his chin high the way the Japanese do. "Your landlord is not pleased with the harvest this year," he said. "You are in debt to him now." He held out the envelope. "These orders are for you and your sister. They are what you must do to repay him. Take them."

With a small bow, Soo-hee took the orders.

The soldier looked at me in a way that made me glad I hadn't told him what I thought about serving Japan. "You better take care of your little sister," he said to Soo-hee. "She could get you all in trouble." He gave a quick nod and then went to his motorcycle. He turned it around and started it with a kick. He drove away down the road, and the snake's tail rose high again behind him.

"What is it?" I asked. "What do the papers say?"

Soo-hee tucked the envelope inside her dress. "Don't worry about them, little sister," she said. "We must soak the vegetables soon or they won't be ready to make kimchi in the morning." She headed to the back of the house.

"But, *onni*, big sister, the soldier said they were orders for you and me. What do they say?"

"Hush, Jae-hee!" Soo-hee said, turning on her heel. "You must learn to do the right thing. Mother will read them tonight when she comes home from the factory. *Ummah* should see them first. Now go back to your chores."

Soo-hee always scolded me like Mother did, and I didn't like being told what to do. So I stomped inside the house and pulled the nappa cabbage from under the sink. As I prepared it for the kimchi, I worried about the papers tucked away in Soo-hee's dress. I guessed they were orders to work in a factory during the winter months. When our skinny Japanese landlord with the big ears had come to collect that year's crop, he had told us the Japanese needed more workers to support their war efforts. "We are winning glorious battles against the Americans!" he had said, climbing inside his old truck filled with the vegetables we had worked so hard to grow. "If you do what you're told, the filthy Americans will be pushed back across the ocean, never to trouble us again."

His truck started with a groan, and it took him several tries to find the right gear. As the truck wobbled down the road, he stuck his head out the window, and I thought his ears might flap in the wind. "Then you will be rewarded for the sacrifices you have made," he said. "You will be glad you are Japanese subjects!"

◆ ◆ ◆

By the time the sun had set over the valley in the west and the evening turned cold, Soo-hee and I had two pots of vegetables soaking in brine. Our farm was the biggest for miles around. When I was a young girl, I thought our big white house was a palace and the fields that surrounded it our palace gardens. Father was the emperor, Mother was the empress, and I was their beautiful princess. Our neighbors in their small, low houses with fields that were nothing more than patches were the peasants in our kingdom. And to be honest, that's often how I treated them.

But now, our beautiful house was dirty from years of neglect, and some of the roof tiles were falling off. Weeds had taken over the fields. And in spite of our hard work over the summer, we didn't have enough to feed us through the winter. In the months to come, Mother would have to beg for an extra sack of rice, just like our neighbors did every year.

It seemed like we had to wait forever for Mother to come home. Soo-hee and I sat at a low table and ate nappa cabbage and a handful of rice for our evening meal. Our house had an open main room with a kitchen, eating area, and family sitting area. It was here where Mother taught us how to read and write. In the back of the kitchen, a huge iron cookstove fed heat to the home's *ondol*, the under-floor heating system. The floor was wood plank, polished smooth from the feet of generations of my ancestors. In the kitchen were two wooden stools, and in the eating area was a low table. Sliding latticed doors separated a sleeping room from the main room. The sleeping room had grass goza mats on the floor and an ornate cabinet that Mother had refused to sell, even though Father said we should. I was glad she hadn't.

When we finished eating, Soo-hee set some rice and vegetables on the table for Mother. Soon she would be walking up the road with the other women from the uniform factory where she had worked every day since the harvest. Mother was very smart—too smart to work in a uniform factory. She loved to read. Our house had many books that she and Appa were very proud of. We had books in Chinese and Japanese as well as a few in Hangul, even though the Japanese banned them. We had the great novels, the teachings of Confucius, Chinese poetry. Even western literature like Shakespeare, Tolstoy, and Dickens translated into Hangul, Chinese, or Japanese.

My favorite was Dickens. I would sit in our living area after fin-
ishing a book and close my eyes to try to picture the eccentric Miss
Havisham and the devious Compeyson from *Great Expectations*, or the
cobblestone streets of London and Fagin and the Artful Dodger from
Oliver Twist. It was wonderful. After a long day of work in the fields, the
four of us would read until we couldn't keep our eyes open anymore. It
was through these books that I learned to speak Japanese and Chinese
so well.

When I was young, the provincial government insisted that all
Koreans speak Japanese. I didn't like Japanese—it sounded like they
were angry when they talked, and maybe they were. I didn't want to
sound like that, and I didn't want to be told what to do, so I spoke
Korean. Mother insisted we speak Japanese when they were around, but
Soo-hee wasn't good with languages like I was, and that was a problem.

Soo-hee was born in the year of the rabbit, but she was not lovely
like others with the rabbit sign. She was plain and awkward, as if somehow the elegant features of Father and Mother had cancelled each other
out. She was quiet and gentle, except, of course, when she was scolding
me. I believed that Mother liked her best, and just the same, I believed
Father liked me best, although I could tell he loved Soo-hee very much.

Soo-hee wasn't clever, either. Sometimes she didn't understand a
joke and would sit there with a confused look on her face while everyone else laughed. Mother and Father had to help her more than me
with her reading and writing. And they told me I had to help her with
Japanese.

So to pass time, Soo-hee and I sat on the great room floor, and I
tried to help her learn Japanese. "What is the word for 'sheep'?" I asked.

Soo-hee thought for a while and then shook her head.

I snorted. "Why is it so hard for you to learn these? *Hitsuji* is the
word for sheep. What about 'tree'?"

"I know that one," Soo-hee answered. "It's *moku*."

"Yes!" I said. "See? It's easy! You look for patterns, things you already know that you can connect the words to. And to pronounce them right, you pretend you're Japanese. It's like acting."

"Do you mean like this?" Soo-hee stood and puffed out her chest. "You must speak Japanese!" she said in Korean.

That made me giggle, and I stood, too. "Yes, like that!" I said. "But do it in Japanese." I puffed out my chest as Soo-hee had done. "You are now Japanese subjects!" I said in Japanese, wagging my finger. "You must learn to obey!"

Both of us laughed, careful to cover our mouths. But our laughing died quickly, and Soo-hee turned melancholy. "You will have to speak Japanese for me, little sister," she said. "I can understand most of what they say, but I can't bring up the words when I have to."

"Why do I have to do it?" I said. "Why can I learn it and you can't? The white crane must have left you at the door. You're not my real sister."

Soo-hee smiled at me, but it was an embarrassed smile. I had hurt my sister's *kibun*—her feelings and honor. I quickly said, "I'm sorry, Onni."

"Jae-hee," Soo-hee said gently, "you are smart like Mother and Father. You are luckier than me, and prettier, too. And you were born in the year of the dragon. You must be careful with these things you have been given."

She was right. I wasn't always careful with what I said out loud. My words often got me in trouble with Mother and sometimes even with Father. "I'm just mad that we always have to do what they say," I said.

Soo-hee put her arm around me. "Don't be stubborn, little sister. We have to be careful with the Japanese."

"I hate them," I said.

A full moon was rising over the aspen trees when Mother trudged up the road. Grime smeared her face, and she looked like what I imagined a Dickens character looked like after a long day of work in a London factory. Soo-hee and I pulled aside the tarpaulin and ran to greet her. Our mother—her name was Suh Bo-sun—was dressed in her old wool coat and faded purple scarf. She smiled when she saw us. "My babies, *ye deulah*," she said. "How are my babies today?" Mother always called us "her babies."

"*Ummah! Ummah!*" I blurted out. "The soldier came on his motorcycle today with orders. He said they are for Soo-hee and me."

"Jae-hee!" Soo-hee scolded. "We must first show our mother respect!"

I sighed, but bowed to our mother with Soo-hee. Then Mother led us inside the house. "Orders?" she said. "What do they say?"

"Soo-hee said we couldn't look at them until you got home," I said. "Can we look at them now?"

"Little sister, you must learn to hold your tongue!" Soo-hee scolded. "Mother is hungry. Let her eat."

Mother slowly removed her scarf and sat at the table without taking off her coat. Soo-hee placed the rice and vegetables we had made in front of her.

"Let me see the orders, Soo-hee," Mother said, ignoring the food.

"Mother," Soo-hee said, "you should eat first. We can read them later."

"Daughter!" Mother scolded. Then, more gently, she said, "Let me see the orders."

Soo-hee bowed. She was always more respectful than I was. She reached inside her dress and pulled out the yellow envelope. She handed it to Mother.

Mother read the orders to herself, and her shoulders sagged. She gave the orders to me. "Here," she said, "you read Japanese, too. Make sure we understand them correctly."

The orders were signed by the same official who had signed Father's orders a year earlier. As I read them, I said aloud, "We are to report to the Japanese military headquarters in Sinuiju tomorrow, where we will be sent to work in a boot factory. We will live in a dormitory. They will subtract rent and the cost of the meals from our wages. Anything left over will go to our landlord."

I pushed the papers back at Mother. "I am not going. They can't make me."

Mother stared at the orders in her hand. "You must go," she said, shaking her head. "We don't have enough food for the winter. And you must always do what the Japanese say."

"But how will we plant the crops in the spring?" I asked. Mother could not possibly plant them by herself.

Mother didn't answer. After a while, Soo-hee said, "Hush, Jae-hee. You ask too many questions."

Eventually Mother folded the orders into the envelope and laid it on the table. "Go, girls. Prepare for bed," she said gently. "Prepare for bed and come back to me. Tonight I will comb your hair with the comb with the two-headed dragon."

SIX

Soo-hee and I went outside to the well to wash. I was anxious to see the comb with the two-headed dragon, so I hurried through the task. Soo-hee glared at me sideways from the basin. "Take care to wash especially well tonight, little sister," she said.

Normally I would have said that I was clean enough, but I could tell this wasn't a time I should argue. So I dipped my washrag into the water again and rubbed soap into it until bubbles came up. I brought it to my face and scrubbed, careful not to miss any part of my head. Then I scrubbed my neck, shoulders, arms, legs, and feet, and every inch of my torso. I pumped clean water from the well and thoroughly rinsed myself with it. When I was finally done, Soo-hee nodded her approval.

We went into the house to change for bed. As we walked through the kitchen, Mother was building a fire in the iron stove. That surprised me. We only burned wood on the coldest days of winter. Mother had washed the factory grime from her face and had changed into her silk hanbok that she only wore on special occasions before the Japanese outlawed them. The top part, the *jeogori*, covered her shoulders and arms. It was ebony except for a narrow white collar and wide white cuffs that covered her hands. The long skirt, the *chima*, was pure white with gentle mountain scenes hand-painted above the hem. Whenever I saw Mother in her hanbok with her gentle features and round face, I thought she must be the most beautiful woman in the world.

As I looked at her kneeling on our kitchen floor, I thought that now, too. She held her back straight and kept her eyes forward as she had before Father left home. When they were together, she was like the earth, and Father was like the sky. Together, they were the whole world to me. I looked up to my father the way you look at a hawk high above and wonder what it's like to fly. With a simple nod or a word of encouragement, he made me believe that I could fly, too. I would go out to our front yard, throw my arms wide, and pretend to soar like a hawk. Father would lean against the front door watching me and laugh.

It was Mother who, like the roots of an oak tree, kept me grounded. She lectured me that to soar as I pretended to required hard work and discipline, traits she said I had yet to acquire. But since the Japanese had taken my father away, there was no sky to balance Mother's earthly reprimands about the traits I was lacking. At times she tried to make me feel like Father did—I could tell she knew I missed him. But she was the earth, not the sky, and her encouragements always came out like a lecture.

I wondered why Mother wanted to comb our hair with the special comb that night. I thought probably she was going to instruct us on how to behave at the boot factory. I went to the sleeping room and pulled on my nightclothes. When I returned to the kitchen, the fire was high.

Next to Mother, on the table, was the comb with the two-headed dragon. I had only seen it a few times before. When I was young, Mother would comb our hair with it during the Korean New Year, before we paid our respects to our grandparents. Father was always away when she did, visiting a friend or helping the village men butcher a pig for the New Year's celebration.

I had always wondered where Mother had gotten the magnificent comb with the gold spine and the strange two-headed dragon. I asked her about it once when she was combing our hair with it. Soo-hee scolded me for asking too many questions, but I could tell she wanted to know, too. Mother had said we were too young to understand.

Then, when I was eight years old, Japanese soldiers came in one of their trucks and forced Father to sign papers giving our farm to the skinny landlord with the big ears. They told us we had to celebrate the New Year the Japanese way or they would punish us. Mother did not comb our hair with the special comb that year, and I never saw it again. I thought she had sold it along with our furniture to buy rice. But now there it was, on the table before me.

Mother told us to come and sit in front of her so she could comb our hair. Soo-hee was the eldest, so she got to go first. She knelt in front of Mother, facing the fire, while I sat close. As the fire danced on the wood in the open stove, Mother pulled up the sleeves of her hanbok and carefully combed Soo-hee's hair with the beautiful comb. Its gold spine gleamed in Mother's hand, and the dragon was white as new snow. Ummah worked slowly, carefully teasing out Soo-hee's tangles.

"You never told us where you got the comb, Ummah," I said as I watched her work on Soo-hee. "You said we were too young. Will you tell us now, please?"

Mother didn't answer, and I thought Soo-hee would scold me for asking questions again, but she didn't. Mother combed Soo-hee's hair until it was smooth and shiny. And then it was my turn. I knelt with my back toward Mother. The comb pressed against my scalp. The fire threw black shadows against the kitchen walls. Our house was pleasantly warm and smelled of burning aspen wood.

Then Mother began in a faraway voice. "My grandmother gave the comb to me after Soo-hee was born," she said. "Back then, our family owned the fields behind the house all the way to the tall trees. We raised pigs and cattle. We grew potatoes and nappa cabbage, and carrots, radishes, and onions. When I was a young girl, my father had to hire twenty men to bring in the harvest."

I remained perfectly still as Mother combed my hair and told her story. Soo-hee, her hair gleaming in the firelight, knelt off to my side facing Mother as the wood crackled.

"My grandparents had two sons," Mother continued. "Their youngest, my uncle, went to Manchuria to join the forces there that opposed the Japanese occupation of our country. The Japanese killed him, so my father was the only child, and I was his only daughter. My grandmother told me that is why she gave me the comb—because I was her only female descendant."

"Where did she get it, Ummah?" I asked. "Who gave it to your grandmother?"

"Hush, Jae-hee," Soo-hee said. "Let Ummah tell the story."

Mother continued. "It was given to her by her mother. Your great-great-grandmother is the one who had it made. She was an important woman who lived in Seoul. When the Japanese became powerful, your great-great-grandmother sent her children here. She gave them this land and sent people along to watch over them. She visited from Seoul when she could, and one day she gave her daughter this comb. Her daughter was your great-grandmother—my grandmother—who gave me the comb."

"Our great-great-grandmother had it made?" I asked. "She must have been very rich. A yangban! Why did she give her daughter the comb?"

"She said the dragon had magic to help her," Mother said. "She told me it must be passed on to daughters to help them, too." Mother finished combing my hair and turned me around. The blaze from the fire shimmered orange off her hanbok, making it look like she was on fire. She looked at me and then at Soo-hee. "It was supposed to help me," she said.

"How was it supposed to help you, Mother?" I asked.

She did not answer. After a while, Soo-hee said, "You can tell us when we come back from the boot factory. We must go to bed now. Tomorrow we have a long journey." Soo-hee pulled at my sleeve. I wanted to ask more questions, but Mother just stared into the fire. Soo-hee and I bowed to her and went to our mats to sleep.

◆ ◆ ◆

I lay on my sleeping mat next to Soo-hee and tried to imagine my great-great-grandmother, the important lady, the yangban, who could afford to have such a fine comb made for her daughter. I pictured her strolling along a tree-lined boulevard in Seoul dressed in a flowing silk robe. She had long black hair smartly folded on top of her head and pinned with an ornate binyeo. As she walked down the wide boulevard, everyone bowed to her out of respect, even the most powerful men.

I wished my great-great-grandmother was still alive so she could stop the Japanese from making Soo-hee and me work in the boot factory. I wondered how the comb was supposed to help my mother. I hoped it would help me someday.

I lay awake for a long time waiting for Mother to come to bed. The floor was hot from the ondol heating system in our house. I kicked a leg out from under the blanket, but the air outside was hot, too. I peeked through an opening in the latticed doors and saw an orange glow coming from the kitchen.

I crawled off my mat and went to the kitchen. The fire was high, and the room was hot. Mother sat next to the fire still dressed in her hanbok. A stack of wood was at her side. I asked her why she was burning all the wood. She stared at the fire and didn't answer me.

I pulled on the sleeve of her hanbok. "Ummah, Ummah, what is wrong? Come to bed now. You have to go to work tomorrow."

Mother turned to me and ran a hand along my hair. "No," she said sadly, "I will not give them any more."

It frightened me to see my mother so sad, so I quickly went back to my mat. When I crawled under the blanket, Soo-hee was awake. "Soo-hee," I whispered, "Ummah is burning all the wood."

Soo-hee put a hand on my arm. "I know. Go to sleep, little sister."

I closed my eyes, and eventually I fell into a fitful sleep.

The next morning, Soo-hee tugged at my arm to get me out of bed. "Jae-hee, wake up!" she said. "We must make the kimchi before we leave."

The house was cold, and I didn't want to get up. I rolled into my blanket, but Soo-hee pulled it off me. She scolded me again to get up. "We don't have much time," she said.

I sat up and rubbed my eyes open. It was still dark outside, and everything inside the house was in shadows. I peered into the kitchen. The fire had burned out, and the wood was gone. The figure of my mother, still in her hanbok, sat in the cold room staring at nothing. Her eyes looked like the eyes of old Mr. Lee when Soo-hee and I found him behind his house dead from starvation.

As the light from the rising sun turned the aspen trees flame orange, I helped Soo-hee drain the brine from the nappa cabbage and daikons. Soo-hee told me to take care to rinse the vegetables well, but we only had time to rinse them twice instead of three times like we usually did. We made a red sauce from garlic, ginger, and hot peppers. The spices stung my hands. We tossed in the vegetables and put the mixture into two large onggis. We dragged them to the back of the house and buried them in deep holes. By the time we were done, the sun was over the top of the aspen trees, and the sky was deep blue. Soo-hee said we had to go.

At the well, I washed the kimchi sauce from my hands. I went to the sleeping room and braided my hair. I wrapped an extra set of clothes in a cloth sack and set it next to Soo-hee's in the kitchen. While Mother continued to stare into the cold stove, Soo-hee packed a handful of rice and kimchi in a hide bag. She brewed some bori cha.

I sidled up to Soo-hee. "What's wrong with Mother?" I asked. It wasn't at all like Mother to be quiet like that.

"She is very tired," Soo-hee said, pouring bori cha into our cups. "Now drink your tea and eat some rice."

The bori cha Soo-hee made was strong and bitter, the way Mother used to make it for Father. I didn't like it strong and refused to drink it when it was like that. But that day I drank it, and although I wasn't hungry, I ate a little rice. The comb was on the table where Mother had left it the night before. It was the most beautiful thing I had ever seen. I stared at the two-headed dragon, and it stared back at me. I brought my face close, and something made me turn an ear to it. For a moment, I thought I heard the dragon speak to me.

"Come, little sister," Soo-hee said. "We must say good-bye to Mother."

The dragon had hypnotized me, and I didn't answer Soo-hee. "Jae-hee!" she said. "We do not have much time!"

"Yes, Onni, I'm coming," I said. I forced myself away from the comb and joined Soo-hee in front of Mother.

Soo-hee bowed low. "We are leaving to work in the boot factory, Mother. We made kimchi and buried it in the back of the house where the Japanese will not find it. We buried the rice there, too. We will write if we can." She bowed again. Mother continued to stare into the ashes.

I stood in front of Mother to bow. Instead of bowing, I took her by the shoulders and shook her hard. "Mother, wake up!" I insisted. "You have to go to work!" She didn't move, and I took a step back, afraid that my mother's spell would never be broken.

Soo-hee took me by the arm and pulled me toward the tarpaulin door. We gathered our sacks and walked out of the house, leaving our mother inside, alone.

◆ ◆ ◆

The sun had climbed over the hills in the east, and the morning air was warming as we walked past the persimmon tree onto the dirt road. I slipped my hand inside Soo-hee's as we started down the road toward Sinuiju. We had gone only a little way when there was a rush of noise behind us. We turned to see Mother running toward us. Her feet were bare, and her white hanbok billowed out. When she got to us, she stopped suddenly. I was glad to see that she was normal again. But then I saw that she wasn't. Her eyes were wild and scary.

"Here," she panted, "take it!" In her hand was the comb with the two-headed dragon. She held it out to Soo-hee.

"Mother, I am sorry," Soo-hee said. "I cannot. The Japanese will steal it."

"I do not want it anymore," Mother hissed.

When Soo-hee didn't take it, Mother took Soo-hee's hand and pressed the comb into it. "Do not let go of it," she said. "It has not helped me. Perhaps it will help you. And then you must pass it on to your daughter someday." She gave Soo-hee a firm nod.

Mother turned to me and took me by the shoulders. "Jae-hee, listen to your onni," she said. "Do as she says. It is important that you do." She let go of me and stood straight. She looked from Soo-hee to me. Her mouth opened, her brow furrowed, and I was afraid that she might cry in front of me for the first time in my life. "My babies," she said. "Ye deulah." Then she lifted her hanbok and walked to the house without looking back.

Soo-hee held the comb as if it were a baby bird that she didn't know where to put. Then she pushed the comb into her sack and took my hand again.

"Come, little sister," she said. "We have a very long journey."

SEVEN

"We have come to work in the boot factory," I said in Japanese to the soldier behind the desk. On the soldier's arm was a white armband with Japanese characters that identified him as Kempei tai, the Japanese military police. Soo-hee held our orders out to him.

We were standing in a large room with high ceilings, wide plank floors, and many desks. Dozens of Koreans stood in lines, waiting to speak to soldiers sitting at the desks. On the wall hung the Japanese flag with its big red circle like a giant eye that never closed, watching everything we did. Outside the window, the daylight was fading, turning everything gray.

The kempei, a small man with a bald head, glanced up from his work. "Address me as 'sir.' I am Kempei tai, and you must show respect."

"Yes, sir," Soo-hee said in Japanese.

"Let me see your orders," the kempei said with a hand out. He took the orders, scanned them, and nodded. "Yes. You've come to the right place. The truck to take girls to the boot factory will be leaving in a little while. Wait over there with the others." He pointed to an open area where five other girls sat on the floor. Soo-hee and I went and sat with them.

It had taken us all day to walk down the dirt road to Sinuiju, and we hadn't arrived until the sun was low. Father had said he would take me to Sinuiju someday, but he hadn't been able to before he left home. I had imagined the city having tall, shimmering buildings, shiny cars speeding along on paved streets, and elegant ladies on walkways carrying pink parasols, just like in the books I had read with Mother and Father. But when we arrived, all I saw were low, shabby buildings and noisy military trucks cutting ruts in dirt roads. And there were hundreds of Korean workers who looked to me like scruffy dogs slinking home after a beating.

We had stopped at a boarding house on the outskirts of the city and asked an old man sitting on the steps where we should go with our orders. He pointed down the road without looking up. "Military command," he had said. "The two-story building with the Japanese flag."

We finally found the imposing stucco building flying the Japanese flag high above. I hated that flag. It reminded me that we all were their subjects. We went inside with our orders, and a soldier directed us to the kempei's desk.

As we sat on the hard floor waiting for the truck to take us to the boot factory, I studied the other girls. They were all pretty and young, and their eyes darted about nervously. It concerned me that I was the youngest. I moved closer to Soo-hee.

Soo-hee leaned into the circle of girls and whispered in Korean, "Are all of you going to the boot factory, too?"

"Yes," whispered an older girl with light skin. "That is what our orders say."

"I thought the factory was here in Sinuiju," whispered Soo-hee, "but the kempei said we will be going on a truck."

"Quiet over there!" shouted the kempei from his desk. "No talking!"

We bowed our heads and stayed silent, waiting for the truck to arrive.

◆ ◆ ◆

An hour later, the bald kempei approached us, followed by a Japanese regular army soldier with dark eyes and a thick chin. "This man has come to take you to the boot factory," the kempei said. "Follow me."

I was glad to get off the hard floor. I was hungry and very anxious to see the boot factory and where we would live. We followed the soldiers outside. The sun had set, turning everything in Sinuiju an inky black. In front of us was a large green truck with a canvas top. The soldier with the thick chin helped us into the back. Inside were crates of supplies and sacks of rice. There was only a small area for us to sit. He handed one of the girls a water jug and slammed the truck gate closed as the bald kempei walked back inside the building.

We huddled together and stared at each other wide-eyed. The crates and sacks of rice hovered over us. The engine roared to life, and the truck lurched forward. Several girls let out a squeal. We grabbed each other and held on. The truck rumbled down the street, and over the top of the truck gate, I could see that we were heading out of the city. Soon we were in the country rolling past farms and rice paddies. Sinuiju's lights faded in the distance.

"Soo-hee," I asked, "where are we going?"

"I don't know," Soo-hee answered. "But I don't think we're going to the boot factory in Sinuiju."

The older girl with light-colored skin shook her head. "I knew we weren't going there," she said. "My mother said that girls our age are sent to Seoul to work in the textile mill. At first I didn't want to go, but she told me I had to. She said it's easy work, and we get as much rice as we want."

I leaned forward, eager to learn more from the older girl. I was excited about going to Seoul. Ever since I was a little girl, I had always wanted to see the big city on the Han River that I had read about in our books. Even Father had never been to Seoul. And the older girl said the work we would do would be easy.

Soo-hee didn't seem to be so curious about what the older girl had to say and pulled me back next to her. The older girl asked me what my name was.

"I am Jae-hee," I said, "and this is my onni, Soo-hee."

"My name is Jin-sook," she said. "My mother said that all we need to do is obey the Japanese." Jin-sook addressed all the girls. "Listen to me and do what I say." Jin-sook looked like she was the oldest, so everyone except Soo-hee nodded. No one said anything more as the boxes and sacks of rice swayed over our heads.

The truck rolled on as we all huddled close. Outside, the sky was dark and the stars twinkled. The diesel fumes and the swaying of the truck made me sleepy. I was hungry, cold, and thirsty, too. I leaned into Soo-hee, and she pulled me close. Someone passed the water jug. When it came to Soo-hee, she handed it to me without taking a drink. "Take my share, little sister," she whispered. "I'm not thirsty." I took two swallows and passed the jug on.

Eventually I fell asleep.

◆ ◆ ◆

I jerked awake in the middle of an odd dream where the dragon from Mother's comb was chasing me. The truck had stopped, and outside it was deathly quiet. It was dark and nothing moved. I rubbed the dream from my eyes. "Where are we?" I asked in Korean. "What's happening?"

"Shush!" Jin-sook whispered. "You'll get us all shot."

A light came from around the side of the truck and pointed in at us. The light illuminated the driver's thick chin and bushy eyebrows from below. His eyes were wide and wild. He looked like the villain from a Chinese puppet show. He reached in and lowered the truck gate with a rattle. He said, "You, come with me."

I was terrified he was talking to me, but the driver reached in and grabbed a tall girl I had heard one of the girls call Sun-hi. "The rest of you stay put," the driver barked, "or I will cut off your ears."

Sun-hi cried out, "Where are you taking me?"

"Quiet!" the driver commanded. There was a slap and a muffled cry. The light disappeared into the darkness. I sat close to Soo-hee and trembled. I could feel Soo-hee trembling, too.

A short way from the truck Sun-hi cried out again. "No," she said. "Please, no!"

There was another slap and the sound of tearing fabric. "Quiet," the driver barked. "Better get used to it, you Korean whore."

I tried not to listen to Sun-hi's cries, but like a coyote's howl in the middle of the night, it was the only sound I could hear. After a few minutes, Sun-hi stopped crying, and the driver grunted. He started breathing hard, and then grunted again and again. Then he was quiet.

Eventually the light pointed in at us again. I was terribly afraid. I looked out the back of the truck to see where I should run in case the driver came for me next. All I saw was smothering blackness. I pushed myself tight against Soo-hee and blinked back tears. All the girls sat perfectly still. The driver shoved Sun-hi into the truck, and she flopped down next to me and curled into a tight ball like a cat protecting itself from the cold. Her dress was ripped, and her hair hung in strings over her face. A streak of blood ran down her chin.

The driver slammed the truck gate closed and went to the front again. The engine started, and the truck jerked forward.

As the truck rolled along and we sat in the darkness, one girl started to cry. "I thought you said we would be all right," she said to Jin-sook. Jin-sook looked as terrified as the rest of us and didn't answer. Two other girls began to cry. I was about to cry, too, but before I could, Soo-hee drew me close and whispered, "Do not cry, Jae-hee. We must be strong. We must be strong, or we will die."

And that's when I knew that my life had changed forever. For the first time, I was going to have to be strong. Until now, my parents and Soo-hee had always taken care of me. I had never really worried about anything. But now I was in a place that I couldn't have even imagined just a day earlier. I was going to have to do what Soo-hee said. So I pushed my cries down, and when I did, I felt my insides harden a little. I brought my knees up and curled into a tight ball like Sun-hi. I thought about the comb with the two-headed dragon. I hoped that if I stayed strong, the dragon would protect me and spare me Sun-hi's fate.

But as the truck rolled on toward our destination, I wondered if the comb was nothing. After all, Mother had said it didn't protect her. Maybe it was only a trinket she had bought in Sinuiju, and the story about my great-great-grandmother was a tall tale to make Soo-hee and me less afraid about leaving home.

Maybe the comb with the two-headed dragon, hidden in Soo-hee's sack, was nothing at all.

EIGHT

Fear kept me awake for the rest of the night. Whenever I tried to sleep, I saw the driver's wild eyes and heard Sun-hi's awful cries. It was like a frightful nightmare that you just can't shake. As I huddled close to Soo-hee, waiting for morning to come, I wondered if the nightmare would ever go away.

By the time the sun came up, I was farther away from my home than I had ever been before. Outside was a landscape I had never seen. Yellow wheat fields blanketed the flats, and there were only a few trees among the low hills. Far beyond were much larger hills that looked like great rolling waves on the horizon. Above, the sky looked much bigger than at home.

I asked Soo-hee where we were. "I think we're in China," she answered.

At midday we rolled into a town of low stucco buildings with gray-green tiled roofs. Men in strange clothing hauled carts down the narrow, dusty streets. The truck stopped at a long clapboard building at the edge of the village. Tar paper covered the roof instead of tile. The driver came to the back of the truck and lowered the gate. I tried to hide behind Soo-hee.

He ordered everyone out and told us to form a line with our backs to the building. I climbed out with the other girls as the driver pulled Sun-hi out of the truck and made her stand with us. My legs ached from sitting so long, and the bright sun hurt my eyes. I stayed close to Soo-hee. I looked up. Standing before us was a thin Japanese officer with sharp black eyes and a pointed nose. His cap came down to just over his eyes. Above the bill was a lieutenant's insignia. His uniform was army green, and he wore the white armband with the red Japanese characters of the Kempei tai. His jacket had brass buttons, and a wide leather belt was pulled tight around his slim waist. He wore black boots that came up to his knees.

As we formed a line, he slapped a shinai against his boots. The bamboo blade made a thwacking sound with each strike. Off to the side, a young regular army soldier in a plain green uniform leaned against the narrow building. In his hands was a rifle.

"What happened to this one?" the lieutenant said, pointing his shinai at Sun-hi.

The driver straightened. "The clumsy girl fell out of the truck when we stopped to piss, Lieutenant."

"Really? That had better be all that happened to her, Corporal."

I wanted to tell the kempei what the driver had done to Sun-hi, but I stayed quiet.

"Lieutenant, sir," the driver said, "I must unload these supplies at once and take injured soldiers to the hospital in Pushun." He gave a quick bow and ran back to his truck. The engine started, and the truck rumbled off.

Out of the corner of my eye, I saw Jin-sook step forward with her head lowered. "Honorable sir," she said in Japanese, "please forgive a girl for being so bold, but there has been a mistake! Our orders said we were to work in the boot factory in Sinuiju."

The lieutenant glowered at Jin-sook. "Come here," he said.

Keeping her head low, Jin-sook approached the officer. He lifted her chin with the tip of his shinai. "A mistake was made?"

"Yes, sir," she answered. "We were to go to the boot fa—"

With a quick motion, he punched Jin-sook in the stomach with the butt of his shinai. She gasped and fell to her knees. "I heard you the first time, girl. Stand up."

Holding her stomach, Jin-sook struggled to her feet. She gasped for air. The lieutenant pointed his shinai at her. "Your disrespect has earned you a beating. But I can't spoil you now, can I? Not before the officers have you. Go back in line with the others."

Back home, I had heard other girls talk about how the Japanese beat Koreans who showed them disrespect, but I hadn't believed them. I thought they were rumors started by the Japanese to make us obey. But now I was seeing it with my own eyes. It was terrifying, and it frightened me to realize how disrespectful I had been to the Japanese. I worried about what else I didn't know about them.

Jin-sook, still holding her stomach, stepped back in the line. The lieutenant drew in a long breath through his nose and pointed his chin out. He began inspecting the girls. He slapped his shinai against his leg with each step. "I am Lieutenant Tanaka," he said in a clipped, authoritative way. "I'm the kempei in charge of this comfort station. You are our new volunteers. You will only speak to me when I ask you a question. You will only speak Japanese." He came to me. I lowered my eyes to the high black boots of the Kempei tai.

The kempei lifted my chin with a finger. "You're a young one. Pretty, too. What's your name?"

"Hong Jae-hee, sir," I answered.

The kempei grabbed my chin and pushed his fingers hard into my jaw. He forced me to look at him. "That is a Korean name," he said, "and you are a Japanese subject. You have a Japanese name. What is it?"

"Namiko Iwata, sir," I said quickly.

"Namiko Iwata. Yes." He let go of my chin, and I lowered my eyes again. The kempei walked on.

"You will obey my orders without question," he continued to all the girls. "If you do not, you will earn a beating. If you run away, we will catch you, beat you, and then shoot you. Anyway, I assure you, here there is nowhere to run."

Jin-sook stepped forward again and dropped to her knees in the yellow dirt. She bowed her head. "Kind sir, please hear a worthless girl," she cried. "We should not be here! We are not volunteers for your comfort station. Please, sir, send us back with the truck. Please!"

"Private Ishida!" Lieutenant Tanaka barked.

The young soldier leaning against his rifle snapped to attention. "Yes, sir?"

"Take these other girls to be examined by the doctor. Then bring them to the courtyard." He pointed his shinai at Jin-sook. "I'll take this one. Surely the officers won't mind one spoiled girl to show them all discipline."

Lieutenant Tanaka grabbed Jin-sook by the hair and pulled her around the other side of the building. She twisted and sobbed. "I'm sorry, sir," she cried. "I will not say anything more. Please! I'm sorry."

Private Ishida ordered the rest of us to leave our packs against the building and follow him. I laid my sack next to Soo-hee's and followed the girls down a narrow dirt path as Jin-sook pleaded with the kempei.

I had never seen a doctor when I was young. Back home, when someone got sick, they called a woman from the valley who, after examining the patient, prescribed special herbs. But I had never needed her. So I didn't know what to do when a nurse dressed in white took me inside a room with tile walls and a bright light while the other girls sat quietly in the infirmary's hallway. The nurse pushed me in front of a fat Japanese doctor who sat on a wooden stool next to a cot. He wore a gray linen smock that went down to his knees and was tied in the back.

The nurse left, and the doctor said, "Take off your clothes."

I wasn't sure if I had heard him correctly. "Sir?" I said, keeping my eyes low.

"I said take off your clothes. Do it now."

"You want me to take off my clothes?" I asked.

The doctor leaned in and slapped me hard across my face. It was the first time anyone had struck me. The shock of it took my breath away. "I'm a doctor. I have to examine you," he said. "Do as I say now, or I'll send you to Lieutenant Tanaka for a beating."

I didn't want the doctor to slap me again, and I surely didn't want a beating, so I slowly unbuttoned my shirt and pants. I untied my undergarments and let them fall to the floor. I had never been naked in front of a man before. I started to tremble.

"Come closer," the doctor said. I took a step toward him. The doctor ran his thick hands along my torso. He pressed his fingers into my neck, stomach, and chest. He squeezed my breasts. I flinched with each touch. He made me turn around, and he put his cold stethoscope on my back and told me to breathe in slowly. I did as he said, but I couldn't stop trembling.

The doctor pointed at the cot and told me to lie there on my back. "Pull your knees up and spread your legs open."

I couldn't believe what he was telling me to do. "What are you going to do to me?" I asked.

"I need to see if you are a virgin. Now stop asking questions and do as you're told."

I still felt the sting of the doctor's slap, and the kempei and his shinai were fresh in my mind. So I closed my eyes and did what the doctor told me to do. My body tensed as the doctor probed me with his fingers. I dug my fingernails into the palms of my hands and stifled a sob.

After a few long seconds he stopped. "You're a virgin," he said. "I would expect it, someone as young as you, but you can never be sure. How long have you been bleeding?"

"Sir?" I asked.

"Your monthly bleed. How long have you had it?"

"Five times."

"Good. You're clean," the doctor said, going to a porcelain basin. "You have good skin and pleasing features. I'm sure Colonel Matsumoto will want you first, someone so young, so pretty. Do what he tells you and you'll be all right. Now get dressed and go back with the others."

I quickly dressed as the doctor washed his hands. "Doctor," I said, "what will the colonel ask me to do?"

"Nothing you can't handle," he said without looking up.

"But what if I don't want to do it?" I asked.

The doctor turned from the basin. "Don't talk back, girl, and do what he tells you. Now go."

I ran back to the hallway and sat on the cold tile floor next to Soo-hee. I thought about what had happened to Sun-hi in the truck and how the kempei had punched Jin-sook in the stomach. I was terrified that awful things like that would happen to me, too. And I wasn't as sure as the doctor was that I would be able to handle it.

Private Ishida, his rifle in hand, led us back down the narrow path to the barracks. "Listen to me," he said. "Do not cross the lieutenant, or you will pay the price! Only speak Japanese. And don't disappoint the senior officers, either. Do you understand?"

"Yes, sir," we replied in unison.

We came to the barracks where the truck had dropped us off. Lieutenant Tanaka was waiting for us. Jin-sook was not with him. He ordered us to take our things and follow him. We gathered our sacks and went with him to where he had dragged Jin-sook. We came to a courtyard closed off by three long barracks, each with ten doors, closely spaced. Two wooden steps led to each door. There were no windows in the barracks. The yellow dirt in the courtyard was hard and dry. You could see hundreds of footprints in the dust.

In the center of the courtyard, Jin-sook stood with her wrists and ankles tied to a post. She was naked, and she trembled visibly. She breathed in shallow sobs. We all gasped and covered our mouths when we saw her. Sun-hi began to cry quietly.

Japanese women, some dressed in colorful yukatas, fanned themselves on the steps of the largest barracks. Others leaned against the walls. When we came in the courtyard, they filed out.

Lieutenant Tanaka pointed his shinai at the ground twenty feet in front of the post and ordered us to form a line facing Jin-sook. I couldn't take my eyes off her as I stood at the end of the line next to Soo-hee.

Lieutenant Tanaka faced us. "You are all fortunate!" he said with a thin smile. "You will learn what happens to a Korean girl who doesn't please her kempei. You will watch the lesson without closing your eyes. If you cry, you will earn a beating. If you faint, you will earn a beating. If you vomit or piss yourself or do anything other than watch the lesson, you will earn a beating. Watch now, and learn from your kempei."

The bright sun beat down on us, and time stood still as Lieutenant Tanaka approached Jin-sook with his shinai at his side. She sobbed and pleaded with the kempei not to beat her. She said she was sorry and wouldn't talk back anymore. He didn't seem to hear her.

Lieutenant Tanaka stood in front of Jin-sook and slowly raised his shinai. Then he struck her across her thighs. The sound of the lieutenant's shinai against Jin-sook's skin made me shiver. It was like both the crack of a whip and thud of a club. Jin-sook's body stiffened. Her eyes went wide and her mouth opened, but no sound came out.

Lieutenant Tanaka brought the shinai down again on the same place, and Jin-sook let out a long, jagged scream. She shook violently against the post. Lieutenant Tanaka struck her thighs again. Then again and again and again. Jin-sook screamed and jerked with each blow. She jerked against the ropes like a wild pig caught in a trap. Angry red welts swelled on her thighs. Urine ran down her legs.

My own thighs jerked with each strike of the shinai, as if Lieutenant Tanaka was beating me. I wanted desperately to close my eyes and put my hands over my ears to make the beating stop. But I was so shocked and horrified at what I was seeing that I could not do either. Bile rose in my throat, and I was afraid I would vomit. I wanted to cry, but I pushed it down inside my stomach as Soo-hee had told me to.

Then Lieutenant Tanaka struck Jin-sook on her shins. With this blow, Jin-sook's body stiffened again, her mouth opened wide, and she took in a short gulp of air. Lieutenant Tanaka hit her in the same place, and Jin-sook let out a long, mournful shriek. Mucus ran from her nose, and her hair was wild and tangled. Lieutenant Tanaka struck her shins over and over, each blow causing Jin-sook to scream horribly. Finally Jin-sook slumped unconscious against the post, her black hair falling like a veil over her face. Lieutenant Tanaka lowered his shinai and faced us.

I couldn't breathe. The courtyard and the barracks and the sun and the sky—everything was spinning, and I couldn't make it stop. I thought I was going to faint. Out of the corner of my eye, I saw Sun-hi fall to the ground. Lieutenant Tanaka pointed his shinai at her. "That girl has earned a beating," he said. "Private, make a note. We will do it tomorrow."

Lieutenant Tanaka strolled down the line of girls with his shinai at his side. "I have given you a valuable lesson. What do you say to your kempei for this lesson?"

No one answered.

"I asked a question!" Lieutenant Tanaka barked, slapping his shinai hard against his boot. "Someone answer, or you will all earn a beating."

I didn't know what to say, and I was terrified that I was going to get a beating like Jin-sook.

Then Soo-hee took a step forward and bowed low. "Kempei, sir," she said in broken Japanese, "thank you for this lesson."

Lieutenant Tanaka looked down his pointed nose at Soo-hee. "What is your name, girl?"

"Okimi Iwata, sir," Soo-hee said with another low bow.

"You're welcome, Okimi Iwata. Go back in line." Soo-hee stepped back.

"Now," Lieutenant Tanaka said, "all of you, wash and change into yukatas. The geishas will assign you to rooms. The senior officers return from maneuvers tonight."

As Lieutenant Tanaka headed out of the courtyard, over his shoulder he said, "Be ready for them."

NINE

After Lieutenant Tanaka left the courtyard, I gripped Soo-hee's hand hard. I asked her what was happening to us.

"Quiet!" Private Ishida barked, going to Jin-sook at the post. "Don't talk! If Lieutenant Tanaka hears you, you will get a beating!" I lowered my head.

"Seiko! Maori!" the private shouted. "Get the others and come help with the new girls." The Japanese women reappeared from behind their barracks. All except the two the private had called to help him took their places again on the steps and began fanning themselves as if nothing had happened. They didn't seem to notice Jin-sook lying naked and unconscious at the post. I couldn't believe that such a horrible thing seemed normal to them.

Sun-hi, lying on the ground, moaned and grabbed at Soo-hee's leg. Soo-hee helped her to her feet. When Sun-hi saw Jin-sook slumped at the post, she began to sob uncontrollably. "No!" Soo-hee said in a sharp whisper. "Do not cry." The tall girl drew in a shaky breath and fell quiet.

Private Ishida ordered Maori to get water for Jin-sook. "She needs to go to the infirmary," he said. He kneeled next to the unconscious girl and untied her from the post. He told the other geishas to show us our rooms and where to wash. "They need yukatas for the officers tonight," he said.

A Japanese woman in a dark blue yukata grabbed me by the arm. "I am Seiko," she said. "Come with me." She was at least seven years older than Soo-hee. She had shoulder-length hair, long eyelashes, and a petite nose. She wore makeup, something I had only seen actors wear at the New Year's festival. She wore Japanese zori on her feet and walked with short, deliberate steps. She led me to a narrow door at the end of one of the barracks. "Listen to me," she said. "This is where you work. From one o'clock to five, it's the enlisted men. They get ten minutes each. From five to seven, you have the noncommissioned officers. They get a half hour. At eight, you will go to one of the senior officers' quarters and stay as long as he wants you. Today you're lucky—you only have the senior officers. The troops return from maneuvers tomorrow. Then you will put in a full day's work."

Seiko continued, "You wash in the latrine next to the infirmary. Take a yukata from the room nearby. You must wear it when you work. We prepare food in the kitchen next to the geishas' barracks. You will be assigned cleaning, cooking, and laundry duty tomorrow.

"And one more thing," Seiko said, poking me in my chest with her finger. "Always remember you are a Korean. Do as we say, or you will get a beating just like your friend over there. Now put your things in your room and follow me to the latrine."

I went inside the room. It was dark and small and stunk like a toilet. Strips of sunlight showed through gaps between the boards in the floors and walls. The door hung loosely on leather hinges. Covering the floor was a small, thin mat. There was a chamber pot in one corner and, in the other, a stool. A candle rested on a small shelf. I had never seen such a disgusting room for someone to live in. The chicken coop behind our house was nicer than this.

I placed my sack on the mat. I turned to Seiko. "What kind of work do we do here?"

Seiko scoffed at me. "You *are* a stupid Korean. You're an *ianfu*—a comfort woman. You are here to service the soldiers."

Ianfu. I had heard the word once before, years earlier, when I overheard Mother and Father talking in hushed tones about what had happened to an older girl who lived near us. I had wondered what it meant, so I asked Soo-hee. She had told me to forget I heard the word, but I never did.

Now I was beginning to understand, and my stomach turned into a knot. I had never been with a man before. I had never even imagined what it would be like. I thought about what had happened to Sun-hi in the truck only hours earlier. I could still hear her cries and see how she rolled up into a tight ball when the driver threw her back in the truck after he had used her. She hadn't been the same since. And I knew I would not be the same, either.

I looked beyond the barracks over the brown wheat fields. The distance between the hills was much greater than the hills outside Sinuiju. And beyond them were bigger hills on the horizon. I remembered Lieutenant Tanaka's words: *there is nowhere to run.* I glanced at the post in the middle of the courtyard, and a shiver of pain went through my legs.

I looked back at Seiko, who glared at me. "Thank you, ma'am," I said with a respectful bow.

◆　◆　◆

An hour later, I had washed, and even though I wasn't hungry, I had eaten a small bowl of broth with a few mushy azuki beans. In a small room next to the latrine, I took a pair of white tabi socks and straw zori sandals. I saw a green yukata with small white and pink flowers. I always looked good in green, so I thought I should take that one. The yukata was too large for my slender frame, and I tripped on the hem while walking back to the courtyard. Lounging on their steps, the Japanese women laughed at me without covering their mouths.

"Look at that poor little chicken," one of them said. "She will squawk when the officers pluck her."

The women laughed again, except for Seiko, who stared at me and said, "Yes. And the officers will be here soon."

When I entered the courtyard, the other Korean girls were standing in front of their barracks. They looked awkward in their yukatas, and there was terror in their eyes.

Soo-hee, wearing a yellow yukata, was on a step at the end of the barracks. I ran to her. I told her I was scared.

"We all are," Soo-hee said. She scanned the other girls and told me to follow her.

As the Japanese women and Private Ishida looked on, Soo-hee gathered the girls around her. Then she said in a low voice, "We're in a terrible place. We have to do what they say, or we will die. But we have each other, and we must stay strong."

"But I do not know what to do!" a younger girl cried.

Soo-hee nodded. "What's your name?"

"Midori Sato," she answered.

"No, no. What's your Korean name?"

"Mee-su," the girl said.

"I don't know what to do either, Mee-su," Soo-hee said. "The doctor said we would be all right if we do what they say. I think we should."

"But I don't know how," Mee-su said.

Soo-hee put a hand on Mee-su's shoulder. "You have to try. Remember what I said. Be strong." Mee-su choked back a sob, and Soo-hee looked each of the girls in the eye. "We must be strong. We must help each other."

With Soo-hee's words, I felt a little less afraid. And that's when I realized that though she wasn't as pretty as Mother or as clever as Father,

Soo-hee was like both of them in one person—the sky and the earth. Like Mother, she kept my feet on the ground. We were in a terrible place, and I would have to learn discipline to survive. But like Father, she made me believe I could do it.

Mee-su wiped her eyes and no longer cried. The girls went back to their steps, and I could tell they felt better, too. Sun-hi, however, still trembled.

Soo-hee led me back to my step. She tugged at the sleeve of my yukata and told me to come closer. "Take this," she whispered. She opened her hand, and inside was the comb with the two-headed dragon. "Mother said that it will protect us."

"But, Soo-hee, Mother gave it to you."

"You were born in the year of the dragon," Soo-hee said. "This comb with the dragon is a sign for you. Take it, little sister."

I wrapped my hand around the comb. It was the first time I had ever held it. It was heavy and cool in my hand and felt like something important. But after what had happened to Jin-sook, I doubted if a comb could help me.

"Where will I hide it?" I asked.

"In your chamber pot," Soo-hee said. "No one will find it there. Put it there now."

I slid the comb inside my yukata and went to my room. I did as Soo-hee said and dropped it inside my chamber pot.

We waited in the courtyard exchanging nervous glances until it started to grow dark. Then Lieutenant Tanaka walked in with his shinai at his side. Private Ishida grabbed his rifle and stood straight. The Japanese women continued to lounge on their steps. Now that the sun had set, it was cooling quickly. There was no breeze, and I could hear the rumble of trucks in the village. We huddled close, except for Sun-hi, who stood off to the side and stared at the ground.

With his shinai, Lieutenant Tanaka pointed at the yellow dirt in front of him. He ordered us to form a line and stand straight with our hands at our sides. He said we were not to talk. "The officers are coming," he said.

I heard male voices and laughter from behind the barracks. The voices grew louder, and a group of men entered the courtyard. The wind blew dust into a swirl in the center of the yard. It reminded me of the soldier on the motorcycle and the snake's tail from two days earlier. A man a half head taller than the rest led them. I had seen Japanese senior officers before, but never anyone like him. He had square shoulders, smooth skin, and a strong chin like you see on important men. Just the sight of him made me fear him.

"Attention!" Lieutenant Tanaka barked. He and Private Ishida snapped to attention. The Japanese women stayed seated on their steps.

The square-shouldered officer approached Lieutenant Tanaka. "Lieutenant, I see we have new girls," he said.

"Yes, Colonel," Lieutenant Tanaka said crisply and with a slight bow. "One was disrespectful and had to be disciplined. She is in the infirmary. The doctor reports all the rest are virgins except the one at the end." He pointed at Sun-hi.

"Let's take a look," the colonel said. With his hands behind his back, he slowly examined each girl. I thought he was looking for something wrong with us. I was afraid that when he examined me, he would see my flaws and that I would suffer some terrible fate. Then, when he finally came to me, he stopped. I bowed my head low and looked at his feet. His boots were polished, clean, and tied tight. Under my yukata, my knees shook.

"This is a young one," he said. "Is she clean, Lieutenant?"

"Yes, sir. She is the youngest. Her name is Namiko Iwata."

The colonel lifted my chin with a finger and examined my face from side to side. The shaking in my knees spread to my legs. The courtyard spun around me, and I thought I would faint. The wind blew up another snake tail in the courtyard. "You have a pretty face, Namiko Iwata," he said, his eyes fixed on me. "Pretty and delicate, like an aristocrat."

He let go of my chin and turned to Lieutenant Tanaka. "This one," he said.

TEN

August 2008. Seoul, South Korea

"He raped me," my birth grandmother says, glaring at me from across her table. I want to look away, but I don't dare. "They took me to his quarters, where he raped me. I was fourteen years old. I didn't know what sex was. I had only been menstruating for five months. Five months! How could I know? How could I know?"

"You couldn't possibly," I say. It's hot and humid inside her small apartment. I need to fan myself, but I don't. Not now. Not with Mrs. Hong reliving her horrible rape. Her beautiful yellow hanbok doesn't cover her shame. It is written on her face and is deep in her eyes.

"He raped me in the cruelest way," she continues. "I'm sorry to tell you this, but you must know. First, he told me to take off my clothes in front of him while he watched. I wanted to say no, but I had just seen how they'd beaten Jin-sook. I was terrified, so I did what he said. I stood there naked and helpless like a baby. I shook with fear. Then he made me undress him. I had to start with his boots—those polished, clean boots that he tied so tight. I had to unbutton his shirt, then his trousers. He made me kneel and take off his undergarments as he stood over me, naked. He told me to look at him. He thought I would be impressed. I had never seen a naked man before. I had only imagined what they were like. I desperately wanted to run away, back to the hills behind our farm where Soo-hee and I used to run among the aspen trees."

She locks her hands into a single fist and places them on top of the table. Her eyes never leave me, and I almost feel like she's accusing me of raping her. "Then he touched me. Everywhere. He ran his hands over my hair, my face, my neck, my breasts, my stomach, my legs, my genitals. He pushed me down and forced himself inside me. He pierced me and made me bleed. He pushed over and over again. Each thrust hurt more than the previous one. I cannot describe the agony. It was worse than pain. It was pain and terror and humiliation and shame all together. I wanted to die. I tried to resist, but when I did, he just laughed at me. He was a strong man. I was a girl. And he was the Japanese colonel."

She clenches her fingers so hard I think they might break. The pain on her face never eases. She continues, "But what made the colonel so cruel was that as he raped me he made me stare into his eyes. When I shut them, he ordered me to keep them open. 'Look at me, girl,' he ordered. 'Keep your eyes open and look at me!' So I looked into his eyes as he raped me. Can you imagine how humiliating that was? Can you?"

"No, ma'am," I answer, "I can't."

"He did not use a condom," she says. "He didn't have to. I was a virgin, and he was the first to rape me. So when he orgasmed, I felt his slime crawl inside every cell of my body like maggots. I could feel it spoil me, turn me rotten. And I knew he would always be in me. Always. Do you know what the worst part of it was?"

"I'm sorry," I say, "I don't."

"The worst part is I thought it was my fault. I had been so proud and stubborn and sure of myself. But when the colonel raped me, I lost everything. I could only think of my grandparents, my mother and father, and Soo-hee. I blamed myself for not having the discipline

Mother told me I needed. I was overcome with shame, but I did nothing wrong, nothing wrong. It doesn't make sense, does it?"

"No," I answer, "it doesn't make any sense at all."

She places her hands in two curves on the low table and turns to the purple flower in the glass bowl. Her eyes are watery. "Do you know what I did when it was over, when he was done with me and told me to leave?"

"No, ma'am."

"I bowed and thanked him," she says in a whisper. She shakes her head. "I don't know why I did that. I wanted to spit on him, scream at him, tell him how much I hated him and all the Japanese. But I had to do the right thing, like Mother said. So I thanked him. It seemed to please him that I did."

We're silent for a long time. The air in her apartment doesn't move. My birth grandmother, who earlier was so proud, now looks completely humiliated. She's hunched over and stares down at her feet as if someone forced her to confess some heinous crime she committed. I don't know what to say. I've never met anyone who's been raped before. I never even got close to it. Of course, sometimes I get nervous when I'm alone on the street at night or when there's a sketchy-looking guy in a hallway. But this? I never knew how devastating rape could be. But I can see it now and feel it, too—in my grandmother.

Eventually the pain in her face goes away, and she straightens up. "Would you like some bori cha, Ja-young?" she asks.

"Bori cha? You mentioned it in your story. I don't know what it is."

She frowns. "Americans think all Koreans drink the same tea as the Chinese and Japanese. However, many traditional Koreans, like me, prefer bori cha. It is roasted barley tea. You must have some."

"Sure," I say. "Thank you."

She puts a teapot on the stove and tosses in a handful of what looks like black tea. She takes two cups from the cupboard and brings them to the table. She moves gracefully in her hanbok. "I like my bori cha strong," she says. "I didn't like it strong when I was young, but I do now. It has become fashionable for our young people to drink coffee like the Americans. I don't like coffee. It isn't Korean, and I am afraid I'm a traditionalist. I think Korea needs to hold on to its traditions, don't you?"

"Of course."

"What do you know about our traditions, Ja-young?"

"Not much, I guess," I confess.

"You should know more about Korea. Yes, you were raised in America. But an important part of you is here," she says, tapping a finger on the table. "You cannot escape it."

I can't escape it? I'm not sure I want it. I'd rather be just an American, like my backpack-toting suburban friends. But when I'm alone in my room and look in the mirror, I see someone different. The woman in the mirror is Korean. It's in her face, her eyes, and her hair. Maybe it's in her blood, too.

The teapot starts whistling, and Mrs. Hong gets it from the stove. She pours the tea through a strainer into our cups. The aroma fills the room. I take a sip, and it's really strong and bitter. It isn't anything like the weak tea served on our tour. As I drink it, I feel cooler and more relaxed.

"Tell me, what do you think of my story so far?" Mrs. Hong asks over the top of her cup. Now she looks as if what she's told me is nothing more than a light tale from her childhood. It still upsets me, and her sudden new demeanor creeps me out, like maybe she's a little off, if you know what I mean. But seriously, who wouldn't be after going through what she did?

"It's . . . horrible," I say. Outside the wind blows, sending a breeze through the window. It gives some relief from the heat—or maybe it's the bori cha.

She stares at me. I sense that she's sizing me up to see if she's made the right decision to give me the comb. I don't want to disappoint her, so I say, "Go on, please. Tell me the rest of your story."

She smiles, but her eyes turn hard. "I have only just begun!" she says. She puts her cup on the table and her hands in her lap.

She continues, "The day after the colonel raped me, the troops came, and I quickly learned what to do. They had made me an ianfu—a comfort woman. I learned a trick, too. I examined the men's boots before they raped me. As I said, the colonel had his boots tied tight. That was a warning sign. His type of cruelty was the worst. It was psychological as well as physical. Whenever I saw someone with boots tied tight, I knew I would be humiliated.

"But there were many others. A soldier with dirty, untied boots would be careless and quick. A soldier who kept his boots on would often hurt me. If his boots were clean and polished, it would be someone who wanted me to pretend I was enjoying him.

"Examining their boots was just something I did," she says with a wave. "But knowing what was going to happen to me did not help. In fact, it made it worse. It was like a torturer telling you what he was going to do to you next. By looking at their boots, I knew how they would rape me.

"And," she says, "I was raped thousands of times."

ELEVEN

August 1945. Dongfeng, Manchuria

When the soldier with the dirty, untied boots left my room, there was one more waiting at my step. There was always a long line at my door before the soldiers went off to their maneuvers. Kempei told us the soldiers needed to purge themselves so if they died in battle, they could enter the afterlife pure. "You're doing a great service for these men," he said. "And for Japan and for the emperor."

I had been serving Japan and the emperor nonstop since midday, and it was now early evening. Even with the six new Korean girls Lieutenant Tanaka had brought in, my line was always the longest. At ten minutes apiece—the soldiers' allotted time—I had serviced over thirty men that day. I was sore and exhausted and had to force myself to serve one more soldier.

That man was Corporal Kaori. He was a big man, and he liked to hurt me. He said he wanted to be the last in line so no one would rush him. But I knew it was because being last, he could do what he wanted to me.

I invited Corporal Kaori in with a bow and closed my door behind him. I saw he had his boots tied tight and that there was hardness in his eyes. I knew I had to be careful.

As the corporal unbuttoned his trousers, I knelt on the floor and washed off the condom the last soldier used. I gave the cleaned condom to him. I lay back on my mat and opened my yukata. My candle was at its afternoon low, and the faint shadows it threw against the walls told me I was nearly done with my work for the enlisted men.

I heard the soft patter of mice scurrying about under the barracks and reminded myself to bring rice that night so I could feel their tiny paws as I fed them through the knothole in the floorboard. I looked up and focused on the gap in the ceiling where the melting snow dripped through in springtime and the wind blew in dust in the summer. Day after day, month after month, I had tried to push myself through that gap to where I would be free from the darkness of my tiny, stinking room, free from what I was forced to do there, free so I could soar like a hawk in the open air as Father had made me believe I could do. I never made it through, but I had to believe that I could.

I knew I wouldn't now. Not with Kaori in my room. As the corporal pulled down his trousers without taking off his boots, I tried to close my nose to the stench of semen in my room made unbearable by the summer heat. My sweat dripped onto the mat, already drenched from the sweat of dozens of men. The foul bedding clung to my back. I placed my hand against the wall that separated me from my comfort women sisters to remind me that I did not suffer alone.

Kaori pulled his large penis through his underwear, and I stroked it to get it stiff. It wasn't working. "Faster, girl," he ordered. "Don't you know how I like it?" He pulled my hair, sending spikes of pain into my scalp.

I knew what I had to do to get him going. "Come on, big man," I snarled. "Hurt me some more."

His eyes flashed excitement, and he slapped me hard.

"Yes, that's right," I said, clenching my jaw. "It's what you want." I stroked him faster, and his huge penis grew. He fumbled with the condom. I took it from him and put it on. He mounted me and tried to push inside me, but he wasn't stiff enough.

"Pinch me," I said. He pinched my nipples hard and slapped me again. My eyes filled with tears. I continued to stroke him. He grew stiff and finally was able to push inside me. His bulk overwhelmed me, and my body jerked with each of his thrusts. Corporal Kaori slapped me again and put his hand around my throat. His eyes grew wide, and he grinned lasciviously.

He was choking me. Hard. I gasped and could feel my face turn red. I tried to tell him to let go, but I couldn't push the words past his grip. I grabbed his arm and squirmed, but his weight kept me pinned to the mat, and my struggles only aroused him more. I saw stars, and everything started to go black.

Then with a convulsion that banged my head in the wall, he was done. He released his hand from my neck and climbed off me. I turned to the side and coughed. I took in air in big gulps. Eventually the stars went away. I clung to the wall and forced myself to stand in the corner.

Kaori removed his condom and dropped it inside my chamber pot. As he pulled up his trousers, I bowed and said a weak thank you. The corporal grunted and left my room.

I clutched the clothes hook on the back of my door to keep myself from collapsing. It took several minutes until I could breathe normally again. Then I picked up my obi and looked at the clothes hook. I admit I thought about doing it. One end of the obi around the clothes hook, the other around my neck. After all, Sun-hi had done it not more than a week after we arrived at the comfort station. She had tied the knots, relaxed her legs, and let herself go. It must have taken great strength for Sun-hi to let herself hang until her obi choked the life from her. I wondered if I could do it, too.

I let go of the clothes hook. I wiped the sweat off my forehead and rubbed the pain from my neck. I wrapped myself in my yukata and tied it closed with my obi. I reached inside my chamber pot, and among the used condoms and semen, I felt for the comb with the two-headed dragon. I took it out and wiped it clean on my bedding. I looked at the two-headed dragon. Mother had said that it would protect us. I was keeping it hidden from the Japanese, but so far it had not protected me from anything.

I slipped the comb under my mat and gathered the sweat-soaked bedding. I picked up the chamber pot and headed out the door. Outside, the sun was bright. It was hot, and the sky was hazy blue. Swarms of big black flies buzzed around the barracks. In the courtyard, the slick mud of spring had turned hard from the sun and the boots of thousands of men. And the wind blew as it did every day at the comfort station.

Seiko and the other Japanese geishas were lounging on their steps, fanning themselves, when I walked by. "You have another night with the colonel," Seiko said to me. "I don't know why he wants a Korean whore like you when he could have a good Japanese geisha like me. He must like the way you use your stone face on him." The other Japanese women laughed without covering their mouths.

I blushed at Seiko's taunting. The colonel had only forced me to do that once. He had just returned from visiting his family in Japan and was upset about something. I never found out what it was. After I undressed him as I usually did, he pushed my face into him. I fought back, but he was so strong, and I was afraid he would break my neck. So I did it. I had to.

Afterward, the colonel turned quiet, almost as if he was ashamed. When I rose to leave, he asked me to stay. That was the first time I stayed the entire night with the colonel. Since then, we spent more time talking than having sex. He gave me Japanese books to read during the long breaks when the soldiers were away. I think the other Korean girls and even the geishas were jealous of me.

As I walked back to my room, Private Ishida was resting in the shade. He nodded to me, and I returned a small bow. I liked the private. He was handsome, but he never used the girls. The geishas teased him and tried to lure him into their rooms. He played along with them but never took their bait. He always warned the Korean girls when the kempei was coming, and he helped me with my Japanese. His rifle was constantly by his side, but I was sure he had never used it.

When I got to the latrine, I emptied my chamber pot and rinsed it out. I washed my hands. In the room next to the latrine, I left my bedding on the pile of dirty laundry and took a clean set. I headed back to the barracks. Seiko and the other Japanese women glared at me. I made sure to keep my eyes low. When I got to my room, I set the chamber pot at the foot of my mat and spread the clean bedding so it would be ready for the next day. I retrieved the comb from under my mat and dropped it inside my chamber pot.

◆ ◆ ◆

I went to the latrine to wash before dinner. The latrine was an open outhouse fifty feet behind the barracks. There was a wooden deck with three holes for the girls to squat over. To the side, on wooden frames, were three chipped and stained metal washbasins. Soo-hee, dressed in her yellow yukata, was washing laundry in one of them. I went to stand next to her.

"I think Kaori will kill me someday," I said, staring into my washbasin.

"I will talk to the kempei about him again," Soo-hee said.

"No, don't," I said quickly, remembering the times the kempei had punched Soo-hee for asking for something. "It is not so bad." I began to wash in the gray water.

"I hear the war is going badly for the Japanese," Soo-hee said. "The Americans are winning in the east. Maybe it will all end soon."

"Then what will we do?" I asked.

"We will go home," Soo-hee said.

"I do not want to go home after what we've done here," I said. "What will Mother and Father think? We have dishonored them."

Soo-hee put a hand on my arm. "Don't worry about what Mother and Father will think. You just need to stay strong a little while longer."

Stay strong? What for? So I could be raped another day? Growing up on the farm, I thought I was strong. I could work all day in the fields alongside Father and Mother and Soo-hee and go days without a full meal when the rice was low. But for the past two years, the effort to make it through each day took everything out of me. I was nothing more than a toilet to the Japanese, and that's exactly how I saw myself. I was doing my best to stay strong, but I wasn't sure how much longer I could.

Soo-hee returned to her basin and looked at me out of the corner of her eye. "This dirty water reminds me of the day that pig got away from Father and Mr. Lee from up the road. They were butchering it for the New Year's feast. Do you remember?"

"Yes, I think so," I answered.

Soo-hee continued, "It was raining that day, and the pig slipped out of their arms. Mr. Lee said they should put out cabbage for it and catch it that way. But Appa was impatient and chased after it."

Soo-hee began to chuckle, and I could feel a smile forming on my face. She continued, "Father chased that pig all around the pen. He slipped and fell in the mud twice before he caught it. And Mr. Lee refused to help."

Soo-hee laughed. "Appa was covered with mud when he got home. Ummah was angry with him for tracking mud inside the house. She made him take off all his clothes and wash outside at the well. He was so mad he had three helpings of roast pig that night!"

We laughed together, careful to cover our mouths as we did. But our laughs quickly went away. As I dried my hands, I looked at my onni's face. "How is your cheek?" I asked.

"It's healing," Soo-hee answered, turning to the basin.

The ugly purple and yellow bruise on Soo-hee's cheek made my heart sink. Three days earlier, Lieutenant Tanaka had punched Soo-hee when she asked the kempei if a new girl could see the doctor about a pain in her stomach. It was only the latest cruelty that my onni had had to suffer at the hands of Lieutenant Tanaka.

"I'm sorry," I said.

"What for?"

"You should have kept the comb. Then you would have better luck, and the kempei wouldn't be so mean to you."

"No, it is better that you have it. It has given you good luck. You are the colonel's favorite."

"It is not so lucky that I am," I said.

Soo-hee stared vacantly at the basin. "Little sister," she said, "I have something to tell you."

"Oh?" I said. "What is it?"

Soo-hee took in a long breath. "I've missed my monthly bleed. My breasts are sore. I'm sick in my stomach in the morning. I think I am pregnant."

My heart stopped. "Onni, are you sure?" I asked.

"Yes. I have to tell Lieutenant Tanaka. He's the only one who doesn't use a condom with me. There is no saying what he will do."

I felt like the ground was opening up and swallowing me. "Soo-hee, they will give you an abortion with a wire, just like they did with Maori and Yo-ee before they died."

"Not everyone who has an abortion dies, Jae-hee. Bo-yun and Mee-su were just fine after their abortions. And Jin-sook was only sick for a month before she came back to work."

I gripped Soo-hee's arm. "You have to take the comb! It will give you good luck like it has for me."

Soo-hee shook her head. "No. You keep it."

"But, Soo-hee, if you die, I will die, too. I'll hang myself with my obi like Sun-hi did."

"Do not talk like that!" Soo-hee snapped. "You will do no such thing."

I lowered my eyes and took a few deep breaths. "When will you tell Lieutenant Tanaka?" I asked.

"I'm supposed to be with him tonight. I will tell him before then. The longer I wait, the riskier the abortion will be. I should have it tomorrow."

"I'm with the colonel tonight," I said. "I'll ask him to send you to the hospital in Pushun."

"He will not do that. Doctor Watanabe will do the abortion."

"Soo-hee, you cannot die. You cannot!" I wanted to cry.

Soo-hee put her hand on me. "I will be all right, little sister. I will not leave you here alone. Now, take care to wash thoroughly for the colonel tonight."

I washed myself with the dirty water and rinsed with it, too. When I was done, I didn't feel clean, but Soo-hee nodded her approval anyway.

As I sat on the step to my room in the fading light, waiting for my time with the colonel, I tried not to think about what life at the comfort station would be like if Doctor Watanabe's abortion killed Soo-hee. I wouldn't be able to do it anymore. I could not possibly go on. I desperately wanted the doctor to send her to the hospital in Pushun for the abortion. But I knew he would not. He didn't even send the geishas there when they got sick.

Suddenly, down the barracks, a roar came from Soo-hee's room. It was Lieutenant Tanaka. I stepped into the courtyard and stared at Soo-hee's door. It swung open, and Lieutenant Tanaka backed out, dragging Soo-hee by the hair. He pushed her down to the dirt and kicked her in the chest. Soo-hee quickly got to her hands and knees and lowered her head to the lieutenant. "I'm sorry, Kempei," she said.

I brought my hand to my mouth to stifle a cry. I watched in horror as Lieutenant Tanaka kicked Soo-hee a second time and growled, "You whore! We must take care of this." He grabbed my onni by the hair and marched toward the infirmary. Soo-hee got to her feet, stumbled and fell, and scrambled to her feet again. Lieutenant Tanaka never slowed as he dragged Soo-hee to the infirmary to see Doctor Watanabe.

TWELVE

The colonel's private quarters were in a wealthy merchant's house near the center of Dongfeng. The comfort station was on the outskirts of town near the wheat fields. I think they put us out there so when they went about their war business, they could pretend we did not exist. The colonel's quarters were a fifteen-minute walk along the road that the trucks used when the soldiers went on maneuvers. In the winter and spring, the trucks made the road a muddy mess. When the comfort women went to be with the officers, they had to take off their tabi and zori and lift their yukatas high to keep them clean. In the summer and fall, the fine yellow dust was the problem. The other girls didn't mind the dust, but I would walk in the ditch alongside the road to avoid it. I had to be clean for the colonel.

I lounged on the daybed alongside the colonel in his quarters. The room had oak paneling, and a large Chinese rug covered the floor. There was a poster bed and a desk with carved legs. Next to the desk was a small table and the daybed where I lay. On the table was a picture of the colonel's family—his wife with an upper-class smile, a pugnacious-looking boy about eight years old, and a girl only a few years younger than me dressed in a pretty white kimono. Next to the picture was a bowl containing two round amanatsu. Their citrus smell filled the room.

The colonel lay on the bed next to me. His men said he was a brilliant military tactician. It was rumored he was being considered for an even higher rank. He worked long hours, and I never saw him when he wasn't deep in thought about something. It is true that he could be cruel to me, but he could be surprisingly gentle, too. He no longer humiliated me when he raped me and almost seemed ashamed afterward. But he still raped me nearly every night he was in Dongfeng.

I moved my legs alongside his muscular frame. The smooth skin on his chest shimmered with the afterglow of sex. His head rested on a dakimakura pillow, and he stared at the ceiling, where a fan with blades made from woven grass slowly rotated.

I hadn't slept the night before, thinking about how to convince him to send Soo-hee to the hospital in Pushun for her abortion. I ran a finger over the table next to the bed. "Colonel, sir, have you gotten a letter from your family in Nagasaki?" I asked.

"I received a letter yesterday," he answered.

"That's wonderful. What do they say?"

"Nothing you need to know."

I wrapped my yukata around me and reclined on the silk bed covers. "When will you see your family again?" I asked.

"I do not know," he said. "I cannot see the future. It might not be for a long time. Why do you care?"

"I have heard the war is ending."

The colonel glared at me. "Who told you that?"

"I'm sorry, sir. It is just a silly rumor."

The colonel looked at the ceiling again. He folded his arms over his bare chest. "Eat some amanatsu," he ordered. "They were shipped from Kumamato for the senior officers. I doubt you get much fruit at the comfort station."

I put a hand on the colonel's leg. It was warm and dewy. "Thank you for taking care of me." I picked up one of the yellow fruits. "What will happen when the war ends? I mean, when Japan has defeated the Americans?"

"We will rule all of Asia, of course," the colonel said.

"Yes, of course. I mean, sir, what will happen to the comfort women when the troops return to Japan?"

The colonel pulled his head off the pillow. "Why do you ask such questions? Am I a prophet? How do I know what will happen to anyone when the war ends?"

He was right. I was asking too many questions again. I lowered my head. "Please forgive a silly girl for asking stupid questions," I said.

The colonel reclined on the dakimakura pillow. "You haven't eaten any amanatsu. Eat some. You are too thin."

"Thank you, sir." As I peeled the fruit, I let my yukata slip open, revealing my breast.

The colonel eyed my breast, and the fan on the ceiling turned. "I don't eat amanatsu this time of year," he said, staring. "They are sour. Take as much as you want." He returned his gaze to the ceiling.

I ate a section of the fruit. It was indeed sour, but I ate it anyway.

"Colonel, sir," I said, "may I ask for something?"

"Ask."

"Sir, my sister is pregnant. Doctor Watanabe is giving her an abortion. Please, sir, have her sent to the hospital at Pushun for the abortion. She will be better off there."

The colonel shook his head. "I will not do that."

"Please, sir, as a favor to me."

With a powerful swipe of his arm, he pushed me off the bed. I fell on the floor with a thud, and what was left of the amanatsu tumbled across the Chinese rug. "Why should I care what happens to a Korean girl?" he said. "I only serve the emperor."

I scrambled to my knees and crawled to him. I brought my face over his thighs and began to unbutton his underwear. He looked down at me as I pulled his penis from beneath his underwear and began to stroke him. He didn't respond, so I brought my face in close. The musty smell from the sex we'd had earlier was strong on him.

The colonel leaned back and grabbed a bottle of sake off the night-stand. "It will not work," he said evenly.

"Please, sir," I pleaded, "I will do anything."

The colonel pulled the cork from the bottle and reached for a glass as if I wasn't there. "Leave me. Now," he said.

I removed my hands from him and slowly stood. As the colonel poured a glass of sake, I bowed and pulled on my tabi. At the door, I slipped on my zori and left the colonel alone in his quarters.

I walked between the low stucco buildings toward the comfort station with my head down. I took the narrow path next to the infirmary. I stopped and put a hand on the infirmary wall. Inside was Soo-hee, waiting for her abortion.

I had tried. I had been willing to do anything. But I had failed, and now my onni's life was in the fat hands of Doctor Watanabe.

◆ ◆ ◆

"You're clean," Doctor Watanabe told me as I lay with my legs spread on his cot inside the infirmary's tiled inspection room. "I don't know how you do it. All girls eventually get pregnant or contract some kind of disease, but not you. You're lucky."

I was seeing the doctor for my monthly inspection for venereal disease. Every month the fat doctor would put on his linen smock and poke and probe me, looking for signs of disease. The soldiers were supposed to use condoms with us, but the Japanese were low on supplies, and we had to reuse the condoms until they broke. They usually lasted only two or three times, and all the girls got venereal disease except me. Perhaps Mother's comb with the two-headed dragon was giving me luck after all.

"Doctor, sir," I said as I rose from the cot and pulled on my short pants, "may I see my sister before the troops come back tomorrow? I will be too busy to see her after that. She is only upstairs from here. Please, sir?"

"No. She is too sick for visitors," the doctor answered from his washbasin.

"Sir, she is my sister."

"Don't talk back, girl," the doctor said over his shoulder. "I said no."

I lowered my eyes. "Will she be all right?" I asked. "Will she recover from the abortion?"

"She's bleeding inside," the doctor answered, drying his hands on a towel. "I don't have time to do an operation. If she doesn't stop bleeding on her own, she will die."

The doctor's words hit me like a punch in the stomach. I stopped buttoning my shirt. "She must go to the hospital in Pushun!" I cried. "Please, Doctor, send her there."

The doctor turned his fat frame toward me. His eyes were red and his face sagged. "Do you think they will take a girl when they have so many soldiers to care for? They will laugh at me for sending her."

"Can anything be done? Please, Doctor."

The doctor motioned for the nurse to send in the next girl. He ordered me to go back to the comfort station. "There is nothing I can do for your sister," he said.

THIRTEEN

The kempei never allowed us to be outside the comfort station, except when we were in the village with the officers and for the monthly checkups in the infirmary. The punishment for getting caught anywhere outside the comfort station was a beating from Lieutenant Tanaka. And if he thought a Korean girl was trying to escape, he would have her shot. So when the soldiers were away, we spent weeks at a time sitting on our steps looking out at the courtyard. Sometimes we tried to make up games to play to pass the time, but they never amounted to much. We were sex slaves to the Japanese, and a silly game could not help us to forget it.

Since they were Japanese, the geishas could go anywhere they wanted to, and when they weren't working, they often went into town for days at a time, leaving us alone. What they did there, I don't know. I was just glad they weren't there to taunt us and call us names, a game they took great pleasure in.

The only respite I had from the boredom was when the colonel gave me books to read. I had to read them inside my room so the other girls wouldn't be jealous of me. In order to see, I had to crack the door open to let light in. In the summer, with the door mostly closed, my room became hot, and the wind blew in dust. I could only read for a short while before I had to open the door all the way to let fresh air in. In the winter, the freezing wind would pour in through the opening, so I could only read a short time then, too. But I still read as much as I could.

We had small chores to do every day, so after my visit to the doctor, I gathered my bedding and went to the laundry. The laundry was four poles supporting a corrugated metal roof next to the latrine. Three metal washtubs sat on low wooden tables. Behind the laundry were wire clotheslines strung from posts. Several sets of bedding dried in the warm sun.

As I washed a stack of them, Jin-sook and Mee-su came in, each carrying an armful of the geishas' laundry. Jin-sook was tall and sinewy and looked at you from down her nose. Mee-su was small and thin. She never looked you in the eye. She was often the last one chosen by the officers.

Mee-su asked me what I had heard about Soo-hee.

"She is no better," I answered.

"She's a fool," Jin-sook said, dropping soiled bedding into a tub. "She pushes the kempei too much. She should do as I do. Make friends with them."

"The Japanese are not our friends, Jin-sook," I said.

"You pretend they aren't," she said, "but you have become friends with the colonel. He gives you books, and you never get a beating. I became friends with Lieutenant Tanaka and haven't gotten a beating since we came here. I have made friends with the geishas, too."

"You are their slave," Mee-su said, kneading the laundry into the soapy water. "You do everything they say."

"That's not true," Jin-sook said. "I just . . . respect them."

"Well, I'm glad Soo-hee stands up to the kempei," Mee-su said. "We will all be in trouble if she dies."

"She will not die," I said, looking at the tub. "I have a plan."

"A plan?" Jin-sook said. "What is it?"

Yes, I had a plan, but I was not going to tell anyone, especially not Jin-sook. Without answering her, I gathered my laundry and headed to the clothesline. "Be careful," Mee-su said. "Kempei is watching you."

I hung the wet bedding on the line and took a clean set from the closet next to the latrine. I headed back to the barracks. When I got to the courtyard, Lieutenant Tanaka was sitting in a chair leaning against the geishas' barracks. The geishas were back from town, which told me the soldiers would be returning soon. Lieutenant Tanaka's shinai rested in his lap. Private Ishida, looking bored, leaned against a wall with his cap over his eyes. Tanaka bent forward as I walked by. "Come here, girl," he said.

I walked to him and lowered my head. His high black boots were freshly polished.

"Look at me," he said. I looked at him. His eyes were small and sharp. "You're not going to cause trouble for me if your sister dies, are you, Namiko Iwata?" He stroked my thigh with his shinai.

"No, Kempei," I answered.

"You won't do something stupid like run away or hurt one of the men?"

"No, Kempei."

"Good, because Colonel Matsumoto cannot help you if you do. I am Kempei tai," he said, pointing at his white armband with the red characters, "the military police. The colonel has no authority over me. So do as I say, or you will earn yourself a beating." He tapped my thigh with his shinai. "And I will give you a good one. Understand, girl?"

"Yes, Kempei."

"Go on now. The troops are returning tomorrow morning. They need you. It is a great service you do for them." He leaned his chair back against the stucco wall.

As I carried my laundry to my room, I glanced at Private Ishida, who turned away.

◆ ◆ ◆

After I had spread my bedding, I went to the courtyard. It was hot and humid. Storm clouds were forming in the west. The girls had put on their yukatas and were waiting on their steps for the soldiers to arrive.

I went to the geishas' barracks and inched open Seiko's door. "Seiko," I said with a slight bow, "I need your help." Inside, Seiko was preparing her room. It was twice as large as mine and had a small window overlooking the courtyard. Inside was a table and a lamp. Instead of a mat on the floor, there was a low bed with a mattress.

"Why should I help you?" Seiko asked.

"Please. I need to see Soo-hee. She's dying."

"I don't care," Seiko said.

"Seiko, you and I, we are not so different. I heard you crying in your room the night Maori died."

Seiko spread clean bedding across her mattress. "Maori was a good Japanese woman. Soo-hee is a Korean."

I was desperate for Seiko's help to make my plan work. It was the only way I could think of to see my sister. "Seiko," I pleaded, "I promise to be your servant for a month if you help me. Please."

Seiko sat in her chair and snapped open her fan. She stared at me as she fanned herself with quick, short strokes. "I will not do anything that will get me in trouble."

"You are Japanese, and Doctor Watanabe is a regular customer of yours. Talk to him. Tell him if Soo-hee sees me, she will recover and return to work. He will listen to you."

"If I do that, you will be my servant for a month?"

"Yes, I promise. I'll do anything you say."

"What if the doctor says no?"

"You are his favorite. If you ask, he will agree."

Seiko snapped her fan closed and returned to making her bed. "Okay. I will talk to him," she said over her shoulder. "I'll let you know what he says."

"Thank you, Seiko." I bowed as I backed out of her room.

◆ ◆ ◆

A while later, Seiko came to me from across the courtyard. She told me she had good news. She had talked with Doctor Watanabe and persuaded him to let me see Soo-hee. She said she cleared it with the kempei, too. "And now you must be my servant for a month," she said.

My heart skipped. "Thank you, Seiko."

"Lieutenant Tanaka said you should go before the soldiers come. You have a half hour. And then come back here. You can start working for me right away."

I bowed and thanked Seiko again. I ran to my room and closed the door. I reached inside my chamber pot and grabbed the comb with the two-headed dragon. The dragon was so white and the gold spine so bright that I knew it would give Soo-hee good luck. I slipped it inside a fold of my yukata and quickly headed for the infirmary.

In the courtyard, the comfort women rested on their steps, fanning themselves in the summer heat. Mee-su and the other girls watched as I crossed the courtyard. From her step, Mee-su slowly shook her head at me.

When I got to the infirmary, I didn't see Doctor Watanabe or Lieutenant Tanaka inside. I hadn't seen Seiko talk with the doctor or the kempei. I thought Seiko might be setting me up, but I didn't care. I was already in the infirmary, and Soo-hee was on a bed on the second floor. I had to give her the comb.

I hurried up the stairs to the infirmary ward. At the end of the hallway, a Japanese nurse sat at a desk writing on a chart. I snuck across the hall to a large white room with a long row of evenly spaced cots.

Sheets hanging from metal rods surrounded several of them. High on the wall, small windows opened out to the town. I did a quick scan of the cots, but didn't see Soo-hee.

A bandaged soldier sitting on the floor next to his cot lifted his head. He asked if I had come for him. I told him I was here to visit my sister.

"When you're done, come see me," he said with a grin. "You can help with my recovery."

I walked down the long room. My zori slapped against the tile floor. Another soldier lifted his head off the pillow and nodded at me. A third rolled over and pulled his blanket over his shoulders.

In a corner, separated from the soldiers by a white sheet, I saw someone lying on a mat on the tile floor. I approached and saw it was Soo-hee. My poor onni's face was pale except for gray circles around her eyes. Her lips were chapped, and her hair was greasy and tangled. I knelt next to her and took her hand. It was clammy and cold.

Soo-hee opened her eyes. "Little sister," she said weakly, "why are you here? You will get in trouble."

"Seiko talked to the doctor, and he said it was okay."

"Do not trust her, Jae-hee."

I brushed a strand of hair from Soo-hee's face. "Onni, you look so sick."

Soo-hee's eyes became cloudy, and she pushed her head in the pillow. "Jae-hee, I do not think I will recover. I said I would never leave you. I'm sorry." Tears welled in her eyes.

I came in close. "No, you will not die," I whispered. "I've brought the comb." I scanned the room and saw that no one was watching us. I reached inside my yukata and pulled out the comb with the two-headed dragon. I slipped it into Soo-hee's hand. "Here," I said, "take it."

Soo-hee shook her head. "No. If I die, they will take it. And then the dragon can't protect you." She pushed the comb back at me.

"But, Soo-hee, Mother gave it to you. If you have it, it will help you. It has not helped me."

"It has helped you, little sister. You must believe in it."

Suddenly Soo-hee's eyes grew wide.

"What do we have here?" a voice boomed from behind me. I spun around and saw the high black boots of the Kempei tai.

"Kempei, sir," I said with a gasp. "The doctor gave me permission to visit my sister."

Lieutenant Tanaka stepped past me and peered down at Soo-hee. "What do you have there in your hand?" Soo-hee wrapped her fingers around the comb. He bent down and slapped her hard. He pulled the comb from her grasp.

"No!" I cried, lunging for it. My cry echoed off the infirmary walls.

Lieutenant Tanaka grabbed a fistful of my hair and held me away. I ignored the pain and fought for the comb, but he was too strong. He held the comb up and examined it. "My, my," he said. "You have been hiding it all this time? You should have given it to your kempei."

I stopped struggling, but Lieutenant Tanaka held on to my hair. "Please, sir, let Soo-hee have it," I pleaded. "It will help her get well."

"Oh no, I cannot do that. Colonel Matsumoto should see it, don't you agree? I'll give it to him when I tell him why you will not be with him tonight."

"Kempei," I said, "Seiko asked the doctor for permission for me to come here. He said I could."

"That's not what Seiko told me. She said you asked her to watch out for me so you could sneak in here against orders. Come," he said with a jerk of my hair, "let's go see Colonel Matsumoto."

As Lieutenant Tanaka dragged me down the infirmary ward toward the stairs, Soo-hee pushed herself up on an elbow. "Kempei, sir," she said, "the comb is mine, not Jae-hee's. I should be punished for hiding it."

Lieutenant Tanaka looked down at Soo-hee. "If you're going to die, girl, do it more quickly," he said evenly. "And don't worry about your sister. I will take care of her."

FOURTEEN

I thought that when the lieutenant caught me in the infirmary, I would get my first beating from him straight away. I had always been terrified of a beating from the lieutenant ever since I watched Jin-sook scream and urinate on herself that first day at the comfort station. And I had had to fight to stay upright all three times the kempei had beaten Soo hee. The lieutenant had beaten most of the other girls, too, and he always made us watch when he did. You would think that after seeing so many beatings I might have gotten used to it. But it was always the same—shocking and terribly frightening to see.

So I was relieved when the lieutenant took me to the colonel instead of marching me to the post in the comfort station courtyard. I dared to hope that the colonel would order him not to discipline me.

Lieutenant Tanaka had a firm grip on my arm as we stood in Colonel Matsumoto's office. The colonel was studying maps spread across his desk. Dark, rough-hewn wooden beams crisscrossed the high ceiling. Windows with Chinese latticework overlooked a courtyard in the center of Dongfeng. A photograph of Emperor Hirohito hung on a wall; a map of Manchuria hung on another. The white and red military flag of Japan stood in a corner. The colonel had not bathed after his return from the battlefield, and dust covered his green field uniform.

There were dark circles around his eyes, and fatigue creased his smooth face.

"Colonel, sir," Lieutenant Tanaka said, standing at attention, "this girl disobeyed orders and must be punished."

"What did she do?" the colonel asked without looking up from his maps.

"She was in a restricted area against my orders."

"Where?"

"In the infirmary, sir."

"The infirmary?"

"Yes, sir. Visiting her sister."

"That is not a serious offense, Lieutenant," the colonel said. "Why do you bother me with it? I have much more important matters to attend to."

"Sir, you asked for her tonight. I thought you should know why she won't be available."

"Really, Lieutenant, is this necessary?"

"Sir, there's something else you should know. This one has been hiding a comb." He pulled the comb with the two-headed dragon from his jacket pocket and placed it on the colonel's desk.

The colonel gave the lieutenant a hard look. "A comb, Lieutenant? With what is happening in the war, you are concerned that this girl has been hiding a comb?"

"Sir, it shows a lack of discipline."

The colonel pushed away from his desk and began to pace across the wood-planked floor. He looked like a man with so much on his mind that some of it had to get out. "Our homeland is under attack, Lieutenant," he bellowed. "We fight the Americans in the east, the Chinese in the south, and now the Russians in the north. They are less than one hundred miles away, and they are advancing with ten divisions." He placed his palms on the desk and leaned toward Tanaka. "The Russians are well equipped and well trained. We do not have the forces or the equipment to—" The colonel held his eyes on the lieutenant for a moment, and then he took a quick look at me. He sat down and stared at his desk.

Eventually he noticed the comb. He picked it up and examined it. "Where did you get this, girl?" he asked.

I bowed. "From my mother, sir. It has been in our family for a long time."

The colonel brought it close to his face. "It . . . it has a two-headed dragon, and its feet have five toes," he whispered.

"Sir?" I said.

"Two-headed dragon, with five toes." He looked at me wide-eyed, then turned to Lieutenant Tanaka. "Do not discipline this girl, Lieutenant."

Lieutenant Tanaka stiffened and pointed to his white armband. "Sir, I am Kempei tai, and I am responsible for the comfort station. I take orders from my own officers. I'm only telling you because she is scheduled with you tonight."

"Yes, you are Kempei tai," Colonel Matsumoto said with a glare, "and I am a colonel, Lieutenant."

"Yes, sir, but I must maintain discipline. For the emperor. For Japan."

"For the emperor. For Japan," the colonel repeated slowly. He looked at the comb and ran his finger along the gold spine. He slipped it into his shirt pocket and looked away. Then he said, "Very well, I will take Seiko tonight, Lieutenant."

Lieutenant Tanaka gave a small nod. "Yes, sir." He grabbed me, pushing his fingers hard into my arm. As Lieutenant Tanaka dragged me to the door, I looked over my shoulder at the colonel. Behind his huge desk and alongside the flag of Japan, he was no longer the terrifying man I had seen that first day at the comfort station.

As he dragged me into the courtyard, Lieutenant Tanaka called for Private Ishida. "Get the rope," he said. "I have a lesson to give." The private jumped to his feet. Our eyes met, and he hesitated a moment. Then he quickly disappeared around the back of the barracks.

Lieutenant Tanaka pushed me toward the post. I fell to the yellow dirt, and he stood over me with his shinai at his side. He ordered me to take off my clothes. I untied my obi and let my yukata fall to the ground. As I pushed off my zori and tabi, I looked out over the courtyard, past the golden wheat fields, over the rolling hills, south toward Korea. I tried to remember the place where Soo-hee and I made kimchi in the kitchen of our home, where our mother had combed my hair in front of the fire. I tried to remember our big white house and the green fields behind it I knew as a child. But no images came, only the bleakness of this place where I had been dying each day for the past two years.

Private Ishida returned with the ropes and handed them to Lieutenant Tanaka. The private didn't look as I untied my undergarments and let them fall to the ground.

Lieutenant Tanaka ordered the private to gather the other Korean girls. Then he pushed me against the post. I pressed my back against the wood, which was warmed from the summer sun. I offered no resistance as he tied my hands and ankles tight to the post. The wind swept over my body. It honestly felt good. The afternoon sun honestly felt good on my naked body. The smooth dirt soothed my feet, and the air tasted sweet. I closed my eyes for a minute and heard soft booms to the west. I wondered if it was the Russian cannons.

The other girls gathered in the courtyard and stood in a line facing me. When Mee-su saw me tied to the post, she brought her hand to her mouth, but quickly took her place with the others. Seiko and a few other Japanese women sat on their steps and watched as Lieutenant Tanaka finished with the ropes. He began pacing in front of the girls.

"This girl has earned a beating," he said, slapping his shinai against his boot harder than usual. "When will you learn that you must not displease your kempei?" He pointed his shinai at the girls. "Do you think I enjoy this? Do you think I *want* to beat you? No! I give you these lessons for your sake, so you will learn to be good Japanese subjects. Soon we will win the war, and you will be glad you are on our side. Now you will watch the punishment without closing your eyes."

Lieutenant Tanaka approached me. His thin lips curled up at the ends, but his eyes were cold and lifeless like a doll's eyes. I took in a breath and relaxed against the post. I looked south toward Korea.

Then he raised his shinai and brought it down hard on my thighs with that horrible crack and thud. The blow shot white-hot flames down my legs and up my back. My stomach clenched hard, and my lungs and throat seized, sending sharp needles of fire into my head and nose. The lieutenant struck me again in the same place, and each flame from the first blow exploded into a thousand more. My lungs let go, and a huge, jagged cry boiled up to my throat. But before it could escape, I grabbed it and choked it back down. And as the kempei beat me, I kept my cries inside, where I was dead like stone.

◆　◆　◆

I could barely make out Private Ishida's face as he carried me to the infirmary. He kept his eyes forward and muttered something under his breath about Lieutenant Tanaka. As he carried me up the stairs, the fire in my legs made me moan. The private stopped and gently shifted my weight in his arms, which eased my pain a little. He slowed his pace and carried me across the ward. He laid me next to Soo-hee.

I couldn't move my legs, and my eyes didn't focus. My head was heavy on the mat.

"Onni," I said, "I'm sorry."

"Don't be sorry, Jae-hee," my onni said. "You did not do anything wrong."

"I was strong," I said. "I didn't cry."

93

Soo-hee reached over and stroked my hair. "I know," Soo-hee said. Her eyes were red, and her face was pale. A tear ran down her cheek. "You were strong and brave. You did the right thing."

"Soo-hee," I moaned, "they've taken the comb."

"Hush, little sister," Soo-hee whispered. "Hush and go to sleep."

Four days later, I lay on my mat staring at the ceiling of my stinking room as soldier after soldier raped me. The bone-deep ache in my legs from Lieutenant Tanaka's beating combined with the fiery burn between them was almost too much to bear. To protect my thighs, I had to spread my legs wide, which made the soldiers' thrusts more painful. Eventually I found a position that delivered the pain evenly between my bruised thighs and raw vagina so I could keep going.

For the past two days, an endless line of soldiers had circulated in and out of our courtyard as cannon fire boomed in the distance. The soldiers were crueler than usual. They slapped me, pulled my hair, and mounted me roughly, desperate to purify their souls before they went off to battle.

As another filthy soldier climbed on top of me, I thought of Soo-hee. I had been able to spend only one night with her on the infirmary's cold tile floor before Lieutenant Tanaka saw that Private Ishida had placed us together. He made Doctor Watanabe put us at opposite ends of the ward. When I saw her last, my onni was pale and weak, but she was still alive, fighting for her life.

At last there were no more soldiers at my step. I struggled to make my aching legs work as I pushed myself off the mat. I wrapped my yukata around me and picked up my chamber pot that no longer hid the comb with the two-headed dragon. When I pushed my door open, Lieutenant Tanaka was standing at the foot of the step with his shinai at his side. "You have the colonel again tonight, Namiko Iwata," he said.

"Yes, Kempei," I replied, trying not to show how weak I was.

"Oh, and I'm sorry to tell you, Doctor Watanabe reports that your sister is not doing well. He says she has only days to live. And in case you're thinking about sneaking out to see her again, I've told Private Ishida to keep a close eye on you and shoot you if you get near the infirmary."

"Yes, Kempei."

"Now go clean up for the colonel," Lieutenant Tanaka said, walking away. "Do your job well. He is under a lot of stress and needs to stay strong for Japan."

And then I finally saw the end. If Soo-hee died, I would die, too. I would hang myself with my obi like Sun-hi did. After two years of being raped, I had enough strength left to do it. The end did not make me sad or anxious. It only made me glad that my nightmare would soon be over.

When I headed to the latrine, I saw that Seiko and the other Japanese women were gone. Private Ishida leaned against the barracks wall as I walked by. He looked in the direction of Lieutenant Tanaka and then at me. I thought he wanted to say something, but he stayed silent. I heard trucks on the road and movement in the village. The cannon fire in the distance was louder than it was in the morning.

I prepared myself carefully for the colonel that day, just like I did that last day at home two years earlier. I washed my yukata and zori and hung them in the sun to dry. I washed my hair and brushed it until it was smooth. I changed out the dirty water in the basin with clean water from the well. I rubbed the coarse soap into my washrag and scrubbed every inch of me until my skin was red. I fetched more fresh water and rinsed myself clean. I picked a splinter of wood from one of the posts that held up the latrine and pricked my finger with it. I squeezed out several drops of blood and rubbed them into my cheeks for rouge as Soo-hee had taught me to do so the colonel would always choose me. I retrieved my yukata from the clothesline. I put it on and smoothed it with my hand. I pinned my hair back with a lotus blossom barrette that the colonel had given me.

And when I was done, I stood at the basin and held my arms at my sides, my fingers straight alongside my legs and my back bent ever so slightly—the pose the geishas used. I closed my eyes. Standing there, I was no longer that stupid, arrogant girl living on the big farm outside of Sinuiju. They had beaten that out of me. I was no longer Korean or even a woman. No, I was a comfort woman—a whore for the Japanese Imperial Army. And I was the colonel's favorite.

I was ready for him.

FIFTEEN

I think I might have been beautiful when I went to be with the colonel that night. I was pretty and young, and I knew how to please a man.

When I got to his room, the colonel was sitting in his short-legged chair with the carved back. He wore his dress whites with a high, stiff collar and a colonel's red epaulets on each shoulder. There were rows of polished medals on his breast pocket, and around his waist was a shiny white belt. He had washed his face and combed his hair. He looked comfortable in his regalia.

An empty bottle of sake lay on its side on the rosewood table. There was another full bottle and two glasses next to it. He had moved the picture of his family from his desk to the table where he sat. The latticed windows were open to the street below, and a breeze blew in.

I had never seen the colonel in a formal uniform. I wondered if there had been a mistake and I was supposed to be with someone else that night. But when he saw me, he ordered me to come in. He nodded toward the daybed and ordered me to sit. I removed my zori and placed them by the door. I sat on the edge of the bed and lowered my eyes.

"I see you are walking with a limp," the colonel said. "Lieutenant Tanaka must have given you a good beating the other day."

"Yes, sir," I said.

He shook his head lazily. "He says he is doing his job like an honorable Japanese soldier. But he does not know what honor is. Perhaps someday I will show him." He lifted his glass from the table and drank the remaining sake in it. He grabbed the full bottle, uncorked it, and poured more into his glass.

The colonel laughed lightly. "Drink some sake with me. It will ease your pain."

"Sir?" I said. He had never offered me any before.

He filled the other glass and held it out to me. "Here," he said. "Sake. Drink it."

I took the glass and held it in my lap. Outside the window, the wind made the trees sway.

"Drink it!" the colonel ordered. "It's white sake from Japan, not the yellow swill they have here. Drink!"

I flashed a flirtatious smiled at him and took a sip of his sake. I'd never had liquor before. It cut my tongue and burned my throat. I wanted to spit it out, but for the colonel, I swallowed it.

"Good Japanese sake," the colonel said, lifting his glass and admiring the clear liquid inside. "I've been saving it for someone special, and you are it! Drink more, girl."

I took another drink. This time it didn't burn as much, and it made me feel warm.

The colonel lifted the picture of his family and gazed at it. "Have you ever been to Japan, girl?" he asked. His speech was slurred. "No, of course you haven't. I will tell you about it. It is beautiful, not like this godforsaken country. My country has snow-capped mountains, blue seas, beautiful green islands, modern cities teeming with people and automobiles. We were the greatest country in the world!" He carefully set the picture down on the table and smiled sadly. "Drink to Japan, girl."

I took another drink.

He leaned toward me unsteadily. The glass of sake dangled between his middle finger and thumb, and he pointed at me with his index finger. "It was a compelling idea," he said. "An empire from the Indian Ocean to the Bering Sea. From the Pacific Islands to China and India. Think of what we could have had! Think of what we could have done! We would have ruled the East for a thousand years!" He grinned at the thought, leaned back, and downed the contents of his glass. He filled it again.

He waved his free hand. "Everyone would have prospered. Not just the Japanese but all Asians. Especially you Koreans. The sacrifices we asked of you were no greater than our own. And you would have been rewarded!" The colonel glared. "But you did not appreciate what we were doing for you."

"I'm sorry, sir," I said. "I do not care about that." I had never spoken to the colonel like that, but I was feeling light-headed. I loosened my obi and opened my yukata a little, but the colonel didn't notice. His face was red and his eyes swam. The wind outside blew hard, making the window bump against the wall.

The colonel swayed as if the wind were blowing him, too. "Of course you don't care," he said. "You are a stupid Korean! Let us drink a toast. Let's drink to Korea! Big drink this time." He raised his glass to me, and together we drank.

He grabbed his glass and the bottle and came to the bed. He loomed over me. "Here, more sake for you," he said, pouring more in my glass.

The room was starting to move, and I was getting nauseous. I wasn't thinking clearly. "Sir," I said, "don't you want to have sex with me? I cleaned myself especially well for you today."

He took a step toward me and struck me with the back of his hand. I fell to the floor, spilling the sake on his Chinese rug. The blow hurt, but in a strange, dull way. I tasted blood in my mouth.

The colonel picked up my glass and filled it to the top. "I said drink!" he roared. "I will drink to Korea, and you will drink to Japan." I lifted myself onto the daybed, and he handed me the glass. I brought it to my mouth and took a drink. The sake no longer burned.

The colonel leaned toward me unsteadily. He unbuttoned his collar. "Lieutenant Tanaka. Kempei," he said, slurring the word. "His job was to turn you into good Japanese subjects. He did not do a very good job, did he?"

"Yes, sir. I mean, no, sir," I said.

"Ha, ha, ha!" the colonel laughed again. He swayed in front of me. Or perhaps it was me who was swaying. He slid into a chair. "It is unfortunate for him. And for you and for Japan. Take another drink," he ordered.

We drank together, the colonel emptying his glass.

"Korea had things Japan needed," he said. "Minerals, protection from the Chinese and mongrel Russians! You are ignorant peasants and needed us, too. If you had done what we asked, it would have worked. It would have worked!" He pointed a finger at me. "It's your fault. You and your damned comb."

I wasn't sure I had heard him right. "My comb, sir?" I heard myself say. "If you don't want to have sex with me, sir, I should go back to the comfort station."

"You cannot go there," he said. "You must stay here tonight. Do you hear me?"

I didn't understand what was going on. If he didn't want to have me, I didn't want to be with him. I didn't care if my impudence got me shot. "Sir, I am going back to the comfort station now." I tried to stand.

He stumbled toward me with the sake bottle and a scowl on his face. He grabbed my cheeks with his thumb and fingers. He pushed me down and opened my mouth. He shoved the bottle in. "Shut up and drink with me, girl!" He emptied the sake down my throat. I swallowed what I could and choked on the rest. He pulled the bottle away, and I coughed and sputtered. Sake dribbled down my chin and onto my yukata.

"Please, sir," I heard myself say, "let me go."

"No! Didn't you hear me? Don't you understand what I'm doing? I am saving you."

"I don't want to be saved," I said.

He threw the bottle aside, and it shattered against the wall. He struck me in the face with his fist. The pain was dull, as if something hard had hit me softly, or something soft had hit me hard. I wasn't sure. "You whore," I heard him say. "It's your fault! You made us do it! You made *me* do it." He hit me again, and the room spun.

I thought I should say I was sorry—sorry for being a stupid Korean, sorry for not being a good Japanese subject, sorry for not being able to please him.

Outside, the trees swayed in the wind. I felt another blow against my face. There were stars in my head, and then everything went dark.

I heard rain falling on the street outside the window. I opened my eyes and turned to the side. It was daylight. My head pounded, and my mouth was dry. I pressed a finger against my lip. It was tender and puffy. I couldn't see well out of my left eye.

I lifted my head and looked around. I couldn't tell if I was alone. A strong wind blew in from the window behind the colonel's desk. I stood unsteadily and wrapped my yukata around me. It stunk like sake. I tried to focus on the door, but the room moved. My stomach convulsed, and I fell to my knees next to the bed and retched. Green bile spewed from me onto the Chinese rug. I retched three times more. My head pounded so hard with each one, I was afraid I would pass out again. I spit sour bile from my mouth. Eventually I caught my breath, and the room stopped moving.

I looked up and thought I saw something on the bed. I forced my eyes to focus on it. On the white linen, where I couldn't miss it, was the comb with the two-headed dragon.

I stood uneasily and looked around the room. I thought I might be dreaming. The desk chair was on its side. Empty drawers were scattered around the room. The military flag of Japan lay on the floor, ripped in half.

The pounding in my head eased a little. I looked again at the comb. The gold spine glistened, and the dragon reached for me like it did the day I left home. I picked it up and slid it inside my yukata. I stumbled to the door. I slipped my feet into my zori and went out into the rain. The shower of cold rain brought me out of my fog a little, and I saw that the entire village was on the move. Military trucks rumbled slowly along the narrow streets. Lines of soldiers walked alongside the trucks with their heads down and rain dripping from their helmets. They were all marching east.

I dragged myself through the muddy streets toward the comfort station. I smelled something burning as I reached the back of the latrine. I peered around the corner at the comfort station. One of the barracks was on fire, and Private Ishida was setting fire to another. Lieutenant Tanaka paced in the middle of the courtyard. The Korean girls stood in a line, facing the back end of a canvas-covered green truck. The rain made their hair and clothes cling to their bodies.

"Where is Namiko Iwata?" the lieutenant shouted above the rain. "Where is Jae-hee? I want to know!"

Jin-sook stepped forward and bowed. "She did not come back last night, sir."

Lieutenant Tanaka took a step toward Jin-sook. He lifted her head with the tip of his shinai. "You wouldn't lie to me, would you, girl?"

"No, sir," she answered. "Not me."

The kempei lowered his shinai. "Jae-hee was with the colonel last night," he said. "Well, well. I think our leader has gone soft. I had better see about that. Carry on, Private," he said to Private Ishida. As he walked away, he threw his shinai in the burning barracks.

Private Ishida hesitated a moment, but then went to the truck and lifted the canvas flap. He stepped away, and from inside the darkness, a machine gun opened fire.

SIXTEEN

They killed five of my ianfu sisters immediately. Three girls froze in fright, and soon the thundering, heavy-caliber gun found them and put them down like the first five.

Jin-sook fell to her knees. "No!" she cried. "Why me?" The gunner put several bullets in her, throwing her body into the mud with her legs twisted underneath her. Mee-su ran screaming toward the latrine with her hands over her ears. Private Ishida lifted his rifle and shot her in the back. She flopped to the mud, arms out, limp as a rag doll. Then the machine gun was silent, and there was only the smell of gunpowder and the splatter of rain falling on mud.

Private Ishida lowered his rifle and stared at the lifeless body of Mee-su. His mouth was open and his head cocked to the side as if he was trying to understand what he had just done. He stared for several seconds. Then he looked directly at me. I held his eyes, stepped out from behind the latrine, and faced him without fear. He raised his rifle, but he did not shoot. I reached inside my yukata and pulled out the comb. I held it in my hand. As I looked down the barrel of Private Ishida's rifle, I saw all the women in my family who, like me, had once held the comb in their hands. I saw them all the way back to my great-great-grandmother, the yangban who'd had the comb made. And they told me to run.

So I ran. As fast as my sore legs could carry me, I ran behind the latrine toward the village. To my left was the laundry and in front of me the white walls of the infirmary. I slipped in the mud, pushed myself up, and ran inside the infirmary. I ran up the stairs to the ward. It was empty except for Soo-hee. My zori slapped against the tile floor and echoed against the walls as I ran to her. I grabbed her arm. "Soo-hee," I panted. "They're shooting us! We have to run!"

Soo-hee's eyes were sunken, and her skin was as pale as snow. "I can't," she said weakly.

I tugged harder. "You have to. They will kill us!" Soo-hee winced in pain, and I let go of her arm.

I stood over Soo-hee with the comb in my hand and saw that she was too weak to move. And then I knew it was truly over. I lay on the cold tile floor next to my onni. I put my head close to hers. "Okay," I said. "We will die together."

Soo-hee took in a pained breath. "Jae-hee," she said. "You must go without me."

I shook my head. "No, Soo-hee. I cannot." I was finally at peace. I was ready to die.

With effort, Soo-hee pushed herself up on an elbow. "Yes, you can, Jae-hee. You have the comb with the dragon there in your hand. You were born in the year of the dragon. You can survive this. The comb will protect you."

I opened my hand and looked at the comb. "I do not believe in the comb," I said. "It didn't help Mother, and it did not save us from this."

"You can still be saved," Soo-hee said, "and then you can tell them what happened here."

"I don't want anyone to know what happened here," I said.

"Then," Soo-hee said, "they will get away with it."

I heard footsteps from the stairway at the other end of the ward. Men were talking in clipped voices. Soo-hee touched my arm. "You must go," she whispered. "Please do this for me. Do it for all of us."

I glanced down the long corridor, then back at my sister. Her eyes were sunken and sad. I so wanted to stay with Soo-hee, to let it all be over.

The footsteps grew louder. "Oh, Soo-hee," I said.

"Good-bye, little sister," Soo-hee said, lying back down. "Go now. Hurry!"

I reached over and stroked Soo-hee's hair. I gave her one last look and pushed down another cry. Then, with the comb in my hand, I ran for the door.

My legs no longer hurt, and my head didn't pound. I ran down the stairs and out into the street. The rain was falling hard among the colorless procession of soldiers. I didn't see Private Ishida or Lieutenant Tanaka. I cut between two buildings, and the roofs dripped rainwater on me. I ran through a courtyard and between two more buildings. I came to a grass strip separating the village from a wheat field. I looked to my left, then to my right, and ran for the field.

From somewhere behind me, Lieutenant Tanaka shouted, "There she is! Shoot! SHOOT HER!"

A rifle shot rang out, and mud splattered a circle near my feet. I ran as fast as I could and reached the wheat field. There was another shot. The bullet snapped through the stalks alongside me. I ran into the field. Mud grabbed at my zori, so I let them slip off. I ran and ran, but the stiff, sharp wheat stalks cut my feet. I dropped to my hands and knees and crawled, gripping the comb as I went. Boots splashed in the mud behind me. I crawled with all my strength, but I kept slipping in the mud. The footsteps came closer. Over my shoulder, I saw Private Ishida scanning the wheat field for me, his rifle in both hands. He spotted me and ran up to me. I rolled over on my back in the cold mud. The private aimed his rifle at me.

I held the comb in front of me. Rain struck my face and ran in my eyes. I blinked it away and met the eyes of Private Ishida. "Private," I said, "your people have already killed me many times. Let me live this once."

He held his aim. Rain dripped off the rifle barrel and the bill of his cap. He held nervous eyes on me for several seconds. Then he whispered, "They'll shoot me if they find out. Stay here until we leave." He pulled the rifle barrel a few inches to the left and fired twice into the ground, making mud splatter on my face. He ran back to the village.

I couldn't breathe. My ears rang from the rifle shots, and I wondered if I was still alive. Eventually the ringing went away, and all I heard was rain patting on the ground next to me. I pulled my arms and legs to my chest. I wanted to cry, but I hadn't allowed myself to cry for so long, I didn't know how to, so tears never came.

Darkness. The rain had stopped, and the air was still. I lay on my side, my knees to my chest, shivering in the cold, sticky mud. Inky clouds slid away, revealing bright stars in a moonless sky. The only sound I heard was a dog barking somewhere in the village.

I pushed myself to my knees and then unsteadily to my feet. There was no movement in the village and no lights. I held the comb with the two-headed dragon tight in my fist.

I walked barefoot through the wheat field, across the grass to the village. The burn in my thighs from Lieutenant Tanaka's beating had come back, making it difficult to walk. The bruises on my face from Colonel Matsumoto's blows had turned into a sharp ache. I stumbled down Dongfeng's abandoned streets to the infirmary. I pulled myself up the dark stairs to the ward and went to where Soo-hee had been. I pulled aside the white sheet. She wasn't there.

I left the infirmary and went to the comfort station. They had burned the barracks to the ground. A few lonely flames danced among the smoldering remains. And there I saw the bodies of the eleven girls lying in a jagged line, lifeless, like mounds of dirt.

I stood in the courtyard, and all the cries I had pushed down for so long roiled and raged inside me. The stone in my stomach cracked. I closed my eyes, fell to my knees, threw back my head, and opened my throat. And all my cries burst out.

I kneeled on the muddy ground with my face to the sky, and a thousand cries met a thousand stars in the moonless Manchurian night. I cried for my innocence and for each time they called me a whore. I cried for the dead girls who had been my sisters. I cried for my mother and father. And I cried for Soo-hee. The cries ripped out my stomach, my lungs, and my heart until there was nothing left inside, and I collapsed, empty, to the mud.

◆ ◆ ◆

Daylight. The smell of burned wood. The sticky wet of mud underneath me. A crow cawed nearby. The stillness of death.

I drew a breath and opened my eyes. The sun was at its midmorning angle. The air was calm. Here and there, thin lines of smoke drifted up from the barracks' charred remains. A crow perched on the dead body of Mee-su, pecking at her eyes. There was the sound of a truck behind me. A truck door opened, and I heard footsteps in the mud. The crow cawed and slapped its wings in flight. I heard voices in a strange language.

A boot like I had never seen before—dirty and well used—kicked me. A voice said something I didn't understand. The boot kicked again, sending pain into my ribs. I lifted my head and looked to where the voice had come from. I saw a man's face.

His eyes were blue.

SEVENTEEN

August 2008. Seoul, South Korea

Mrs. Hong is giving me an "I-told-you-so" stare. I look into my empty teacup. I guess I didn't know what to expect when I agreed to hear her story about the comb with the two-headed dragon. Maybe something about a rich ancestor or a found treasure. I'd hoped it would be something that would help me. For sure, I hadn't expected a story like this. "I didn't know anything about the comfort women," I say. After I say it, I realize I sound incredibly lame.

"I am telling you," she replies, "because you must know."

"To fulfill your promise to your sister," I say. "To tell what happened to you."

"Yes, but you must also know because you are a Korean. You should know what happened to your country. You need to know your people. Anyway, you have only heard part of my story. There is more, much more I have to tell you."

There's more? She's still dressed in her yellow hanbok, sitting upright in her chair, ready to go on. Me? I need to stop. I'm tired and confused. I now have more questions than when I got here. It just doesn't make sense—the gold comb in the hands of this poor woman, her incredible story. I need time to process this.

A breeze blows through the window, and clouds are forming outside. It smells like it does before it rains. I look down at the street. I check my watch. It's 12:45. The cab won't be here for over two hours, and I have no other way to get back to the hotel.

I look around Mrs. Hong's apartment. It's the exact opposite of my room in Minnesota. Nothing's out of place. The spread on her bed is tucked in drum tight. The walls and small refrigerator are spotless. The window is clean inside and out. The floor looks like she sweeps it every morning, although I'm sure it doesn't need it.

I look at her. In her face are the lines and scars of her story. In her eyes is her pain. In her shoulders, draped by the chima of her hanbok, is dignity and grace that tells me there is indeed more to her story. I want to hear it.

"Ma'am," I say, "I'll listen to the rest of your story. But what is it about this comb? I mean, it's just an heirloom, right?"

Mrs. Hong shakes her head. "It is important that you take the time to understand what it is so you know what it means for you."

"I'm sorry, but I don't know if I should take it," I say. "I don't want to break any laws."

Suddenly there's a loud knock on the door. A man's voice shouts something in Korean. My eyes snap to Mrs. Hong. "The police," she whispers. Her weird smile rattles me as much as the knocking at the door. "They're here for the comb!"

I look at the table where Mrs. Hong set the package with the comb. It isn't there. The knocking turns into pounding. My heart starts racing. "Anna," Mrs. Hong says with a stern look, "listen carefully. Tell them that you went to an address that came with the comb and gave it back to the person who gave it to you. Then you came to visit me. Do you understand?"

"Why?" I ask.

"They cannot have the comb," she says.

Mrs. Hong goes to the door and opens it. In the hallway are two men. Mrs. Hong bows, but the men push past her into the apartment. The taller one is dressed in a smooth suit and looks like a government man you see on TV. The other guy is bald and looks like an Asian version of Bruce Willis. He's wearing a sports coat a size too small that shows off his impressive biceps. Two policemen follow them in. I quickly stand as Government Man comes up to me.

"Are you Anna Carlson?" Government Man asks. His English is well practiced with only a slight trace of an accent.

I shoot a nervous look at Mrs. Hong. "Yes," I say.

"And this is your grandmother, Hong Jae-hee?" Government Man asks, pointing at Mrs. Hong.

"Yes, it is. Who are you?"

"My name is Mr. Kwan," he answers. "I'm here for the comb you showed Dr. Kim yesterday. It might be a valuable Korean artifact. I wanted to talk to you at the hotel this morning, but your father said you were sick and had to stay in bed. But now we find you here. You lied. So where is the comb?"

"I . . . I don't have it. I gave it back. Are you with the police?"

Mr. Kwan takes out his ID and shows it to me. It is in Hangul, so I can't read it, but it looks official enough. He tells me he's with the Korean National Police. He asks who I gave the comb to. I'm starting to wonder if it's a good idea to go along with Mrs. Hong's lie.

"There was an address with it," I say quickly. "I went there and gave it back. Then I came here to visit my grandmother." My knees are shaking, and I don't want Mr. Kwan to see, so I move closer to the table.

"I don't believe you," Mr. Kwan replies, noticing my move to hide my shaking knees. "Anyway, it doesn't matter. If the comb is here, we will find it." He motions Bruce Willis over to me. As the policemen start to search the apartment, Bruce motions for me to raise my arms.

"Are you going to frisk me?" I ask unsteadily.

"Yes, we are," Mr. Kwan answers. I can't believe it. I'm ten thousand miles from home in a country where I don't speak the language. I think I might be in serious trouble. I see Bruce has a metal-detecting wand, so thank God he doesn't have to touch me. He waves the thing over my entire body. When he's satisfied that I don't have the comb, he turns to Mrs. Hong. Her twisted grin makes me even more nervous. Bruce says something to her in Korean and waves his wand over her. He doesn't find anything on her, either.

Mr. Kwan points to the table. "Both of you sit," he orders.

We sit at the table, and Mr. Kwan stands over us with his arms folded as the policemen search the apartment. They're amazingly thorough. They disassemble parts of the stove, pour the bori cha down the drain and look inside the pot, remove the trap in the sink, wave the wand over every inch of the bed mat. They wand all of Mrs. Hong's clothing, pour out the rice from the burlap bag in the cupboard, examine the light fixture in the ceiling, turn over the table and chairs. They look everywhere, but when they're done, they haven't found the comb. I begin to wonder myself where it is.

Finally the police are done, and Bruce Willis shrugs. Mr. Kwan turns to me. He asks me if I remember the address where I took the comb and how I got there. I say I don't remember and don't know where it was. He asks me to describe the comb, and I give him a general description of it. He writes everything I say on his pad.

Then he asks, "Did the dragon have five toes? Try to remember. This is important."

I remember Mrs. Hong's story that Colonel Matsumoto was amazed that the dragon had five toes, but I didn't notice it myself. "I don't remember seeing that," I say, thankful that I can finally tell him the truth about something.

"So you gave the comb back and then you came here?" he asks. "Why?"

"To meet my grandmother. To hear her story."

"Her story?" he says. "I can only imagine what she is telling you. But you should know that if she was an honorable woman, she would live in the comfort woman home in Gwangju instead of this place."

He turns to Mrs. Hong. "I have read your papers, Hong Jae-hee," he says in English, probably to discredit Mrs. Hong in front of me. "What are you hiding? Why do you live in this place and not at the House of Sharing? You would be honored there along with the other comfort women."

Mrs. Hong glares at him but doesn't say anything. Mr. Kwan says, "Perhaps it is because you were a *chinilpa*?"

I don't know what a *chinilpa* is, but the way Mr. Kwan slurred the word, it sounds like a gross insult. He turns back to me, and I swallow hard. "Is she the one who gave you the comb?" he asks. "Answer me."

I'm starting to panic. I don't want to tell the truth, but I don't want to lie, either. Mr. Kwan motions to Bruce, who comes and stands behind me. Mr. Kwan puts his hands on the table and looks me straight in the eye. He's scowling, making me wish I'd never come here. He tells me people have stolen Korea's national treasures for thousands of years. He says it's illegal to take artifacts out of Korea and that I'll be in a lot of trouble if I do. He says the comb might be very important to Korea. "Now I want answers," he says. "I ask you again. Is this the person who gave you the comb?"

I feel the hulking presence of Bruce behind me, and I'm about to cry. "I—I—" I stammer.

Mr. Kwan slams his fist on the table, making both me and the teacups jump. "Answer me!" he barks. "You know where it is, and I want you to tell me. Now!"

Tears are welling in my eyes. I can't breathe. If these men want to hurt me, there's nothing I can do to stop them. I take a deep breath, ready to tell them everything they want to know.

Then in a flash, Mrs. Hong is on her feet, pushing Mr. Kwan toward the door. "Get out!" she screams. "Get out of my apartment this minute!"

Mr. Kwan steps back, surprised at her rage. "Ma'am, do not get in our way. This is an official matter."

She takes an angry step toward him. "Do you think I'm afraid of you?" she growls. "Do you think you can do anything to me that has not already been done? You are nothing! I have suffered all my life for Korea. I can suffer a lot more." She steps up to Mr. Kwan until she is inches away from his face. "She doesn't have the comb, and you have searched my apartment. Now go, find who has it instead of threatening me and my granddaughter!"

Mr. Kwan locks eyes with Mrs. Hong. Then he blinks twice. After a few long seconds, he turns to me and asks what my plans are for the rest of the day. I tell him that after I'm done here, I plan to buy a celadon pot and then go to the hotel to catch the bus for the airport.

"Good," he says. "Be sure you are on your flight tonight, or I will have you arrested. Is that clear?"

I assure him he's very clear. I'm seriously relieved that I'm off the hook. He shoots another look at Mrs. Hong, who hasn't backed away an inch. He turns to leave but stops midstep. "Oh, and by the way, the best place to buy a celadon pot is at Kosney department store, not from the shops on the streets. The quality is much better. It's worth the higher price."

"I'll . . . ah . . . look into that," I say. He gives me a diplomatic smile, and then he and the others leave.

Mrs. Hong comes back to the table. All the anger she showed only seconds earlier is gone. She asks if I'm all right.

I shake my head. My heart is pounding. The apartment is shrinking in on me, and I'm suffocating. "They—they were going to hurt me," I gasp. "I have to go." I grab my purse and push away from the table.

"No, stay," she says. "You will be fine."

"No, I'm not fine!" I cry. "I have to get out of here." I head for the door.

"If you leave now, Ja-young, you will prove that I was wrong about you," she says.

Wrong about me? She doesn't know the first thing about me. And honestly, I don't know anything for sure about her, either. I turn back to her. "Look, my name is Anna, and I'm sorry if I'm afraid, but I can't do this." I fight back tears as I march to the door and pull on my shoes.

As I reach for the door handle, she says, "It is your fear that will prevent you from becoming who you are meant to be." I grip the door handle hard but don't turn it.

"Don't you want to know, Anna?" she asks gently.

EIGHTEEN

Who am I meant to be? Good question, Mrs. Hong. Am I the backward Anna or the forward Anna? Am I the American me or the Korean woman I see in the mirror?

She tells me to come back to the table. "You are safe here," she says.

I let go of the door handle and slowly push my shoes off. I go back and sit with her. She's perfectly composed, which is only a little reassuring. She points at the blossom in the bowl on the windowsill. "It's beautiful in the sunlight, don't you think?" she asks.

"Yeah, I guess," I say.

"Every two or three days I get a new one at the market even though I can't afford it. Notice how the sun brings out the colors. You can see the veins in each petal." I don't look at it that closely.

"That blossom started as a seed," she continues. "It was buried deep in the cold, dark ground. One day when the soil was warm and moist, the little seed split apart and began to climb to a world it could not see. Imagine the courage it had! It did not know what it would find when it broke through the surface. The scorching sun? The gardener's blade? The crushing hoof of a cow? But the seed courageously pushed on so that one day it could become a beautiful flower."

She points a finger at me. "You must have the courage of the seed, Anna. Without it, you will stay buried. You will rot and die. It does not matter how smart you are, or how pretty, or if you have money and many friends. If you do not have courage, you will never blossom into the flower you were meant to be."

"I don't have much courage," I say.

She raises an eyebrow. "You have more than you think. It took a great deal of courage to come here today. And you didn't tell that awful man what he wanted to know."

"I was about to tell him everything," I admit.

"Perhaps. But you didn't." She goes to the kitchen area and starts to clean up the mess the police made. "Tell me, Anna," she says, putting things back in their place, "do you know what kind of flower it is?"

I glance at it. "It looks like a hibiscus," I say. "We have a bush in our backyard."

"Very good. You are correct. It is in the hibiscus family." She gets out a rag and carefully wipes down the kitchen countertop. "In Korea we call it a *mugunghwa* blossom. Have you ever heard of it?"

"I think one of our tour guides told us it's used in Korean architecture. Something about the House of Yi."

She's at the stove that the police took apart. They put it back together, mostly, but Mrs. Hong is readjusting what they did and at the same time cleaning it as thoroughly as most people do only once every one or two years. "Did the guide tell you anything more?" she asks.

"I don't remember," I say. I'm losing the battle against my nerves. I don't want to talk about the mugunghwa blossom or the House of Yi. I'm afraid that Mr. Kwan and Bruce Willis will come crashing back in and arrest me. I just want to get away.

Mrs. Hong turns from the stove and frowns at me. "You need to pay attention," she says. "The mugunghwa was the symbol of the Chosŏn Dynasty of Korea. The House of Yi was our ruling family from the fourteenth century until the Japanese annexed our country in 1910 and turned Korea into a slave state."

"Yes, it was a terrible thing the Japanese did," I say.

"The Americans, too," Mrs. Hong says.

"The Americans?"

She looks around her apartment and wrings her hands. "I'll have to clean more thoroughly later," she says.

"Seriously?" I say. "It looks fine to me. Perfect, in fact."

She sighs. Then she puts another pot of bori cha on the stove.

She comes to the table and sits across from me. "Ja-young, for all of our history, world powers, including America, have exploited us. Do you remember how the Russo-Japanese war ended?"

"No. I haven't studied history."

"You should," she says. "The US negotiated the treaty in 1905. However, to get the Japanese to sign, and so Tokyo would not challenge America in the Philippines, your President Roosevelt secretly agreed to let Japan occupy Korea. And that is just what they did. They took our country and said Korea was now part of Japan. Of course, because of that secret agreement, America did nothing. The result was thirty-five years of horrible oppression of my people—like being raped by their soldiers."

"But Americans didn't rape you," I say.

"No," she snaps back, "but they let it happen to protect their own interests."

She lets her point sink in. Then she goes to the stove, pours two cups of bori cha, and brings them to the table. The aroma fills the room. I take a sip, and immediately the strong, bitter liquid calms my nerves. Mrs. Hong sits in her chair, relaxed and poised.

She turns her attention to the blossom again. "The mugunghwa is not only beautiful, it has a pleasant fragrance, too. Smell it."

"What? You want me to smell it?"

"Yes," she answers.

I lean over and take a sniff.

"No, no," she says. "Take the bowl in both of your hands, and smell it that way."

I lift the bowl from the sill and bring it to my nose. The fragrance is earthy and sweet. "I see what you mean," I say.

Before I can put the bowl back, she lifts an end of the windowsill. There's a small compartment underneath. She reaches inside and lifts out the package of coarse brown cloth. I have no idea when she put it there. It must have been sometime during her story about the comfort station when I wasn't looking. Dumbstruck, I continue to hold the bowl with the mugunghwa blossom in my hands.

She giggles like a kid who just got away with something. "I have lived in this apartment for thirty-five years," she says. "Practically since the building was new. I have hidden the comb here all that time. I knew they wouldn't find it."

She sets the package on the table and pulls on the twine. The cloth falls open, and there's the comb with the two-headed dragon.

"By the way," I say, setting the blossom back on the sill, "you said there were two things you wanted me to do. One was to hear your story. What's the other thing? You haven't said yet."

She moves the mugunghwa blossom to the table next to the comb and the two photographs. "Listen to the rest of my story first."

I'm still a bit shook up, but her confidence reassures me. I lean back, ready to listen again.

"Where were we before we were so rudely interrupted?" she asks.

"The Japanese left, and the Russians had come."

"Ah yes." She nods. She holds her teacup in both hands. "The communists. How disappointing."

NINETEEN

September 1945. Dongfeng, Manchuria

For two years in Dongfeng when I dared to dream, I sat in my tiny room and dreamed of the day I would be free and could go back home. I thought it would be the happiest day of my life. But when the day finally came, I was lost and alone. With the Japanese, I always knew what I had to do—laundry in the morning before the soldiers came, cooking on the days the geishas assigned it to me, servicing the soldiers all afternoon and night. I wasn't allowed to go anywhere outside the comfort station except the infirmary for my monthly inspection and the officers' quarters at night. My routine was simple, and my world was small. But now it was gone, and I didn't know what to do.

And I was afraid. I was afraid of the Russians with their strange, guttural language. I was afraid the Japanese might come back and kill me. I was afraid someone would discover what I had done there for the previous two years.

So for days I hid among the low stucco buildings of Dongfeng still dressed in my green yukata. I snuck from empty house to empty house, staying far away from the comfort station. I ate what food I could find, and each night I took shelter in one of the abandoned houses, curled up in a dark corner, and tried to sleep. I never really slept well then. Whenever I drifted off, I saw the machine gun cutting down my Korean sisters or the face of Soo-hee when she said good-bye. Any loud noise made me hide for hours.

One day I went inside a house that had a mirror and saw my reflection. At first I didn't recognize myself. But gradually I could see it was me who was dressed in the green yukata. I was horrified. I immediately stripped it off and searched the house until I found regular clothes.

I do not know how many days I lived like that. It might have been weeks. But eventually the Russians caught me and took me to their headquarters in Colonel Matsumoto's office. When they pushed me in front of the thick-browed Russian officer sitting at Colonel Matsumoto's desk, I thought they were going to accuse me of helping the Japanese. I was afraid they were going to shoot me. In Japanese, the officer asked me what I was doing in Dongfeng. I couldn't answer his question. I honestly did not know what to tell him. He asked me where I was from.

"My family farm outside Sinuiju," I answered.

"Korea," he said. "Were you one of the Korean girls?"

"Yes," I answered, looking at my feet.

"What were you doing here?"

I was too numb and confused to tell him what happened at the comfort station. And I'm not sure I had the words even if I hadn't been confused. "Have you found Soo-hee?" is all I could think to say. "She is two years older than me."

"You're the only one we found alive," the officer said. "The Japanese have surrendered. They're gone. Go back to your home. You can't stay here."

I didn't know exactly where my home was from Dongfeng, so I asked the Russian officer. He told me it was 280 miles to Sinuiju and that there was no transportation. Apparently I'd have to walk the entire way. The officer told his soldiers to give me some rice, and then he sent me on my way.

I wrapped the rice along with the comb in a wool blanket. I looked south toward Korea. I was afraid to go back home where I would have to tell my mother and father I had been an ianfu. How could they possibly understand? But I longed to see them again and have things the way they were before. So I lifted the blanket sack to my shoulder and asked an old Chinese farmer which way it was to Korea. The farmer pointed down the dusty road that ran alongside the comfort station, and I set off.

After a mile, I turned onto a two-way road. I looked back at the low, tile-roof buildings of Dongfeng and thought of the eleven girls I knew there, my ianfu sisters. I thought of my onni, Soo-hee. Somehow I had survived, and I wondered why. Perhaps it was because I had been born in the year of the dragon. Maybe the comb had brought me good luck after all. Whatever the reason, I had to go on. I had to go on for them. So I joined a thin gray column of refugees with bundles on their backs, pots and utensils tied to their waists, and children in tow. There were young and old, Chinese and Koreans, bent under their loads, going east, going south—going home.

◆　◆　◆

I walked for many miles each day. Then on the third day, a Russian soldier offered me a ride on the back of his flatbed truck. I was tired and my feet were sore, so I climbed up and hung on. After a few miles, the driver stopped where there was no one on the road. He pulled me off the truck and led me to the ditch. I lay in the dewy grass and looked up at the sky as I had looked up at the ceiling of my room in the comfort station all that time. I knew what I had to do. So I opened my dress as the driver unbuttoned his trousers. He went to mount me, but he wasn't stiff yet.

"Slap me," I said in Japanese.

He looked at me, confused. "Slap me hard!" I yelled. I took his hand and made him slap my face. "Pinch me!" I demanded. I brought his fingers to my breasts and made him pinch me. "Come on!" I screamed at him. "I know what you like. Aren't you a man?"

He pulled back, confused, and started to button his trousers. He was rejecting me. Yes, I wasn't able to wash myself for him, but I was the one who always had the longest lines at the comfort station, and I was the colonel's favorite. Didn't he know? I flew into a rage. I jumped on him. I scratched his face and spit on him. I screamed at him, nasty words that I learned from the Japanese geishas. I punched him in the nose, making it bleed. He punched me back, throwing me hard to the ground.

"What's the matter?" I said, looking up at him. "Don't you want me?" He walked backward to his truck mumbling something in Russian. He climbed in and drove off, leaving me alone in the ditch.

I sat in the tall grass and watched the truck disappear down the road. And then I laughed. I laughed out loud at the stupid Russian driver who thought I wouldn't know what to do. I faced toward Dongfeng and laughed at the thousands of Japanese men who'd had me. I laughed at the arrogant geishas who had done exactly what we did, only for money. I laughed at all of them without covering my mouth. And then I stood up and screamed. I screamed so hard that it hurt my throat. My scream echoed off the hills, and I laughed again at the echo of my scream, this time careful to cover my mouth as I did.

After a while, standing there in that field with my dress wide open, I wanted to cry. Instead, I buttoned my dress and lifted my sack and marched on.

On the eighth day, I ran out of food. My legs ached from walking. My feet were on fire with blisters and bleeding, and my stomach growled constantly. I was weak with fatigue. I stopped for the day alongside two elderly Chinese women. They told me they were going to Dandong, China, across the Yalu River from Sinuiju. I spoke Chinese to them, and it was the first time in two years that someone other than my Korean sisters was nice to me. They gave me some rice and a pair of tabi for my raw feet. They said I could travel with them.

At night before we went to sleep, one of the women asked, "What did you do in Dongfeng?"

I didn't know what to say. I was exhausted and confused, and nothing about the past two years made any sense. After a few long moments, I said, "My sister and I worked for the Japanese."

"What did you do for them?" the woman asked.

"I—I—" I stumbled. "We were supposed to work in the boot factory," I finally said.

The other woman raised an eyebrow. "You worked for the Japanese in a boot factory?"

"We did not volunteer," I said quickly. "We were not *chinilpa*. They made us do it."

The women exchanged glances and said nothing more. They crawled under their blankets to go to sleep. When I awoke the next morning, they were gone.

◆ ◆ ◆

Midday on the fourteenth day, I arrived at the outskirts of Sinuiju. I had run out of food and water again. My stomach had stopped growling a day earlier, and my tongue was thick and dry. In spite of the effort it had taken to get this far, I wanted to keep going, farther away from Dongfeng. I forced myself up the long road to our farm. I was desperate to get home. I wanted to see my mother and father again. I wanted Soo-hee to be there, too. But the last time I had seen my onni, she had been close to death. It wasn't possible that she had recovered and found her way home. No, it wasn't possible at all.

My heart raced when I saw our big stucco house with the tarpaulin door. The gray-green roof tile was crooked and broken from neglect.

Someone had cut down the persimmon tree, and weeds grew in the yard. The front window was broken.

I stood in the road a long time looking at our house. I tried to think of what I would say to my mother and father if they were inside. How could I possibly tell them all the terrible things I had done? I thought about turning around and going back to Sinuiju.

Finally I went to the house and stepped inside. It was musty and dark. "Ummah?" I called out hesitantly. "Appa?" My calls echoed off the walls. There was no answer. Cobwebs grabbed at my face. "Soo-hee?"

I went to the back of the house. In the field, tall weeds cast long shadows in the setting sun. I went to the well and took a long drink of water. I took off my clothes and washed myself. I scrubbed and scrubbed until my skin was raw, but I didn't feel clean. I washed my clothes and laid them out to dry. I went inside the house and wrapped myself in a blanket. I lay on the floor of the big room, curled up, and went to sleep, alone.

The next morning, hunger pains knotted my stomach. I dressed, went out back, and dug up the onggis of rice and vegetables that Soo-hee and I had buried two years earlier. They had not been touched. I opened one. The brine and spices had not preserved the vegetables, and they were rotten. The stench of them almost made me retch.

I opened the other onggi. The rice was unspoiled, so I dragged it inside the house. I made a fire with dried weeds and brought some water to boil in a pan I had found inside the stove. I threw in some rice. As the rice cooked, I went out and found some carrots and potatoes growing wild in the field. I dug them up and took them to the house. I washed them and sliced them with a rusty knife from the kitchen drawer. When the rice finished cooking, I ate it with the raw carrots and potatoes. Eventually my hunger pangs went away.

I looked around the house. There was a thick coat of dust on the floor and cobwebs in the ceiling. In the main room, only one chair and the low table remained. I went to the sleeping area. Mother's cabinet was gone. But where it once stood, I saw a photograph of my family taken during the New Year's celebration when I was just four years old. My family, dressed in hanboks, stared out at me from the photo. Father stood tall with his beautiful young wife at his side. Soo-hee and I, innocent young girls, stood in front of our parents holding hands. I was so happy to have found the photograph, but for some reason, it made me cry.

I put the photograph inside my dress and went out to the field to dig up more potatoes and carrots. I found some garlic and dug it up, too. I gathered dried weeds and sticks. I took it all back to the house and made a fire in the stove. Soon the home's ondol system warmed the floors. Next to the stove, I found some ground bori cha and Father's tin cup. I filled the cup with water and a handful of bori cha and put it over the fire to steep. Soon I had bori cha, bitter and strong.

I went to work cleaning the house. I swept the floor and spent an hour scrubbing the kitchen sink. I brushed the cobwebs from the ceiling and spent another hour cleaning the soot from the stove. I made several trips to the field, all the way back to the tall aspen trees, and gathered wood and brought it back to the house. I stacked it neatly next to the stove.

Then I scrubbed myself again until my skin was raw, as I had done the day before. I braided my hair and washed my clothes again. When night came, I sat at the table drinking bori cha and stared out the window. I desperately tried to remember what it was like when Father and Mother and Soo-hee were still there and we read books by the firelight, but the images never came.

TWENTY

The next day I went to work on the outside of the house. I pulled weeds in the yard and climbed up on the roof to straighten the tiles. I scrubbed the stucco walls until my knuckles bled. I raked the yard smooth with a tree branch.

In the days and weeks that followed, I searched on my hands and knees for the tiniest speck of dirt in the house, and when I found one, I cleaned the entire house again. Mother had always liked a clean house. And Father had always been proud of his fields, so each day I pulled weeds and picked stones from the field behind the house until not even a pebble was out of place.

I gathered wood and vegetables until I had as much as we used to put up for the winter. Every night I scrubbed myself raw and washed my clothes and carefully braided my hair as I did when I was a young girl and waited by the fire for them to come home. And I tried to remember my life the way it was before.

Then one evening after the sun had set, an old woman came up the road and stopped by where the persimmon tree had been. *"Anyohaseyo,"* the woman said. "Are you the girl who used to live here?"

"Anyohaseyo," I said with a bow. "Yes, I am. Do you know where my family is?"

"I'm cold and need to rest," she said. "May I come into your house?" Age and hard labor had bent her. Her clothing was tattered and torn. Her eyes were deep inside their sockets. She looked like an apparition, and I thought I might be hallucinating. I showed her in and invited her to sit at the table. She coughed deeply several times and sat heavily in the chair. I started a fire in the stove that threw deep shadows against the wall.

I offered her rice and carrots. She devoured them as if she hadn't eaten in years. After she finished, she sat for a while, as if she had to gather strength. Then she eyed me through strands of gray hair. "I live down the road," she said in a low voice. "What is your name?"

"I am Hong Jae-hee," I answered. "My father is Hong Kwan-bae and my mother, Suh Bo-sun. The Japanese sent my sister and me away to work in the boot factory. The Russians told me to come home and wait here. Please tell me what you know about my family."

The woman had another coughing spell, making her tattered clothes shake and sending dust into the firelight. It took her a full minute to recover. "I knew your mother," she said finally. "We worked at the uniform factory together."

"You know my mother?" My heart pounded. I moved closer to the woman. "Where is she? Please tell me."

"I am sorry to tell you, young one, when you and your sister went away, your mother . . ." The woman lowered her eyes. Her breathing was long and labored. Her words came out as if a spirit possessed her. "Your mother knew before you left home that your father had been killed in the Philippines. The Japanese never sent him to Pyongyang like they said. They forced him to be a soldier and fight for them. She never told you that he had died.

"And," the woman said, "your mother is dead, too."

I clearly heard the word "dead," but it was only a sound floating in the evening air. "Dead," I repeated, trying to understand what it meant.

"Yes," the woman said. "One very cold day about two years ago, your mother hadn't been to work for many days. The women from the factory found her sitting under the persimmon tree, dead from the cold." She pointed a bony finger outside the window. "We buried her in the tall grass just north of your house."

"No," I heard myself say. "You must be mistaken. It couldn't be my mother you buried." Then I remembered Mother had burned all the wood the night before Soo-hee and I had left for Sinuiju. I remembered her saying she refused to give the Japanese anything more.

The woman stood to leave. Her clothes hung heavily on her. "Go to Sinuiju," she said. "The new government is taking a census. You have to give them your information. Perhaps you can find work there." The woman thanked me for the rice and carrots and disappeared through the tarpaulin door.

For a long time I sat alone and wanted to believe that the old woman was just a dream. The fire cast its light inside my clean house, and through the window I could see a full moon rising. The tarpaulin door fluttered in the evening breeze.

Eventually the old woman's words sunk in. It wasn't a dream after all. My mother and father were dead. At first I was glad that they were gone so I wouldn't have to tell them about Dongfeng. Then I was overcome with loss. Everyone I once loved was gone, and I knew my life would never again be like it was, like I so desperately wanted it to be again. And I cried. Through my tears, I tried to see my future without Soo-hee by my side or my parents' gentle love. But all I could see was the darkness of being alone. I wondered how I could go on, what I had to live for. I wished I was dead like the rest of my family.

And as I sat at the table, I finally remembered. I remembered the meals that my family had shared after a hard day's work in the fields. I remembered my joy in seeing my grandparents when they visited during the New Year. I remembered how Soo-hee and I played in our front yard and my mother teaching us to read in the great room. I remembered trying to teach Soo-hee to speak Japanese and getting frustrated with her. And I was sad, but also thankful that I could remember again.

And after I had remembered it all, I retrieved the comb from underneath my blanket and took it to the fire. I looked at the dragon with its claws and two heads. I thought of my great-great-grandmother and my ancestors who had passed the comb to their daughters. Their spirits had brought it to me, and I was now responsible to all those who had carried it before me.

I sat in front of the fire and let down my hair. And I combed it with the comb with the two-headed dragon.

◆ ◆ ◆

Growing up, I never thought much about Korean traditions. I participated in them, of course, because that was what my family did. Being young, I saw them as just something we had to do because we were Korean. But now that my family was gone, our traditions were important to me.

So the next day I rose before dawn and didn't clean the house for the first time in weeks because Koreans do no work during the time of mourning. I didn't cook rice, and I didn't eat. I wore my hair down as we did when my grandparents died.

I took a handful of rice and carrots and my father's tin cup out to the field with the tall grass and found the mound of dirt where they had buried my mother. I tossed three handfuls of dirt on my mother's grave, the *chwit'o* ritual that I had seen done at funerals when I was young. I took great care to smooth the ground and clean it of pebbles. With my eyes low, I placed the rice and carrots on the grave to nourish my mother's spirit for its long journey.

I touched the cool earth and raised my eyes up. And in the aspen trees beyond the field I had so perfectly cleaned, I saw the faces of my father and my grandparents and all my ancestors. And in front of them all, I saw the face of my mother.

"Thank you, Mother," I said softly. "Thank you for all you did for me and for teaching me to read and write. I am sorry for what I did in Dongfeng, and I'm sorry I couldn't save Soo-hee. I have the comb you gave us. I will take care of it as you said we should." I placed Father's cup on the mound. "I am leaving Father's cup so you can give it to him when your spirits meet. Please tell him I miss him very much." I took a handful of dirt and let it trickle through my fingers. I stayed a minute more, quiet and respectful, as I should have been when I was young.

I went back to the house, made a sack out of my blanket, and packed it with rice, carrots, potatoes, the photograph of my family, and the comb. I dragged the onggi of rice to the front of the house where the old woman would find it. And then I set off.

The sun had climbed over the hills in the east, and the morning air was warming when I walked past where the persimmon tree had been. I turned toward Sinuiju. After weeks of meals and hard work, I was strong and made good time. I was in Sinuiju by early afternoon.

I went to the two-story military headquarters where the Japanese had been two years earlier. A Korean flag had replaced the white flag with a red circle. I went into the building and to the large open room with the wood-planked floor. A few uniformed Russian soldiers worked at desks, but most of the people inside were Korean. I was glad the Japanese were gone. But honestly, it felt a little strange.

I approached a middle-aged female clerk sitting at a desk under a sign that read "Records" in Hangul. It was the first time since I was a little girl I had seen a sign in Hangul. "My name is Hong Jae-hee," I said in Japanese. "I have come for the census."

The clerk peered over glasses perched on the end of her nose. "Why are you talking in Japanese?" she said.

I lowered my eyes. "I am sorry," I said in Korean.

She turned back to the papers on her desk. "We only take census in the morning," she said without emotion. "You will have to come back tomorrow."

"Please excuse me, ma'am," I said. "If I must wait until tomorrow, do you know where I can stay tonight? I don't have anyone here."

"I don't know," the clerk said.

As I turned to leave, a man stood from a desk behind the clerk. "Wait," he said. "Perhaps I can help."

The clerk lowered her head as the man approached.

"I'm in charge of the census," he said. "Come to my desk. I'll take your information." He smiled. It was the first time a man had smiled pleasantly at me in over two years.

TWENTY-ONE

This man was like no other I had ever seen. His skin was smooth, his hair long and shiny. Over his medium build, he wore an unusual, loose cotton shirt. He wore leather slip-on shoes, the likes of which I had never seen before.

I wondered why he had singled me out. I hadn't had a chance to clean up, and I was certainly a mess. He pointed to a chair next to his desk and told me to sit. He asked my name as he retrieved a sheet of paper and a pen from a drawer. I sat straight-backed with my hands in my lap. I gave him my name, and he wrote it down.

He asked my age. "I'm sorry," I said. "I don't know. What month is it?"

"September," he said with a smile that reminded me of Father when he laughed at me for saying something funny. "Almost October."

"Then I am just seventeen."

"Where do you live?"

"On my father's farm, up the road, east about twenty miles."

"Father's and mother's names?"

"They are dead, sir," I said.

He looked at me, and I saw kindness in his eyes, but I was not sure if I could trust him. "I'm sorry," he said. "The Japanese killed many people. I'm in charge of gathering information about what they did here in Sinuiju. Please, tell me their names and how they died."

I did, and the man wrote it down, careful not to miss any details. Then he asked, "Do you have any brothers or sisters?"

"Yes, a sister, Soo-hee. She is . . . was my onni. She was two years older."

"Where is she?"

"I think she is dead, too, sir."

"I'm sorry. How did she die?"

"The Japanese took her away," I said. "To China."

"I see." He nodded as if he understood and wrote something on the paper. "What did you do during this time?"

I hesitated. I didn't want to lie, but I couldn't tell him I was a comfort woman. So I said, "I worked in the boot factory."

"The boot factory?" he asked.

"Yes, sir," I answered.

"I see." The man smiled his smile again, and this time he didn't write anything down. He put the paper on top of a large stack, then put his pen in the holder on the desk. "I heard you say you don't have anywhere to stay here in Sinuiju," he said.

"Yes, sir. I came for the census, and I was told I could find work here."

The man leaned back and folded his arms across his chest. "The city is full of people with nowhere to go. And there's not much work, either."

He eyed me for a long time, making me feel as if I had done something wrong. I thought he might be looking at me sexually, like the soldiers at the comfort station. Finally he said, "Perhaps you can help me, and I can help you, too. My wife is pregnant. It's been difficult for her. She gets tired easily. We have an apartment with one of our friends near the river. If you would like, you can work for us for food and a place to stay."

I thought of all the men I had known over the past two years—Colonel Matsumoto, Corporal Kaori, Lieutenant Tanaka. I wondered if this man was like them. But I couldn't walk back home, not this late in the day. And there was honesty in him. Or perhaps I only wanted to believe him. "I would be grateful for the work," I said with a bow.

"Good. My name is Pak Jin-mo. Wait over there on that bench. I'll be done here soon."

Thirty minutes later, Jin-mo stuffed some books in a canvas satchel and threw it over his shoulder. He led me from the military headquarters to an area of town by the shipyards on the Yalu River. An evening breeze blew from the south, and the day was pleasantly warm. The shipyard was crawling with men unloading supplies and military equipment from large gray ships. The ships were flying the same Russian flag that had flown over Dongfeng after the Japanese had fled. There were Russian soldiers in this area of Sinuiju and, to my surprise, Korean men in military uniforms. The city and especially the people were not the same as when Soo-hee and I were here two years earlier. There was something in the air like before the New Year celebrations when I was a girl. It was an expectant buzz.

We came to Jin-mo's apartment. As we pushed through a door leading to a set of stairs, Jin-mo stopped and whispered, "Don't tell anyone you worked in the boot factory. Just tell them you lived on your parents' farm. Okay?"

I nodded. I looked up the stairs and wondered what I would find behind the door. I thought about running back to my home in the hills. But Jin-mo's eyes met mine, and he said, "It's all right. Don't be afraid." I decided I had to trust him.

He led me up the stairs to a two-room apartment overlooking the river. When we stepped through the door, I was relieved to see a woman at the stove. A man about Jin-mo's age sat on the floor in front of an old radio.

"Hello, comrades," Jin-mo said, kicking off his leather shoes. When they saw me, the man lifted himself onto a crutch and the woman turned from the stove. Her pregnant belly protruded from underneath her blue blouse.

"This is Hong Jae-hee. The Japanese killed her family, and she has nowhere to go. She can help Ki-soo." Jin-mo pointed at the pregnant woman. "This is my wife, Choi Ki-soo. And that's my comrade, Park Seung-yo."

I bowed to them. Choi Ki-soo, tall and pretty with hair down to the middle of her back, was expressionless as she said, *"Anyohaseyo."* She wore simple pajamalike pants that went to just above her ankles. She wore zori without tabi. I could see in her face the weathered hardness that I had seen in the comfort women in Dongfeng.

Park Seung-yo stood in front of the radio and nodded his greeting. He had only one leg, and the wooden crutch he leaned on was worn smooth and shiny. He was short, and his frame was square. After I bowed to him, he curled his leg and stump underneath him. Then he began to fiddle with the knobs and antenna on the radio. Faint whistles and static came from the speaker.

Jin-mo pointed to the floor next to Seung-yo. "You'll have to stay in this room with Seung-yo," he said. "Ki and I have the other room. After dinner, we'll find a mat for you." Jin-mo walked over to Ki-soo and put his arm around her bloated stomach. I was surprised and embarrassed at the open display of affection. It was not how proper Koreans behaved.

As Ki-soo continued to stir the rice, Jin-mo disappeared through a door into the other room. I took off my tabi and put my cloth sack on the floor next to the wall. The apartment was neat and clean, with windows overlooking the street below and the harbor beyond. The wooden furniture was simple. On one wall was a cabinet filled with many books like we used to have at home.

I went to Ki-soo. "May I help?" I asked.

She didn't look up. "It's almost done," she said. "I was able to get a chicken on the dock and onions for bulgogi. I need to eat meat for the baby. Where are you from?"

"I lived on my parents' farm east of here."

"Jin-mo said your family is dead."

"Yes, they are."

Ki-soo pressed a hand into the small of her back. "How did they die?"

"My father was sent to fight for the Japanese and died in battle. They sent my sister to China, and she died there. My mother was killed by the Japanese."

"Japanese pigs," Ki-soo said. Then she looked sideways at me, making me uncomfortable. "And you, so young and pretty, you stayed at the farm after your mother died?"

"Yes," I answered.

After a few moments, Ki-soo said, "Get chopsticks and bowls from the cupboard. Jin likes to eat right away when he gets home."

◆ ◆ ◆

During the meal, Jin-mo, Seung-yo, and Ki-soo fell into a passionate discussion about the rich, the poor, property, and workers. Mother said that it was an insult to the cook if young people talked while the elders ate. Soo-hee often pinched me under the table when I did. So I didn't talk and concentrated on my food. Over the past few years, I had forgotten what good food tasted like. In Dongfeng, the comfort women rarely ate meat, and when we did, it was often tough, boiled horse meat. But here, the chicken bulgogi was delicious. It tasted like the meals I'd had with my family when I was a young girl.

Jin-mo sat close to Ki-soo at the low table. He did more talking than eating, waving his chopsticks in the air to make a point. The meal lasted a long time. Ki-soo kept looking at me out of the corner of her eye, which made me nervous. Seung-yo, with his good leg tucked underneath him and his stump out front, devoured his food and talked with his mouth full. Then, when Jin-mo, the eldest male, finished eating, everyone stopped. I helped clear the table while Jin-mo and Seung-yo tinkered with the radio antenna. Finally Jin-mo exclaimed, "Got it!" A faint voice came over the radio's speaker.

The high-pitched voice was saying something in Korean. Ki-soo lowered herself to the floor next to Jin-mo, and I sat behind Seung-yo. I could only catch a few words above the static, but the others listened carefully, especially Jin-mo. Every once in a while, he nodded in agreement with what the person on the radio was saying. Eventually the voice signed off, and in its place, tinny music played.

Jin-mo turned off the radio. "We have to go to Pyongyang soon," he said, looking pleased. "The party is gathering there. The Russians are supporting us. We will be the new government of Korea."

"I'm not going," Seung-yo said, lighting a cigarette.

Jin-mo leaned forward. "Seung-yo," he said, "why not?"

"I can't go to Pyongyang with one leg. It was all I could do to make it to Sinuiju. Anyway, this is my home. It's where I grew up. Maybe my family will come back someday." He took a pull on the cigarette and blew smoke toward the ceiling.

Ki-soo pushed herself off the floor without expression. She went to the other room and closed the door. Jin-mo continued to stare at Seung-yo. "I can get a car to go to Pyongyang. You must go. The party needs you. Korea needs you."

Seung-yo returned Jin-mo's stare. "I have given plenty to Korea already," he said. "I just want to rest for a while. I'll find something to do here. I'll stay in this apartment." He took another puff from his cigarette.

"But, Seung-yo, this is our opportunity!" Jin-mo said, raising his palms. "It is what we've been fighting for. All those years in the hills, and now Korea will be free, and we will be the leaders. You cannot quit now."

"I'm staying," Seung-yo said simply. He pulled himself over to the corner and curled up on his mat. He took a book out from under the mat and began to read, his cigarette dangling from his lip.

Jin-mo and I sat in front of the radio. He sighed and regarded me with his liquid-soft eyes. "What do I do with you?" he said.

I lowered my head. "Perhaps I should leave."

"And go where?"

He was right. I had nowhere to go. And everyone I had known before I left home was gone. It was as if fate had plucked me from my old life and dropped me here. Though I didn't know these people or what their intentions were, I had to depend on them, like a stray dog seeking shelter from the cold.

There was a long, uncomfortable silence. Then Jin-mo asked, "Can you read?"

"Yes, sir," I said. "My mother taught me to read Hangul and Chinese. I know Japanese, too. Mother always said I had a good ear for languages."

"Oh? Do you speak them well?"

"I speak Japanese and Chinese fluently," I said, looking into his eyes. "I have already learned some Russian and English, too."

A sly smile spread over Jin-mo's face. "Okay," he said in Chinese, "tell me, what did you think of our dinner tonight?"

I could feel the corners of my mouth turn up. "I thought it was delicious," I answered in Chinese, careful to pronounce the words correctly. "I haven't had chicken in a long time."

Jin-mo's grin grew to a full smile. In Japanese, he asked, "What do you think of our apartment? Is it . . . um . . ." In Korean: "What's the Japanese word for 'satisfactory'?"

I straightened and put out my chin. "*Juubun* is the word." In Japanese, I added, "And I think your apartment is indeed satisfactory. I like the view of the river."

Jin-mo laughed, and my heart skipped a beat. "And you're learning Russian, too?" he asked, switching back to Korean.

I nodded. "I haven't heard it much, but I already know many words. Their sentences come together in a strange way. When I hear more, I will learn it quickly."

Jin-mo shook his head. "You have a remarkable talent indeed. Perhaps you can come to Pyongyang with us. We could use your help."

"Why are you going to Pyongyang? Why don't you stay here?"

"Because with the Japanese finally gone, Korea will be free and independent for the first time since they took our country from us. We can do it with a new kind of government, one that represents all Koreans—not just the wealthy, not only the landholders, but the working people, too."

"I don't know anything about governments," I said.

The door from the other room opened and Ki-soo leaned out. "Jin, are you coming?" She had a hand on her belly.

"In a minute," Jin-mo said. Ki-soo's face flashed disapproval. She gave me a look that made me feel like I shouldn't be here. Then she slipped back inside the room and shut the door.

Before I could say I wanted to leave, Jin-mo said, "I have something for you." He went to the bookshelf and took out a small, well-used book. "This is my most prized possession. It is one of the few copies of *The Communist Manifesto* translated into Hangul. It's by a man named Karl Marx. Read it, and we can talk more." He handed me the book.

"Thank you," I said.

Jin-mo moved toward the room where Ki-soo was. "We won't leave for Pyongyang for a few weeks. In the meantime, help Ki-soo around the apartment and read that book. Then you can decide if you want to go to Pyongyang with us and join the Communist Party."

I took the book and the blanket Jin-mo handed me and went to a corner. Seung-yo curled up on his mat. Soon he was snoring softly. I wrapped the blanket around me. I looked around the apartment and sighed. This would be my home for a while. I was thankful for a warm place to lie with people I could talk to. Jin-mo seemed kind, and Ki-soo—well, I would have to be careful with her.

I opened the book Jin-mo gave me. I hadn't seen a book written in Hangul since I had left home two years earlier. I ran my finger over the letters and words. There were handwritten notes in the margins, and many sentences were underlined. I was glad to have a book to read to black out my nightmares of Dongfeng.

And I prayed that these people would never find out what I did there.

TWENTY-TWO

Two weeks later, Jin-mo, Ki-soo, and I drove to Pyongyang in a tiny, beat-up Fiat that Jin-mo had borrowed from a government official he knew in Sinuiju. He had bartered with a Russian soldier for just enough gasoline to make the 150-mile trip. I'm not sure what Jin-mo had to give him, but it must have been something very dear because gasoline was hard to come by.

We packed the car, said a heartfelt good-bye to Seung-yo, and set off. Jin-mo drove and Ki-soo sat in the passenger side with her hand on her belly. I was wedged in the backseat next to several old suitcases, two bedrolls, pots and pans, and Jin-mo's duffel bag stuffed with his books. On my lap was a musty suitcase that Jin-mo had given me. Inside were some old clothes from Ki-soo, Jin-mo's copy of *The Communist Manifesto*, the photograph of my family, and, tucked within the lining where no one could see it, the comb with the two-headed dragon.

It was my first ride in a car. Of course, I had ridden in trucks before—you cannot very well grow up on a farm without riding in a truck once in a while—but never a car. The Fiat smelled of exhaust fumes, and the ride over the rutted road was bumpy. The engine sounded as if it was complaining constantly, and I worried that we were not going to make it to Pyongyang.

At first I was scared to be going so far from home again with these people that I didn't know well. But the farther south we went, the better I felt. Every mile was another mile away from Dongfeng and the comfort station.

And then, many miles out of Sinuiju, I saw the Yellow Sea for the first time. I had learned about the sea from my parents' books and Father's stories. I had tried to picture water stretching so far that it looked like it was spilling off the edge of the earth. Now it was there in front of me, outside the car window. I pressed against the glass for a better look.

It was wonderful. The blue-green sea sparkled under the morning sun, and the sea air smelled fresh and clean. A large freighter with its stacks trailing thick black smoke steamed along on the horizon. Closer in, dozens of fishing boats bobbed and pulled their nets. Still closer, great waves reached for the shore like foamy white fangs, then crashed against the cliffs with a thunderous roar, only to retreat again to the sea, gathering themselves for another surge. I could not take my eyes off it.

After a while, the road turned south. The little Fiat seemed to have accepted its chore and was not complaining as loudly. We traveled across a broad plain with rice paddies reaching all the way up the hills. Dozens of workers in pointed straw hats, their black pants rolled over their knees, skillfully swung long cane poles, knocking the rice grains into baskets. Others balanced baskets full of rice on their shoulders and carried them to carts waiting on the edge of the fields.

Eventually the road rose from the rice paddies into farm fields like those behind my home. The smell of onions and garlic filled the air. It made me feel like a girl again. Workers stuffed sacks with carrots and beets. It reminded me of harvest time on our farm when I was a little girl. It seemed so very many years ago.

In another field, cattle grazed lazily on the fall grass. I felt a surge of pride for this land and for my country, and I realized Colonel Matsumoto was right. Korea was indeed a great country. Now I understood why the

Japanese wanted it for themselves and had to be forced to leave. And now that they were gone, I thought perhaps someday Korea could be great again.

"How much have you read of Marx?" Jin-mo asked with an elbow over the front seat. I snapped out of my spell. *The Communist Manifesto* had been difficult to read. It was dense and filled with words I didn't know. Jin-mo and even Ki-soo had helped me with the new words. Still, I had read so much growing up that I was able to finish it and understand most of the ideas. But I was afraid of exposing too much of myself, so I didn't let them know that.

"It is very difficult," I answered.

"Don't worry," Jin-mo said. "It was difficult for me when I first read it. I got through it, and you will, too."

Ki-soo let out a snort. "Why do you bother? She's too young."

Jin-mo slid his elbow off the seat and gripped the steering wheel with both hands. "I was her age when I first read it. You were only a year older. Anyway, we'll build the party on the shoulders of the young. They are the future of Korea."

Ki-soo turned her pretty face to the side window and didn't say anything.

During the two weeks in Sinuiju, Jin-mo, Ki-soo, and Seung-yo had passionate discussions at night in the apartment about governments, workers, and the future. They used each other's shortened names—"Ki," "Seung," and "Jin"—which sounded strange and impolite to me. It was not the way proper Koreans addressed each other. They discussed what would happen to Korea now that the Japanese were gone. Jin-mo tried to include me in their discussions, and I participated as much as I could. The ideas were new, but they seemed to make sense. The discussions felt like those my family had about one of our books after a hard day's work on the farm.

I had learned that Jin-mo, Ki-soo, and Seung-yo were rebels and had fought the Japanese with other Koreans in the mountains of northern China. It had been a dangerous, hardscrabble life that had cost Seung-yo his left leg and many of their friends their lives. They had been part of a group led by a man named Kim Il-sung, who they said had fought bravely and who had convinced the Russians to enter the war against the Japanese. The radio in the apartment had given them news that Kim Il-sung, with Russia's support, was in charge of a provisional government in Pyongyang. Jin-mo had been close to comrade Kim and was going to Pyongyang to secure an important position in the new government there. He had said he could get a job for me, too.

Jin-mo turned to me. "It's an exciting time in Korea, Jae-hee. A new beginning. Soon the party will take over, and Korea will become a modern country. You'll see."

Ki-soo folded her arms across her bloated belly and continued to look out her side window. "I wouldn't be so sure," she said under her breath.

Jin-mo tensed. "Why do you have to be that way, Ki?" he demanded. "Why are you always so cynical?"

"Because I don't trust them," she said, suddenly facing him. "I don't just believe everything they say."

I sank low in my seat. I had never heard a woman talk back to a man like Ki-soo did to Jin-mo. Mother had never talked to Father like that. But Jin-mo and Ki-soo argued often, and it usually ended with Ki-soo slamming the door to her room and Jin-mo staring blankly at Seung-yo and me.

"Look, Ki, this isn't going to be easy," Jin-mo said. "We'll have to work together, or other countries will push us around just like they always have. Communism is our chance. No more Japanese, no more Chinese. And the Russians and the Americans have agreed to leave once we establish a government."

"I'm not sure it will work," Ki-soo said.

"What's the alternative?" Jin-mo said, shaking his head. "Capitalism? Money and power in the hands of a few greedy men?

It plunged the world into a ten-year depression that the Japanese and Germans took full advantage of. It caused the war. We have to find a better way. Communism is it."

"A classless society based on common ownership of the means of production," Ki-soo said, as if she were reading from Marx.

"Exactly," Jin-mo said. "It's what has made Russia powerful. And there are communist movements in a dozen other countries, too. China will be next, and countries in Asia and Europe will follow. There's even a communist movement in America. And right now in Korea, we can make it happen without a civil war."

"Changes like this are never bloodless, Jin. And who will lead this new government? Your friend Kim Il-sung? I don't trust *comrade* Kim," Ki-soo said, twisting the word "comrade."

"He fought against the Japanese, Ki, when others ran away to America or Europe."

Ki-soo faced the window again and said nothing more for a long time. The car climbed into hills terraced with more rice paddies.

Finally, with a nod to me, Ki-soo asked, "What are you going to do with her in Pyongyang?"

"She can help with the baby."

"I don't need help with the baby."

"Then she can help in the new government. She is great with languages. She speaks Japanese better than I do. Chinese, too. I've never seen anything like it."

"Is she going to live with us?" Ki-soo asked. Her eyes flashed.

"She lost her family, Ki."

"Half of Korea lost their family during the Japanese occupation. You aren't going to invite all of them to live with us, are you?"

Jin-mo gripped the steering wheel hard as the car bumped along the road and crested another hill. I sank low in my seat as Pyongyang loomed in the distance. I hoped we would get there soon so I could get out of the car, away from Ki-soo.

Finally Ki-soo said, "I have to piss again. This traveling isn't good for the baby."

Without a word, Jin-mo pulled the car to the side of the road and let it idle while Ki-soo got out and squatted in the ditch.

◆　◆　◆

Pyongyang. I had heard about the great city with tall buildings on the Taedong River. Father had been there once and had told us all about it. But after my disappointment in seeing Sinuiju for the first time, my expectations were low. But Pyongyang was different. It was a marvelous city teeming with people on bicycles, on foot, in cars, in rickshaws, on boardwalks, and on the streets, all rushing to get somewhere. I wondered where they were all going and why they had to hurry so to get there. Hundreds of electric wires on tall posts ran along the streets. We didn't have electricity on our farm. I never saw the need for it, so I couldn't imagine what all that electricity was for. Buildings— some so big they looked like palaces—were everywhere. The sounds, the sights, the smells, the *energy* were like nothing I had ever imagined.

Jin-mo produced a map from the glove box and gave it to Ki-soo. She did her best to help Jin-mo navigate around the cars and bicyclists on the busy streets. The Fiat rolled through the heavy traffic before we finally came to a stop in front of a four-story stone building with stairs leading to an entrance supported by tall pillars. I had never seen a building so massive. I thought that it must be the biggest building in the world.

"This is it!" Jin-mo said excitedly. "You two stay here while I check in."

He changed his shirt, brushed his hair smooth, and slipped on his leather shoes. Then he disappeared inside the building while Ki-soo and I stayed in the car. Ki-soo kept her back to me, staring out the car window at the people on the street. After a while, she said into the window, "I will not let Jin-mo destroy me and my baby." I didn't know what Jin-mo would do to destroy her. But the tone of her voice was more grave than usual for her. I pushed into my seat among the suitcases and bedrolls and prayed that Jin-mo would return soon.

An hour later, Jin-mo came running out of the building and jumped into the car. He held some papers in his hand. "It's all arranged," he said with a nod. "We have a furnished apartment close to here. I report to work the day after tomorrow. I think I will be able to get a job for you, too, Jae-hee."

As he started the car, he turned to Ki-soo, then to me. The joy in his smile made my heart beat fast. "Welcome to the new Korea," he said.

TWENTY-THREE

Jin-mo was true to his word and got a job for me working for the provisional government in the massive building where he also worked. He said it was a job translating important documents from the Japanese occupation into Hangul. Although I could read and write well in both Japanese and Hangul, I had never done anything like translations before. I did not believe I was qualified, and I didn't want to accept the position. But Jin-mo was enthusiastic and so happy for me that I had to take it, although I was very nervous.

Jin-mo was apparently an important man, because the government had given him a furnished, western-style apartment across the street from a park filled with giant willow trees. There were five rooms—a large main room with European upholstered furniture and a fireplace, a bedroom where Jin-mo and Ki-soo slept, a kitchen with a cast-iron stove, a bathroom with a porcelain sink and tub, and a tiny room off the back where I slept on a small, low bed. The apartment was on the street level and had windows in the main room that overlooked the park. Instead of ondul heating, there were radiators that brought in hot water from a boiler somewhere in the building. There were electric lights and an electric clock on the fireplace mantle. Since we arrived, the electricity had gone out several times, and when it came back on, the first thing Jin-mo did was reset the clock.

It was my first day of work. I hadn't slept well the night before, worrying about how I would do on my new job. I got out of bed and headed for the bathroom. Jin-mo, who worked impossibly long hours, had already left for the day. I had to get into the bathroom before Ki-soo. Once she got it, I would have to wait a long time until she was done. Even when I got in first, if she wanted to use it, I would have to let her have it. I was thankful that she was far along in her pregnancy and usually slept late.

Once in the bathroom, I washed myself thoroughly as I had always done for Colonel Matsumoto. There was hot water, but I had to be careful not to use too much of it, or there wouldn't be enough for Ki-soo. I thought about pricking my finger with a needle for blood to use as rouge and lipstick, but I didn't know if the women in Pyongyang wore makeup, and I didn't want to look like a prostitute. I put on a dress that Ki-soo had passed down to me. I had to take it in at the chest and waist and take up the hem. It was still too big for me, but it was the only appropriate clothing I had.

I wasn't sure what to do with my hair. I didn't want to look silly by making it too fancy, but I did not want to look like a peasant girl, either. Ki-soo casually pinned her hair up when she lounged around the apartment, but I didn't think that would be appropriate for work. I thought about leaving my hair down and pinning it in the back. I had seen women on the Pyongyang streets with their hair like that. But it seemed pretentious to me. In the end, I braided it as I had always done when I worked in the fields back home.

I looked at myself in the mirror above the sink. I was not sure that I was pretty anymore. I thought I might be completely out of place among the big-city workers in the big building.

A few days earlier, Ki-soo had mentioned an area in Pyongyang where girls worked as prostitutes. I do not know why she told me about it, and she only mentioned it that one time. Now, as I looked at my reflection in the mirror, I thought I should find that place. It was something I knew, something I was good at. I would fit in there. But Jin-mo had gotten this job for me. I did not want to disappoint him.

There was a knock on the door. "I need the bathroom," Ki-soo said from outside. I quickly opened the door and bowed my head. As I moved past her, she paused to look at me, and I thought she was going to laugh at how I had done my hair. Instead, she said, "You look fine. Good luck." And then she went inside the bathroom and closed the door.

◆　◆　◆

When I stepped into the provisional government headquarters building, I had to stop to take it all in. You could have fit our entire farmhouse inside the reception area with plenty of room to spare. The floor was marble. Brass chandeliers with electric lights hung from the ceiling. There were people scurrying about in every direction, some carrying papers and folders. They all looked very serious.

I went up to a young lady behind a desk. She was wearing a shirt and dress that looked like a uniform. I was relieved to see she had her hair braided like mine. I asked her where I could find Mr. Chee, the man Jin-mo said I would work for. "The third floor," she said, pointing to a staircase. She went back to her work and didn't seem to notice that my dress was too big for me.

I went up the stairs that were wider than any staircase I could have ever imagined. On the third floor was a large bull pen area. People were busily working at desks, and even more were rushing around. Along the outside of the bull pen were offices with windows that looked out over the street. There were file cabinets everywhere. I could not comprehend what they were all for.

I bowed to a man sitting at one of the desks and asked him where I could find Mr. Chee. He pointed to where a small, bookish man was pacing behind several men sitting at desks. "That is Mr. Chee," the man said.

I approached Mr. Chee. He wore a western-style wool suit over a white shirt and a gray tie. "I am Hong Jae-hee," I said with a low bow. "Mr. Pak said I should come here this morning to work for you. I am honored, sir."

As the others looked on, he regarded me over the top of his reading glasses. "You're the one they told me was so good with languages," he said. "Japanese and Chinese, they said. Well, we don't have much work in those languages. English is what's important now. Do you know it?"

"No, sir, I do not," I answered, keeping my eyes low. "But Mother always said I have a good ear for languages." The men sitting at the desks exchanged glances, and I felt stupid for saying it.

Mr. Chee took off his reading glasses. "English is very different, so I don't expect you'll be able to learn it anytime soon. But they told me I had to use you, so I'll give you an English dictionary and some other books to get you started. Maybe in several years, if you work hard, you will be useful to me. For the time being, you'll have to work on Japanese documents."

He pointed at a desk near the edge of the bull pen. "There are documents on that desk in Japanese. Translate them into Hangul, and let me know when you're done. If you're as smart as they say you are, it should take you less than three hours. Then you can leave."

"Thank you, sir," I said with another bow. Mr. Chee put his reading glasses on and turned back to the men, signaling that he was done with me. I went to the desk he had pointed to. I looked around at the other people in the bull pen. I thought they would all be staring at me, at how I was dressed or how I had done my hair. But no one seemed to notice.

I picked up one of the documents I had to translate. They were government papers, nothing like the books we read at home or the ones that Colonel Matsumoto had given me. The language was flowery and grand, and I was concerned that they had given me such important documents to work on. I picked up a paper and pencil and started, determined to do my best. There were words I did not know that I circled on the translations. I made a list of them on a pad of paper so I could learn them later.

In spite of the lofty language and the words I didn't know, the translations were easy, and I finished in less than two hours. I offered them to Mr. Chee, who told me to leave them at my desk and then turned back to his work without saying anything more. I assumed that I was done for the day and headed down the staircase to go home.

◆ ◆ ◆

It was a little after midday when I walked through the grand reception area out into the city of Pyongyang. I felt guilty about being so free and thought that I should hurry back to the apartment straight away like I always did in Dongfeng after being with the colonel. But here, I was not restricted to just one place. Here, I could go anywhere I wanted to. It was a lovely fall day, and Pyongyang was so grand and new to me, I decided to take a walk to see it. The freedom was exciting, but a little scary, too.

I walked along the boulevard jammed with cars and trucks and bicycles and rickshaws carrying boxes and sacks and all sorts of things I had never seen before. They rattled and roared down both sides of the street. The trucks belched out smoke, making the air heavy with the smell of exhaust fumes. The sidewalks were full of people hurrying about in every direction. There were men in suits like Mr. Chee wore, and some women wore fancy coats and dresses. Everyone seemed to be in such a rush, just like inside the provisional government building. I wondered what was so important that they had to practically run to get to where they were going. They reminded me of the ants I used to watch in the yellow dirt of the comfort station courtyard.

There were shops along the boulevard that had big windows with words on them. In some windows, the words were in Hangul. Others had Japanese characters that men were scraping off and replacing with Hangul.

There was a bakery with more types of bread than I had ever seen in my life. I saw a clothing store and stared at dresses and shoes that I was sure I would never be able to afford. I came to a bookstore that had hundreds of books inside. I smiled at the thought of all those books to read.

I turned a corner and stopped in my tracks. There in front of me was a building with more electric lights than I thought could be in all of Pyongyang. The building took up half the block and had a pagoda roof. I thought it must be a palace. There was a marquee with huge letters in Hangul that said, "Gone with the Wind." There were many people waiting in a line to go inside. I went to the front of the building. On the wall was a poster of a man holding a woman in his arms. And then I realized that I was standing in front of a cinema.

Of course, I had heard of movies before, but growing up where I did, I never got to see one. Father saw a movie once in Sinuiju and told us about it. It sounded almost unbelievable, and I immediately wanted to go. Colonel Matsumoto had talked about movies, too, but at the comfort station, I didn't dare dream that I would ever be able to see one.

And now, here in front of me was a cinema. It was more spectacular than I ever dreamed. I could barely breathe just looking at it. I tried to envision all the wonders and new worlds that I could discover inside. I looked at the entrance. A sign said the fee to get in was ten won. It might as well have been a million, because I didn't have any money. I looked again at the poster. It said the movie was in English with subtitles in Hangul. I recalled that Mr. Chee said I needed to learn English. I vowed to find the money someday to see my first movie.

I pushed myself away from the cinema and started down the street again. I wanted to see more of Pyongyang. I went a block and then two and then three. I stared through store windows and watched the people and cars hurry by. I was sure this was the most wonderful city in the world.

Suddenly there was a scuffle a ways down the sidewalk in front of me. I saw Korean soldiers with red armbands and white stars push a man through a door out to the street. The man held his arms over the top of his head. A soldier lifted a baton and brought it down hard on the man, who let out a cry and fell to the ground. People around me covered their ears and ran away. But I did not. I stayed where I was and watched the beating as Lieutenant Tanaka had trained me to do.

The soldier hit the man again and again. The sound of the baton hitting flesh, the terror in the man's eyes, and his horrible cries made the grand city of Pyongyang melt away, and I was in the comfort station courtyard again. Finally a soldier grabbed the man by the arm and forced him to stand. His face was bloody, and he was unsteady on his feet. The soldiers escorted him up the street past me. As they walked by, the soldier with the baton glared at me, and for a moment I thought I was looking at Lieutenant Tanaka again.

And when they were gone, I ran through the streets of Pyongyang, all the way home.

TWENTY-FOUR

Two years later

It was another late night in the provisional government headquarters building. I sat at my desk, helping translate English documents into Hangul for the meeting two floors above. The meeting was between delegations from the American-controlled South and the Russian-controlled North. The two sides were trying to reconcile their differences and unify Korea under one government. It was the third day of meetings, and according to Jin-mo, a delegate for the North, they were not going well. My desk was in the middle of the translation department. It was dark except for the area around me. Mr. Chee paced behind me, reading our translations aloud.

I had learned that Mr. Chee had been educated at a college in England and lived in London before the war. When World War II broke out, he couldn't get back to Korea and was stuck there during the bombing of London. When the war was over, he made his way back to his family in Pyongyang. Since he spoke English well, and since he was an educated man, the provisional government put him in charge of translations.

When I had first started in his department, Mr. Chee had been angry that Jin-mo's friends forced him to work with someone so young. For the first six months, he only gave me low-level documents to translate from Japanese into Hangul. I became very good at it, and soon Mr. Chee saw that I wasn't as useless as he had thought I would be. He gave me several English-language books and encouraged me to study them.

And I did. I was determined to put the shame of Dongfeng behind me. I desperately wanted to prove that I could do something more than lie on my back and let men rape me. And I didn't want to disappoint Jin-mo. So I worked very hard at learning English.

I studied every day and late at night when I should have been sleeping. I never took a day off. I learned dozens of new words each day and researched their meanings and precise pronunciations. I was obsessed with English grammar. I read everything I could get my hands on in English. I hardly ever ate a meal without a book in front of me. I snuck away to the cinema two or three times each week to watch movies in English with subtitles in Hangul. I saw *Gone with the Wind* four times and read the book in English three times, making notes in the margins of nearly every page. I practically memorized a book on English grammar that Jin-mo gave me. I used my dictionaries and thesaurus so much, they fell apart. I listened very carefully to Mr. Chee and the translators when they spoke English.

And I had a gift. It's hard to explain, but I only needed to hear a word once and I was able to recall its meaning, remember the context, the correct pronunciation, and everything about its usage. People said I was a genius, and I suppose I was. But they didn't see how hard I worked at it.

And that's why I became better at English than anyone else in the translation department. In fact, I became so good that Mr. Chee had to make me his top translator.

My success didn't help my nightmares about the comfort station, however. I often woke up in the middle of the night in a cold sweat. I could still clearly see the machine gun cut down my Korean sisters that last, horrible day. I could feel the sting in my thighs where Lieutenant Tanaka had beaten me and the ache between my legs where Colonel Matsumoto and a thousand men had raped me. And every day I yearned for my sister, Soo-hee. I could only forget about Dongfeng when I was at the cinema or studying English. I suppose that's why I worked so hard.

As I sat at my desk, Mr. Chee was pacing behind me. He was reading our translation of a document they needed upstairs. "What do they mean by this phrase?" he asked, lifting his reading glasses to his eyes. "*A dictatorship of the proletariat through which the socialization of the means of production can be realized.*'"

"It's the basis for a communist government," I said. "It means the workers will build a government that controls economic production for the benefit of everyone."

"Why do they call it a dictatorship?" he asked.

"It's a Marxist idea," I answered. "He believed the workers need to take complete control from the proletariat capitalists for a more fair economy."

"How do you know all of this?" Mr. Chee asked, shaking his head. "Never mind," he said quickly with a wave. "Let's just get the translation done. They're waiting for it."

We worked for a while longer, tossing phrases and words back and forth. When we finally agreed on the translation, I wrote it out and handed it to Mr. Chee. As he read it, he said, "You need to stay. They could go all night again." I bowed and said I would. He smiled a tired thank you and hurriedly headed to the stairs to deliver the translations to the delegation.

I leaned over my desk and laid my head on my arms. I closed my eyes, and words in Hangul and English danced awkwardly in my head. Soon I fell into a restless sleep.

◆ ◆ ◆

"Jae-hee!" someone said over the impossibly long line of Japanese sol-diers in my dream. "Wake up! It's time to go." I forced my eyes open and lifted my head. Jin-mo's handsome face replaced the faces of the Japanese soldiers in the comfort station. "You fell asleep again," he said. "Come, we have to go. Ki will be worried about us."

I walked with Jin-mo through the vacant streets toward his apart-ment six blocks from the provisional government headquarters. We had made this walk together nearly every night since we'd started working there. At first I was uncomfortable being alone with a man who was not my husband. But over time I realized that Jin-mo was a gentle, kind man. He had a way of talking to me that made me feel like Father did. And his passion for Korea and his ideas for a new kind of government were infectious. I felt alive around him and had feelings for him I had never known before.

As we walked in the cool spring air, I asked, "How did the meeting go today?"

Jin-mo sighed. It worried me how sunken his eyes had become and how his back was beginning to bend. "Not well," he said softly. "Both sides feel they have the legitimate right to rule the entire peninsula. Neither is willing to give ground."

"What is going to happen?"

"If the Americans and Russians would leave us alone, maybe we could work something out," he said. "They have both agreed to leave this year if we can form a unified government. But the Russians want a communist government, and the Americans won't tolerate it. They want to make a stand against communism here in Korea. It's turning into a stalemate."

We walked for a while in silence. The park was on our right, and there was very little traffic on the street. There was a gentle night breeze.

"What side do you think is right?" I asked. As soon as I asked it, I wished I hadn't. I was asking too many questions again, especially in Pyongyang, where questions like mine were discouraged. But it did not appear to bother Jin-mo.

"I used to think it was the North," he said. "This is where Korea was born. We have more industry here than they do in the South. And as you know, I believe a socialist government would be right for us. But what is most important is that we come together under *one* government. We've been divided our entire history—the North aligned with the Chinese, the South with the Japanese. This is our chance to be one nation if the Russians and the Americans don't keep us divided."

"What must we do?"

"I've presented ideas, but my comrades won't listen. They're inflexible. They won't compromise, and I think they are wrong." Jin-mo raised an eyebrow. "Of course, my comments are just between you and me."

I nodded, pleased that he had taken me into his confidence. "Of course," I said.

When we came to the apartment, there was a black car with a driver inside parked out front. Jin-mo gave the car an uneasy look. He quickly opened the apartment door, and I followed him inside.

Jin-mo and I removed our shoes and stepped inside the main room. Ki-soo sat on the sofa with her legs folded underneath her. Her eyes were red. On the sofa next to Ki-soo was her winter coat, and on the floor in front of her was a suitcase. Lying next to her was their two-year-old son, Suk-ju. The little boy was leaning against his mother, sleeping. He wore a traveling coat.

Jin-mo saw the suitcase and stopped. "What is this?" he asked.

Ki-soo said, "I cannot risk it anymore, Jin. I'm leaving, and I'm taking Suk-ju with me."

"What do you mean?" Jin-mo asked. "What can't you risk anymore?"

Little Suk-ju pressed his face into his mother's side and moaned.

Ki-soo said, "I don't want to talk about it. You will wake Suk-ju."

"If you're leaving, when *will* we talk about it?" Jin-mo asked, trying to keep his voice down.

Suk-ju opened his eyes and reached his little hands to his mother. "Ummah?" he said.

I stepped forward. "I will take him so you can talk." Ki-soo looked at me angrily, but she let me take the boy.

Suk-ju wrapped his arms around my neck as I carried him to my room and closed the door. My room, small as it was, was still twice as large as the room I had at the comfort station. There was no window, but it was warm in the winter and cool during the hot summer months. There was a low bed, a wooden chair, a small table with a lamp on it, and a mirror above. The walls were light brown plaster, and a plain rug covered the wood floor. I spent a lot of time in that room reading books, studying English, and sleeping when I couldn't study anymore. I knew that room well—everything except the ceiling. I could not say if the ceiling was plaster, wood, or solid gold. I refused to look at it because looking up at the ceiling brought back the horrors of what they did to me in my room at the comfort station.

I sat on my bed and held Suk-ju close. The boy was warm against my breast. Over the previous year and a half, I had come to love this little boy as if he were my own. I took great delight in everything he did—the way he clung to my finger when he was just a few days old, his first steps, his first words, his mischievous toddler grin, his eyes, soft and intelligent like his father's. My heart ached at the thought of never seeing him again if Ki-soo took him away. I pressed him close to me.

Suk-ju fell back to sleep while the voices of Jin-mo and Ki-soo— low at first—argued in the living room. I tried not to listen, but the voices grew loud. Jin-mo and Ki-soo argued often. Sometimes their arguments got very heated. I always went to my room, closed the door, and ignored them. But now Ki-soo said she was leaving, and I could sense that this argument would be a bad one.

"I said you could not reason with these people, Jin-mo!" I heard Ki-soo say. "It's going to be a bloody dictatorship, just like in Russia with Stalin."

"I'm being careful, Ki. We have to try."

"You have made too many compromises."

"Look, the Russians have agreed to leave in a few months. It will be different then."

"Different? Your leader is murdering people, Jin-mo! Once the Russians leave, it will only get worse."

"The South is murdering their dissidents, too, Ki."

"So that makes it right? What happens when the murdering comes here, to our home? What happens when they decide *you* are a dissident?"

"I work for them. They won't do anything to us."

"Don't be so sure. You have enemies. You are on the wrong side of this."

"I'm not the only one. And I won't stop trying. It's the only way we can bring our people together. We cannot give up. We can still make it work."

There was silence for a while, and I thought the arguing was over. But then there was a crash of porcelain breaking. In my arms, Suk-ju jerked but didn't wake up.

"You and your ideals!" Ki-soo shouted.

"Keep your voice down, Ki."

"No, I will not! You said you were going to get rid of her a year ago."

"She doesn't have anywhere to go. Anyway, she loves Suk-ju, and he loves her. I'm not going to just throw her out."

"I told you I will not allow it!"

"Ki-soo, nothing has happened between us."

"I don't care. Go ahead. Live with your pretty little *chinilpa*, your comfort woman whore."

And there it was, the words "comfort woman" and "*chinilpa*." Every nerve in my body snapped to life. All the images of the comfort station—the post in the courtyard, my tiny, stinking room, the machine gun on that last, horrible day—came rushing back. I felt unclean. I hadn't told anyone about what I had done in Dongfeng. How had the secret I kept for nearly two years possibly have gotten out? *How could they know?*

I squeezed Suk-ju hard into my body, as if holding on to him could keep me where I was, in Pyongyang instead of back at the comfort station. He gave out a moan, and I loosened my hold on him a little. There was another crash from the living room. Suk-ju twisted his little head and began to wake up.

"Shut up, Ki!" Jin-mo said from the main room. "We have to help each other."

"That's not why you won't get rid of her."

"What do you mean by that?"

"You know what I mean."

"Okay, go ahead. Leave."

"I'm taking Suk-ju."

I heard the sound of footsteps marching to my door. I squeezed Suk-ju close to me. The door flew open, and Suk-ju jerked awake. Ki-soo pulled her son from me. She marched out to the living room. She grabbed her coat and suitcase and stomped out of the apartment with her son.

For a long time, I sat on my mat with my knees to my chin. I felt dirty and wanted to go to the bathroom to wash myself. Ki-soo's words "comfort woman whore" rang in my ears. I hadn't heard those words in more than two years. I put my hands on my head and tried to make them go away, but they stayed, like the insults they had thrown at me every day at the comfort station.

Finally I rose, cracked open my door, and peeked into the living room. Jin-mo was in a chair in the shadows looking at nothing. Outside the window, the willows swayed gently in the night breeze.

I went to the kitchen and got a broom and dustpan. I started to sweep up the shards from the broken celadon pot. "Leave it," Jin-mo said from the darkness. "It's my responsibility."

I set the broom down and went back to my room. I shut the door and sat on my low bed as the horrors of Dongfeng surrounded me again.

TWENTY-FIVE

"You run this upstairs while we start on the other one," Mr. Chee said. "Hurry!"

I grabbed the proclamation that the translation team had just finished and ran to the stairs leading to the fourth floor of the government headquarters. It was midday, and the building was abuzz with activity. People in the translation department examined documents or talked on telephones. Others flitted from desk to desk, carrying file folders. They all stopped and stared when I ran by with the papers.

As I climbed the stairs, I sensed a pending doom for the meeting on the fourth floor—and for the chance to unify Korea. The document in my hand was a proclamation from the Southern delegation declaring they were going forward with national elections as directed by the United Nations. And they would do it with or without the North's consent. It further stated that as far as the South was concerned, these elections would determine who had the right to govern all of Korea, North and South.

The translation department was feverishly working on a similar proclamation from the North. It stated that the North would not recognize the elections in the South, which they believed the Americans would rig to elect the pro-American puppet, Syngman Rhee. It said the North would hold separate elections under the supervision of the Soviet Union. And just like the South, as far as the North was concerned, *their* elections would determine who had the right to govern the entire peninsula. It was, as Jin-mo had feared, a stalemate.

I reached the fourth floor and ran to the huge, two-story, mahogany-paneled anteroom of the great meeting hall. I heard voices arguing on the other side of the giant wooden doors. A clutch of bureaucrats sat at desks, shuffling papers or talking softly to each other. They looked up as I approached. I went to a desk by the door to the meeting hall and bowed to the man sitting there. I offered the translations. The stern-faced man took the proclamation, read it over, and said, "Where's the one from the North?"

"Sir," I said with another bow, "we have not finished it. It will be done soon."

Suddenly the huge double doors swung open, and a group of men carrying briefcases came marching out with their eyes resolutely forward. I quickly stepped aside to let them pass. Half the bureaucrats in the anteroom scrambled to their feet, stuffed papers into their briefcases, and ran after them.

Inside the great hall, Jin-mo and the other delegates from the North stood at the door staring at the backs of the men who were leaving. Jin-mo ran his hands through his hair. A bureaucrat asked aloud, "What do we do now?"

Jin-mo and the others turned to their lead delegate. The man said, "Issue our proclamation."

I watched Jin-mo as he went to his desk and stuffed papers into his briefcase. Then he headed out of the great hall. As he walked past me he said, "Let's go home."

"It's over," Jin-mo said, sitting with me on a bench in the park outside our apartment. There were new lines in his face, and the circles under his eyes were darker than before. I worried about his health. "There will be no reconciliation," he said. "Korea is officially a divided nation."

It was a glorious spring day. Pyongyang's famous giant willows had leafed out. They looked like enormous green trolls with wispy arms reaching to the ground. The sun was high and warm, but the sadness on Jin-mo's face made it feel like midwinter.

"You did your best," I said, facing him.

He scoffed. "My best was not good enough. Now the only way to unify Korea is through a civil war. With the Americans and Soviets involved, it might lead to another world war. And they both have nuclear weapons. Fools! Why wouldn't they listen to me?" He closed his eyes and shook his head.

How could I know what to say? I had read about the global conflict called the Cold War. I knew that Korea was an important battleground. I had also read about nuclear bombs and their ability to destroy entire cities. But could Korea be the cause of another world war? Surely Jin-mo was exaggerating.

Jin-mo stared at his hands. He was so handsome with his smooth skin and shiny black hair. It made me sad that he never smiled anymore. I wondered if his sadness was from losing the fight for a unified Korea or from losing Ki-soo and Suk-ju.

"Have you heard from Ki-soo?" I asked. Perhaps I shouldn't have asked that—I still asked too many questions—but I wanted to know.

He told me he hadn't. "She will not change her mind," he said.

"I am sorry, Jin-mo."

He turned to me. "I've been avoiding asking you this, Jae-hee. How much did you hear of our argument the night Ki left?"

I looked out over the park and the willows. "I heard everything," I answered.

"Then you heard what she called you."

It was then that I knew that I had heard Ki-soo correctly two weeks earlier. She had called me a comfort woman and a *chinilpa*. Apparently they had known all along the secret I had tried so desperately to hide.

I felt my shoulders sag. I looked at the ground. I wanted to find a place to hide. "How did you know?" I asked.

"I knew when I first met you," he said. "You told me you worked in the boot factory at Sinuiju. Jae-hee, there was no boot factory there. It was a cruel joke by the Japanese. When they said they were sending a girl to the boot factory, they meant they were sending her to a comfort station. When you said you worked there, I knew you had been a comfort woman."

I felt so stupid for not knowing this. Boot factory. How fitting. It was like the Japanese were humiliating me all over again. I exhaled a sob. "I'm sorry I lied," I said. "I did not want anybody to know."

Jin-mo turned to me. "I only told Ki because she wanted me to kick you out. She said she didn't want an old-fashioned marriage like that. I thought she would feel sorry for you when I told her what you'd been through, but it only made her angrier."

"I was tricked into it," I said quickly. "The Japanese sent orders for me and my sister to report to work at the boot factory. We didn't know they were sending us to work in a comfort station. We were not *chinilpa*. We did not want to do it. They forced us to. We would have been shot."

"I know," Jin-mo said. "I know. They forced tens of thousands of girls into their comfort stations. You have nothing to be ashamed of."

I had nothing to be ashamed of? Now that I had learned that Jin-mo knew my secret all along, all I felt was shame. All the work I had done over the past two years was for nothing. I wasn't a valuable worker for the provisional government. I wasn't an honorable citizen of Korea. I was a *chinilpa*, a comfort woman whore who had let the Japanese use me like a toilet.

And Jin-mo knew what I had done! I couldn't bear to look at him. "I should go," I said. "I should find another place to live. It would be the right thing to do." I stood up from the bench. I wanted to run as fast as I could to someplace where no one knew who I was.

"I don't want you to leave," Jin-mo said. He reached out and gently touched my arm. At his touch, the images of the men who had slapped me, punched me, and raped me for two years flashed in my mind, and I recoiled.

He took his hand away. "I'm sorry," he said. "Please know, Jae-hee, I will never hurt you."

I knew he wouldn't. My reaction had been instinctive, and I wished I had not pulled away. His words, *I don't want you to leave,* gave me something to hold on to. I no longer wanted to run away. I wanted to continue my work. I wanted to be an honorable citizen. And I wanted Jin-mo.

I sat on the bench again. "I'm sorry I made Ki-soo leave," I said.

"You aren't the reason she left," he said. "I am. We weren't meant for each other. I'm an idealist, and she is a cynic. I wanted to bring Korea together, and I put it above everything else, including my family. I'm not going to change, Jae-hee. Neither is she."

Jin-mo looked at his feet. I could still feel the place on my arm where he had touched me. I hoped he would touch me again, and if he did, I would not recoil. After a few seconds I asked, "Shall I stay?"

"Yes," he said. "I want you to. Very much."

We said nothing more as we walked home among the giant willows of Pyongyang.

◆ ◆ ◆

For many months, I had dreamt about marrying Jin-mo. I pictured the two of us walking along the big boulevard in Pyongyang or going to the cinema together like other couples. I saw us having a child together, or maybe two. I daydreamed about us being happy in the apartment by the park as my mother and father had been on our farm. Yes, I thought about it often, but I never dared believe it would happen.

But that night as I prepared for bed, I sensed a change in the apartment. In a strange way, I was glad that Jin-mo knew my terrible secret. He had said I had nothing to be ashamed of, but I couldn't believe a man like Jin-mo thought it was true. But he had asked me to stay . . .

I put on clean bedclothes and stood before my mirror combing my hair with the comb with the two-headed dragon. I had left my door open to the main room. Jin-mo had a fire going in the fireplace. The apartment was comfortably warm.

Then, beyond my reflection in the mirror, I saw Jin-mo leaning against the doorjamb, watching me. My stomach jumped. The horrors of the comfort station began to rise in my mind, but I pushed them away. I put the comb on the table and turned to him. Our eyes met, and my heart beat fast. He came and stood in front of me. He reached out and stroked my hair. His touch was so tender, and this time, I did not recoil. I pressed my cheek into his hand and closed my eyes. He moved his hand to my shoulder and down my arm. And then he stopped. I opened my eyes and saw he was looking at my comb.

"It's beautiful," he said. He took his hand from me and picked up the comb. As he examined it, his mouth opened. "The dragon," he whispered, "it has two heads, and its feet have five toes."

"Yes," I said. "It has been in our family a long time."

"How long?" he asked.

"For generations."

He looked at the comb again, then handed it to me with a weak smile. He went back to the living room.

I didn't understand why he did not stay in my room. I wanted him to touch me again. I wanted him to make love to me. I followed him with the comb in my hand.

"What's wrong?" I asked. "What does the comb mean?"

He sat in a chair, and I sat on the sofa across from him. The fire in the fireplace crackled. He asked me what I knew about the comb. I told him the story Mother had told me and Soo-hee years earlier. I told him that women in my family had passed the comb on to their daughters for generations. I told him how Mother had given it to Soo-hee and how Soo-hee had given it to me at the comfort station.

"You have had it all this time?" Jin-mo asked.

"Yes. Why? Please tell me."

He didn't answer right away, and I thought he was angry with me for not telling him about the comb. Finally he said, "A dragon is a powerful symbol, as you know. But in Korea, a two-headed dragon is extraordinary. You see the two heads are facing opposite directions, east and west. The head facing east protects Korea from Japan. The head facing west protects us from China. And the dragon protects those who possess it so they can serve Korea."

I moved closer to Jin-mo. I wanted to ask questions, but I stayed quiet and let him continue. "When the Japanese annexed us, they forbid anyone from having that dragon," he said. "They said we were Japanese now and did not need protection from them. So when they found something with the two-headed dragon, they destroyed it and arrested whoever owned it. Nothing with that dragon was thought to have survived."

"I didn't know. It must be very valuable."

"Valuable?" he said. "It is beyond value." Jin-mo focused on the comb as if it had put him under a spell.

I stared at it, too. "Do you believe it?" I asked. "Do you believe a dragon can protect someone?"

He shook his head and then shrugged. "I am an educated man," he said. "I believe in science and history and observation and careful analysis. I am not given to superstition. Normally I would not believe such a thing. But honestly, I do not know what to believe anymore."

Then he looked at me with his mouth slightly open as if he wanted to say more. Instead, he forced a smile. "I should go to bed," he said. "I'm very tired."

My heart sank. I so wanted him to come with me to my room, but I could tell he wouldn't, not tonight. Perhaps not ever. I felt foolish to think that he would. "Yes," I said. "I am tired, too."

I closed my hand around the comb, bowed, and said goodnight. I went to my room and shut the door. I hid the comb in the lining of the old suitcase Jin-mo had given me. I curled up in bed and pulled the blanket to my chin. The familiar guilt I had carried with me since the first day Colonel Matsumoto had raped me came flooding back.

The dragon protects those who possess it so they can serve Korea, Jin-mo had said. I closed my eyes. Just like Mother, it had not protected me. I had been a comfort woman. And surely someone like me would never have the love of a man like Jin-mo.

TWENTY-SIX

Months later

I was cooking rice flour at the cast-iron stove to make dduk with jujube for Jin-mo. I hoped the sweet rice cakes and jelly would entice him to eat something. It was morning, and snow fell in the park outside the apartment.

Jin-mo sat at the low table in the kitchen and stared vacantly into his bori cha. His hair was a mess, and his wrinkled, unwashed clothes drooped on his thinning frame. He had stayed up all night reading his books, scribbling on paper, pacing the living room, and talking aloud to no one. He scared me when he did that. And he was doing it now nearly every night.

"Jin-mo, you have to go to work," I said. "You've missed too many days."

"I do not feel well," he said.

"They are asking about you. I'm running out of excuses."

"Why do they care?" Jin-mo scoffed. "They don't listen to what I say."

"What should I tell them when they ask about you?"

Jin-mo sighed. "Tell them you don't know anything. Tell them we never talk. Tell them you just have a room here. That's what you should say."

I did not know what to say to him to bring him out of his black mood. So I continued to steam the dduk as Jin-mo stared into his bori cha. After a long silence Jin-mo said, "Tell me about your sister."

"What do you want to know?" I asked.

"She was your onni, right?"

"Yes. Two years older."

"And the last time you saw her, she was still alive?"

I set the spoon on the stove. "You've asked the same questions three times this past week, Jin-mo. Yes, she was still alive, but she was almost dead. And the Japanese Kempei tai killed all the Korean girls. I'm sure they killed her, too. Why? Why do you want to know?"

Jin-mo turned away.

I went back to the rice. "I'm making dduk for you. You should eat."

"I'm not hungry."

"Jin-mo, you have to eat," I pleaded.

"No!" he said angrily. He marched into the living room and flopped in the upholstered chair. He picked up a book.

I removed the rice from the stove. It hadn't finished cooking, but it didn't matter. Jin-mo was not going to eat. I poured myself a cup of bori cha, sat at the table, and stared out the window at the snow on the willows. Months earlier, Jin-mo had asked me to stay with him, and I had hoped we would become a couple. It never happened. After he saw the comb with the two-headed dragon, he regarded me with caution, as if I was a fragile thing not to be broken. I yearned to have him touch me, kiss me, make love to me the way it should have been done before the Japanese had raped me. Instead, he had fallen into fits of depression and had lost himself in his books. I orbited around him and felt like a fool.

I finished my bori cha and went to the living room. Jin-mo had curled himself up in his chair, reading. His books and papers were stacked all around him. Even though the sun was up, it was dark in the room except for a lamp next to Jin-mo. He kept the shades on the windows closed all day. I went to the electric clock on the mantle and reset it from when the electricity had gone out two days before. Jin-mo hadn't touched the clock in months. I went to a stack of papers. I picked up something Jin-mo had written and began to read it by the light of the lamp.

"What are you doing?" Jin-mo asked from behind his book.

"I'm reading this."

"Leave it," he said. "Put it back exactly where it was."

"I want to see what you're working on." I held on to the paper.

Jin-mo slammed his book closed. "Put it back!" he yelled. "You're messing up the order."

His tone startled me. He had never talked to me like that before. "I'm messing up the order?" I asked. "What order, Jin-mo? I do not see any order at all."

Jin-mo looked around the room, and his shoulders sagged. "You think I'm mad, don't you?" he asked.

I sat on the couch across from him. "I am worried about you."

He set his jaw. His soft eyes were so sad. "I wasn't wrong," he said. "The compromises I proposed were right for Korea. It was the only way to have one government."

"You cannot compromise with a dictatorship," I said.

"Dictatorship?"

I pushed myself to the edge of the couch. "The way I see it," I said, "Marx's revolution of the proletariat is not possible. That much power will always turn into an oppressive dictatorship. It is human nature. In Korea, the dictator will be Kim Il-sung, just like Stalin is in Russia."

"Yes," he said. "That is a problem, isn't it?" He picked up his book and fell into it again. I thought I had lost him.

As I stood to go to the kitchen, he said, "I'm sorry."

"For what?"

"I'm sorry about me . . . about you and me."

"You and me?" I sat on the couch again.

"Yes," he said. "I'm sure you wanted more. From our relationship, I mean."

I let his words sink in. He was right, I had hoped for more. But as the weeks and months passed without anything happening between us, my hope had faded. And when his depression came and deepened, my hope died completely. I had tried everything, but I couldn't reach him. I had lost him before I ever had him.

"Yes, I did," I said. "But I understand why you cannot love me."

"No, you don't," Jin-mo said, setting his book down. "You think it is because of what you did . . . because of what you were forced to do by the Japanese."

A lump grew in my throat. I turned away.

"That's not why, Jae-hee," he said. "You were just a girl when the Japanese tricked you. How could you know?"

"I could not possibly," I said quickly.

"The Japanese did unspeakable things to us. They murdered our children and the elderly. They forced our women to work long hours in their factories and made our men fight their war. They raped girls like you. It's not your fault. Do you understand? It is not your fault."

I looked at Jin-mo. "Then why don't you want me?" I asked.

"I do," he replied.

I had never had a man say he wanted me before. Not like this. And the man who said it was my beloved Jin-mo. "I want you, too," I heard myself say.

"I'm sorry. I can't," he said, shaking his head. "I cannot fall in love with you."

But I was already in love with him and couldn't wait any longer. I went to his side and took his hand. I lifted his chin so our eyes met. "I love you, Jin-mo."

"Jae-hee. No."

I leaned into him, and we kissed. The sublime tenderness of Jin-mo's lips on mine pushed away the demons of the thousands of men who had raped me. And where the demons had been, a warmth rose. Jin-mo lifted a hand to my back and gently pulled me in close. I ran my hand along the muscles of his smooth back, and the warmth in me grew into a fire. I pushed myself into him and kissed him harder. He wrapped his arms around me, and our bodies met, chest to breast. I fell into his embrace. He lifted me in his arms and carried me to his room.

And there, I made love for the first time in my life.

◆　◆　◆

I lay next to Jin-mo and ran my fingers across his bare chest. I had never felt this way before. I had never even imagined it. I'd had sex thousands of times with thousands of men, but this, this was the first time I felt anything other than pain and shame. For years, I worried that if true love came, the demons of my rapists would haunt me and make love impossible. But in Jin-mo's embrace, the demons never came, and I knew I was meant to love him.

And he loved me, too. I could feel it. It was in his hold, in the way he said my name when we made love. It was in the way he touched me so tenderly, kissed me and held me close. Maybe what I did in Dongfeng, as shameful as it was, was not my fault after all. In his arms, I could believe it was true.

I thought about my sister. Poor Soo-hee never knew the joy of making love. She had only known the pain of forced sex and the humiliation of rape. Perhaps it was because Soo-hee had given me the comb. I hadn't believed in the comb when I was at the comfort station. But now I was living in a great city, doing important work, and in the arms of the man I loved. Perhaps the comb that Soo-hee had given me was good luck after all. *I am sorry, Soo-hee,* I said to myself. *This should have been you.*

"Jin-mo," I said, "why do you ask so many questions about my sister?"

"I just want to know about her."

"Jin-mo," I said, "she is dead."

"You don't know that for sure," he said.

I thought for a moment. He was right—I didn't. Of course, I had often wondered what had happened to Soo-hee after I left her for dead in the infirmary. I knew it would have taken a miracle for her to survive. And it was best not to hope for miracles.

"I do not think it is possible she's still alive," I said.

"It *is* possible," he said. "And I can find out. I am an official in the provisional government. I have access to records."

I pushed myself up on an elbow. "You've looked? What have you learned?"

"Nothing yet."

"Why do you want to know? Tell me."

Jin-mo sighed. "If she is alive, I want to find her, so you will not be alone."

"Alone? But I have you," I said, putting a hand on his shoulder.

Jin-mo pushed me away. He sat on the edge of the bed with his bare back to me. "Listen to me, Jae-hee," he said over his shoulder. "This . . . this was a mistake. We should not have done it. I should have been stronger."

I pulled the blanket over my shoulders. I felt the joy I had known only minutes earlier slipping away. "So everything you said before, about it not being my fault, was a lie?"

He turned to me. "No. I meant what I said. This, what we did, it was beautiful. I have wanted you for a long time. Don't you see? Didn't you feel it?"

"Yes, I did," I answered. "So why was it a mistake?"

He shook his head. "Because I am a marked man. Those fools think I'm their enemy. They want to kill me. But you, Jae-hee, you must go on. That is why I want to find your sister."

While I knew Jin-mo was at odds with people in his party, I did not know he thought they might kill him for it. I was shocked and frightened for him. "If they kill you, they will have to kill me, too," I said. And I meant it.

"I believe you would do that, but I will not let you."

I pushed myself straight. "Then we should run away, Jin-mo, escape to the South. Thousands of people are doing it."

"They will never let me escape, Jae-hee. If you go with me, they will kill you, too. And then they will get your comb."

"My comb?" I said, surprised. "What does my comb have to do with this?"

"They cannot have it. I don't want the dragon to protect them."

"The dragon? Protect them? Do you really believe in the dragon?" I asked.

"I don't really know," Jin-mo said. "It might be true. Think about it. You survived, Jae-hee. When your family and the other comfort women died, *you survived*. And now you must go on."

"But you said the dragon protected those who possessed it so they could help serve Korea. I haven't done anything for Korea."

"Yes, you have," he said simply. "You've done something very important. You survived." He looked at me straight on. "And we should never do this again."

He started to dress. At that moment, I felt Jin-mo slipping away like my family had years earlier. I couldn't imagine not lying with him again, not feeling his touch, not making love to him. Without Jin-mo, my terrible loneliness would return, and I was convinced that next time it would kill me. "I do not care about the comb," I said. "I will throw it away."

He turned to me, and there was anger in his eyes. "Don't say that. You have to keep it, Jae-hee."

"But why me? Why am I responsible for it? Why can't I throw it away and be with you?"

Without answering, Jin-mo finished dressing and went to the main room. I lay on the bed with the blanket to my chin. I loved Jin-mo more than I ever loved anyone. If I had to, I would destroy the comb with the two-headed dragon to hold on to the man I loved.

TWENTY-SEVEN

When I pushed my way out of the apartment to go to work, my stomach churned. I moved to the street in case I had to vomit again. I had to wait a full minute to let my stomach settle.

I had decided not to tell Jin-mo about my morning sickness or that my breasts were swollen and sore. I did not want to burden his troubled mind with the fact that I was pregnant. Over the previous several months, we had made love sporadically, and after each time, Jin-mo berated himself and called himself weak. It frightened me to watch him slip deeper and deeper into his depression. He was missing a lot of work. He slept during the day, and at night, he read his books or filled sheets of paper with notes. He rarely ate and had turned pale and weak. I worried about him.

I worried about what to do with the baby growing inside me. Jin-mo certainly was not able to cope with being a father again, and I was not sure he would even accept our baby in his state of mind. I knew I would be alone with a child to care for. I had heard of a place where I could go to end the pregnancy. But I remembered how Soo-hee's abortion had killed her, and I worried that it could kill me, too. Anyway, I did not want to lose the baby I had made with Jin-mo. I loved him, and

I wanted to have his child. So I went on with the pregnancy and prayed that Jin-mo would get better.

That morning, the March wind was sharp. I wrapped my scarf tight, dropped my shoulders to the wind, and headed to work. I dreaded going to work. It scared me there. Mr. Chee had disappeared months earlier. In hushed conversations, people in the translation department said the communists took him away because he had lived in England and had capitalist's ideas. Others said he had escaped to the South. After he left, the documents and contracts I worked on became increasingly absurd. I didn't want to do it anymore. I wanted to be home to take care of Jin-mo. But with the way things were in Pyongyang, I went to work every day and kept my feelings to myself.

As I rounded a corner onto the boulevard leading to the government building, a convoy of gray-green army trucks belching black smoke in the air rumbled south. In the backs of the trucks, young soldiers clutched rifles and looked out at the pedestrians with fatalistic eyes.

Outside the government building, a group of workers clung to scaffolding around a newly installed granite base on the boulevard. Next to it was a tall crane. There was a lot of construction going on in Pyongyang, and I thought this was just another new project. Then I saw a government official dressed in a black wool coat and fur hat standing next to the scaffolding. The pedestrians bowed to him as they walked by. From behind the scaffolding, the crane lifted a huge iron statue of a man. Its back was to me, and its arms stretched out to the street below. As it rose to the pedestal, it slowly turned toward me, and I saw they were erecting another statue of Kim Il-sung. The massive figure smiled down benevolently at his subjects below. I scoffed at it under my breath.

I hated the communists. They were just like the Japanese. Months earlier, they had set fire to the cinema. They claimed faulty wiring caused it, but everyone knew it was because the communists didn't want them to show the popular American films anymore. So they burned it down and arrested everyone who worked there.

The communists were arrogant and pushy, and there were grave consequences if you did not humbly follow their orders. And they were Koreans—Koreans!—treating their own people like animals. It seemed like we had traded a great evil for a more insidious one.

I went inside the provincial government building and climbed the stairs to the third floor. In the bull pen area, a man I had never seen before was sitting in my chair. He wore wire-rimmed glasses and a black military coat with a major's insignia. Standing next to him was a soldier in a green uniform. The pistol on his belt made me swallow hard.

I wanted to run but went to my desk. I saw my coworkers sneaking nervous glances at me. Without getting up, the man asked if I was Hong Jae-hee. I told him I was. He ordered me to follow him. He picked up his briefcase and marched toward the stairs. His footsteps echoed off the walls. The soldier with the pistol motioned me to follow the major.

They led me to a windowless room on the second floor. Inside was a metal table and two chairs. The soldier stood with his back against the door. The major ordered me to sit. He took off his coat, laid it on the table, and sat in the chair across from me. He took out a pencil and paper from his briefcase. "My name is Major Lee," he said. "I have some questions. I expect you will answer them truthfully."

"Yes, sir," I said.

Major Lee observed me coldly, which sent a shiver through me. He made me feel like the Japanese officers did in Dongfeng—as if he would slap me for the slightest indiscretion. I knew I had to be careful, but I had a lot of practice handling situations like this.

"You are Hong Jae-hee from near Sinuiju," he asked. "Correct?"

"Yes, sir," I answered.

He wrote on his paper. "Your father died in battle fighting for the Japanese, and your mother worked in a uniform factory. Correct?"

"Yes, sir."

"And during this time, your sister, Soo-hee, was sent to a comfort station in Dongfeng, China. Correct?"

I was stunned. How did this man know about Soo-hee? I wondered if he knew about me, too. "Yes, sir," I answered quickly.

"What did you do during this time?"

My stomach began to roil again. I wanted desperately to keep what I did in Dongfeng a secret, but his question hung heavy in the air.

The major leaned over the desk toward me. "I asked a question. You will answer."

My stomach turned into a knot. I tried to think. Ever since the Russians had left North Korea and Kim Il-sung had taken power, people who lied to the new regime had disappeared. And there were rumors that the officials knew if someone was lying. I decided I had to tell the truth. "I worked in the comfort station in Dongfeng, too," I said finally. I lowered my eyes.

Major Lee nodded and wrote something on his paper. The soldier at the door glared at me, bringing back my shame from what I did at the comfort station.

The major continued to ask his questions. He asked about my relationship with Jin-mo. I told him that Jin-mo and I only shared an apartment and that we were not married. "We rarely talk," I said, truthfully. He asked why Jin-mo wasn't coming to work anymore, and I told him it was because he was sick.

And then the major asked, "Do you know why he has been inquiring about your sister?"

My stomach jumped again, and my mind raced. I couldn't imagine why this man thought that Jin-mo's investigation regarding Soo-hee was important. "Sir," I said, "I asked him to. He has learned nothing. I do not think it is possible my sister is alive."

The major nodded. "Yes, I don't believe he found out anything about her." The major wrote some more on his paper, folded it, and pushed it inside his briefcase.

"Very well," he said. "There is one more thing and we will be done."

From his briefcase, he took out a two-page document, a pen, and an ink bottle and placed them on the table. He stretched his lips into a polite smile, but his eyes remained cold behind his wire-rimmed glasses. "It has been determined that you are valuable to the Workers Party of Korea. You have the physical qualities of an ideal Korean woman, and apparently you have great skill with languages. Your supervisors report that you are an obedient worker. We need someone with your skill in the department of education, where you will translate literature supporting our Great Leader. It is an important assignment, and you are fortunate to have been selected for it."

He pushed the document and pen toward me. "First, we must be sure you are qualified. This is a statement of support for Chairman Kim. It states that you believe he alone is the rightful leader of Korea, North and South. It further states that you agree to give him your devotion and are even willing to die for him if asked."

Major Lee's thin smile stretched thinner. "The party is willing to overlook someone's past if that person agrees to support Chairman Kim. I'm sure you will agree with this statement. Please sign where indicated." He uncorked the ink bottle and pointed it at me.

I dipped the pen in the ink and signed the document without reading it. Major Lee blew once on the ink to dry it and put the document in his briefcase. "You have made a wise decision," he said. "And now, this man will show you to your new assignment."

The soldier with the sidearm led me to the Ministry of Education on the third floor. I sat next to a stern woman with thick ankles who regarded me with disdain. I spent the entire day translating into English and Japanese propaganda about Kim Il-sung. The documents pronounced the Dear Leader's incredible bravery when he fought the Japanese during their occupation. They said that he alone had the skill and vision to bring the Korean people together as one nation. The documents made him sound like a god.

I did not question a word and made the translations as accurately as I could.

◆ ◆ ◆

That evening when I left the government building to go home, the wind was still blowing cold. I wrapped my coat tight around me and walked quickly to the apartment. I was anxious to talk to Jin-mo about Major Lee and his questions.

I pushed the apartment door open and took off my shoes. For the first time in months, Jin-mo had opened the drapes to the windows that overlooked the park. The books and papers he had stacked in the living room were gone. Jin-mo crouched in front of a blaze in the fireplace. What remained of his books was in a small stack next to him. The orange flames threw shimmering shadows against the wall.

As I took off my coat, I asked Jin-mo what he was doing. His face reflected the orange flames. He had changed into clean clothes and had brushed his hair smooth.

"I'm burning them," he said in an odd voice. He tossed another book in the fire.

"Why?"

"Because these books do not mean anything anymore."

"Jin-mo," I said, coming to his side, "someone came to talk to me today. Major Lee was his name. I had to tell him what I did in Dongfeng."

Jin-mo stared into the fireplace as the flames caught the pages of the book and rose high. "It's a good thing you did." He nodded. "They probably already knew."

I took his hand. I looked in his face, still handsome through all his misery. "Jin-mo, let's leave Pyongyang. Let's run to the South where no one knows us. We can go tonight."

"It's too late for me," he said.

"But they will kill you here."

"Yes, they will," he replied, his tone matter of fact. He tossed another book on the fire.

The flames were hot against my face. "What should we do?" I asked. "What should we do?"

"You have to go without me."

I pushed his hand away. "No, I won't go alone," I cried. I could feel a tear overrun my eye. "I will not leave you!"

"Jae-hee," he said, "they are probably outside right now. They will not let me get one block from this apartment. And if you're caught trying to escape with me, they will kill you, too."

"I don't care. I will not go without you."

"You have to. They will destroy you here. First your mind, then your soul. In the end, you will not care when they kill you."

He picked up a book and admired it. After he tossed it in the fire, I said, "Jin-mo, I'm pregnant."

He looked into the fire and smiled sadly. "How long?" he asked.

"Three months."

"It is a girl," he said simply.

"How could you know?"

"Because of your comb."

"I don't care about the comb," I said. "I do not believe in the dragon. And I will not have this baby without you."

"Yes," he said. "That's how I will do it."

I shook my head. "Jin-mo, what are you talking about?"

Suddenly Jin-mo grabbed my shoulders and forced me to look at him. "Jae-hee, promise you will do this for me. Promise you will keep the comb and let the dragon protect you."

"No. I will not," I said. "Not if it means losing you."

He gripped me hard. "You must do it. Don't you see? You must survive this. Then someday you can tell them what we tried to do here. Do it for me. Do it for Korea."

I must have winced from his grip because he let go of me. He nodded oddly and smiled another sad smile.

"I thought you didn't believe in the dragon," I said.

"I said I wasn't sure," he replied, picking up the last book. "But now it's all I have to believe in. At least it's something. And who knows? It might be true." He tossed the book in the fire.

Eventually the flames consumed each page, and all that remained of Jin-mo's beloved books were glowing orange embers. He watched as the embers faded to ash and then looked at his feet.

I was overwhelmed with foreboding, and I was so terribly confused. The only thing I knew for certain was that I loved Jin-mo more than I ever thought it possible to love anyone. I took him by the arm and led him to his room. I stripped off his clothes and put him in bed. I took off my clothes, too, and slipped beneath the blankets next to him. He pushed his head into my breast and cried.

TWENTY-EIGHT

They came for Jin-mo when the night was darkest. They were inside the bedroom and were on him before I knew what was happening. Two soldiers dragged him naked from the bed and made him dress. He offered no resistance.

"What are you doing?" I cried as I pulled on my clothes. I scrambled to the living room as they led Jin-mo toward the front door. "Where are you taking him? No! He is sick. Let him go!"

"Halt!" came an order from beside the fireplace. Poking at the ashes of Jin-mo's books was Major Lee. The soldiers stopped at the front door and turned Jin-mo to face him.

The major wore a black coat and fur hat. I hated the way he looked sideways at me through his wire-rimmed glasses. "It has been determined that Mr. Pak is sick and needs rehabilitation," the major said. "Yesterday you told me you were not married to this man. You signed a paper in support of Kim Il-sung and agreed to die for the Great Leader if asked. In return, we have given you an important job in the Workers Party of Korea. You have a fine apartment here. You have done well for someone with your . . . history. Certainly you do not want to give it up for a disillusioned man, do you?"

I was about to say that I would give up everything for the man I loved when Jin-mo pulled himself from the soldiers' grip. "Jae-hee," he said, "remember your duty to Korea." For the first time in months, his eyes were clear. He looked like the man he was when I first saw him in charge of the census in Sinuiju. He looked like a man who believed in ideas. "You can do it," he said. "Do it for Korea. Do it for me." He smiled sadly. "Good-bye, Jae-hee," he said. Then he turned and walked out the door as the soldiers scurried after him.

I loved Jin-mo, I truly did. And I was not afraid to die for him. I desperately wanted to curse at Major Lee and run to Jin-mo's side. But as I watched him disappear out the door, my insides turned to stone just as they had in the comfort station in Dongfeng. The stone took hold of me and froze me in place like the Pyongyang fountains in the winter. I couldn't feel and I couldn't move. And I let them take my beloved Jin-mo away.

Major Lee slowly placed the poker back in the stand. "You've made the right decision," he said, pressing his lips into a smile. "Our Great Leader will not forget. And now I must see to Mr. Pak's care. I hope the rest of your night is quiet." Major Lee followed the soldiers out the door.

Standing there in Jin-mo's apartment, I could not believe what I had just done. I dragged myself to the sofa and covered up with a blanket. I stared into the fireplace and wanted to cry. But my stone-hard heart imprisoned my sobs. I thought about what kind of person I had become. I had tried so hard to put Dongfeng behind me and heal Jin-mo with my love. But I was a comfort woman, and I could never have a man like Jin-mo.

My stomach roiled, and I became nauseous like in the mornings. My skin turned clammy, and I shivered. I threw off the blanket and built a fire in the fireplace. When the flames had taken hold of the wood, I marched to my room and pulled out my suitcase. I reached under the lining and took out the comb with the two-headed dragon.

I took it to the fireplace. In the flame's flickering light, the gold spine glimmered, and the two-headed dragon mocked me with its tongues and claws. I decided I hated it. The comb was nothing more than a cheap trinket, and the power of the two-headed dragon was just a myth. It had brought me only sorrow and loneliness, and death to the ones I loved. How could I have been so naïve to believe it would protect me?

The baby inside me made me nauseous. I decided I hated it, too. I kneeled on the hearth and poked the wood. The flames rose high. I added another log, then another. Soon the flames reached past the flue. I held the comb close to the fire. The heat burned my hand and brought tears to my eyes.

You must pass on the comb, my mother had said. *Do this for me,* Soohee had said. *Do it for Korea,* Jin-mo had said. I could see their faces dancing in the flames. "Damn you!" I shouted at them. "Damn you for making me do this. I am not the one who should!"

The baby pushed against my insides and made me want to vomit. I cocked my hand to throw the comb in the fire. And then the faces in the fire changed to those of Colonel Matsumoto, Lieutenant Tanaka, and Major Lee. They laughed and mocked me. I dropped my arm, and the faces changed back to flames.

I took the comb to the couch and wrapped myself in the blanket again. I did not know why the spirits of my ancestors had brought me to this place. I did not know what I was supposed to do now or how I could go on without Jin-mo. Then I noticed my nausea was gone. The baby rested comfortably in my womb. I watched the fire for a long time, trying to make sense of all that had happened to me since the day I left home with Soo-hee.

Soon I was warm, and a profound weariness that felt like death took hold of me. I lay on the couch to sleep. As I was about to close my eyes, I noticed something on the lowest shelf of the bookshelf. It was one last book that Jin-mo had not burned. I pushed myself off the couch and picked it up. It was Jin-mo's copy of *The Communist Manifesto* in Hangul.

I took it to the couch and opened it. Near the back was an envelope. Inside was money and a note. I took the note out and read it.

> *My dear Jae-hee,*
> *You must leave the North as soon as you can. Go to the Gimhae Hotel just off the Taedong River south of the great square. Ask for a man named Mr. Gah. Tell him you want to see the world. Use those exact words. Pay him what he asks and he will take care of you.*
> *Please forgive me for loving you.*
> *Jin-mo*

I thumbed through the money. It was a substantial sum. I read the note again and memorized the name of the hotel and the phrase I would need to say. Then I picked up the money and tossed the note and book in the fire. I took the comb to the kitchen. I found some cloth, wrapped it around the comb, and tied it with twine. I went to my room and laid out my dress for work the next day. I put the comb, the money, and the photograph of my family in my dress pocket. I went to bed and waited for morning to come.

◆　◆　◆

The next day, I didn't have morning sickness for the first time in a month. I washed thoroughly and dressed. I went to the kitchen. The apartment was eerily still without Jin-mo and his books. I finally cried when I realized I would never see him again, lie by his side, or talk to him about his ideas. I wondered what was happening to him. Had they tortured him or simply killed him right away?

I hated them. The communists had killed my beloved Jin-mo, and they would kill Korea, too. They wanted all of you. It was just like Jin-mo said—first they take your mind, then your soul, and then your life. I remembered what Mother had said about the Japanese the night before I left home—that she wasn't going to give them anything more. I finally knew what she meant. I wasn't going to give the communists anything more, either.

I ate a breakfast of dduk and strong bori cha. I wondered if I should make dduk cakes to bring with me, but thought better of it. Jin-mo's note said Mr. Gah would take care of me. I had to trust that he would.

I put on my coat and went out the door. The sun was making everything bright again. The willows filtered the sun like light through lace. It was almost warm. I headed to the provincial government building, careful not to look over my shoulder or do anything out of the ordinary. When I got there, I looked at the huge new statue of Kim Il-sung. He beamed down at me with outstretched arms. I threw a silent curse at him.

I walked inside and climbed the wide staircase to the Ministry of Education. I bowed a greeting to my supervisor with the thick ankles and sat at my desk. I began to work on a translation proclaiming that Kim Il-sung would be Korea's supreme leader for all eternity.

When my supervisor left the room, I went to the service staircase and down to the street level. I pushed the door open to an alley jammed with military trucks and official government cars. I wound my way to a side street and turned south toward the Taedong River.

TWENTY-NINE

"I want to see the world," I said to Mr. Gah, who was sipping green tea in a back room of the shabby Gimhae Hotel. He was thin and balding and had a lazy lower lip, but his eyes were sharp.

He asked me if I was in trouble with the authorities. The words bumped across his lip, making him sound drunk. I said no, I wasn't in trouble, and that I wanted to go because I didn't have anyone here in the North.

"Do you have someone in the South?" he asked.

"No, sir," I said. "I have no one."

Mr. Gah raised an eyebrow. "So you want to leave because you have no one here. But you have no one there, either? Are you sure you want to go?"

"Sir," I said, "I believe they will kill me here."

"And do you think it will be better for you in the South?"

I held Mr. Gah's stare and thought about his question for a second. Then I said, "I honestly do not know."

Mr. Gah's face spread into a sloppy grin. A chuckle rose from his chest and spilled from his mouth. After a few seconds, he turned serious again.

"There is a fee to see the world," he said in a professional tone.

"I understand. How much?"

"One thousand won."

One thousand won was nearly all Jin-mo had left me. I counted out the money and laid it on the table in front of Mr. Gah. His lazy lip curled unevenly into a smile. He took a sip of tea and wiped his lip with a handkerchief he kept in his hand. "When do you want to go?" he asked.

"I have to leave right away," I answered. "I cannot go back."

Mr. Gah took the money and folded it into his pocket. "You're lucky. We have a truck leaving tonight. Behind the hotel is a shed. Go there and wait."

The shed was an old lean-to with a tin roof built against the back of the hotel. I pulled open the door and slipped in. It was dark inside. I could feel there were others in the shed with me, huddled close to each other. I sat on the floor next to a sack of rice. I could smell the dampness of the Taedong River a few blocks away. Outside the shack, trucks rumbled over the street.

After a few minutes, I could make out the others' faces. It was a man, a woman, and a young boy. I could see fear in their eyes. The man's jaw was set at a defiant slant. The woman clung to his arm and held the boy close.

I smiled at the boy. "What is your name?" I asked.

He blinked at me, then at his mother.

"It's okay," I said. "I am going on a trip, just like you."

The boy eased a little. "My name is Sang-dong."

"Hush," scolded his father. "Children should not talk to strangers."

My heart went out to the frightened boy as he pushed his face into his mother again. He looked a little like Suk-ju, who I hadn't seen since Ki-soo took him away, and who I missed terribly.

Sang-dong's father looked at me suspiciously. "Why are you leaving the North?" he asked.

"They killed the man I loved," I answered.

The man nodded. "There will be a civil war soon, and the South will win with America's help. Maybe Korea can finally be united."

"Yes," I said, "although I hope it can be done without a civil war."

The man said, "I have a brother in Taejon. His name is Yaeng Il-dak. He works for an American contractor there. I haven't heard from him in two years. I'm hoping he can help me get work. What will you do there?" he asked.

I hadn't thought about it. Jin-mo's note had only told me how to escape. It hadn't told me what to do after I did. I had very little money and nothing except the clothes I wore, the comb with the two-headed dragon, and a baby in my belly.

"I do not know what I will do in the South," I answered. "All I know is that I will not stay here."

We said nothing more and waited in the shed all day. My bladder grew full, and I was thirsty. My muscles ached from sitting, but my pregnant stomach was calm. Finally the door opened. By the sun's angle, I could see it would be dark soon.

Mr. Gah leaned in. "Go inside and use the toilet," he said. "Hurry, the truck is coming."

I followed the others inside the hotel. I waited until they were done and then used the toilet myself. I took a long drink from the tap in the basin. I wanted to wash before we left, but I knew we didn't have enough time. When we went back to the lean-to, a military supply truck was waiting for us.

Mr. Gah stood at the tailgate, watching the street. "In here," he said. "Quickly!" He lifted the tarp and helped each of us in. Inside were sacks of food and boxes of military supplies. It reminded me of the truck that took me and Soo-hee to Dongfeng. I was suddenly afraid I was making a terrible mistake.

Mr. Gah held up the corner of the tarp. "Listen carefully," he said. "In four hours, the driver will stop and knock on the cab three times. It is the signal for you to get out. Find a tire on the side of the road. Take the path by it until you come to a fence. Don't go off the path. When you get to the fence, go right fifty yards. There's an opening there. You'll have to look for it. Go through it and follow the path on the other side to the road. Wave down the first truck you see. It will be the South Koreans."

Mr. Gah jutted his lip at us. "Be quiet, keep low, and move quickly. Be sure you stay on the path on both sides of the fence. Understand? Stay on the path! There is a quarter moon tonight, so your chances are good. If you get caught, do not tell them about me, or I will never be able to help anyone again." He dropped the flap and pounded on the truck side.

The truck lurched forward and rolled through the city. After a while, the ride smoothed out over what felt like a paved road. Sang-dong's mother pulled him close, and eventually the boy fell asleep. As evening gave way to night, the back of the truck grew dark and cold. I wrapped my coat tight around me. I worried about what I would find in the South. What the communists said about it made it sound evil. But I knew the North *was* evil, and I didn't want anything more to do with it. I had no choice. I had to make it to the South. I had to believe that my baby and I would be better off there.

Several hours later, the truck came to a stop. Three thuds came from the cab. Sang-dong's father jumped up and crawled out. He helped his wife and son get down. As I stood, the truck began to roll. I placed a hand on the tailgate and jumped. When I landed, my ankle twisted, and I fell. A sharp pain shot up my leg. I stifled a yell and pushed myself to my feet. I tested my ankle. The pain was almost unbearable. I hobbled over to the others, who were crouching low in the ditch.

The truck disappeared over a ridge, and we were alone in the darkness. We were next to a large, open field filled with dead, waist-high weeds. It was very dark and quiet.

"We have to find the path," the man whispered. "Do you see the tire?"

He looked along the ditch one way, then the other. "It's too dark. I'll have to find it," he said. He crawled along the ditch, and a few seconds later he came back. "This way!" he whispered. "Follow me." He lifted his son and took his wife by the hand. They disappeared into the blackness.

I tried to follow them as fast as I could, but each step sent spikes of pain up my leg. A few yards away, I found them crouched next to an old truck tire. Together we crawled out of the ditch to a path among the weeds.

Down the road on the other side of a ridge, we saw a faint dome of light. Then the sound of a truck engine broke the stillness of the night. "Quickly!" the man said, darting forward. I followed them, but the pain in my ankle made me fall behind. I glanced over my shoulder just in time to see a truck crest the ridge and slowly come toward us. On top of the truck was a searchlight sweeping over the field.

I gritted my teeth and quickened my pace. Soon I caught up to the others. The truck came closer. The searchlight cast its beam across the field to our left. The man stopped and crouched low. "I see the fence. It's only a short distance if we go straight for it." He handed Sang-dong to his wife. "I will lead the way. Come quickly."

"No!" I whispered. "Stay on the path." But the man had already disappeared. The woman lifted the boy to her hip and followed him.

I was about to follow when the night sky exploded in a blinding light, throwing me to the ground. The explosion echoed off the hills. I do not know how long I lay there. It might have been only a few seconds, or perhaps it was longer. Eventually I pushed myself to my hands and knees. I shook my head to clear the ringing in my ears. I thought I heard screaming.

The searchlight swept through the weeds next to where the explosion had been. Something moved in front of me. The woman burst through the weeds with the boy in her arms. Blood covered them both. The woman's eyes were wild like an animal's caught in a trap. She thrust the boy at me. "Take him," she cried. I was still dazed and didn't understand what she wanted. The woman pushed the boy into my arms. "Take him!" she hissed through clenched teeth. I took him, and she ran back into the weeds.

The searchlight scanned the area around us. Men were shouting from the road behind me. The boy's eyes were wide. Blood covered his face. He reached for where his mother had gone. "Ummah!" he cried. "Appa!"

I put my hand over his mouth, and he squirmed and fought me. I lifted my head above the weeds. In the distance, I saw the outline of a high fence topped with barbed wire. I left the path and ran for it. The boy continued to wriggle, but I held him tight. When I got to the fence, I tried to remember Mr. Gah's instructions. I couldn't remember if he said to go left or right. I went right as the voices behind me grew louder.

I looked along the fence for an opening, but in the darkness, I couldn't see anything. The searchlight swept the ground behind us. I dropped among the weeds. My hand came off the boy's mouth, and he cried out. I found the boy's mouth again with my hand. "Shhh," I whispered. "Please be quiet." The boy, his eyes wide with fear, stopped struggling. When I took my hand away from his mouth, he stayed quiet.

As the searchlight moved closer, I felt inside my pocket for the comb with the two-headed dragon. It wasn't there. I frantically searched the ground among the weeds, but I could not find it. The searchlight swept over us, exposing something shiny a few feet from me. It was the comb. Then I looked beyond the comb and followed the path of the searchlight. For a split second, the light illuminated the fence, and I could see an opening next to a post. It was small, barely big enough for one person to squeeze through. I grabbed the comb, and with the boy on my hip, I crawled for the opening.

The voices behind me grew louder. "Sergeant, over here!" a man said. There was the sound of boots running. The footsteps stopped where the explosion had been.

"You killed him!" the woman screamed. "You pigs, you killed him!"

At the sound of his mother's voice, the boy jerked up. "Ummah!" he shouted.

"Someone else is over there!" a soldier yelled.

With the comb in one hand and the boy in the other, I ran for the fence. The boy squirmed and shouted for his mother. "Mama!" he cried again. "Mama!" I got to the fence and lifted the wire. I pushed the boy through. I crawled under the fence, grabbed the boy, and ran.

Be sure you stay on the path on both sides of the fence, Mr. Gah had said. I looked at my feet and saw I wasn't on the path. I was terrified that I might step on a mine like the boy's father, but I kept running. The weeds slapped at my legs, and my ankle screamed in pain.

A shot rang out, ripping through the weeds next to me. Then the searchlight found me. Another shot rang out, but this one came from in front of me. "Halt! Stay where you are," a voice said. I stopped and crouched among the weeds. I was breathing hard, and my heart was pounding. The searchlight stayed on me.

There was the sound of footsteps approaching. Suddenly three sets of boots, black and polished, surrounded me. I looked up. Soldiers pointed rifles at the fence behind me.

The searchlight went out. A soldier reached down and took the boy. Another helped me to my feet.

"Be very careful to follow exactly where I step," he said. "Welcome to the Republic of South Korea."

THIRTY

August 2008. Seoul, South Korea

Mrs. Hong doesn't seem to notice me as she stands at her apartment window, telling her story as if the entire world is her audience. The sun has moved around, and It shines on her. In her hanbok, she almost looks like an angel. She has clasped her hands behind her back and sways slightly. I notice the lines on her face are deeper than before, as if her story is aging her.

"I was able to give young Sang-dong to his uncle in Taejon one week after I escaped from the North," she says. "The uncle was not pleased to have another mouth to feed. As a reward for saving his nephew, he gave me a few grains of rice to eat. Then he told me I had to leave." She sighs. "I was on the streets of Taejon with nothing more than the clothes on my back, the comb, and a baby in my belly," she says.

She stays quiet for a while and then turns from the window. "I was able to work for food until several months later, when I gave birth to a girl. It was September 15, 1950, three months to the day after the North invaded the South and started the Korean civil war. It was also the day General MacArthur landed at Inchon to repel the invasion."

"The baby girl," I say, "she was my birth mother?"

Mrs. Hong nods. "Yes. I named her Soo for my sister, Soo-hee, and Bo for my mother, Bo-sun. In Korea, it is not proper to name a child after an elder. But I did it anyway to regain a little of what I had lost. It was selfish, I suppose." She flashes a mischievous grin. "But who would know? Would you like more bori cha?"

"Yes, ma'am," I answer. I'm beginning to get a taste for the bitter tea.

She goes to the stove and fills our cups. She hands me mine and sits at the table across from me, upright with both hands around her cup. Her head nods ever so slightly. I wonder if it's age or if she's psyching herself up to go on.

"Soo-bo was born prematurely," she says. "It was a difficult delivery. I was in labor for eighteen hours during the Battle of the Pusan Perimeter. The North had almost won the war. I was terrified that if they did, they would find me and kill me. So I went to Pusan with the retreating South Korean army.

"Pusan was the war's defining battle," she continues. "The American air force turned the war for the South. There were bombs going off day and night. Thousands died. During that battle, there was an equally violent struggle inside me. But eventually Soo-bo was born. She was sick for a long time. An American army doctor cared for her. Captain Charles Keegan was his name. He was young, not even thirty years old. He was able to find a cotton blanket for Soo-bo, and he gave me food from the American mess so I could nurse. I heard he was killed by a mortar a few months later."

I take a sip of bori cha and try to imagine what it was like back then. "The war must have been awful," I say.

She looks into her teacup and shakes her head. "It should not have happened. The Americans and Russians should have let us be after World War Two. Perhaps then we could have resolved our differences."

I push to the front of my seat. "When we visited Panmunjom, they told us that the Russians gave the North weapons and pushed them to invade the South. The Americans only came in later. To prevent the communists from taking over."

She glares at me. "You are correct," she says. "But then your army drove all the way to the Chinese border. General MacArthur's insolence and disrespect for the Chinese made them believe the Americans were going to invade them, too. So they entered the war on behalf of the North. As a result, the war in my homeland went on for three more bloody years."

"So you think we should have let the communists win?"

"I think the Americans should have been more careful with my country," she answers. "Understand, Ja-young, millions died in that war. Millions! They are not just numbers in a history book. They were families, entire villages, people I knew, my friends and countrymen. And millions more were left homeless with nothing to eat. After centuries of being torn between the Chinese, Japanese, and Russians, and after thirty-five years of a brutal Japanese occupation, all we wanted was to be one country, at peace. Instead, Korea was a pawn in a game fought to a draw by the world's superpowers."

She looks at me like a teacher trying to get through to a stubborn student. I have to look away. I'd never had much interest in history before, but now I'm seeing it from someone who lived it. I'm beginning to understand why Dad says I should take a few history classes in college.

"To answer your question," she says, "we are better off having not let Kim Il-sung rule all of Korea. He became a despot, just like I predicted. Although the corrupt American puppet Syngman Rhee was not much better."

"What happened to you during the war?" I ask.

She sits back and looks into her bori cha again. "I was one of the homeless and destitute. I was fluent in English, as I said, and that helped. But I still struggled. Soo-bo and I were always close to starving. In the middle of a war, a poor young woman with a sick baby is a nuisance to everyone." She lifts her chin. "You need know nothing more, other than we survived through effort and luck."

I think about how hard her life had been at my age and feel guilty for feeling sorry for myself and for being afraid. I mean, really. Compared to what she had to go through, what do I have to be afraid of? "Your life was tough," I say. "I'm sorry."

"Yes, but I survived," she says. "And for me, that is what was important."

She eyes me for a few seconds and then asks, "And what about you, Anna? What is important to you?"

Her question throws me. "I—I'm not sure," I stammer. "I used to think it was being successful, you know? Doing well in school, that sort of thing. But I'm not in school anymore," I confess. "I had to drop out when Mother got sick."

"Do you plan to go back?"

I shake my head. "I really don't know. I haven't got a clue what for."

She continues to stare at me, and I can see she's expecting more of an answer. I fidget and then say, "At one time I was thinking about medical school. I took the premed classes, and I did enough to get in, but I'm not sure if I want to be a doctor. Then I thought about law school. I made a pros and cons list for each one, medical school versus law school. After all that, I thought maybe I should do something completely different, you know? Now, I don't know if I should even finish school."

"You made a pros and cons list?" she asks. "Do you always think things through that way?"

"Yeah. I try to."

"And does it work for you?"

"I guess."

"You have a very good mind, Anna, that is obvious. But you are a Korean, and Koreans make decisions differently. We use our hearts as well as our heads. When we say 'I think,' we point to our hearts.

"So let me tell you what I think," she says, pointing to her heart. "I think you are trying to find what is in your heart, but your head keeps getting in the way. You came to Korea to try to discover something about yourself, something you cannot simply make a pros and cons list for. After I gave you the comb, you came to meet me for the same reason. You did not give in to those government officials even when they threatened you. If you had thought through those decisions—if your heart wasn't tugging at you—you would have never done them.

"So tell me, Anna Carlson," she says, "what does your *heart* say about your future?"

It's a good question. I hadn't really thought about it like that. I shrug. "I really don't know."

She smiles. "After I finish my story, we'll talk more. Are you ready to hear the rest of it?"

"Yes, ma'am," I answer.

She straightens and puts her hands in her lap. She tells me that after the Korean War, South Korea was in chaos and that everyone was angry, looking for people to blame. She says there was a backlash against anyone who might have been sympathetic to the communists. "I was caught in that backlash," she says. "People knew I had worked for the North, so I was blacklisted, unable to get work. They cut me off from assistance. I was in grave danger and had to disappear for a while."

She takes in a breath as if she's about to start again, but she hesitates. She gives an embarrassed smile. I wonder if she'll be able to continue.

Finally she says, "I'm sorry. This last part is hard."

"It's okay," I say. "Maybe we should rest for a while."

She shakes her head. "No. I must finish this."

THIRTY-ONE

April 1954. US Military Base Camp Humphreys, South Korea

I stood in the back room of a bar talking to the bar owner with three-year-old Soo-bo clinging to my side. I could feel my daughter's bones pressing through her dress like a sack filled with sticks. Soo-bo's eyes were sunken and her cheekbones stuck out. She looked the way I had pictured the poor, starving orphans in *Oliver Twist*. And she was fever-ish again.

It had been three days since we'd had anything to eat. For the previous six months I had searched for food in small villages in South Korea, decimated by our civil war. There were thousands of people as desperate as I was, and food was scarce. There was very little to eat, and people lived in crude shelters cobbled from scraps of wood, rocks, and tin. Many of the children, like Soo-bo, were starving.

Eventually an American sergeant in a jeep picked me up and dropped me and Soo-bo off at this bar in a camp town outside an American military base called a *kijichon*. While we waited, the sergeant went inside to talk to someone. A few minutes later, he returned with the bar owner. The bar owner gave me a long look, then handed the sergeant some money. As the sergeant drove off in his jeep toward the military base, the bar owner told me to follow him.

He led us to the room in the back. American jazz pulsed from the barroom on the other side of the wall. The bar owner, a man in his early thirties with green eyes and a deep scar on his cheek, reclined in front of me with his feet on a desk. He had his blond hair cropped short, in the style of a US military man. He told me his name was Alan Smith.

Alan leaned back and inspected me professionally. "We don't give away food here. You hafta earn it. It's called capitalism."

I had read Jin-mo's books written by the world's greatest economists that argued the merits of capitalism versus socialism. I doubted if Alan had read even a single word on the subject. "I see, sir," I said. "How does it work?"

"We give you a loan for your first and last month's rent. We also give an advance for food and clothing. That's the 'capital' part of capitalism, understand? I charge ten percent interest every month. Rent is due at the beginning of the month, no exceptions. A hundred bucks. Another twenty for the bed and chair. Anything you buy we charge against your account. You'll also have to pay for food and laundry."

I was anxious to end the interview so I could get something to eat for Soo-bo. But I didn't want to appear too desperate. "What do I have to do?" I asked.

Alan kept his eyes on me as he worked a toothpick between his teeth. He reminded me of the actor James Cagney, who I had seen in American movies in the cinema in Pyongyang. I think it was because of the way he talked—quick and staccato—and his aggressive mannerisms. "Well, some girls start by helping out around here," he said. "Working the bar, cleaning, laundry, running errands and such. You're lucky. I need someone for that."

"I see. How much will I be able to earn?"

He took his toothpick out and pointed it at me. "Depends on you. That's how capitalism works, see? The more you do, the more you make. I pay fifty cents an hour."

"I understand," I said. I pressed Soo-bo close.

Alan eyed Soo-bo impassively. "'Course, if you can't earn enough just by helping out, you can be a juicy girl. You're older, but you're pretty, and you speak English good. Could make a lotta money. Here's how that works. If a customer wants to spend some private time with you, they pay me what's called a bar fine to take you upstairs. On top of the bar fine, they give you a tip for your services. I get half your tip. It's the same deal for everyone. It's the same at every bar in this kijichon."

I could hear Soo-bo's stomach growl. My stomach clawed at me, too. "No. I won't do that," I said. "I would like the other job, please. Can I start right away?"

Alan grinned, and the scar on his face twisted. "Sure. If that's what you wanna do."

Alan led me and Soo-bo up a set of wooden stairs to a long, dimly lit hallway on the second floor. At the end of the hallway, he opened a door and pointed inside. "Your room," he said.

I stepped inside the room, leading Soo-bo by the hand. It was small—only a little larger than my room at the comfort station. It reeked of stale sweat and semen. The familiar stench ignited my memories of Dongfeng like a match to gasoline. I saw the faces of the men who had raped me and felt the burn between my legs.

Before I could pick up Soo-bo and run out the door, Alan held out a dark green can and an opener. "And here's your lunch," he said. "Should be enough for you and the kid."

Soo-bo grabbed at the can. "Ummah!" she cried. "Food! I'm hungry." Her sunken eyes pleaded with me.

I closed my nose to the stench in the room and took the can and opener. "Thank you," I said.

Alan Smith jammed the toothpick in his mouth. "I need help at the bar this afternoon. Get yourself an outfit at one of the tailors on the street. Can't work dressed like that. This is a classy joint." As he headed down the hallway, he said over his shoulder, "I need the can opener back when you're done with it."

I closed the door and pushed my rucksack beneath the American-style bed. I sat on the floor, pulling Soo-bo's scrawny frame into my lap. As Soo-bo anxiously watched, I opened the can. Inside was a gelatinous, gray-green mass. I picked at it with my fingers and tasted it. It was salty and slimy, but it was something to eat. I scooped out a finger full and fed Soo-bo, who gulped it down without chewing, like a hungry baby bird. In less than a minute, we had eaten the can's entire contents.

Soo-bo, her starving body finally satisfied, drooped with fatigue. I laid her on the bed. I kissed my daughter on the head, and soon she was sound asleep.

The meal made me tired, too, but as I listened to the American servicemen gathering in the bar below, I knew I had to start earning money right away. I left Soo-bo and went downstairs to the only street in the kijichon. At the end of the street was a paved road and a gate to a military base with an American flag flying atop a tall flagpole. Above the entrance, a sign read "Camp Humphreys." Shabby bars lined the street and advertised sex with Korean girls. One said, "Most friendly girls in camp!" Another advertised that their girls would "Fulfill wildest fantasies." I wondered how I had come to this. I thought I had put this behind me. But here I was again, and I prayed that someday I would be free of the comfort station.

I walked a few doors down and turned into a long, narrow tailor shop. A balding man wearing half-glasses was working at a sewing machine. "Do you need an outfit?" he asked without looking up.

"Yes, sir."

"What bar are you with?"

"The Hometown Cat Club."

The man examined me over his glasses. "You need something that makes you look younger," he said. "I recommend a short black dress."

"No," I answered. "I'm not doing that."

He shook his head and laughed. He pointed to the back. "You can choose from that rack. The prices are in dollars. Sizing is extra." He turned back to his sewing machine.

I went to the rack. Hanging from metal hangers were all sorts of provocative women's outfits—long, formal dresses; short, sequined dresses; several Japanese kimonos; and even an American cowgirl outfit. At the end was a green yukata with pretty white and pink flowers.

I ran my hand across the cool green silk of the yukata and tried to think of what I could do other than this. I couldn't think of anything. I felt trapped with nowhere to run, just like in Dongfeng. But if I stayed here, I would be able to hide for a while and feed Soo-bo. I would have a roof over my head, and if I worked hard enough, perhaps I could pay off the debt I now owed. Then I could move to Seoul once things settled down and it was safe for me.

I turned away from the yukata and looked for a more appropriate outfit. On the rack was a simple blue dress with a knee-high hem that was about my size. It was thirty dollars—the cheapest on the rack. I took it and presented it to the balding man. He looked up from his sewing machine. "You sure you want that cheap one? You'd be better off with—"

"I want this one," I said.

The man shrugged. "Okay. Do what you want. What is your name?"

I gave it, and he wrote it down. "I'll charge your account at the bar," he said and returned to his sewing. "Good luck."

THIRTY-TWO

Soo-bo was in a deep sleep when I returned to my room. From the rucksack, I took a blanket and laid it in the corner on the floor. I carried Soo-bo from the bed and put her on the blanket. She moaned and rolled toward the wall. Her bones stuck out from under her dress, but I was relieved to see her sleep like that again.

I took a rag from my rucksack and wiped the window and floor. It was not clean like I wanted it to be, and I resolved to do a more thorough job later. I placed the photograph of my family next to the bed. I grabbed the rucksack to push it under the bed, and the flap opened. Inside was the coarse brown cloth package of the comb with the two-headed dragon. I took it out, unwrapped the comb, and stared at it. I ran my finger over the tiny pieces of ivory that formed the two-headed dragon. I wondered how much it was worth. Perhaps enough to go to Seoul and stay low until I could find a job there. After all, I had a gift for languages, and I had heard that with America's help, South Korea was going to rebuild. Surely someone could use a person like me.

But I had promised Soo-hee and Jin-mo that I would carry on and tell their story. I had promised to keep the comb. So I put it back inside the rucksack and slid it under the bed. I went to the bathroom in the hall and scrubbed myself clean. I brushed my hair and thought about how I should wear it. I decided I did not want to draw attention to myself, so I simply braided it. I put on the blue dress, my tabi and zori, and went downstairs to the Hometown Cat Club bar.

The Hometown Cat Club looked like a bar from an American western movie. Beer and cigarette smoke had stained the plywood floors brown. Behind a long, flimsy bar was the red-and-black emblem for the United States Eighth Army. Tables, rough and leaning, were scattered in front of a large, dirty window that looked out at the kijichon's street. A jukebox played jazz music, and a soldier danced cheek to cheek with a young Korean girl. The room smelled like stale beer.

When I came in, sixteen servicemen and six working girls studied me. Alan Smith, his toothpick jammed in the corner of his mouth, was behind the bar pouring drinks. He motioned for me to come over. He nodded toward three soldiers at a table. "Get their drink orders," he said. "Your job is to keep them drinking. Go."

I approached the table. A young, uniformed lieutenant with thick, dark hair and a slim build smiled at me lasciviously. "Hey, baby," he said, curling an arm around my waist. "You speak-ee English?"

Instead of bowing like I should, I faced him straight on. "As a matter of fact, Lieutenant," I said, careful to pronounce each word correctly, "I am fluent in English."

He smiled broadly at the two soldiers next to him. "Holy shit! D'ju guys hear that? She speaks English like a damn schoolteacher." The soldiers grinned at me expectantly.

"You from America or somethin'?" a stocky sergeant asked. He clutched a mug of beer in one hand and a cigarette in the other. There were gaps between his teeth like on a picket fence.

"No, Sergeant. I have never been to America. I just have a good ear for languages. My name is Jae-hee. I'm here to get your drink orders."

"Fuckin' A," the sergeant said, smiling his picket fence smile. "Good ear for languages, eh? We got ourselves a regular Margaret Mitchell juicy girl here. You ever write a book like *Gone with the Wind*?"

The other soldiers laughed at the sergeant's joke. A man in civilian clothes who had been sitting alone at a table by the window came over and joined the group. He had no left arm. The others stopped laughing when he approached, but they still wore silly grins. "What's going on, men?" the new man asked. "Who's the new girl?"

"Name's Jae-hee, Colonel," the lieutenant said, still clinging to my waist. "Says she's good with languages. Talks like a goddamn English professor, even though she's never been to America."

I was surprised the man was a colonel. He looked young for that rank. He inserted himself between me and the lieutenant. "Where'd you learn to speak English?" he asked.

I looked back at four sets of eyes eagerly awaiting my answer. It was a careless thing, what I did next, but I wanted them to know I wasn't like the other girls there. So I said, "I was a translator for the government for four years. I worked on important contracts, statements, and speeches. In fact, in 1948, I helped translate into English the declaration that established the Republic of South Korea, the country you now occupy. Now, what can I get you men to drink?"

The soldiers looked at each other wide-eyed for several seconds, then burst into laughter. The sergeant knocked over his beer and dropped his cigarette on the floor. The lieutenant almost fell down. Everyone in the Hometown Cat Club stopped and stared at us.

"Where'd you get this one, Al?" sputtered the lieutenant. "She's good!"

The colonel pushed himself farther between me and the others. "Come join me at my table," he said, looking straight at me.

I bowed my head and noticed the colonel was wearing polished shoes tied tightly. My instincts kicked in. *Be careful,* I said to myself. "I'm sorry, sir," I said. "I have to help at the bar."

The colonel said, "Don't worry, Al won't mind. Get these men what they want and put it on my tab. Then come sit with me." He went to his table.

After the soldiers settled down, I took their drink orders and gave them to Alan. I told him the colonel asked me to sit with him.

"Do as he says," Alan replied.

I brought the soldiers their drinks, then went to the colonel's table next to the big window.

The colonel was tall and trim. His eyes were the blue-green of jade and his hair the smooth, dark brown of polished rosewood. He wore pressed khaki slacks and a white safari shirt. The empty sleeve where his left arm had been was neatly pinned to the front of his shirt. He was well tanned.

He told me his name was Colonel Frank Crawford. He had a light Southern accent. He asked what my family name was, and I told him.

"*Anyohaseyo*, Hong Jae-hee," he said. He continued in Korean, "What brings you to the Hometown Cat Club?"

I kept the conversation in Korean, although his Korean was not very good. "I've come here to work. It's difficult to find work in Korea right now."

"What will you do here?"

"I'm helping Mr. Smith at the bar and with his chores."

"You won't make it just doing chores," the colonel said, switching to English. "You'll have to be a juicy girl like the rest."

"I am a very hard worker," I replied.

"It doesn't matter," the colonel said, shaking his head. "There aren't enough hours in the day to earn what you need. Everyone who starts like you is forced to be a juicy girl."

I did some quick math in my head and realized the colonel was right. At fifty cents per hour, I would earn less than ten dollars per day. I was already in debt for the first month's rent, my blue dress, and for the food that Soo-bo and I had just eaten. I would never be able to catch up.

The colonel raised an eyebrow. "Is it true what you said about being a translator before the war?" he asked. "Your English is certainly good enough."

I knew I had to be careful what I told the colonel. As a senior military officer, he would know the names of people that I had worked with. "No, sir," I said. "I was only making a joke."

The colonel looked at me in a way that made me think he did not believe my lie. Then he looked out the window and said, "I've seen a lot of Korea over the past several years. It's a beautiful country, though it's hard to see anything through this filthy window. Where are you from?"

"I am from the North. I escaped to the South after World War Two."

"Do you have family there?" he asked.

"No, sir. They were killed by the Japanese."

The colonel took a sip from his glass and held it in his hand. He was drinking what looked like bourbon. "I'm sorry to hear that. If it wasn't for the damn communists, we'd have the entire peninsula on the right track."

"You mean," I said, "we would all be exploited by capitalists under the American system." As soon as I said this, I regretted it. I was being impertinent, which was not a smart way to be with a senior American army officer. But I did not approve of what the Americans were doing here in this kijichon, and I wanted the colonel to know it.

So yes, I was impertinent with the colonel. Thankfully, the corners of his mouth turned up, and his blue eyes sparkled at my comment. "Do I detect cynicism in you, Hong Jae-hee?"

"With all due respect, Colonel," I said with a slight bow, glad for the opportunity to show some deference, "I do not think it is as simple as you say."

"Ah, you're a philosopher. How interesting."

The colonel set his glass on the table. He regarded me for a moment, making me feel like I was someone special, but also like someone he could buy. Finally he said, "Would you like to dance with me? I'm a very good dancer, even with just one arm. My mother insisted I learn. 'A Southern gentleman should know how to dance with a lady,' she said.

And a Southern gentleman never disappoints his mother." He smiled pleasantly.

"I don't know how to dance," I said quickly.

The colonel stood and held out his hand. "Come," he said. "I'll teach you."

"No, I shouldn't. It isn't right. What about your wife?"

"She divorced me when I volunteered for a third tour in Korea." The colonel took my hand. "Come with me."

The dance floor was a small open square in front of the jukebox. When we took the floor, the soldier and girl who had been dancing there moved to the bar. The colonel leaned over the jukebox and punched a few buttons while I stood alone. I felt everyone staring at me. Soon the jazz song ended and the jukebox began to play a waltz.

The colonel faced me. "I had Al put in some records just for me. The men don't like it. Razz me about it all the time. But I outrank them," he said with a grin. "Now, let me show you how to do a Viennese waltz."

He wrapped his one arm around me and pulled me close. I was embarrassed at being this close to a man I did not know. And we were in public. I was about to push away when he told me to put my hands on his shoulders. I looked at Alan at the bar. He grinned at me and nodded. I decided I had to do what the colonel said. He told me a waltz was a three-count step that I could hear in the music. "One, two, three. One, two, three," he counted with the beat of the music. "Move your feet with mine."

He began to step to the music, taking a step back with his right foot on "one," putting his feet together on "two," and taking a side step with his left foot on "three." Looking down, I tried to mirror his steps. I missed a beat and nearly tripped on his feet.

He held me firmly. "You're doing just fine," he said. "Try again." He moved once more, and I moved with him. After a few more tries, I could feel the music flow through me. I stepped to its rhythm. When

I made a mistake, the colonel pulled me back with the poise of a self-assured leading man. "Keep going. Good," he said when I got it right. His support melted away my self-consciousness, and I began to move with the colonel across the floor as if we were a single dancer.

I looked up from my feet. The room spun around, and I became light-headed. My steps became more natural. I began to surrender to the moment, to the dance with this soldier who embraced me with one arm. I felt free and alive, like I did on the farm when I pretended to fly, and like I did in the arms of Jin-mo.

Then the colonel said, "Look at me. Look into my eyes."

I looked into his jade-blue eyes. Suddenly the image of Colonel Matsumoto flashed in my mind. *Look at me,* he had said as he raped me. *Look into my eyes.* I stopped dancing and pushed back. "I'm sorry, sir," I said. "I cannot do this."

"Is something wrong?"

"Yes . . . I mean, no. I should get back to work."

The colonel nodded politely. "Thank you for dancing with me, Hong Jae-hee," he said with a slight bow. "We'll do this again, I hope."

I bowed back to him and went to join Alan at the bar.

THIRTY-THREE

"Ummah, wake up!" Soo-bo said, inches from my face. I blinked sleep from my eyes. Standing in front of me was my daughter, ready to begin her day. The morning light was still low, and I needed more sleep. I ached from long hours of hard work. But I didn't mind. I had saved Soo-bo from starving.

My daughter had filled out since we arrived at the kijichon ten months earlier. She was still thin and often had long spells of fever. But at the kijichon, she was able to eat every day, and I was greatly relieved. I loved her more than I had ever thought possible. I took sublime joy in reading to her like my mother read to me. I loved her playfulness and her four-year-old mannerisms, watching her grow and learn new things. Still, Soo-bo struggled with the simple lessons I gave her. Sometimes she slipped into long, dark moods, and I worried about her strength.

I stroked Soo-bo's hair. "You're awake so early, little one."

"I'm hungry," my daughter said. "Will you tell me more of our story today?"

I swung myself to the edge of the bed. "Of course," I said. "Where did we leave off?"

"The rich yangban had come from Seoul with a present for her daughter. What is it, Mother? What is the present?"

"You will have to wait to see," I said. "Let's eat breakfast first."

I pulled on a shirt and slacks. I took Soo-bo's hand, and we went down the stairs to the small plywood-walled kitchen behind the bar. It had a newer army refrigerator that Alan had bartered a girl's time for and a propane countertop stove. As Soo-bo waited at the table, I made bori cha and poured myself a cup. I poured Rice Krispies in a bowl with milk and gave it to Soo-bo.

After I had worked for Alan for a while, I encouraged him to trade bar tabs for supplies, so we usually had American foods available. Rice Krispies was Soo-bo's favorite. She loved the characters of Snap, Crackle, and Pop on the box and delighted in the sounds that the cereal made. She wouldn't eat anything else for breakfast. As Soo-bo ate her cereal, I cleaned the kitchen and washed out dozens of foul mugs with stale beer and cigarette butts inside.

As I cleaned, a juicy girl shuffled into the kitchen. She was dressed in baby-blue lingerie, and her hair was a mess. Her name was Dae-ee, and I guessed she was not much more than seventeen years old. She poured herself some bori cha. She looked at Soo-bo, then at me, and I could tell she wanted to talk.

I told Soo-bo to go to our room and wait for me and that we would have more of our story when I got back.

Soo-bo hurried out of the kitchen, and Dae-ee slumped into a chair at the table. Four months earlier, Dae-ee had strolled into the Hometown Cat Club on the arm of a handsome American corporal who had told her he loved her and that he would take her to America and marry her. She had looked with disdain at the juicy girls and only talked to me to order drinks for her man. Days later, when the corporal went back to America without her—undoubtedly with a few hundred dollars in his pocket from Alan—she was alone, penniless, and scared. She had to accept Alan's offer to help me at the bar. But like most girls, she could not get out from under her debts just doing chores. Alan pressured her to pay him, and one month after she arrived, she was working the men as a juicy girl.

"I can't do this anymore, Onni," Dae-ee said, staring at her bori cha. "But I don't know what else to do."

I set the towel on the counter and took the chair across from her. "You should go back to your family," I said. "Chonan is not far from here."

"I cannot. I have shamed them. And I owe Alan too much. I thought if I worked as a juicy girl, I would be able to make more money. But now I owe more than when I started." She began to cry. "What should I do? Tell me, what should I do?"

My heart went out to her. She reminded me of myself when I was young—stubborn and a little too proud. So when Dae-ee started working at the club, I had taken her under my wing and helped her get by. I warned her about becoming a juicy girl, but she didn't listen to me. Now she owed Alan so much that she would never get out from under her debts. Dae-ee, like most other juicy girls, had become nothing more than a sex slave for the Americans, just like I had been for the Japanese.

I reached over and touched Dae-ee's hand. "Don't worry about what you owe Alan. Go back home and face your family. You have to find the strength to do the right thing."

Dae-ee had tears in her eyes. "I can't. I just can't do it."

I looked at my hands. "I have felt that way several times. Honestly, sometimes I feel like it here, too."

Dae-ee's jaw tightened. "You've never had to do what I do," she said.

I gave her a stern look that took her aback. "Do not ever assume you know how others have suffered."

Dae-ee lowered her eyes. "I'm sorry, Onni." She set her bori cha aside and sighed heavily. "I wish I was strong like you." She left the table and trudged up the stairs.

◆ ◆ ◆

Thursday was the colonel's day off, and I hoped to see him in the bar that evening. I gave Soo-bo to Dae-ee. Without Soo-bo in tow, I was able to finish my chores by early afternoon. I washed my blue dress and hung it on the line behind the club to dry. I took a hot bath and scrubbed myself clean. I washed my hair and combed it smooth with the comb with the two-headed dragon.

Late afternoon, I put on my blue dress and went down to the bar. It was early. Only a handful of soldiers were there, and only two juicy girls were working. There were almost always soldiers in the Hometown Cat Club, day and night. On a good night, we could have sixty or seventy men drinking and using the girls. It could get loud and raucous, and sometimes fights would break out over who was next in line for one of the girls. Alan, who I had learned was an ex-marine and an accomplished amateur boxer, would step in and throw the fighters out. It did not matter how big they were or how scrappy, Alan always prevailed.

It was feeling like it was going to be another one of those unruly nights. I went over to the bar to get it ready for the customers. Alan had an elbow on the bar and rested his square head on his thick hand. "When are you going to make some real money, Jae-hee?" he asked. "Been ten months, and you ain't making progress on your debt. You're popular with the men. Any one of them would pay top dollar to have a poke with you."

"I do make money for you, Alan. You just don't pay me for it. Business is way up since I started here. I have offers from other bars."

He plucked a toothpick from a shot glass and examined it. "You'd make a lot more as a juicy girl."

"Who would do all the cooking and cleaning?" I asked. "Who would take care of the girls? This place would fall apart."

"I'd find someone."

No, he would not. Not anyone as good as me, and he knew it. I leaned against the bar. "Dae-ee wants to leave," I said. "Let her go."

"Can't. She has debts."

"She cannot pay them off, and you know it."

"'Cause she's lazy. And she's just another girl." Alan lifted his chin and looked at me. "You, on the other hand, you got somethin' the men want. You'd make a lot of money. Wouldn't be so bad. You'd get used to it."

I shook my head. The girls in the Hometown Cat Club served four or five men per night. In Dongfeng, I'd had forced sex with as many as thirty-five men nearly every day for two years. I never got used to it then, and I certainly would not get used to it now.

Alan chuckled. "Shit, I bet the colonel'd pay five hundred bucks for a night with you. Maybe more. He likes you, and he's got money. Comes from a real rich family in Atlanta. They build houses or somethin'."

"Commercial construction," I said.

"What?"

"His family owns the biggest construction company in Georgia. They build skyscrapers. He told me all about it."

"Is that what you two talk about all the time? Skyscrapers?"

"We talk about a lot of things," I said. "He gives me books to read. We talk about those. You told me I should spend as much time with him as he wants."

"You shouldn't be wastin' time with your damn books. You should do more than talk to the colonel. You'd be able to pay off your debt."

"You and your debt," I sniffed. "This is nothing more than indentured slavery."

Alan pointed his toothpick at me. "Be careful, Jae-hee. I got a good guess why you're here. A few calls and I'd know for sure. Then what'd you do?"

He jammed the toothpick in his mouth. "Beginning of the month," he said, "you owe another rent payment. I ain't letting you out of here until you pay me off, so you better think about how you're going to make more money." He went to the other end of the bar and picked up a magazine.

◆ ◆ ◆

Of course, Alan was right. Just like the colonel had said when I first started, and just like the other girls, I'd never be able to pay off my debt. But I had a roof over my head here and food for Soo-bo. Alan was also right that I could make a lot of money as a juicy girl. The soldiers liked me and made outrageous offers of money to have sex with me. I made it very clear that I did not do that, but it didn't stop them. The only one who never asked was the colonel.

I grabbed a rag and went to the front window. I stood on a chair and wiped the glass clean. I did so every day—on most days, inside and out. I told myself I did it because it was my job to keep the club clean. But I knew it was because the colonel liked to look out the window.

The bar started to fill with soldiers, and the girls came from their rooms to work them. I went from table to table wiping off tabletops and taking drink orders. Jazz music pulsed from the jukebox while the girls started their nightly trek upstairs with men. The Hometown Cat Club ran smoothly because of me. It was clean, I had the bar stocked with good liquor, the beer was always cold, and the jukebox played the latest American records. And I took care of the girls, too. I knew what they needed to do their jobs—good meals, clean laundry, medicine, time off, emotional support—and I saw to it that they got it.

Alan thought I coddled them too much, and I often fought with him about it. But I was stubborn and persistent, and I usually won. Eventually he saw that my approach attracted the best girls to the club, and he agreed to let me do what I wanted. Through my work, I had made it the most popular brothel in the entire kijichon. But when I thought about what I was doing, I was ashamed, too. I was supporting the sexual exploitation of Korean girls.

It was still early when the colonel came in. He usually stayed only an hour or so to drink his bourbon, and he never used the girls. The soldiers were always well mannered when he was there. I smiled when I saw him. He was wearing the same khaki slacks and safari shirt that he always wore. His empty sleeve was pinned to his shirt. He took his table in front of the window. I poured some Old Fitzgerald Kentucky bourbon into a spotless glass and took it to him.

Months earlier, he told me that he drank Old Fitzgerald at home in Georgia. "It's what they serve in the White House," he had said. So I asked the man who sold us liquor to get a case, and I convinced Alan to pay the higher price for it. The bourbon had come three days earlier, and I couldn't wait to surprise the colonel with it. I took the glass to his table.

He said good evening to me in his soft Southern drawl. He asked how business was in the Hometown Cat Club. I told him it was going to be a busy night and took a seat across from him.

"Yes," he said. "Best bar in the kijichon."

He raised his glass and took a sip of bourbon. He looked in the glass, lifted an eyebrow, and took another sip. His jade-blue eyes went wide. "Jae-hee, what have you done? I do believe this is Old Fitz!" he exclaimed.

I grinned and nodded. "Alan was upset at how much it cost. I had to convince him to buy it. He's charging you double."

"Well worth it, well worth it. The drink of presidents. They say General Ulysses Grant drank a glass every day. He was a great warrior, but, as you know, my favorite is Robert E. Lee."

"Yes. You have told me many times," I said.

The colonel sipped more bourbon and took a long look at me. "Thank you," he said. "You always treat me well."

"You are a good customer."

"Good customer? Is that all I am?"

"A special customer," I said.

"So why don't you ever dance with me? You only did that one time."

"I cannot."

"Why not?" he asked. "We've spent a lot of time together, Jae-hee. We've shared a lot. At least, *I've* shared a lot. I think I've earned a dance, don't you? As I recall, you caught on quickly to the Viennese waltz."

I looked into the colonel's eyes. He was a decent man. He was polite, always a Southern gentleman. He was well read on many topics. We spent hours talking about his family and friends back home in his beloved Georgia. He went on and on about "General Robert E. Lee of the Southern Confederacy," as he said. We talked about politics, World War II, and the Korean War. He gave me books to read—his favorite was Ayn Rand's *The Fountainhead*—which we discussed every Thursday night at his table for a month. I honestly enjoyed our talks. They reminded me of the long talks I'd had with Jin-mo about his books and ideas. But just like the juicy girls and their customers, there was no future for me with the colonel. I knew he would go home someday, and I would stay trapped in the kijichon thinking about him, wishing I had not gotten involved with the handsome Southern gentleman.

"It is not proper for a Korean woman to dance with a man who is not her husband," I said. "I'm sorry."

"We're in a kijichon. All sorts of improper things go on here. Dancing is relatively tame, don't you think?"

"It depends on what your ulterior motives are."

"My ulterior motives?" he exclaimed. "With you?"

"Yes."

He shook his head. "I just want to dance."

"And then?"

"There doesn't have to be an 'and then.' We can dance to enjoy dancing." He set his glass on the table. "Why don't you trust me? Is it me, or do you distrust all foreigners?"

"I distrust people who have their soldiers in my country," I answered. "I distrust a military that supports the trafficking of women for sex."

"We don't support it."

"Oh? Then what are these men doing here?"

"We're not the Japanese, Jae-hee," the colonel said.

"What's the difference?" I pointed my chin at the girls in the room. "For them, for the girls, what's the difference between you and the Japanese?"

He looked annoyed. "What would you have us do? Leave? Let the communists take over? It's us or them, Jae-hee. Take your pick."

"So here we are, a divided nation," I said.

The colonel shrugged. "Like I said, take your pick."

The Hometown Cat Club was starting to fill up. Soldiers were coming through the door and ordering their drinks at the bar. Smoke from their cigarettes hung heavy in the air. The girls flirted with the men, trying to get them to go upstairs. The men kept shooting looks at the colonel as if they were reluctant to let loose until he was gone.

The colonel took another sip of Old Fitz and regarded me with a long stare. "So if you feel that way, what are *you* doing here serving drinks to American soldiers?"

"I am trying to pay my debt to Alan."

The colonel sighed. After a long pause, he grinned at me. "You should try some Old Fitz," he said. I was about to say no, but he was already halfway to the bar. He got the bottle and another glass from Alan and brought them to the table. He filled my glass, then his own.

"Come on, try it. Good Kentucky bourbon, not like the swill they have here."

I refused. The colonel looked at me as if I was one of his men. He said, "If you won't dance, then have a drink with me."

I decided I could give him that, so I took a sip. The bourbon cut my tongue and burned my throat.

The colonel lifted his glass and admired the liquid inside. "Good Kentucky bourbon. Liquor like this should only be drunk with someone special, and that's you, Jae-hee! Have another sip."

I took another drink. This time it didn't burn as much, and I started to feel warm.

"Someday you should go to America," the colonel said, pointing his glass at me. "It's beautiful. It has snow-capped mountains, blue oceans, modern cities teeming with people and automobiles. We are the greatest country in the world."

He grinned to himself and raised his glass. "Let's drink a toast. I'll drink to Korea, and you drink to America."

I looked at his handsome face and remembered the night I drank sake with Colonel Matsumoto. Suddenly everything about this place— the soldiers who took advantage of Korean girls, the Eighth Army emblem above the bar, Alan and his book where he kept track of the girls' debts—it all sickened me. I set my glass down and bowed my head. "Thank you for the drink, Colonel, but I should not have any more of your bourbon. And I must get back to work."

I went to a table of soldiers and took their drink orders. As I brought the orders to the bar, I glanced at the colonel. He sat alone, drinking his Old Fitzgerald Kentucky bourbon, the drink of presidents, looking out the window that I had cleaned for him.

THIRTY-FOUR

It was late at night when I hauled a sack full of dirty linens toward the laundry at the far end of the kijichon. Laundry was one of the dozens of chores I had to do to make the Hometown Cat Club run smoothly. I was exhausted and thankful that this was my last chore before I could get a few hours of sleep and start all over again in the morning. As I walked along the street, light shone from inside only one bar. Here and there, a drunken soldier staggered toward Camp Humphreys or slumped against a wall in a stupor.

On the other side of the street, the bartender of the last open bar shoved three soldiers out to the street. One stumbled to the ground. As his companions pointed and laughed at the soldier, the bartender closed the door and switched off the lights.

"What the fuck?" said the soldier who had fallen. He carried a bottle in one hand and reached for his companion with the other. "Ain't there nothin' open in this goddamn place?"

"All shut down with nothin' to do," his companion said, pulling his friend to his feet. I kept walking toward the laundry, hoping they wouldn't see me. But then the third soldier spotted me.

"Well, lookee there," he said. "It's a juicy girl."

One shouted, "Hey you. Wanna make some money?"

I quickened my pace in spite of the heavy load. The three stumbled across the street after me.

"Don't go away," one said. "I'm talking to you."

They caught up to me and surrounded me. I dropped the laundry sack and faced them. They were typical American soldiers—tall, a little pale, and lacking proper manners.

"I'll be damned," another one said. "It's Jae-hee from the Cat Club. She don't screw no one. Not even Crawford." He took a step closer. "Why don't you fuck, girl? You too good for an American?"

"Let me be," I demanded. I was angry that these vulgar men were accosting me. They acted just like the Japanese in Dongfeng.

"Shit, you talk like an American. You should be willing to fuck one."

"Yeah," another said. "I need someone new."

The three pressed in close, and I could smell beer on their breaths. "I am friends with Colonel Crawford," I said quickly. "You don't want to get in trouble. Now leave me alone!"

One of the soldiers laughed. "Colonel Crawford? He ain't the colonel here no more. He shipped out."

"Yeah," another said. "Won't be much help to you now."

A soldier reached for me, and I punched him hard.

He rubbed his nose and said, "You bitch!" And then all three jumped on me. I fought as hard as I could, I really did, but I couldn't fight off all three of them. I tried to scream for help, but they covered my mouth. One of them straddled me and started to unbutton his pants. Another one grabbed my pants and started pulling them down. It was happening to me again. They were raping me. The street was the comfort station courtyard. The buildings were the barracks where the Korean girls lived. The men were the Japanese soldiers like Corporal Kaori.

And there, on the street of the kijichon, I was a comfort woman again.

Then a voice came from behind the soldiers. "Get off of her!" a man shouted. I saw a hand reach in, grab the soldier on top of me, and throw him to the ground. The soldier trying to take off my pants wheeled around, and a fist slammed into his stomach. He collapsed to his knees and gasped for breath.

The third soldier turned. "What're you doin'?" he said.

"Leave her the fuck alone!"

"Jesus, Alan!" the third soldier said, backing away. "Don't hit me."

Alan Smith stood a few feet away, his fists clenched and pure rage in his eyes.

"Take these two assholes and go back to your barracks!" Alan ordered. "And if you pricks ever touch her again, I'll fuckin' tear your heads off and shit down your throats. Understand?"

"We're just havin' fun," the soldier said, helping his friends to their feet.

"Get outta here!" Alan roared. The three scurried away, keeping a wary eye on Alan as they stumbled toward Camp Humphreys.

Alan helped me to my feet. "You all right?"

"Yes, I think so," I said. "They were going to rape me."

"Ah, they're just drunk," Alan said. "Probably couldn'ta done it if you let them."

I blinked at Alan. "What are you doing here?"

"Came to get you. Colonel wants to talk to you. He's in a car outside the club."

"The colonel?"

"Yeah. Wouldn't tell me what it's about. I'll take the laundry. You go."

"Alan," I said, "thank you."

"Better hurry," Alan replied, hoisting the sack of laundry. "Said he didn't have a lotta time."

◆ ◆ ◆

A big black Cadillac sat underneath a lone streetlight outside the Hometown Cat Club. The stars were out, and the kijichon was quiet. A sergeant leaned against the car, smoking a cigarette. "Are you Hong Jae-hee?" he asked as I approached.

"Yes, sir," I replied.

The sergeant dropped his cigarette and ground it out with the toe of his boot. He opened the car door. "Get in," he ordered.

"Where are you taking me?" I asked.

"Nowhere. The general wants to talk to you."

I climbed in, and there in the backseat was Colonel Crawford. In the darkness, I could see that he was wearing a traveling uniform with several rows of service bars and medals above his breast pocket. He held his cap in his lap.

"Hello, Jae-hee," he said. His soft Southern accent made my heart beat a little faster.

"The driver said a general wanted to talk to me," I said.

"A general *is* talking to you. They've made me a general, Jae-hee. I'll be one of the army's youngest. I'm heading to the Pentagon now. I don't have much time."

"I see," I said.

"I was going to tell you last night, but you cut our conversation short."

"Yes, I did. I'm sorry."

The light from the street lamp shone through the car window and fell across the colonel's face as he analyzed me. "Hong Jae-hee," he said. "There's more to you than you let people know. I've done some research."

"Research?" I wondered what the colonel had found out about me. I pushed myself into the car seat and prayed his research hadn't uncovered too much.

"You grew up on your family farm outside Sinuiju," he said. "You had a sister named Soo-hee who was in China during World War Two.

I wasn't able to find out what she did there, but I have an idea. I didn't find out what you did, either."

"I worked on my family farm," I said quickly.

"No, you didn't," he said. "You were in China, too."

And there it was. He knew about Dongfeng. I wanted to jump out of the car and let him leave and take my secret to Washington. But for some reason, I stayed with him. I looked down at my feet.

He looked out the window. "The goddamn Japanese. It was disgraceful what they did to Korea. And I fear that we let them get away with it."

He turned back to me. "You shouldn't blame yourself."

"I'm trying not to," I said.

"Good," he said. "I discovered a few other things about you, too. After World War Two, you worked as a translator in the North, and eventually you escaped to the South. A few months after the Korean War, you showed up here. I presume it was because you had worked for the communists."

"Soo-bo was starving," I said.

"Yes," the colonel said with a shake of his head. "War is cruel."

"More for some than others," I replied.

There was an uncomfortable silence. Then the colonel asked, "Do you think we could have fallen in love, you and me?"

The colonel's bluntness surprised me. He was always such a gentleman. "I—I don't know," I said.

"I'd be a damn liar if I said I didn't think about it. You're a beautiful woman. Intelligent. Graceful. And you have something . . . something special. Maybe in a different time and place."

I kept my eyes low. "A different time and place," I said.

"I'm sorry," the colonel said with a wave. "I don't mean to embarrass you. I guess I'm just saying I'll miss our talks." He smiled tenderly, and I realized I would miss him, too.

"By the way," he said, "I talked to Alan about your debt. I told him to forgive it and let you go. He agreed."

"He did?"

"I didn't give him a choice," the colonel said with a glint in his eye.

"You didn't need to do that," I said.

"It's done. Oh, and I have something for you." The colonel reached inside a briefcase at his feet, took out an envelope, and handed it to me. "Inside is the name and address of the head attorney of a construction company in Seoul. They need a translator. Tell them I referred you." He pointed at the envelope. "There's also a few hundred dollars in there to get you started. It's all I could get my hands on with such short notice."

"I cannot take this," I said.

"Don't let your pride hold you back, Jae-hee. The money is nothing to me. Just take it and leave this place. You don't belong here."

I looked at the envelope. The colonel was right, I had always been too proud. I tucked the envelope into my pocket. "Thank you," I said.

The colonel let out a sigh. "I wish we could've danced just one more time. I don't imagine I'll get to do it much with my new responsibilities."

I looked into his handsome face and his jade-blue eyes. I do not know why I did what I did next. It was instinctual, something that just felt right. I took his hand and said, "Come with me." I opened the car door, and we got out. I led him to a place under the street-light. I faced him and put my hands on his shoulders. "Show me again," I said.

He smiled broadly as he wrapped his arm around my waist. "It's a three-step, remember? One, two, three. One, two, three." He moved his feet, and I moved with him as I had done when we first met. I quickly remembered the steps, and soon we were moving as one. He pulled me in and swung me around. The sergeant, smoking a cigarette and leaning against the car, grinned at us.

The colonel beamed. "Good," he said. "This is good."

And it was good. It was almost like pretending to fly for my father or being in the embrace of Jin-mo. I looked into General Frank Crawford's eyes, and this time, I did not see Colonel Matsumoto. I only saw this good man with one arm who loved his country, General Robert E. Lee of the Confederacy, and Old Fitzgerald bourbon. And I saw someone who could have loved me and who I could have loved in a different time and place.

Under the streetlight, we danced the Viennese waltz, and then he said, "I have to go." We stopped dancing, but held on to each other for a moment longer. "Thank you," he said, stepping away. He gave me a Southern gentleman's bow. "Good-bye, Jae-hee," he said and went back inside the car.

The driver flicked away his cigarette and took his place behind the wheel. The Cadillac pulled onto the road next to the kijichon. And as the car's taillights disappeared into the blackness, I whispered, "Good-bye, Frank."

◆　◆　◆

"You're leavin'?" Alan Smith asked me, standing in my doorway the next morning. Soo-bo clung to my side as I shoved my belongings inside my rucksack. It was morning, and downstairs, the barroom was quiet. "But we made a lotta money, you and me," he said.

"No, Alan, *you* made a lot of money. I did all the work, you did nothing. It's like Karl Marx said in *The Communist Manifesto*: 'The bourgeoisie, veiled by political illusions, control the means of production and instinctively, brutally, exploits the proletariat.'"

Alan cocked his head. "What the fuck are you talkin' about?"

I shook my head. "You should read more, Alan."

"Look," he said, "I'll double your wages. And you'll never have to be a juicy girl. You're a real capitalist, Jae-hee."

"I want you to let Dae-ee go, too," I said.

"Why in the hell would I do that?" Alan asked with a twist of the scar on his face.

"Because I am telling you to."

"You're nuts," Alan said.

I finished stuffing my belongings into my rucksack. "I'm leaving my dress. Give it to your next girl." I took Soo-bo's hand and turned to leave.

"Wait! Okay, look. You can live here for free," Alan said. "I'll even give you a percent of the profits. You're right. I need you."

I tugged at Soo-bo to follow me. I pushed past Alan out to the hallway. "Please stay, Jae-hee," he said.

I went to Dae-ee's door and knocked. After a few seconds, she answered. Her black hair was a mess, and there were dark circles around her eyes. "Do you need me to take Soo-bo?" she asked sleepily.

"I'm leaving the kijichon," I said.

Dae-ee ran a hand through her hair. "What? You can't just leave."

"Yes I can, and you should, too. Don't worry about your debt to Alan. Just leave. Today." I pushed a twenty-dollar bill at her. "Here, this is enough for bus fare to Chonan. There is one this afternoon."

Dae-ee looked puzzled. "But I can't pay you back."

"You do not have to. Go back to your family, Dae-ee. It will be hard, but they will take you back. Go home and never fall in love with an American again. Do you understand? Never again. Now take the money."

Dae-ee stood in the doorway, looking from me to the twenty-dollar bill and back at me again. She took the money. "Thank you, Onni."

"Go home," I said.

I took Soo-bo's hand and went downstairs. I walked out of the Hometown Cat Club into the morning light. Without looking back, I walked down the dirt street to the bus idling at the gate of Camp Humphreys military base.

THIRTY-FIVE

Seoul. It was my first time in South Korea's capital city. I was thrilled to see it. But I was scared, too. As the bus, a wobbly antique filled with poor farmers and American enlisted soldiers on R and R, weaved through the city under the April sky, I saw that the city was much larger than Pyongyang, but it did not look much like it. There were miles of slums with makeshift houses and homeless people staring out from the shadows. There were fewer cars and trucks than in Pyongyang. In places, there were attempts to rebuild from the war. A group of men was erecting bamboo scaffolding on one block, and on another, men were dumping rubble into a rickshaw. In spite of the work, it did not look like they were making much progress.

As I stared out the bus window, I wondered what I was getting myself into. I had heard that thousands of desperate people had flooded into Seoul during the war. Unemployment was very high, and people were starving in the street. If the job at the construction company didn't work out, Soo-bo and I would soon be on the street alongside them.

It was midafternoon when the bus came to a stop outside the Yongsan US Military Garrison in the Itaewon district of Seoul. I was relieved to see this area was less poor than the slums we had driven through. There was an active market here with people buying food and clothing from street vendors and stores. There were trucks and cars going up and down the street. I lifted Soo-bo to my hip and my rucksack to my shoulder. I followed the soldiers off the bus. A swarm of filthy children and women dressed in rags confronted us. They reached out to us with grimy hands and begged for our spare change.

I pushed into the crowd. The beggars took one look at Soo-hee on my hip and let me pass. A half dozen taxis and rickshaws waited on the street. I approached a taxi driver. He asked me what I wanted. I took the address of the construction firm from my pocket and read it to him. I asked if he could take me there. The taxi driver looked past me at the American soldiers trying to escape the beggars. "Go away," he said.

I put Soo-bo on the ground, reached inside my rucksack, and pulled out a five-dollar bill. I showed it to the taxi driver. "I can pay just as well as they can," I said.

The driver looked at the money, then at me. He grinned and told me to get in.

Less than ten minutes later, we stopped in front of a two-story concrete building on a wide boulevard not far from Itaewon. Above the door was a sign that read "Gongson Construction Company." After Soo-bo and I got out, I asked the driver how much I owed.

"Five dollars American," he answered.

"That's too much," I said.

"That's your fare," he answered firmly.

I sighed and gave him the five-dollar bill. I took Soo-bo by the hand, and we entered the building.

Inside, painters on upside-down v-shaped bamboo ladders brushed paint on the walls. The chemical smell of their paint hung in the air. A handful of workers scurried from desk to desk. I approached a middle-aged woman at a makeshift reception desk and told her who I wanted to meet.

"Mr. Han is on the second floor," she said. She pointed at Soo-bo. "You shouldn't take your child up there. Can you leave her with someone and come back?"

"No, ma'am," I answered. "This is my first time in Seoul. I don't know anyone here."

The woman looked around the office. "Well, I don't have much to do right now. I can watch her for a while." She pointed at my rucksack. "You should leave your pack with me, too. You can wash in the bathroom before you see Mr. Han."

I did not know if I could trust this woman. Seoul was a big city, and I had heard rumors at the Hometown Cat Club that crime was rampant here. But I did not have a choice. I had to trust her. "Thank you," I said.

The woman came from behind the reception desk. "My name is Mrs. Min. What's your daughter's name?"

"Her name is Soo-bo. I am Hong Jae-hee."

"It's nice to meet you. Come with me, Soo-bo," Mrs. Min said, extending a hand.

"Anyohaseyo," Soo-bo said as she took Mrs. Min's hand.

I swung my rucksack off my shoulder and put it on the floor behind the reception desk. Inside was everything I owned—my clothes, the money Colonel Crawford had given me, and the comb with the two-headed dragon. Mrs. Min sat Soo-bo at a desk behind her and gave her some paper and a pencil. Soo-bo went to work on a drawing. Mrs. Min watched with obvious delight, and I could see Soo-bo was in good hands. I went to the bathroom and washed. Then I went to the second floor to meet Mr. Han.

I approached a man at a desk who wore thick glasses, a white shirt, and a worn suit coat. I told him I wanted to apply for the translator job. He looked at me as if I was trying to sell him something he didn't want. "You want to work as a translator for our firm?" he asked.

"Yes, sir," I said. "I read, write, and speak several languages. I was referred here by Colonel Crawford of the American Eighth Army."

He cocked his head, then shook it. "I don't know him."

"Aren't you Mr. Han?" I asked.

"No, I am Mr. Park, Mr. Han's assistant," he said. He gave me a smug look. "So you think you can be a translator for our company? Which languages do you know?"

"English, Chinese, and Japanese. I learned Japanese and Chinese as a young girl, and when the Americans came, I learned English, too. I also know some Russian."

Mr. Park raised an eyebrow. "All of them?"

"Yes, sir."

"Fluently?"

"English and Japanese, yes. Colonel Crawford said I should see Mr. Han."

Mr. Park leaned back and grinned. "Mr. Han is not here," he said in English. "Where have you worked before?"

Mr. Park's English was dreadful. His grammar was wrong, and his accent was so bad, I could barely understand him. "I worked as a translator for the government," I replied in my best English. "I worked for a negotiator during the talks between the North and South."

I could see that my excellent English intimidated Mr. Park. His grin fell from his face, and he switched back to Korean. "Did you work for the North or the South?" he asked.

"The South, of course," I said.

"Well. We need a translator, so let's find out how fluent you are." He reached inside his desk, took out some papers and a pencil, and handed them to me. He gave me a contract. He pointed to a wooden table in a corner and told me to do my best at translating it into English. "You have one hour," he said.

I thanked him and took the papers to the table. The language on the contract was similar to the declarations and decrees I had helped to translate for the North Korean government. There were only a few words I didn't know, and I burned them into my mind where I would never forget them. Thirty minutes later, I handed the translation to Mr. Park.

"Are you done already?" he asked.

"Yes, sir."

"And you know Japanese, too?"

"Yes, sir. Even better than English."

Mr. Park stared at my translation and scratched his head. "We will have to look this over. Come back in a week, and we will let you know."

"Thank you, sir. Will I be able to see Mr. Han then?"

"It depends on how good your translation is."

Given the way Mr. Park had spoken English, I was sure that I had passed his test. I bowed again and went downstairs to get Soo-bo. When I reached the reception area, Soo-bo was still drawing pictures, and Mrs. Min was at her desk working on some papers.

"You're back so soon," Mrs. Min said without looking up.

"Yes. Thank you for watching my daughter."

Mrs. Min kept her eyes on her work.

Soo-bo showed me one of her drawings. "Look, Mother," she said. "Here is where we used to live." Within the scratching and scribbling, there was a picture of a bar and me in my blue dress. On top, Soo-bo had written "Cat Club."

I quickly stuffed the drawings into my rucksack and picked up Soo-bo. I thanked Mrs. Min again. She didn't look up, and I could tell she had seen what Soo-bo had drawn.

I hurried outside. I looked one way down the boulevard, then the other. It was late in the afternoon. I was tired and hungry and didn't have anywhere to stay for the night. Soo-bo, even as thin as she was, was heavy on my hip. I could tell that she was tired and hungry, too. I started walking. The boulevard was full of workers going home. I noticed the poorer workers were heading in one direction while well-dressed office workers were heading in the other. I lowered Soo-bo to the sidewalk, and we joined the line of poorer workers.

After many blocks, the line began to thin. We walked into an area of cheap-looking boardinghouses. I scanned the windows and doorways for signs offering rooms to rent. I didn't see any.

Soo-bo tugged on my hand. "I'm hungry," she said.

"I know, little one," I said. "I am, too. We will find something soon." We walked on. It felt like the months after the Korean War when I had to scrounge for food and shelter. I thought about going to Itaewon and catching a bus back to the kijichon. Colonel Crawford was right; I did not belong there. But I was not sure I belonged here, either. There were so many poor people, and desperation hung in the air. My only hope was that I would get the translation job. All I had to do was hang on for just one week.

We walked several more blocks to where the city began turning into a slum. Hopeless-looking people watched us from windows. I quickened my pace. Finally, in the doorway of a dirty, two-story boardinghouse, was a sign, "Room for Rent." I went to the door and knocked. An old woman with several missing teeth answered.

"Forty-five dollars a month, American," the woman said without introducing herself. "First month now and another forty-five dollars as a down payment. If all you have is won, the price is higher and will change every month because of the inflation. Take it or go away."

I did some quick calculations in my head. Ninety dollars was nearly half of what Colonel Crawford had given me. I would need clothes, food, and a sleeping mat for Soo-bo and me. If I didn't get the translation job at Gongson, I would be broke in just a few months.

I looked down the street at the shabby buildings and desperate people. I looked back at the filthy, broken-down boardinghouse and the rude woman with bad teeth who would be my landlady. My stomach growled. Soo-bo leaned against my leg.

"I will take it," I said.

THIRTY-SIX

"We haven't gotten the results in yet," Mrs. Min said from behind the Gongson Construction Company's new reception desk. The fresh paint smell was gone, and the lobby had new upholstered furniture. There was wall-to-wall carpeting on the floor—something I had never seen before—and a fancy light fixture in the ceiling. The place had the feeling of hope.

But the fancy new lobby only served to mock me. It had been two months since I had applied for the translation job and taken their test. I had come back every week since, and Mrs. Min had given me the same answer each time—they had not checked the translation.

"Why is it taking so long?" I pleaded. "Mr. Park told me you would know by now."

Mrs. Min pressed her lips together and picked up some papers. I could tell she only pretended to read them. "I'm sorry," she said. "I have work to do now."

I sighed and walked out the door. Seoul's summer rain had come, and with it, the humidity. The air was heavy, and the skies were a seamless gray. It smelled like it would rain again soon. I turned down the boulevard toward the Itaewon market. I had left Soo-bo with a neighbor, a young woman named Yon-lee, who watched Soo-bo for four won per day. I dropped Soo-bo off when I went to the market or to look for work. So far, I hadn't found any.

I was desperate again, the way I had been during those awful months after the Korean War. Food, clothing, and a mat cost much more in Seoul than I had expected. My landlord demanded the rent on the first of each month. This month's rent was past due, and I did not have it. In fact, I was nearly broke. I was terrified that if I didn't find work soon, Soo-bo and I would be out on the street like the people dressed in rags who begged for my spare change.

I went to the market. The vendors had set up on the street and expertly scanned the people walking by for anyone who might buy something. They looked right past me. The clouds turned dark, and a breeze kicked up. I searched for "Help Wanted" signs in the stores, restaurants, and tailor shops that catered to the American military men. I saw nothing.

I went to the seedier section of Itaewon, where bars and cheap restaurants advertised their goods with sad signs in English with poor grammar. One bar named the Queen of Hearts had a sign next to its door that read, "Girls Wanted." I stopped on the sidewalk facing the bar. On the second floor, a young woman wearing too much makeup stared dispassionately out of a window.

Next to the bar was a pawnshop. Behind the yellowed windows were cheap used watches, jewelry, leather goods, radios, and antiques. A sign in the window said, "Will Buy Anything."

The breeze swelled, and the dark clouds opened up. Rain poured down with a hiss at first, then in loud splatters. The people on the street ran for cover, and soon I was the only one on the sidewalk. I was getting drenched, but I didn't care. I stood facing the bar and pawnshop and let the rain wash over me. My hair matted against my head, and my dress clung to me. After several minutes, I took a step forward.

I pushed open the pawnshop door. Glass cases filled with goods surrounded a small, energetic man. "Good morning, pretty lady. Do you want to buy a watch for your husband? A radio? Jewelry? I have a good price for you."

I stepped to the glass counter. Inside were several antiques. My hair dripped rainwater on the glass. "Do you want something for your home?" the man asked, scooting behind the counter. "I have valuable antiques and a good price for you."

"Your sign says you will buy anything," I said.

The merchant sagged. "What do you have?" he asked.

"I have an antique comb."

"A comb? That's all?"

"Yes."

"I am not interested in an old comb," he said.

"It has a solid gold spine and an ivory inlay of a two-headed dragon."

The man froze for just a second, and I could see that my description of the comb took him by surprise. "Are you sure the dragon has two heads?" he asked.

"Yes, I'm sure. And its feet have five toes."

The man gasped as if I had told him I wanted to sell him the emperor's jewels. "The dragon has five toes?" he whispered. "Are you sure?" He pulled back and smoothed his hair. He smiled professionally. "Now that you mention it, I might be interested in a comb. Do you have it with you?"

I glared at the man. "It's valuable, isn't it?" I asked.

The man shrugged as if he did not know, but I could tell he was putting on an act. "It might be," he said.

I leaned over the counter, pressing both hands on the glass. All of my frustrations over the past two months boiled over. "Tell me," I snarled. "It is an antique comb with a two-headed dragon whose feet have five toes. It's valuable, isn't it?"

The man slowly nodded. "Yes," he said. "If it is what you say, it is very valuable. Do you have such a comb to sell? I will give you a lot for it."

"What does it mean?" I demanded. "A two-headed dragon with five toes. *What does it mean?*"

The man said, "The dragon . . . it protects Korea and the one who possesses it so they may serve Korea."

I stood with my hands on the counter as the merchant stared at me. My clothes and hair still clung to me from the rain, but I did not care. *One Korea,* the man had said. So what Jin-mo told me years earlier was true. The dragon with one head facing east and one facing west protected Korea. And I could get a lot of money for it—certainly enough to live on until I could find a proper job and perhaps enough for a long, long time.

I knew what I had to do. I headed for the door.

"Wait!" the merchant pleaded. "I will give you good money for it!" He followed me outside into the pouring rain. "Bring me the comb," he shouted. "I will give a lot for it. More than you can imagine!"

I walked all the way to the boardinghouse in the rain. When I went inside, my landlord came shuffling up to me. "Rent is past due," the old woman said through the gaps in her teeth. "Forty-five dollars. I have others who can pay. Don't make me kick you out."

"Yes, ma'am. I understand."

"I will come with you to your room. You can pay me now."

I growled at the woman, "I have to get my daughter. And I need to change my clothes. I will pay you later."

The old woman turned away with a huff. "Rent is past due," she squawked over her shoulder. "Pay me tomorrow, or I will kick you out."

I went to Yon-lee's room and knocked. Soo-bo opened the door. "Mother!" she squealed. She grabbed my leg and quickly let go. "You're wet!" she said.

I waved a thank you at Yon-lee.

"You still owe from last week," Yon-lee called after me.

I took Soo-bo down the hallway to our tiny room. It was not much different than the one I had in the kijichon. Instead of smelling like semen and sweat, it smelled like mold and decay. There was no window, and the light was poor. And in spite of my efforts to clean it, the room always felt dirty to me.

As I changed into dry clothes, I asked Soo-bo about her day.

"I read books in English," Soo-bo said proudly. "Mrs. Kim is trying to learn, and I helped her."

I smiled at my daughter. "Someday soon, little one, I will buy you books and teach you many English words. Other languages, too." Soo-bo beamed.

I went to the closet and took out my rucksack. I opened it and picked up the envelope where I kept my money. Only fourteen dollars were left inside. I put the money back into the rucksack. The brown package containing the comb with the two-headed dragon was in the corner. I took it out and held it in my hand.

I shoved the rucksack into the closet and lowered myself onto my mat. Soo-bo sidled up next to me. "What's that, Mother?" she asked, pointing at the package.

"It is a comb, little one."

"Can I see it?" Soo-bo said.

I pulled on the twine and opened the cloth. Soo-bo's eyes went wide when she saw the comb. "Is it the comb our story is about?"

"Yes, it is."

"It's pretty. Can I comb my hair with it?"

I ran my hand over Soo-bo's hair. "No, little one. This comb is too valuable for combing hair."

"Is the story true—the one about the yangban and her daughter?" Soo-bo asked.

I carefully folded the cloth around the comb and tied it closed. "No," I said softly, "it is only a story."

Soo-bo went to a corner and bounced a red ball. Lately she had started to cling after I picked her up from Yon-lee. It worried me that she was eating less, growing thinner, and asking questions about money. I was doing my best to keep my despair hidden from her, but I knew she was sensing it. If we ran out of money and had to live on the street, Soo-bo, with her poor health, would suffer terribly and maybe even die.

I looked at the package containing the comb. If I sold it to the pawnshop merchant, Soo-bo and I would not have to live on the street. And if the comb was what Jin-mo said, why didn't it protect me? Why did I have to suffer just to survive?

Soo-bo stopped bouncing the ball and grew quiet. I could see she was falling into one of her dark moods again. I took the comb from the brown cloth and slipped it inside my dress pocket. I extended a hand to Soo-bo. "Come, little one," I said. "We have to go somewhere."

◆　◆　◆

Outside, the rain had stopped. Oily puddles glistened in the street. People were starting to come out of their cramped rooms to breathe the rain-cleaned air. Soo-bo and I headed toward Itaewon. We walked several blocks into the neighborhood where the boarding-houses were not as shabby. A few blocks farther was the business district and, beyond that, the Itaewon market. I walked with my back straight and my eyes focused ahead. Soo-bo had to run to keep up with me.

I came to a corner. In one direction was the Gongson Construction Company, in the other was the pawnshop. I reached inside my dress pocket and felt the comb. It was smooth and cool. I remembered in the Dongfeng wheat field how it felt in my hand when Private Ishida let me live. I remembered how I had dropped it when I was escaping to the South, and then when I found it, it showed me the way through the fence.

I turned toward the Gongson Construction Company. When I got to the door, I pushed my way into the lobby. I marched up to Mrs. Min and said I wanted to see Mr. Han.

"You—you can't," Mrs. Min said. "He is busy. Anyway, I told you this morning, we don't have the results."

"I do not believe you," I said. I lifted Soo-bo to my hip and marched to the staircase.

"Wait!" Mrs. Min shouted. "You can't go there. Stop!" She swung around the reception desk and came after me.

I was at the top of the stairs before Mrs. Min could catch me. Mr. Park was at his desk. With Soo-bo still on my hip, I marched to him and bowed my head as Mrs. Min came up from behind.

"Sir, I want to see Mr. Han," I said.

"I'm sorry, Mr. Park," Mrs. Min said, panting. "She came in without permission."

Mr. Park frowned. "You can't come in here like this. You have to—"

The office door opened, and a tall, graying-haired man in a smooth blue suit stepped out. Mr. Park stood and bowed. "What's going on here?" asked the man.

"This woman has come in here without permission, sir," Mr. Park said.

The tall man looked at me. "What do you want?"

I lowered Soo-bo to the floor and bowed. I reached inside my pocket and gripped the comb. "Sir, several weeks ago, Mr. Park gave me a contract to translate as a test for a translator position. I have been waiting to hear the results. Colonel Crawford of the American Eighth Army told me that I should give you his name."

"I know the colonel well," the man said. "Tell me what you know about him so I know you're telling the truth."

"Sir," I said, "he enjoys Old Fitzgerald bourbon, and his hero is General Robert E. Lee of the Confederacy of the South."

The man smiled the way people do when they greet an old friend. He looked at Mr. Park. "We still need a translator. Why haven't you checked her work?"

"Sir," Mr. Park said, "Mrs. Min told me this woman was no longer interested in the position."

The man glared at Mrs. Min. "Well, obviously Mrs. Min is wrong." Mrs. Min bowed low and scurried away.

"Do you still have this woman's translation?" the man asked.

"Yes, sir," Mr. Park answered.

"Check it immediately," the gray-haired man said over his shoulder as he walked back inside his office.

I was terribly nervous as I sat in a leather chair in the attorney's newly carpeted office while Soo-bo waited outside. An enormous bookshelf behind Mr. Han's rosewood desk dominated his office. In it were hundreds of scholarly books. At the desk, Mr. Han was reading my translation that, moments earlier, Mr. Park said I had done perfectly.

"I should ask how you met Colonel Crawford," Mr. Han said over the top of his reading glasses, "but I probably do not want to know."

"Sir," I said, "I will do a good job for you."

"I believe you will." He set the translation on the desk and took off his glasses. "Jae-hee, a company lives on the honorable conduct of its employees. I am going to hire you based on Colonel Crawford's recommendation. You might have done things in your past that we should leave in your past. But from now on, you need to uphold the honor of this company."

"I understand, sir. I will. Thank you."

"Good," the attorney said. "Welcome to the Gongson Construction Company."

THIRTY-SEVEN

Ten years later. November 1964. Seoul, South Korea

I sat at a low table in my new sixth-floor apartment in the 315 building and watched with pride as Soo-bo grabbed her book bag, pulled on her coat, and headed for the door. Soo-bo would be fifteen soon, and though she was still thin, she had filled out like a woman. She would never be strong like me, or brilliant like Jin-mo, but she worked very hard at school and had progressed in her studies.

It hadn't been easy to get her into school. Since Soo-bo did not have a father, she was unable to get a family registration. I'd had to go to the local elementary school and pay a bribe to have her admitted. For her middle school entrance exam, I made Soo-bo study long hours, and she had passed. The middle school administrator assumed that Soo-bo had a family registration and let her in. Soon she would take the exams for placement into high school, and I hoped Soo-bo would pass again. But the exam would be more difficult, and in high school, the officials would be careful to check for a family registration. Without one, they would not admit Soo-bo, and her formal education would be over.

"Soo-bo," I said as my daughter opened the door to leave, "you should say good-bye to your mother."

"Oh," Soo-bo said, "I'm sorry." She bowed. "Good-bye, Mother. I am going to school now." She hurried out the door.

I watched Soo-bo leave and smiled to myself. I loved my daughter more than I had loved anyone. For fourteen years, it had been just Soo-bo and me. We had seen terrible hardships together. There were times I thought I would not be able to save her. But I did what I had to do, and somehow, we made it through. I was very proud of her and proud of myself, too. I was a good mother, and I knew it.

I thought about her life compared to mine. At Soo-bo's age, the only education I'd had was from my mother, who taught me to read and write in Hangul, Chinese, and Japanese. If it weren't for my skill with languages, I would have stayed poor as South Korea flourished after General Park Chung-hee overthrew the corrupt government of Syngman Rhee. Now South Korea was hard at work building a modern nation while our children went to school. In a few years, Soo-bo would come to adulthood in a country with endless promise—but only if she passed her exams, and only if I could get her admitted to high school.

I stuffed the translations that I had worked on the night before inside my bag. I was thankful that I had a good job at the Gongson Construction Company. I worked very hard at it. I went to the library every week and checked out books in Japanese, Chinese, and English. I read every night after work, just like I did when I got the first translation job in Pyongyang. I watched foreign films whenever I could. With my language skills, I was a valued employee at Gongson. And I no longer thought of myself as a comfort woman. Yes, I'd let the Japanese exploit and brutalize me for two years, but that was no longer who I was. I was now one of millions of proud South Koreans helping to build a great nation.

Today I wanted to get to work early. Gongson was expanding along with the rest of South Korea, and I had a lot of work to do. Before I left, I picked up the black-and-white photograph of my family sitting in a new frame on the table. "Mother, Father, Soo-hee," I said to the images as I did every morning before leaving for work, "thank you for sending your spirits to help me. I will always do my best to honor you." I set the photo on the table. I left my apartment and headed to work.

◆ ◆ ◆

Two years earlier, Gongson had moved to a four-story glass and steel building in Itaewon. In Seoul's construction boom, Gongson was growing fast. It now employed several hundred people, and they were hiring new employees every week. The company hummed with energy, and I was thrilled to be a part of it.

I greeted Mrs. Min in the lobby. "Good morning, Mrs. Min. Isn't it a lovely day?" She pretended not to notice me as she had done every day for the past ten years.

When I got to my desk, Mr. Han, the senior attorney for Gongson, was already outside his office waiting for me. The gray-haired man wore his customary smooth blue suit and a worried look below his thick gray hair. He held a stack of documents out to me and told me I had to finish translating them today. "This is the most important deal our firm has ever done," he said. "If we can get this loan at a favorable rate, we can expand into other industries and become a conglomerate, a true chaebol!"

"Yes, sir," I said with a respectful bow. I took the documents to my desk. "Are we doing them in English when we are done with the Japanese?"

"No, we do not need them in English. We're only dealing with the Japanese on this one. We want to keep the Americans out of it. Anyway," he said slyly, "Diashi Bank is anxious to do business with us. Hopefully they will give us a good rate."

"I will get them done today, sir," I said.

"Good," Mr. Han said with a quick nod. "Oh, by the way, the bank's negotiators will be here tomorrow morning. We need your help interpreting. You're good at reading Japanese men."

Mr. Han went inside his office and closed the door while I sat at my desk and seethed. Yes, I knew all about the Japanese. They were ruthless and cruel and arrogant and bigoted. Even atomic bombs on Hiroshima and Nagasaki and a seven-year American occupation had not subdued their conceit. And after General Park overthrew the Korean government, he moved away from the Americans and normalized relations with Japan. Korean businesses were now turning to the Japanese to help build their industries. *Why are we doing business with these people?* I fumed. *Don't you remember what they did to us? Don't you know what they did to me?*

I closed my eyes, and the images of the machine gun murdering the Korean girls in the comfort station courtyard burned in my mind. My stomach turned. I wanted to throw the contracts on the floor and storm out the door. I wanted to march into the South Korean Ministry of Foreign Affairs and tell them what the Japanese had done to me. I wanted to reach out to thousands of other women who I had heard the Japanese had also raped and tortured as comfort women.

Then I remembered Soo-bo and the long hours she had to study to pass her exams. I remembered how I had promised my ancestors that I would honor them. I thought of my new apartment and how I didn't have to struggle just to survive. So I went to work translating the contract. I took my time, consulted my dictionaries, and made sure I got everything just right. In the margins, I made notes where the language was ambiguous and where Mr. Han should be careful.

By midafternoon, I was done and gave the contract to Mr. Han. "Good work, Jae-hee," he said. "Don't forget, we need you to interpret tomorrow. Wear something the Japanese men will like. You know how they are."

"Yes, sir," I said, taking care to hide my disgust.

After Mr. Han went back to his office, the telephone on my desk rang, and I answered it.

"Jae-hee," a voice said, "I want to see you after work. Can you meet me?" The caller was Choi Chul-sun, a senior manager at Gongson, and I was sure he was in love with me. He was a friend of the founder's son. We had been dating for nearly two years, going out to dinner and to the movies on the weekends. He was always painfully polite. Lately, he had been dropping hints about taking our relationship further.

"Chul-sun, I cannot see you tonight. I have an important meeting tomorrow."

"Yes, I know about the meeting with Diashi Bank. But this is important, too."

"I also have to get home to Soo-bo," I said.

"I will pay for a cab. You'll be home at your usual time."

"Well, okay," I said. "For just a little while. Where shall we meet?"

He told me to meet him outside at the corner in twenty minutes. I told him I would see him then and hung up the phone. Over the next twenty minutes, I worked on a translation of a letter to an American subcontractor and put it in my "out" basket. I put on my coat and headed to the lobby.

On the way out, I passed the steno pool. Moon-kum, a thick, middle-aged woman, looked up as I walked by. "Are you going to see Choi Chul-sun again tonight, Jae-hee?" she teased. "When are you going to marry him and make him a real man?"

The other women looked up from their typewriters and grinned. "He is not so handsome," Moon-kum continued, "but he makes good money. He will be a vice president someday. What more do you want?" The other women covered their mouths and giggled.

"Why do I need a man?" I said, throwing my hair to the side. "I have everything I need. Men are nothing but a burden to a woman. And," I whispered loudly, "they have bad odors."

The women laughed, careful to cover their mouths. I smiled at them and took the stairs down to the lobby.

When I reached the corner outside the building, Chul-sun was already waiting for me. As a senior manager in the accounting department, Choi Chul-sun dressed well, but it did not help his looks. His expensive suit, white shirt, and red tie hung awkwardly on his bony frame. His skin was pocked, and his thin hair was graying prematurely.

He blushed as I approached. "Jae-hee," he said. "Seeing you pleases me." He motioned down the street. The sidewalk was crammed with people heading home. The November air was dry, but not too cold. Chul-sun took my arm. "I thought we could go to Namsan Park," he said. "I will pay a cab to take you home. It's not too cold for you, is it?"

"No, I am comfortable."

We walked six blocks to Namsan Park. All around, the city was under construction. Office buildings, apartments, shopping centers, and restaurants were springing up everywhere. Dozens of construction cranes punctured the Seoul skyline. Workers laid new streets and put up electrical lines. Hundreds of cars and trucks and buses motored over the new streets. There was talk of putting in a subway system. Seoul was pulsing with growth.

Chul-sun and I exchanged small talk as we walked. I could see he was nervous, and I did my best to make him relax. It had been that way ever since we first went out two years before. That day, he picked me up in a cab and took me to an expensive new restaurant near the Han River. At first he was terribly nervous and blushed a lot. But I used my skill at talking with men to put him at ease. Since then we had gone out on dates nearly every weekend, and Chul-sun had become more comfortable around me. He told me that he was from a wealthy merchant family from Seoul and had gone to school for accounting after World War II. He had worked in procurement for the South Korean army during the Korean War and, for the past nine years, had worked for Gongson Construction. He was a proud, respected senior manager and had a bright future.

I had told him about my family farm outside Sinuiju, how the Japanese had sent my father and sister away, and how my mother had died. I told him about Soo-bo's father and how I had escaped to the South. I told him how I got my job with Gongson. But I never told him about the two years I had spent in Dongfeng, or that I worked for the communists, or about the year I had worked in the kijichon. I prayed that he would never find out.

We entered the west end of Namsan Park. To the east, Mount Namsan rose gracefully in the low November sun. Young couples walked side by side over the gravel pathways. In an open field, an old man dressed in white practiced taekkyeon with slow, graceful movements.

A man in a shabby coat sat hunched on a park bench. He extended his hand for spare change as we walked by. Chul-sun kicked gravel at him and scoffed. "Why do they let these people in the park?" he said.

"He doesn't have anywhere to go," I replied.

"It does not look good for Korea," Chul-sun said. "They should get rid of them." I wanted to say something to Chul-sun about how it was to be poor, but in Korea, it was not proper for women to disagree with a man in public. And I did not want to reveal too much about my past. So I said nothing.

We walked on. Eventually Chul-sun let go of my arm. "Jae-hee," he said, his lanky frame tipping forward, "um . . . how was work today?"

"It was very busy. I worked on the Diashi contracts."

"Good. Good," Chul-sun said. "That is an important meeting tomorrow."

We started walking again. We walked in silence for a while longer, and I could see that Chul-sun was very nervous. Finally I said, "What is it, Chul-sun? You did not bring me here just for a walk."

He nodded. "Yes, there is something. Something very important I want to ask you."

"I see," I replied. "What is it?"

Chul-sun drew his hand over his balding head and blushed. He scanned the path in front of him as if the question he wanted to ask was lost among the gravel.

I took his arm and turned him to face me. "Chul-sun, ask your question."

He shook his head. "I want to do this right like a proper Korean man should, but you have no father, so I can't ask him first, so I have to ask you directly, which is not the way it should be done, and now I cannot remember what I was going to say."

I gently touched his arm. "I understand. Just ask."

He took a deep breath and blurted, "Jae-hee, I would be honored if you would marry me. I will make a good husband." He looked at me wide-eyed, as if my answer would decide if he lived or died.

I looked back at Chul-sun and smiled to myself. I did not love him, not like I loved Jin-mo. But he was a good man, and he wanted me very much. With him as my husband, I would be a respectable citizen in the new, prosperous South Korea. Soo-bo would have a family registration so she could go on to high school. With luck, maybe she could even go to the university someday. Given my history, a successful man like Chul-sun was more than I could have ever expected.

I lowered my eyes. "Yes, Chul-sun," I said with a bow. "I will be honored to be your wife."

THIRTY-EIGHT

The next morning, I put on the dress that best showed off my slender legs. I applied more makeup than usual and carefully brushed my hair, flicking my wrist with the brush to make it curl at the end. I looked at my reflection in the mirror. At thirty-four, I was still able to turn men's heads. But I was disgusted to have to put on such a display for the Japanese men. They made my stomach turn.

I walked out of the 315 apartment building along with Soo-bo. We said good-bye at the street, and I watched my daughter march off to school. I pulled my coat tight against the November chill and headed for my bus. As I walked, I pushed aside my anger about dealing with the Japanese. After all, for the first time since Dongfeng, I was going to be respectable. The night before, I had agreed to marry Chul-sun.

A block from my bus stop was a dress shop. I stopped at the window and peered in. In the back were colorful wedding hanboks with long chima skirts and jeogori blouses. I spotted a red one. I looked good in red. Off to the side were intricate ceremonial headdresses and wedding sashes with brightly embroidered flowers. I pressed against the window to get a better look. My heart beat a little faster as I tried to picture myself dressed in the red hanbok holding the arm of a proud Chul-sun in front of his family and our friends from Gongson. I smiled as I imagined an excited Soo-bo wearing the blue hanbok, and the young men at the wedding staring at her when they thought no one was looking.

I heard the bus to Itaewon pull up a quarter block away. I ran and caught it as it started to pull out. I thanked the driver for stopping for me and then took a seat near the back. When I settled in my seat, I quietly laughed at myself for almost missing my bus to look at wedding dresses.

As the bus wound its way through the bustling Yeongdeungpo-gu district and crossed yet another new bridge over the Han River into Itaewon, I prepared myself for the meeting ahead. It was difficult working meetings with the Japanese. They used word tricks and deception to gain an edge. Even though Mr. Han and the executives of Gongson spoke Japanese, they depended on me to read their counterparts' body language and catch the nuances of what they were saying. I was good at it, and today I was determined not to let the Japanese get away with anything.

◆ ◆ ◆

The Gongson Construction Company had designed their fourth-floor conference room to impress people. It had mahogany paneling, a huge Chinese rug, and a western-style table that sat twelve people with enough room to spread papers around. Wall-to-wall windows overlooked the boulevard four stories below, and sunlight poured in, making the room bright. I stood in the corner while the company's executives took their places at the table. Mr. Han caught my eye and gave me a firm look to remind me how important this meeting was. I bowed my head to indicate I understood.

Three Japanese executives from Diashi Bank entered the room. I kept my eyes respectfully low as the executives greeted each other and exchanged business cards in a grand show of respect. I carefully examined the shoes of the Japanese bankers. One wore shoes that were coming untied, and I knew he would be sloppy in his negotiations. Another had shoes that were smudged and unpolished, and I knew that what he said would be unimportant. The third wore shoes that were perfectly polished and tied tight. He would be the one to watch out for.

The executives took their places at the table, the Japanese with their backs to the window and the Koreans on the other side. They shuffled through papers and made notes in the margins. They scrutinized their counterparts on the other side of the table. I stood behind the Koreans, keeping my eyes on the Chinese rug. Then the president of Gongson stood and cleared his throat, and the room went silent. He gave a short speech in Japanese about how honored they were to have an opportunity to do business with a firm as respected as Diashi Bank. I cringed when he said Korea was lucky to have such good friends as the Japanese.

Next, the Japanese executive with the smudged shoes stood to introduce their head negotiator. I smiled to myself at their grandstanding. While Gongson's president merely gave a speech, the Japanese had to introduce the head of their team. I had to admit, they knew how to take the upper hand.

I stepped forward, ready to interpret. "Gentlemen," the junior executive said bombastically, "you are very fortunate to have one of Diashi Bank's top executives to meet with you today. Normally he would not get involved in a transaction this small. However, since you are a new customer, he has graciously agreed to be here. He is a man of great intellect and importance. I am pleased to introduce to you Diashi Bank's senior vice president, Mr. Tanaka."

Every nerve in my body snapped to life. Had I heard the man correctly? Had he said *Tanaka*? I slowly raised my eyes and watched as the senior vice president stood to make his speech. When I saw him, my heart stopped. He wore an expensive black suit and a tie the same red color as the Japanese flag. He had filled out some in the past twenty years, and his hair was gray and thinning. But he still had the pointed nose, the cold, sharp eyes, and the air of authority. It was my kempei, Lieutenant Tanaka. I could almost see him slapping his shinai against his black boots.

I stood in the Gongson conference room with my eyes low and began to tremble. My breathing was difficult, and the walls closed in. My legs ached where he had beaten me that last week in Dongfeng. I squeezed my eyes shut and forced myself to take a deep breath.

At the head of the table, Lieutenant Tanaka paced back and forth while he delivered his speech in his clipped tone, just as he had done in front of the Korean girls in Dongfeng. I heard only a few words of his speech: "You are fortunate . . . discipline . . . obey." The kempei's words swept me back to the comfort station. I could picture the terror in Jin-sook's eyes when he tied her to the post that first day. I could hear the girls' sobs as they lay in their tiny rooms at night. I could see Soo-hee's ashen face as she lay dying on the infirmary floor. And there, standing in the opulent Gongson conference room, I was a comfort woman again.

I took another glance at the kempei strutting and posturing in front of his audience, and another fear gripped me. I had never told anyone except Jin-mo about my two years in the comfort station. Lieutenant Tanaka could reveal my terrible secret or use it as an advantage in these negotiations. But I had been just a girl in Dongfeng, and now I was a mature woman. Perhaps he wouldn't recognize me. I struggled to keep my composure and kept my head bowed low.

Lieutenant Tanaka finished his speech and took his seat. I moved to a place out of his line of sight as the negotiations began. The Japanese carefully answered questions about the loan contract, and they themselves asked pointed questions about how Gongson would use and repay the money. Several times Mr. Han asked me to clarify what the Japanese meant in a phrase or statement. Each time, as I stepped forward and answered, I glanced at the kempei. He never saw me.

But I saw him. I tried to imagine how different from my life his had been since Dongfeng. There he was, a senior executive of a large

Japanese bank. Unlike me, he never knew how it felt when you had no food for your starving child. He never had to worry about where he would sleep at night or how to stay warm during winter. He never knew desperation so suffocating it took all your strength not to surrender to it.

And unlike me, in spite of what he had done, he had respect. It didn't matter that he had beaten girls and overseen their systematic rape. It didn't matter that he had them murdered. And it did not matter that *I* was innocent and *he* was guilty. He had respect, and I did not. I wanted to scream out at the injustice of it. I wanted to tell everyone in the room what this man had done. But I did not dare, because if I did, it would expose my own terrible secret. So I stood there only feet away from my kempei and obediently did my job in silence.

The meeting progressed, each side angling for an advantage and gaining none. After two hours, both sides agreed to the final contract language. They decided to reconvene later that evening to celebrate with drinks and dinner at Seoul's most expensive restaurant. As they rose and bowed to each other, Mr. Han, standing next to Lieutenant Tanaka, motioned for me to come over. I approached with my head lowered. Lieutenant Tanaka was talking to the president of Gongson with his chin raised and chest out, the way he had talked to the girls in Dongfeng.

"Yes, sir?" I said softly.

"I want to be sure we are clear on these maturity dates. Please look them over in both languages. That will be all, Jae-hee."

I froze. Mr. Han had said my name aloud. I glanced at Lieutenant Tanaka, and our eyes met for a split second. He showed a flash of recognition. I quickly went to my place behind the executives. After a short while, all the men left, leaving me alone in the mahogany-paneled conference room.

I took a seat at the table to collect myself. I was sure Lieutenant Tanaka had recognized me. It was in his eyes. For just a flash, a look of surprise had replaced his cold arrogance. And . . . what else did I see? Was it fear? Could it be that, like me, he didn't want anyone to know what he had done in Dongfeng twenty years earlier?

I quickly gathered my papers. As I was about to leave, the conference room door opened and Lieutenant Tanaka stepped in. He closed the door behind him. I lowered my eyes as he took a seat at the table and stretched his legs out in front of him. Sunlight shone on him through the conference room windows, and he looked like a ghost—or a god—in the bright light.

"Namiko Iwata," he said, punctuating each syllable of the name. "I suppose I should call you Jae-hee. Imagine my surprise at seeing you here." He nodded toward the door. "I told Mr. Han that I wanted to talk to you alone about the contracts. They probably think I'm courting you for sex. How ironic."

I kept my head lowered. I tried not to show any emotions, but under my dress, my knees shook.

"Don't worry," the kempei said. "It would be in both our interests if no one knew what happened in Dongfeng."

"Yes, Kempei," I heard myself say.

"Good. As long as you hold your part of the bargain, I will see that your company gets a favorable rate on this contract. I will even tell them I am impressed with your work."

"Thank you, Kempei."

He slowly traced a circle on the table with his finger. "I have a wife now, and a daughter. Her name is Miwa."

"How old is she, sir?" I asked.

"She is fourteen."

"That is how old I was when . . . when we first met."

He stopped tracing the circle and looked down his sharp nose at me as he had done a thousand times before. "It was a war, Jae-hee," he said. "We had a duty to fulfill. I had mine, and you had yours."

I looked up. "My duty, Kempei?"

"Yes, of course! The comfort women had a duty to the men and to Japan." He pointed his chin at me as if I should naturally agree.

I returned his stare. "Then why did you kill them, sir?"

There was a sudden blankness in his face. He blinked twice and said simply, "I do not remember doing that."

It took a moment for the vacant look on his face to go away. Then he rose to leave. "Do you still have that comb with the two-headed dragon?" he asked. "Colonel Matsumoto said he gave it back to you."

I thought about the comb hidden under the windowsill of my apartment. "No, Kempei. I had to sell it to feed my daughter."

"Too bad. I remember the dragon had five toes. I did not know what it meant at the time. But it does not matter now. I hope you got a good price for it."

"I did, Kempei."

"Good. I had better get back. They'll start to wonder what we are doing in here." He turned to leave. Then he turned back. "One more thing," he said. "Give my greetings to your sister. I always did like her. I trust she is well."

I quickly lifted my head. "Sir," I said, "Soo-hee died in Dongfeng. Didn't she?" My knees stopped shaking.

A thin smile stretched across Lieutenant Tanaka's face. He shook his head. "You don't know, do you?"

"I don't know about what, Kempei? Please tell me, sir."

Lieutenant Tanaka laughed quietly and put his hands on the back of a chair. "Well," he said, "when the Japanese left Dongfeng, Doctor Watanabe insisted that they take all his patients to Pushun, including your sister, Okimi Iwata. No one thought she would make it, but in Pushun, she had an operation and eventually made a full recovery. When I went home to Japan several months later, she was trying to get back to Korea. Don't tell me after all these years you never knew."

"No, Kempei, I did not."

"My guess is she is in the North somewhere. So there you go. Your old kempei has given you valuable information to reward you for a job well done."

"Thank you, Kempei."

Lieutenant Tanaka regarded me for a moment. "Remember our agreement," he said. "No one needs to know about Dongfeng."

"Yes, Kempei," I said.

Lieutenant Tanaka tapped the back of the chair twice and went out the door.

I lowered myself onto a chair and stared at the door. Was it possible that Soo-hee was alive? Or was this a cruel joke by the cruelest man I had ever known?

After a while, I gathered my papers and left the conference room. It *was* possible Soo-hee was alive. I hadn't seen her since I fled from Private Ishida. And when I returned to the infirmary, she was gone. Lieutenant Tanaka might be telling the truth. I had to find out. But how? The North and South were bitter enemies with an impenetrable border between them. Yet there were rumors of underground networks that families could use to pass letters to each other.

As I went back to my desk, I resolved to find my sister, whom I hadn't seen in twenty years.

THIRTY-NINE

"What did you and your sister do in Dongfeng?" Mr. Lee asked, peering over his glasses from his metal desk in the Department of Family Records. Mr. Lee's desk sign identified him as the Administrator of Records. He had a slight paunch, and his white shirt was gray from being washed too many times. His office was on the second floor of one of South Korea's new government buildings in Seoul's Jongno district, a twenty-minute bus ride north of Itaewon. The building's design was midcentury modern, and the beautiful structure was one of the many statements from the General Park government that South Korea was going to be a great, modern nation.

For the past fifteen minutes, Mr. Lee had been asking me questions so he could complete his form. He hadn't even bothered to look up until I mentioned Dongfeng. I told him we worked for the Japanese there, hoping he would accept my answer and move on, but he asked me to be more specific.

While he held his pen over his form, I wondered what I should tell him about the comfort station. What people had done during the Japanese occupation was something proper Koreans did not discuss. But I had come here to see if Lieutenant Tanaka had told me the truth about Soo-hee and if there was information about her. So I had to tell Mr. Lee about Dongfeng.

"My sister and I received orders from the Japanese military command to report to work at a boot factory in Sinuiju," I said. "The orders were a trick. They put us in a truck and shipped us to Dongfeng. They forced us to become comfort women. That is what we did there."

Mr. Lee glared at me for several seconds and then pushed the papers aside without writing anything more. "I cannot help you," he said flatly.

"Why?"

"Because we have no records of that sort of thing happening."

"It is what happened," I said, keeping my voice low. "I spent two years there. If we had not done it, we would have been shot."

Mr. Lee looked from side to side, as if he were afraid someone was listening. "You should not talk about it," he said. "The Japanese are our allies now. They're helping us. There is no need to bring up what happened twenty years ago. I am not putting it in the records."

"That's fine, but please see if you have anything about my sister. Her name is Hong Soo-hee. She was from Sinuiju."

"Look," Mr. Lee said, taking off his glasses and leaning forward as if he were getting ready for a fight. "Families were scattered after World War Two and again after the Korean War. Millions died. The chances of your sister still being alive are small. The chances of you finding her if she is alive are even smaller. I will not waste my time looking for something from someone who is probably dead."

If this man thought he could intimidate me, he was mistaken. In my life, I had faced much more intimidating men than a government clerk. So I moved to the edge of my chair and met his eyes with mine. "Mr. Lee," I said directly, "isn't that what this department is for? Helping family members find each other? You have thousands of files here. You can at least look. Just because the Japanese forced me to be a comfort woman does not mean you don't have to help me. Why do you make me suffer for what the Japanese did to me? Now do your job and help me."

Mr. Lee backed away, and I could see that I had taken the upper hand. He sighed. "Okay, I will look if it will get you to leave. I doubt if I will find anything. What was your sister's name again?"

I gave it to him, and he wrote it down. He said it would take some time, and I told him I would wait.

Mr. Lee disappeared into a huge open area filled with tall beige file drawers and long shelves packed with boxes. I looked at the form on Mr. Lee's desk. I was glad he didn't want to write down what Soo-hee and I had done in Dongfeng. But as I waited for him to return, I wondered why it had to be that way. For years, there had been hushed talk throughout Korea about tens of thousands of women who the Japanese had forced to be comfort women. Apparently there were many more like me who the Japanese had raped and tortured. Now the Koreans and Japanese were allies, and we were sweeping aside the atrocities of their brutal occupation. No one wanted to hear about our suffering. I knew why. Just like me, Koreans did not want to admit what the Japanese had done to us. We were ashamed.

Ten minutes later, Mr. Lee returned, scratching his head and holding a wrinkled envelope. "I found something," he said. "Before the Korean War—in May of 1950, to be exact—there was a letter delivered to this department by a Park Seung-yo from Sinuiju who had escaped to the South. Apparently Mr. Park lived with you at one time. He delivered this letter." Mr. Lee looked at me over his glasses as he handed the envelope to me.

The letter was water-stained and yellowed with age. On the back was a government label with the name "Hong Soo-hee: Sinuiju" and a file number. On the front, handwritten in smudged ink, was: "For Hong Jae-hee, born twenty miles east of Sinuiju, last seen in Sinuiju, October 1945."

I pressed the envelope to my chest. My heart beat fast knowing my onni was alive. Lieutenant Tanaka hadn't lied. Soo-hee had recovered from her botched abortion and was living somewhere in North Korea.

I opened the envelope. Inside was a letter dated April 1949.

> *Jae-hee,*
>
> *If you are reading this letter, you know I survived my illness in Dongfeng. After several years in China, I returned to Sinuiju to look for you. I made inquiries and found this man with one leg, Park Seung-yo, who said he knew you. So I am sending this letter with him, hoping to find you some day.*
>
> *I have learned that Mother and Father are dead. You and I are all that is left of our family. Please write to me in Sinuiju. Perhaps we can be together again someday.*
>
> *Take care, Little Sister,*
> *Your onni, Soo-hee.*

I read the letter twice more. I nodded to myself and asked Mr. Lee how I could get a letter to my sister in the North.

He shook his head. "It is impossible. Communicating with people in the North is prohibited."

"But my sister is alive," I said. "I must get a letter to her. I've heard it can be done. Help me. Please."

Mr. Lee eyed me carefully. Then he motioned for me to lean in close. "I'm not supposed to tell you this, but . . . there is an underground network. It is not cheap, and if you are caught, you will be arrested."

"I understand. How do I do it?"

He told me about a Chinaman named Dr. Wu who could be found in a warehouse in Songdong. He wrote down an address and gave it to me. He told me to tell Dr. Wu that he sent me. "Don't get caught," he said, "and do not tell anyone where you got this information."

I thanked him and assured him I would be careful. I took the address and letter, then left the government building to catch a cab for Songdong.

◆　◆　◆

The address was for the Daegu Refrigerated Warehouse, and the taxi driver drove right to it through the late afternoon traffic. As the cab waited for me, I entered the warehouse through an open dock door. Workers noisily moved crates of vegetables from trucks to refrigerated rooms. The warehouse had the pungent smell of onions, which reminded me of our family farm. I climbed a set of open wooden stairs to a second-floor office filled with file cabinets and cardboard boxes. A thin man sat at the office's only desk. When he saw me, he asked who I was.

"My name is Hong Jae-hee. I am looking for Dr. Wu. Mr. Lee sent me."

"What do you want with Dr. Wu?" he asked.

"I was told he could help me get a letter to a family member in the North."

"Contact with people in the North is against the law. Go away."

I started to leave, but turned back before I got to the door. "I have money," I said.

The thin man didn't respond, and I went to leave again. As I opened the door, the man said, "It will cost a lot of money."

"I will pay whatever it takes," I said.

The man finally looked at me. "How do I know you aren't from the police?"

I thought for a moment. Then I shook my head and said, "I guess you don't. But I assure you, I only want to find my sister. I just learned she is alive. I have not seen her in twenty years."

The man licked his lips. He told me to wait and went through a door. After a minute, he came out and pointed at the door he had just come through. "Dr. Wu will see you in there," he said.

I walked through the door. It was dark inside, and there was the sweet smell of incense. When my eyes adjusted to the dark, it was as if I had stepped into another world. Persian rugs covered the floors, and beautiful Chinese tapestries with scenes of cranes and snow-capped mountains hung on the walls. In the center of the room was a massive rosewood desk with thick carved legs. In front of the desk were matching chairs with embroidered cushions. Sitting in the shadows at the desk was a rotund man wearing a maroon smoking jacket. Between his stubby fingers was a long cigarette holder tipped with a thin cigarette. Smoke drifted up from the end.

I went to the desk and bowed. The man motioned to the chair in front of his desk. "What is your name, woman?" he asked in a husky voice. He had no trace of a Chinese accent.

"Hong Jae-hee," I answered.

From inside the shadows, the man nodded. "The Hong clan. From the North. Mostly farmers, if I'm not mistaken." He took a puff from his cigarette. The tip glowed orange.

"Yes, my family had a farm outside of Sinuiju."

"Sinuiju. I cannot say I like the place." He angled his head and blew cigarette smoke toward the ceiling. "I prefer the Chinese city of Dandong across the Yalu River. The Great Wall begins there, and it has a lovely park on Wihwa Island. I am told you have a sister who you want to find."

"Yes, sir," I said. "The Department of Family Records had a letter on file. I think my sister might be in Sinuiju. I want to get a letter to her."

Dr. Wu leaned his bulk over the rosewood desk, and his round face came out of the shadows. His eyes were white and lifeless. "It costs a lot of money to get a letter to someone in the North. We do not know where she is or if she is even alive. We have to avoid the authorities on both sides of the border. It is all very . . . complicated."

"I understand, sir."

He leaned back into the shadows and took in a long draw from his cigarette. He angled his head in the manner of a man who has been blind all his life. "If I agree to do this for you, it will cost two hundred thousand won or one thousand American dollars, if you prefer. And I make no guarantees. The chances are your sister is dead. So many of your people died in the civil war. Are you sure you want to do this?"

"Yes, sir. I think I can get the money."

He took another pull from his cigarette. "Where will you get that kind of money, woman?"

"I work for the Gongson Construction Company."

"What do you do there?"

"I am an interpreter."

"What languages?"

"Japanese and English. I also speak Chinese."

"Impressive!" Mr. Wu said. "When did you get separated from your sister?"

I peered into the shadows at the bulk of Dr. Wu. I hesitated only a moment and then answered, "We were comfort women in Dongfeng. The Japanese tricked us into working for them. I thought they had killed my sister, but as I said, today I learned she is alive."

Dr. Wu pointed his cigarette in my direction. "I doubt you earn enough as an interpreter for the Gongson Construction Company, but if you can raise the money, I will help you. When you have it, bring it here with your letter and everything you know about your sister. We will get back to you if we find her."

"How long will it take?" I asked.

Dr. Wu leaned forward, exposing his lifeless eyes again. "Months," he said with a blind man's grin.

"Thank you, sir." I bowed and hurried out.

I climbed in the cab and gave the driver the address of my apartment. I thought about my strange meeting with Mr. Wu, the blind Chinese man who was going to help me find Soo-hee. Two hundred thousand won. I didn't have that much money. But I knew one person who could give it to me.

FORTY

Chul-sun and I planned our wedding as we ate dinner at one of the new, expensive restaurants in Itaewon. The restaurant's glass front overlooked Gyeongnidan Street, which had dozens of American-influenced shops and restaurants. In spite of the cold, the narrow street was crowded with young people dressed in American-style coats and shoes window-shopping. Many couples held each other close to keep warm, which was not something traditional Koreans would do in public. South Korea was becoming a modern city, and the people were changing, too. I knew it was inevitable, but I regretted that we were losing our Korean heritage.

When we had been seated at the restaurant, Chul-sun had ordered a bottle of plum wine and an elaborate meal. The waiter had spread several dishes of banchan before us on the low table. We sat close to each other on mats. Since I had agreed to marry him, Chul-sun walked with his shoulders back and his chin held high. The pockmarks on his face didn't show as much, and his clothes seemed to fit better. He didn't blush anymore and was starting to assert himself with me.

Chul-sun took a sip of wine. "I want a traditional wedding," he said, holding his glass out. "I do not care what it costs. I want both of us to wear new hanboks. I want a *moja* for my head, just like the yang-ban wear. We will have a formal tea ceremony and a wedding feast at a hotel. Bulgogi, galbi, mandu, bibimbap, gamjatang and jajangmyeon, banchan and all the trimmings. We will invite my family, our friends, and people from Gongson. It will be a grand wedding."

I picked at my food. "Maybe we shouldn't spend so much," I said. "It could be expensive."

"It *will* be expensive," he replied.

I took Chul-sun's hand and gave it a squeeze. A flash of excitement crossed his eyes. "We will have other expenses, too," I said. "We will need money to send Soo-bo to school and . . . for other things."

"Yes, yes, I know. Don't worry. We will have enough."

After a long silence, Chul-sun said, "Jae-hee, now that we're engaged, it would not be wrong if you went home with me tonight."

I lowered my eyes. "I must get home to Soo-bo," I said.

He lifted his chin at me. "It's still early. I will pay a cab to take you home. You will be back to Soo-bo in plenty of time. Come home with me, Jae-hee, just for a little while."

I peered into his face and saw how deeply he wanted me. But I wondered if he would still want me if he knew my secrets. Would he still want to take me home, make love to me, go through with the elaborate wedding, and take me as his wife? And what did it say about me if I kept my secret from him? Our marriage would be based on a lie.

I looked at my hands. "Chul-sun," I said softly, "I have to tell you where I went yesterday. I went to the Department of Family Records and discovered that my sister is alive and living in the North. I want to get a letter to her, but it costs a lot of money."

"You told me your sister died when you lived in Sinuiju."

"Yes, Chul-sun, that is what I told you."

"I don't understand," he said.

I put down my chopsticks. "Let's go for a walk."

A cold wind was blowing from the north as we left the restaurant. I took Chul-sun's arm and pulled myself close to him like the other couples on the street. He stayed focused on the sidewalk. I pointed down a side street away from the crowd. I told him I wanted to marry him and have a grand wedding with a reception, a tea ceremony, and all of our friends, just like he wanted.

"But there is something you have to tell me first," he said.

"Yes, there is," I replied.

"Okay, tell me."

I could have made up a story about how Soo-hee had been taken away to work in a comfort station while I stayed on the family farm. But I had to know if Chul-sun loved me for who I really was, just like Jin-mo had. If he did, perhaps I could love him, too. So as we walked, I told Chul-sun everything I had kept secret for so long. Everything—the comfort station, my work for the communists, the kijichon. For the first time since I had escaped to the South, I exposed my true self, my ugly history. And when I finished, I knew that I had done the right thing. I prayed that Chul-sun would understand.

At the end, I said, "If you still want to marry me after what I have told you, I will go home with you tonight."

I waited for his answer. After a while, he said, "You should have said no."

"What do you mean?"

He stopped and turned to me. His chin was set hard, as if I had just insulted him. "You should have said no, Jae-hee. When you realized the Japanese had tricked you, you should have let them shoot you. You should not have worked for the communists, and you should have never gone to the kijichon."

"I should have let them shoot me? Chul-sun, listen to what you are saying."

"I know what I'm saying," he said angrily. "I am saying the honorable thing to have done is to have said no!"

As we stood on the sidewalk, the streets and buildings of Seoul began to melt away, and in their place, I saw the comfort station, the huge iron statue of Kim Il-sung, and the Hometown Cat Club. The people on the sidewalk became the Japanese soldiers who had raped me, the North Korean soldiers who had carried Jin-mo off to prison, and the American soldiers in the kijichon. They all had a firm hold on me. I desperately longed for Chul-sun, the man who wanted to marry me, to reach out and pull me away from their grip.

"Chul-sun," I begged, "please understand. If I had refused any of those times, I would have died. I was only fourteen years old in Dongfeng. I was too young to know. In Pyongyang, everything was so . . . so confusing. And at the kijichon, Soo-bo was starving. I could not let her die. Please, please accept my confession. Love me for who I am, and I will love you, too. Then we will be married and have a grand wedding."

I searched Chul-sun's face for his answer. He wiped his nose on the back of his sleeve. "I told my family about our engagement," he said. His voice was jagged and hard. "I made a big show of it! And now I have lost face. They will think I am a fool! I will never be able to look them in the eyes again."

"We do not need to tell them," I said. "Only you need to know. But you *had* to know. Don't you see? It is the only way I can be sure you accept me for who I really am. It is the only way I can marry you."

Chul-sun shook his head. "The receptionist, Mrs. Min, she knows, too. She told me you worked in a kijichon. I did not believe her. I didn't think it was possible, but she was right. She knows!"

My head began to spin. Chul-sun grabbed me and pushed me into a wall. His fingers dug into my arms. His eyes were wide like Corporal Kaori's were when he raped me. "How can I love you after what you've done?" he shouted. "You have dishonored me." He squeezed my arms harder, and I was afraid he was going to hurt me. Then, with a shove, he let go and stepped back. He looked down the street. "I cannot marry you. You are not who I thought you were."

The faces of my past swirled around me. I closed my eyes to try to make them stop. But Chul-sun was right. I was not who he thought I was. I had tried to keep everything a secret, but my past would always be part of me. I wished I could go back and refuse to obey the orders to work in the boot factory as I had wanted to do. It had set my life on an arc that decades of honorable living could not bend straight. "Chul-sun," I pleaded with my eyes still closed, "how could I have known the right thing to do? How?"

"You should have said no!" he said. "And you should have said no to me, too." He gave me a long, pained look, and then he walked away.

Eventually the people and buildings in the street returned to normal. I headed for home. As I slowly walked through the busy streets of Itaewon and then over the long Mapo Bridge, I thought about my life and all that I had done. I wondered if I had made the right choices.

I stopped halfway across the bridge and looked back at the city. The lights of Seoul twinkled all around me. Below me, the Han River slowly rolled to the sea. Then and there, I decided Chul-sun was wrong. Yes, I needed his money to get a letter to Soo-hee. I wanted to marry him so Soo-ho could go to high school. I even wanted to get married for myself. But if I denied that I had been a comfort woman, I would betray Soo-hee and all of my sisters who had died in the comfort station. No, I had a higher duty to fulfill than to uphold Korea's reputation. After all, important men like Chul-sun and those who wanted to bury the Japanese atrocities so they could build their nation were doing a fine job of that. But telling what happened to us—how we struggled and how we were able to survive—was the only way Korea would become a great nation.

I finally realized how I was to serve Korea. The two-headed dragon had protected me so I could tell my story as Soo-hee and Jin-mo had said I should. They had been right all along. It was a grave responsibility, and I did not know how I would do it. But as I walked the rest of the way home, I vowed I would find a way.

The next day, the final loan agreement with Diashi Bank came through, and the terms were more favorable than anyone at Gongson had hoped for. The entire company throbbed with excitement. Gongson would soon be one of South Korea's chaebols, and everyone from senior executives to message runners did their jobs with their chests out and chins held high.

One reason given for the excellent terms from Diashi was that their chief negotiator had been impressed with me. For one day, I was a hero among the women in the steno pool. "You will be made a manager soon," Moon-kum teased as I walked by. "Then you won't talk to us anymore."

"Yes," I replied, acting like I was a manager already. "Someday I will take over the company. And when I do, I will fire all the men." The women laughed at my joke, covering their mouths as they did.

All that day, Mr. Han smiled openly at me the way a proud father smiles at a successful son. At noon, I ate my lunch on a bench in Namsan Park near where Chul-sun had proposed. I did not hear from him or see him all day. In the afternoon, Mr. Han told me that I could go home early, so I left Gongson and took a cab instead of the bus. That evening, I helped Soo-bo with her homework and went to bed early.

The next morning, when I walked by the steno pool, Moon-kum and the other women kept their eyes on their typewriters. When I said hello, no one returned my greeting. When I got to my desk, there were no contracts to work on.

Mr. Han leaned out of his office. His face was cheerless, and I could see something bad was about to happen. He told me to come in his office and close the door.

The firing was quick and perfunctory. Mr. Han gave no reason, but I understood why. Chul-sun had persuaded his friends in senior management that I was not an honorable employee. I received no severance pay for my ten years of service. I had no pension. At the end, Mr. Han held out an envelope. "Here is your back pay," he said. "You must leave immediately."

I took the envelope and looked at Mr. Han. I could see that though he was trying to hide it, firing me was hard for him. I almost felt sorrier for him than I did for myself. I looked down at the envelope. "I always did my best, sir," I said. "Ever since I was fourteen, I have tried to do the right thing."

The gray-haired attorney's eyes softened, and he nodded. "The actions that society deems respectable—what Confucius called *li*—is not always the most righteous. We must be loyal to our families, our ancestors, and our country first—your *yi*— and only you can determine what your *yi* is."

He smiled sadly. "Thank you for your good work, Jae-hee. Personally, I am sorry to see you go."

I knew then that Mr. Han was a great man, like Jin-mo and Colonel Crawford, and perhaps even like young Private Ishida. It made me sad that I would never see him again. I bowed low. I got my coat and headed home. And I held my head high as I walked through the Gongson Construction Company lobby past Mrs. Min.

FORTY-ONE

Ten years later

I handed out yellow pamphlets in front of the history department on the new Seoul National University campus. The university was Korea's top academic institution and had just moved to the Gwanak district in the south of Seoul. The buildings were new and impressive, and the entire campus was alive with possibility. There was a spring breeze blowing through campus, and I had to hold the pamphlets tight to my chest so they wouldn't blow away. The akebia were in bloom, and the air was heavy with their chocolate smell. All around me, intelligent-looking students carrying books braced themselves against the wind as they rushed to their classes. I pushed pamphlets at them as they walked by. Every so often, a student reached out and took one. It was my third day at the university, and I had only a small stack of pamphlets left.

I'd had the four-page pamphlets printed in a shop not far from my apartment. When the shop owner read it, he refused to do the job. I agreed not to tell anyone where I had them printed and gave him one hundred extra won. He quickly printed them and gave them to me in a plain paper sack.

I was pleased with what I had written. The headline read, "Japanese Sex Slaves. We Were Not Volunteers." The pamphlet explained how the Japanese military had forced me and thousands of others to be comfort women. It proposed that the Korean government force Tokyo to acknowledge their war crimes against Korean women and make reparations. So far, however, no one had responded to my proposal.

I pushed a pamphlet at a female student with short black hair. I wanted to scold her when she stuffed it in her bag without reading it. I watched as she walked to her class. She was part of the new pop generation and wore long, wide-bottomed slacks and a matching jacket over a blouse with a large scarf around the collar. She looked bright, happy, and confident. Of course she did. She had her entire life before her. Her prospects in the modern Republic of Korea were good.

As she disappeared inside the history building, I thought about how different my own life was at her age. I was smart and had an exceptional gift for languages. I would have thrived at a great university like this. Perhaps I could have become an attorney, a negotiator, or a diplomat. But fate had other plans for me.

And fate had other plans for my daughter, Soo-bo, too. I would have given anything to get Soo-bo into a university like this. But without a father to get a family registration, Soo-bo had to quit her studies after Chul-sun broke off our engagement. And without an education, Soo-bo had to work menial jobs to supplement my government welfare check. Even with her income, we just barely paid the rent, and sometimes at the end of the month, we had to skip meals. Our life wasn't even as good as the one I had had in those last hard years on the farm in Sinuiju.

The breeze kicked up, and I held my pamphlets tight. A middle-aged man in a suit trotted toward me down the concrete stairs of the history building. He held one of my pamphlets in his hand. He asked me what I was doing.

"I am telling the truth," I answered.

The man's hair was thick and gray, and he wore scholarly glasses. "I don't want to get you into trouble," he said, "so I'm asking you to leave."

"Why?" I asked. "This is the perfect place to hand out my pamphlets. It talks about an important part of Korea's history. These students should know. All Koreans should know."

The man glared at me. "Do not tell me what these students should know. I am the head of the history department here."

I felt my jaw tighten. "You are?" I asked. "Then certainly you understand how important it is to expose what the Japanese did to me and thousands of other Korean girls. It is your history, too, Professor."

"What is or is not our history is what historians like me say it is," the professor said, jabbing a finger at me. "And I say it did not happen. Now leave."

A good Korean woman would have bowed to a man in authority and done what the professor said. But his arrogance infuriated me. I'd had enough arrogant men in my life, and I was not about to back down to this one. "But it *did* happen," I countered. "It happened to me and my sister. Why do you deny it? Why?"

I could see that the professor was not used to having someone argue with him. He looked both flustered and insulted. After a moment, he leaned into me and said, "Look, we are a modern nation now. If the rest of the world doesn't respect us, we will never become a world power. So please, take your pamphlets and leave, or I will have to call the police."

"I will not," I said. "I won't leave, and I will not stop. I refuse to be a proper Korean and suffer in silence for the rest of my life. As a nation, we're a little too good at being the victim, Professor. Korea will never be great until we stop letting others use us. And it begins with making those who raped us admit what they did."

The professor took a step back and shrugged. "Very well," he said. "I'm sorry." He turned and trotted back up the stairs.

I watched the head of the history department of Korea's most prestigious university disappear inside the building, and my blood boiled. Respect? To my fellow Koreans, respect was more important than the truth. But we would never have respect if we based it on a lie. And anyway, what did I do that was so disrespectful? Read the pamphlet. *We were not volunteers!*

I turned to look for more students to hand my pamphlets to. Standing several steps away was an attractive, middle-aged woman who was obviously not a student. She looked both ways and then came to me. Our eyes met for a second, and she handed me one hundred won. Then she quickly walked away without saying a word.

I went after her. "Wait!" I said, holding the money out. "Why are you giving me this?"

The woman quickened her pace. I ran and caught up to her. "Stop," I pleaded. "Please. I just want to talk to you."

I placed a hand on the woman's arm. She shrugged it away. "Leave me alone," she said. "I gave you the money, that's all I can do."

I kept pace for a few steps more, and then I stopped. The breeze let up for a moment, and the air was still. And then I said loud enough for the woman to hear, "They told me I was going to work in a boot factory. How did they take you?"

The woman stopped with her back to me. She stood for several seconds and then dropped her head. She turned and said, "They came for me in the middle of the night. My grandfather tried to stop them, but they hit him with their rifles and knocked him unconscious. They sent me to the Philippines, where they raped me for three years. I was only fifteen years old."

I went to the woman and put a hand on her arm. "I hear there are thousands of us," I said. "Maybe hundreds of thousands."

"Yes," the woman said. "I have heard the same thing."

"If we work together, we can make the Japanese admit what they did."

The woman shook her head. "I have a husband," she said simply. Her eyes pleaded with me to understand. Then she turned and walked away.

I clenched my teeth and marched to my spot in front of the history department. I thrust my yellow pamphlets at students. A male student looked at me disapprovingly. I pushed a pamphlet at him. "You have to know about this," I said angrily. "If you don't, it could happen to your wife or daughter." The student walked away shaking his head.

A female student came by and looked at me questioningly. "Korea will never be great until we admit this," I said to her. "Take it and read it." She took a pamphlet. She read the headline.

"I've heard rumors about this. Did it really happen?"

"Yes," I said. "It happened to me."

"Why don't they want us to know about it?" the young woman asked.

Before I could launch into a lecture about truth and respect, a man shouted at me from the stairs of the history building. "You there with the pamphlets," he said, "stop what you're doing." Two policemen ran down the stairs toward me. The young woman shoved the pamphlet back into my hand and hurried away.

The policemen came up to me and took my pamphlets. "What are you doing?" I protested. "I am not doing anything illegal."

They took me by the arm and led me toward the street. "Someone wants to talk to you," one said.

As we walked past a trash can, they threw away my pamphlets, and I could see there were already dozens of them inside.

I sat in a small, windowless room in the central government building. Across from me was an average-looking man in a plain suit who introduced himself as Mr. Cho, an agent for the national police in the Department of National Security. He told me I was not to hand out my pamphlets anymore. "In fact," he said, "you are not to go to the university ever again. Am I clear?"

I pushed myself to the edge of my chair. This man did not frighten me, and I was not about to do what he said. "I am only telling the truth about what happened to me. I will not stop."

Mr. Cho tapped on the table and said, "Ms. Hong, you have an interesting record. It seems you've had a dishonorable past."

"I have not done anything dishonorable, sir. That is what I'm trying to say."

"I see. And how does your family feel about what you're doing?"

"My family?"

"Our records show that you have a sister living in the North," Mr. Cho said. "She is probably a communist, just like you. Have you been in contact with her?"

"I am not a communist, sir. And I have not seen my sister for twenty-seven years. She might not even be alive."

Mr. Cho raised an eyebrow. "And then there is your daughter, Soo-bo."

I hesitated for a second. I stared at Mr. Cho. "What about her?"

"According to our records, she was born five months after you escaped to South Korea. Her father must be your lover in the North, Pak Jin-mo. And that means she is the daughter of a well-known communist."

"Leave Soo-bo out of this," I said quickly.

Mr. Cho nodded. "We will gladly do that. All you need to do is stop stirring up controversy. If you do, no one needs to know who your daughter's father is."

I hated them for what they were doing to me. I wanted to fight back, march to Seoul University and shout my story from the top of the history building stairs so everyone would hear. I did not care what people thought of me. I did not care what they would do to me. But I had to think of Soo-bo. If I went on, everyone would know that she was the daughter of a comfort woman, and her life would be even harder than it was now. I could not put her through it. She had suffered enough.

I stared at Mr. Cho for a while longer. Then I nodded my agreement.

"Good," Mr. Cho said. "And now, Ms. Hong, you may go."

FORTY-TWO

Fourteen years later

My poor Soo-bo did not have a good life. She would soon enter middle age and had depended on me her entire life. Her hair was thin, and she was gangly, awkward, and pale. She never made it past middle school and was only able to get menial jobs at menial wages. She did not read much, and unlike most people her age, she never went out at night or on weekends. She was plain, simple, and poor. But I loved her as only a mother could.

I should have found a husband for my daughter. I tried, but no one would have her. So when she got pregnant by a man from her work, it was my fault. I should have met him. But Soo-bo never talked about him, and I didn't know she was seeing him until it was too late. And she never saw him again after she told him she was pregnant.

When we visited the hospital for her maternal exam, the doctors recommended Soo-bo have an abortion. Her heart was weak, they said, and they warned that a difficult delivery might kill her.

I was afraid that Soo-bo was considering having the abortion, so I decided to take her to Gyeongbok Palace. I had to dig to the bottom of my satchel for the won I had been saving for food until my government check arrived. I counted it out. There was just enough for cab fare. The bus would cost far less. But it would require two transfers and take over an hour each way, and that would be too much for Soo-bo in her condition.

It was a clear spring day when the cab dropped us off at the Gwanghwamun Gate. Behind its drab concrete entrance was the massive Japanese Government-General Building that the Japanese built during their occupation. Its towering brass dome and massive stone walls obscured the palace behind it. The Japanese had put it up just there, in front of the royal palace, so that all Koreans would know who was in charge. Like most Koreans, I hated the building. It was ugly and vulgar and an insult to all Koreans.

We walked around the building into the palace courtyard. There, trees and grass were green, and flowers were in bloom. Before us were several buildings, some old and a few under construction. The buildings' tiled roofs curved gracefully upward, like the wings of giant herons rising into the sky. The walkways and courtyards were paved with stones. Beyond the palace grounds, Mount Bukhansan rose like a giant palace guard. I looked around at Korea's most important place and was at peace. Here, I felt the spirit of my ancestors. Here, I knew what it was to be Korean.

"Why did you bring me here, Ummah?" Soo-bo asked as we walked.

"I wanted you to see this place," I answered. "It was the home of the Chosŏn Dynasty for five hundred years."

"I know. It is where Empress Myeongseong was murdered by the Japanese."

"On October 8, 1895," I said. "Tell me if you get tired."

"I'm okay for now."

We slowly strolled past a pavilion with a long porch. Here and there, tourists took snapshots of each other or gazed in awe at the colorful buildings.

Finally I said, "I want to talk to you about something."

"Oh? What is it?"

"You cannot have an abortion."

"But the doctor said I could die if I have the baby."

I looked at the gravel path. "Yes, I know," I said.

I pointed at the palace grounds. "See this place? One hundred years ago, there were many more buildings here. Hundreds more. I have seen pictures and a map of what used to be. Beautiful, majestic buildings for the emperor and empress and the royal family. They said there was no other place like it in all of Korea."

"Hundreds of buildings?" Soo-bo exclaimed. "I can't imagine. What happened to them?"

"The Japanese destroyed all but ten during their occupation. There is talk of rebuilding every one. They also want to tear down the Japanese Government-General Building and rebuild the Gwanghwamun Gate. I hope they do."

"What does this have to do with me having an abortion?"

I looked up at Mount Bukhansan while we walked. "Do you remember the comb with the two-headed dragon?" I asked.

"Yes, of course."

"Do you remember the story I told you about it?"

"Yes. The one about the rich yangban who sent her daughter away and gave her the comb."

I took Soo-bo's arm. "Come. I want to show you something."

We walked to a series of connected buildings dominated by a tall tower with five pagoda roofs, one on top of the other in layers like the branches of a great pine tree. We entered one of them. Inside was the National Museum of Korea. Glass cases filled with artifacts lined the corridors, and folk art hung on the walls. Each had a plaque describing its history.

"I come here on Tuesdays," I said. "It's free, and I can spend as much time as I want. There are things in here that remind me of my childhood."

I led Soo-bo down a corridor filled with exhibits of Korean treasures and armament. We stopped at a glass case containing a sword with detailed etchings and a gold rim along the scabbard. "See this sword?" I asked. "Look at the etchings."

Soo-bo examined the scabbard. "It has the same dragon as your comb!"

I nodded. "That is right. Read the plaque. Read it aloud."

Soo-bo leaned in and read, "In 1967, this sword was found hidden in the wall of a home once owned by a wealthy merchant. Historians believe the two-headed dragon with one head facing east and one facing west protects Korea and those who served our country. Some believed Empress Myeongseong created the symbol of the two-headed dragon, although there is no evidence she did. During their occupation of Korea, the Japanese destroyed all items they could find bearing the two-headed dragon. This sword is the only known surviving artifact."

Soo-bo stepped back. "What does it mean, Mother?"

"Before you were born, your father told me what the dragon stood for. I didn't know if it was true, but I kept the comb for years. When I discovered this sword, I knew that what he said was true."

I pointed at the sword. "Look at one more thing. How many toes does the dragon have?"

Soo-bo pressed against the case. "Four. It has four toes."

"Correct," I said. I smoothed her hair and nodded toward the exit. "Come. You look tired. Let's find a place to rest."

We went outside to the courtyard and sat on the steps of the tall building with five roofs. We looked south over Seoul and the towering new office buildings and apartments. A lazy haze hung over the city. People strolled across the grounds in front of us.

After I let a few people pass, I reached inside the pocket of my dress and took out a package. I loosened the twine and unfolded the brown cloth. Inside was the comb with the two-headed dragon.

"You still have it!" Soo-bo said. "I thought you sold it years ago."

"The story about the yangban from Seoul," I said, "I didn't make it up. My mother gave this comb to my sister and me. She got it from her grandmother, and her grandmother got it from her mother. My mother's great-grandmother, your third great-grandmother, was the one who had the comb made."

"Who was she?"

"Look at the dragon," I said. "How many toes does it have?"

Soo-bo examined the comb. "Five," she said.

"That is right," I said. "A five-toed dragon." I faced Soo-bo. "I didn't know what it meant until one day I asked a docent why the dragon on the sword had four toes. She told me that most dragons on artifacts have only three. They knew the merchant who owned the sword was a very important man because the dragon had four toes. I asked her, 'What if a dragon had five toes?' She said that dragons with five toes were only used for items belonging to the emperor and empress."

Soo-bo cocked her head. "Does that mean . . . ?"

"Yes, Soo-bo. The comb is proof that Empress Myeongseong created the symbol of the two-headed dragon and that we are her descendants. Through this comb, she has given us a responsibility to serve Korea."

Soo-bo took a few minutes to take in what she had just learned. Then she asked, "But how can I serve Korea, Mother?"

I took my daughter's hand. "Soo-bo, you are my joy. You are the only thing that has given me lasting happiness since I was a young girl. I love you, and it would break my heart if I ever lost you. But we are royalty, my daughter, and our first duty is to our country. I think you were meant to have this baby. The dragon will protect you."

I folded the cloth around the comb and gave it to Soo-bo.

She took it and stared at the package. "Do you really believe in the dragon, Mother? Do you believe it will protect me?"

It was the question that had defined my life for forty years. Did I believe the comb with the two-headed dragon, passed down from

Korea's greatest empress, had the power to protect those who possessed it? Did I believe that I was a link in a royal chain and that it was my duty to pass the comb on to my daughter? I knew the answer. With the comb, I had survived while others had perished, just like Mother, Soo-hee, and Jin-mo had said. The dragon must have protected me, and I had to believe it would protect Soo-bo, too. "Yes," I said. "I believe in the comb with the two-headed dragon."

Soo-bo nodded. "Then I will have the baby," she said.

We sat for a long time without talking, surrounded by the grandeur of Gyeongbok Palace. All around were the spirits of Korea. I prayed to them to spare my daughter.

Eventually I stood and extended a hand to Soo-bo. We had to get home so she could rest. We walked arm in arm under the Gwanghwamun Gate, back into the great city of Seoul.

FORTY-THREE

It scared me how weak Soo-bo became as her stomach swelled with the baby. It was as if the fetus was sucking the life from her, and I wondered if I had done the right thing when I talked her out of having an abortion. The doctors grew increasingly worried, too, and insisted that Soo-bo end her pregnancy. She refused. She slept long hours and forced down food even when she wasn't hungry. Every morning and night in our apartment in the 315 building, she did the breathing exercises the nurses had taught her. She studied books on how to deliver a healthy baby. I was so very proud of her. But I worried about her, too.

One night after a meal of rice and vegetables, Soo-bo went into labor. As she held her stomach and tried to breathe like she did in the exercises, I ran to the pay phone in the lobby and called a cab. It came in less than five minutes.

Earlier that afternoon, there had been a rain shower, and when I helped Soo-bo into the cab, the city lights twinkled off inky-black puddles. The rain had brought in cool air, and everything smelled clean. I prayed that it was a good sign for Soo-bo. As the cab wound through traffic on its way to the hospital, Soo-bo grimaced in pain from a contraction. I held her hand. "The doctor will give you something for the pain," I said.

"It's okay, Mother," Soo-bo replied. "It is a good pain."

As the cab pulled up to the emergency room door, Soo-bo's water broke. There was a lot of blood in it. A nurse helped her into a wheelchair. When she saw how weak Soo-bo was, the nurse called for the doctor immediately. She pulled me aside and asked how long Soo-bo had been in labor.

The concern on the nurse's face filled me with fear. "Less than an hour," I said. "We came as soon as it started."

"She shouldn't be in this much pain," the nurse said. "And there should not be this much blood."

They wheeled Soo-bo inside a blue-tiled delivery room with a large bank of lights. The nurse stripped off Soo-bo's clothes, dressed her in a hospital gown, and laid her in a bed with stirrups for her feet. She gave Soo-bo a shot for her pain and spread a blue sheet over her. I stood at my daughter's side and held her hand.

As another contraction started to build in Soo-bo, the doctor entered the room. He asked about Soo-bo's condition.

"She's in a lot of pain," the nurse replied, "and she's been in labor for less than an hour. Her blood pressure and heart rate are very high."

The doctor picked up Soo-bo's wrist and felt for her pulse. "What can you tell me about her?" he asked.

"Her heart is weak," I answered.

The doctor dropped Soo-bo's arm. "Yes, it is," he said gravely. He ordered the nurse to get a heart monitor and some help. "Now!" he barked.

As the nurse ran out, the doctor lifted the blue sheet and looked between Soo-bo's scrawny legs. "The baby is breeched," he said, "and the mother has lost too much blood for a Cesarean."

Soo-bo arched her back from a contraction, and her body shook. The twisted pain in her face made me hate myself for making her have this baby.

"Breathe!" the doctor ordered from under the sheet. "Get her to breathe," he said to me.

I leaned over my daughter. "Soo-bo, you have to breathe. Deep breaths like the book said."

Soo-bo closed her eyes and tried to take in deep breaths, but it only came in gasps. She gripped the bed with both hands. Beads of sweat formed on her forehead.

"Nurse!" the doctor yelled toward the door. "Get that heart monitor in here!"

I squeezed Soo-bo's arm. "Breathe, Soo-bo," I begged. "Please, breathe."

After a few minutes, the contraction subsided, and Soo-bo sank into the bed. Her face was ashen, and sweat matted her hair. The doctor put his stethoscope over her heart. "We need to turn the baby," he said. "But the mother's heart is arrhythmic. We have to change our approach before the next contraction. I'll be right back."

The doctor ran out of the room, shouting angry orders at the staff outside. Soo-bo blinked her eyes open and looked at me.

"Am I doing it right, Mother?" she asked.

I stroked her sweat-soaked hair. "Yes, my daughter. You are doing it just right."

"Good," she said. "What should I name my baby?"

"Her name should be Ja-young."

"Why should she be named Ja-young, Mother?"

I leaned in close and wiped my daughter's brow. "Because it is a royal name. She should have a royal name."

Soo-bo smiled and nodded. "Ja-young. Yes, that is a good name. I will name my baby Ja-young."

Then Soo-bo asked, "Do you have the comb? I should hold it so the dragon will protect me."

My heart stopped. In the panic to get to the hospital, I had forgotten to take the comb from its place under the windowsill in our apartment. I couldn't give it to Soo-bo.

Suddenly the door to the delivery room flew open, and the doctor and nurse rushed through. Another contraction began to build in Soo-bo. She closed her eyes and gritted her teeth. Her back arched high.

"We're too late," the doctor said from between Soo-bo's legs. "We don't have time for anything else. What's her pulse?"

The nurse held Soo-bo's wrist and answered, "I can't get a reading."

I watched in horror as Soo-bo's body convulsed as if an unseen spirit was shaking her. She clawed at the bed. Her eyes rolled back, and her mouth opened. She did not breathe, and neither did I. As I stood there in the blue-tiled delivery room watching my daughter writhe in pain, I prayed to the spirits of my ancestors to save her. I prayed to Myeongseong, Korea's great empress. And I prayed that the two-headed dragon had the magic to protect Soo-bo even when she couldn't hold it.

"Her heart stopped!" the nurse said.

I stared at my precious daughter. "Soo-bo," I whispered.

A second doctor and two nurses burst into the room with a heart monitor and oxygen. The doctor went to Soo-bo's side and hooked up the monitor while one of the nurses put the oxygen mask over Soo-bo's face. The other nurse took me by the arm. "You have to go outside now, ma'am," she insisted. "Quickly."

As the nurse led me to the door, I looked at Soo-bo one more time. "My baby," I said. "Ye deulah."

I was numb as I stared at the delivery room door. I do not know how long I sat there. On the other side, the doctors and nurses worked on Soo-bo. Medical staff rushed in and out. Time seemed to stop, and I was afraid that I had made a tragic mistake by convincing my daughter to have her baby. I had told her the dragon would protect her, but now I didn't know if it would. In times like this, it was hard for me to believe that Soo-bo and I were direct descendants of Empress Myeongseong, responsible to carry on the legacy of the two-headed dragon. Certainly I believed in the spirits of my ancestors. I could feel them inside me and see them in the people and land of my country. But if Soo-bo and I were a part of their grand scheme, why didn't they help us? Why did we have to suffer and die for Korea?

Eventually the doctor pushed his way out the door and slowly walked toward me. Blood covered his lab coat, and his eyes were sunken. He bowed to me. "We did everything we could," he said. "Her heart just wasn't strong enough. We could not save her."

I was unable to move or to breathe or to see anything beyond his words. My sweet, sweet Soo-bo. The child I carried close in my womb, who suckled and slept at my breast, who I taught to walk and read, who I loved so much that the loving hurt me inside. My daughter was dead, and I had killed her because of the cursed comb and my duty to Korea. I wished I could go back and refuse to take the comb from Soo-hee in the comfort station. But I had accepted it, and now it had cost me everything.

I heard myself say, "What about the baby?"

"She is fine," the doctor answered. "Strong, in fact. A beautiful girl. Would you like to hold her?"

The doctor stepped aside, and I saw in a nurse's arms a bundle wrapped in a yellow blanket. Slowly I rose to my feet. The nurse stepped forward and gave me the baby. I pressed her to my breast. Beneath the blanket, I could feel her short breaths. I softly ran my hand over her smooth, warm head. With a finger, I traced the lines of her high cheekbones and her delicate nose. I pressed my finger into the baby's hand, and she gripped it with long fingers. I could feel the spirit of Korea strong inside her.

"She is an empress," I whispered. "Her name is Ja-young." I looked up at the nurse. "Be sure she is given that name."

I looked back at the baby and reached into the depths of my soul for one final bit of strength. "And an empress needs a family where she can grow strong so that she can do what she must do." Then I pushed down one last cry and held the baby out to the nurse. "Please," I said, struggling to push the words out, "I would like to put my granddaughter up for adoption."

FORTY-FOUR

August 2008. Seoul, South Korea

The comb with the two-headed dragon sits on the table between Mrs. Hong and me. The magnificent comb with the gold spine and ivory dragon gleams in the evening light. Next to it are the mugunghwa blossom and the photographs of my grandmother's family and her daughter —my birth mother, Soo-bo.

"Now do you understand why I sent you away?" Mrs. Hong says. "I had nothing left to give. I died the day Soo-bo died, just like my mother did when Soo-hee and I left home. So I made the decision to have you adopted. I didn't know if I would ever see you again. But I believed that if the dragon was true, if everything I had suffered through was part of a grand enterprise to make Korea great, then the spirits of my ancestors would bring you back to me someday. And here you are, my granddaughter, here you are. I believe in the two-headed dragon, and I believe it is your destiny to have the comb."

I shake my head. "I don't know."

Mrs. Hong sighs and looks at me. "Why did you come to Korea?" she asks.

"To see where I was born. To meet my birth mother. To learn what it means for me to be Korean."

"And what have you learned?"

I think of Mrs. Hong's story and all the things I saw on our trip. Nothing adds up to any real answer. "I can't say for sure," I say.

"You should know about Empress Myeongseong," Mrs. Hong says. She folds her hands in her lap. "Her name was Min Ja-young. She was born in 1851 to a poor clan from Seoul. She was very beautiful and quite intelligent. At fifteen years old, her family arranged for her to marry Yi Myeong-bok, the boy king of the House of Yi. The king was lazy and incompetent, so Ja-young taught herself history, science, politics, and religion. She had a good ear for languages and learned to speak Japanese, Chinese, English, and Russian. Eventually she acquired great power. She promoted education, modernization, freedom of the press, the arts, and equality for women. They say she modeled herself after Queen Victoria of England."

Mrs. Hong puts her hands around the bowl that holds the mugung-hwa. She admires the purple blossom. "The empress took power during a time when Korea was being fought over by the Chinese and Japanese. She was a skilled diplomat and was able to keep both powers in check. But the Japanese were powerful and threatened to take Korea for themselves. That is when she created the secret society of the two-headed dragon. She employed skilled artisans to make artifacts with the dragon for members of the society and her family. She had shamans instill magic in them."

Mrs. Hong takes her hands from the bowl and picks up the comb. "Isn't it interesting that the empress had a comb made for herself instead of a sword or some other kind of armament? Look at it. It is a woman's comb. You can tell by the long tines. The empress knew that if her secret got out, the Japanese would kill her and persecute her son. So she gave the comb to her daughter."

"At the history museum, they told us she only had a son," I say.

"You are correct. You were paying attention. Good. Yes, history books say she only had a son. But it is not true. You see, back then, it was common for the royal family to say the first child died if it was a girl. Then they would keep the girl cloistered in the palace. It turned out to be a fortunate thing. When the empress learned the Japanese planned to assassinate her, she moved her daughter to our family farm and gave her this comb with the two-headed dragon."

Mrs. Hong sets the comb on the table. Her eyes narrow. "On October 8, 1895, the shameful Japanese murdered my great-great-grandmother, your fourth great-grandmother. Assassins snuck into Gyeongbok Palace where the empress was sleeping. They dragged her out of bed and hacked her to death. The assassination marked the beginning of Japanese dominance in Korea and our darkest hour."

"When you learned about the two-headed dragon, why didn't you just give the comb to the government?" I ask.

"Because it was as Mr. Han said when he dismissed me from Gongson Construction: my *yi* was what was most important. I have a duty to Korea and to my ancestors and to my descendants." She points to the comb. "Look at the dragon. The heads do not just look east and west. They also look backward and forward. It is a symbol they do not explain at the museum. You see, in Korea, when we look back, we see all of our ancestors all the way back to the three kingdoms to Tan'gun, the father of Korea, who reigned four thousand five hundred years ago. Each of our ancestors has given us a duty that we must fulfill. And when we look forward, we see the generations of our descendants. We love them like grandparents, but expect them to honor their duty to us as we have honored our duty to our ancestors. It is a single, unbroken chain. If I gave the comb away, I would have broken that chain and not fulfilled my duty to Korea."

"And you think I have a duty to Korea, too? But I'm an American, not a Korean."

Mrs. Hong taps a finger at me. "Do you think because you were raised in America that you are not Korean? Then why did you come here? And why did you come to my apartment to hear my story? Just like me, you were born in the year of the dragon. The spirits of your ancestors are strong inside you. You have a duty to them—a duty to Korea. You must tell my story for Soo-hee, for Jin-mo, for Korea. And for me. As long as you serve Korea, the dragon will protect you."

I run a hand through my hair and stare at the comb. The dragon stares back at me. I don't know. Her story seems a bit too much, if you know what I mean. But when I see the lines in her face and the pain in her eyes, I think it has to be true.

"Ja-young," she says, "now that you have heard my story, you must decide what to do. You have to decide before you go back to America."

Back to America. I check my watch. It's 4:30 p.m. "Oh no!" I say, jumping up from the table. "Excuse me, ma'am. The bus has already left for the airport. Mr. Kwan said he'd arrest me if I miss my flight." I grab my purse.

Mrs. Hong's eyes plead with me. "I have sacrificed everything for Korea," she says. "Take the comb. Tell our story."

I shake my head. "I just don't know."

She puts her hand over her chest. "Ja-young . . . Anna, what does your heart say?"

I try to search my heart, but I'm conflicted, unsure, and afraid, like I have been since Mother died. I look at the comb. It's a Korean comb, made by Korea's most important queen. But I'm an American and have been since I was a baby. I don't know anything else. Yet in the mirror, I see the Korean woman. There is a yearning in her eyes. Her heart aches for something that I can't explain.

I pick up the comb and hold it in my hand. I think perhaps it speaks to the woman in the mirror. I think she wants me to take it. I nod slowly. "Okay. I'll take it. Maybe you should send it to me."

"I am afraid that is no longer possible. Now that the government knows who I am, they will be watching me. You have to find another way."

"They're watching me, too," I say. "But I have an idea." I can't believe what I'm planning to do. It makes me nervous, but excited, too. For the first time in a long time, I'm taking charge, and I like it.

Mrs. Hong takes the comb from me and gives it one last look. Then she ties the brown cloth around it and says, "I told you there were two things I wanted you to do for me. One was to hear my story. There is one more thing as well."

"Oh yeah. You never said what it was."

"I want you to help me see my onni before I die."

Of course. Mrs. Hong never saw Soo-hee after Dongfeng, and now that she's given me the comb, the only thing she has left to do is to see her sister again. "I'm not sure I can do that," I say.

"I believe you can," she says. Yeah. The way I'm feeling all of a sudden, I think I can, too.

I stand before her with the comb in my hand. Our eyes meet one last time, and I bow low.

◆ ◆ ◆

I run outside, and, thank God, my taxi driver is waiting for me. He complains that he waited for an hour and a half. I toss a hundred dollars at him and tell him to take me to the Kosney store by our hotel. "Hurry," I say.

We speed through the streets of Seoul, and when we get to Kosney, I tell my driver to wait for me. The huge department store looks a lot like Macy's, only all the signs are in Hangul and the prices are in won. As I run down an aisle, a clerk says something to me in Korean.

"What?" I say.

"I am sorry," she replies in English, "we are closing soon, ma'am."

I ask where the celadon pots are. She tells me they're on the second floor and points to an escalator. I take the escalator two stairs at a time and find the area with the blue-green pots. I run up to the counter, and a clerk greets me in Korean. I tell her I want to buy two pots.

"Two?" she asks in English.

"Yes. A large one and a small one."

She takes my order and information, and I pay for the pots with the cash Dad gave me. I grab the box and run back out to the taxi. I tell the cabbie to take me to the Sejong Hotel. When we pull up to the hotel, Dad is standing at the front door with our suitcases waiting for me. He looks panicked.

"Anna, thank God," he says. "Where have you been? The bus left over an hour ago. We won't make our flight!"

"Get in," I say, waving him into the taxi. "We might still make it."

Dad shoves our suitcases in the back of the cab, and we cram inside the backseat. I put the box with the celadon pot between us. "Incheon Airport," Dad says. "As fast as you can."

The driver throws the car into gear, and we race onto the street. Even though it's rush hour, the traffic moves. The driver swerves from lane to lane to make good time. Over the top of the box, Dad asks, "You gave the comb back, right?"

"No," I answer.

His brow furrows. "Some government officials came to the hotel looking for it. They searched our room and asked a lot of questions. They might be waiting for us at the airport. Anna, you'll get in trouble if you have it."

"Don't worry," I say, trying to sound convincing.

Twenty minutes later, we pull up to the drop-off zone in front of the giant glass and steel half-dome of the Incheon airport. The flight leaves in thirty minutes, and we were supposed to have checked in over an hour ago. Dad jerks the suitcases from the trunk and pushes a hundred dollars at the cabbie. I take my celadon pot, and we sprint toward the ticket counter. When we get there, I freeze. Waiting for us are Mr. Kwan, Bruce Willis, and several airport security guards.

FORTY-FIVE

Mr. Kwan sees me before I can turn away. He marches up to us. "We have been waiting for you," he says with his diplomatic smile. "If you had been any later, we would've let the plane go and arrested you. I will have the airline hold the plane for you, and if you do not have the comb, I will let you go back to America. You should check in first," he says, pointing to the ticket counter.

Other travelers gawk at us as two male security agents take our luggage and the box with my celadon pot. Dad and I go to the counter and give our passports and tickets to the agent. Mr. Kwan steps up and says something to an official-looking man. The official bows to Mr. Kwan and then shoots an angry look at us. He disappears around the back of a glass panel behind the ticket counter.

After the check-in agent hands us our boarding passes, Mr. Kwan tells us to follow him. We walk through the modern terminal, past a duty-free and a Louis Vuitton store. There's the obligatory McDonald's, too. We come to a door just off the entrance to the concourse. An airport security guard unlocks the door with a key attached to his belt, and Mr. Kwan points us inside.

The lights in the room are bright and hurt my eyes. There's a long metal table, an airport luggage scanner, and a people scanner that leads to an outside door. I try not to stare at the security guard who opens the box with the celadon pot. Another guard lifts our suitcases onto the table and zips them open. They begin sifting through the contents, searching the pockets, our shoes, Dad's shaving kit, our toiletries—everywhere we might have hidden the comb. One by one, they pass everything through the scanner while a third guard stares into a monitor. Bruce Willis has his back against the door and watches everything.

As the guards pick through our luggage, Mr. Kwan tells us that they have to frisk us, and then we have to go through the people scanner. A guard stands next to him with a metal detecting wand. Mr. Kwan explains that the "examination," as he calls it, is necessary to ensure we're not taking the comb out of the country. "I assure you," he says, "if you have it, we will find it."

"This isn't right," Dad complains.

"Of course," Mr. Kwan says, "if one of you has the comb, you can give it to me now and avoid this unpleasantness."

Dad glances at me, but I say nothing. After a few seconds, Mr. Kwan tells Dad to take off his shoes and raise his arms. The security guard runs his wand up and down Dad's body and legs. When he's finished, Mr. Kwan tells Dad to walk through the scanner. Dad does, and the light on top turns green. Mr. Kwan points to the door. "Wait for your daughter in the concourse," he says.

Dad looks worried. "It's all right," I say. "I'll be there in a minute." Dad frowns and goes out the door.

Mr. Kwan tells me to take off my shoes. I give them to a guard, who runs them through the scanner. The guard with the wand steps up to me and waves it over me like he did with Dad and the way they did in Mrs. Hong's apartment. This time I'm strangely calm, almost as if this is happening to someone else. I'm not embarrassed or the least bit afraid. I feel like someone I don't know is controlling me.

I stare at Mr. Kwan. "So it's true, isn't it?" I say. "The two-headed dragon is a powerful symbol for Korea."

"It is just a valuable artifact," he says as the guard wands my legs.

"No, it's more than that," I hear myself say. "A five-toed dragon with two heads. It's a symbol from Empress Myeongseong."

The security guard finishes frisking me and hands me my shoes. "Is that what your grandmother told you?" Mr. Kwan asks.

"Yeah, it is," I say, pulling on my shoes. "She said the comb has been in our family for generations. She said that I'm a descendant of Empress Myeongseong."

Mr. Kwan shakes his head. "I read your adoption papers, Ms. Carlson. Just because she gave you the same name as the empress does not make you related to her. Many Koreans say they are descendants of royalty."

"Yes," I say, "but she had the comb with a five-toed dragon that you want so badly, didn't she?"

Mr. Kwan nods almost imperceptibly. "Yes, she did."

I stand before the people scanner with my eyes still locked on Mr. Kwan. He raises his chin. "I see you bought a celadon pot," he says.

The corners of my mouth turn up. "I got it at Kosney," I say. "I heard the quality is much better than the ones on the street."

For the first time since I met him, he gives me a genuine smile. And then he says, "Take care of yourself, Ja-young."

I'm completely at ease as I walk through the scanner and the light turns green.

◆ ◆ ◆

Dad and I sprint to our gate carrying our suitcases and my celadon pot. When we get to the gangway, a luggage handler is waiting for us. He takes our bags, and we board the plane. As we find our seats, the other passengers glare at us for delaying their flight.

After we settle in, Dad whispers, "What happened? Where were you all day? And what happened to the . . . package?"

"It's safe," I answer. "I'll tell you all about it when we get home." Dad gives me one of those looks that parents give their kids, but he lets it slide.

We have two seats together over the wing. Dad's on the aisle and I'm at the window. The airplane pulls away from the gate and rumbles down the runway. Soon we're crossing over the Korean peninsula toward the Sea of Japan. A monitor on the bulkhead shows our progress with a yellow line over a map of the North Pacific. I'm relieved to be going home.

An hour into our flight, we've crossed over the Japanese island of Hokkaido. The monitor says we're cruising at thirty-eight thousand feet heading toward the Aleutian Islands. The airplane hums quietly, and there're only a few overhead lights on. Dad is sleeping. Asleep, he finally looks peaceful.

I'm wiped out. I can't even begin to grasp all that's happened on this trip. I know there'll be plenty of time to think it through when we get home, so I set it all aside. I look out the window at a billion stars.

My eyes are heavy, so I turn off the light and pull the blanket to my chin. I curl up in the seat, and soon I'm asleep. As we head home, the people and places of my Korean grandmother's life story fill my dreams.

FORTY-SIX

When I was growing up, my family didn't have a big house or fancy cars or a cabin on a lake "Up North." We didn't spend money on boats or snowmobiles or ATVs like many of our friends did. We didn't buy the latest fashions. But I didn't mind. We traveled instead.

Dad always said that to understand the world, you had to smell it. So by the time I graduated from high school, I'd smelled Europe and Canada three times each, Mexico and the Caribbean twice each, Central America, Kenya, Australia, and New Zealand. I'd been in forty-one states (airports don't count) and had my US National Park passport book stamped twenty-nine times.

And now I've smelled Korea, the country where I was born.

When I get home, it's as if I've stepped into some alternative universe. Everything's bigger and more alive. Cars are shinier, buildings are taller, the sky is bluer, and the summer air seems positively musky with life. Yet at the same time, everything seems somehow more manageable, kind of like when you're in the zone playing sports. I can't explain why, really. I suppose it's because I have a new context to put it all into—my birth grandmother's amazing life and the new knowledge I have of the people I share DNA with. For the first time since Mother died, I'm looking forward to the next chapter in my life.

The day after we get home, I tell Dad that the woman who gave me the comb was my birth grandmother. I tell him her incredible story and that I promised to try to help her meet her sister someday. I decide not to tell him about me being a descendant of Empress Myeongseong or that Mrs. Hong says I have to serve Korea somehow. I feel guilty about keeping it from him, but honestly, I really don't know if any of it is true.

Dad listens carefully and asks questions. I answer them as best as I can. Then he asks about the comb. I tell him it's just a family heirloom that Mrs. Hong wants me to have to remind me of my Korean heritage. "Why were those government officials so intent on it?" he asks.

"It's just an heirloom, Dad," I repeat. He raises an eyebrow, but doesn't ask any more questions.

That night I think about going back to college to finish my senior year. When I left, Northwestern said they'd let me come back. Dad says I should do it, but I decide to stay home and enroll at the University of Minnesota instead. I log on to the U's website to see what my class options are. I'm still not sure what I should take, and the deadline is only a few days away. I bring up my list of pros and cons for medical school versus law school. Medical school and residency would be an expensive, ten-year grind. But in the end, I'd have a prestigious job and a good income. Law school would be a piece of cake compared to medical school. It'd be three years of school and a few years as a law associate. But a career in law isn't exactly a sure thing like medicine is.

Or I could do something completely different. I don't know.

My choices on the computer monitor stare at me. I search my heart for the right answer like Mrs. Hong said I should. It's not telling me anything. So I log off. I still have a few days.

It saddens me when Dad falls back into his miserable routine. Each day he leaves for work early and comes home in time to sit in the living room with the shades closed. When he puts on his grilling apron to make dinner, he makes the same things each week. On Monday, it's Mother's goulash. On Tuesday, it's Mother's baked tilapia. Wednesday, it's her parmesan chicken . . . and so on. Every week it's the same thing, and every recipe is Mother's. When I offer to make something different, Dad says, "No. I'll do it."

◆ ◆ ◆

One day, I do a search for the Korean embassy, and I see there's a consulate in Minneapolis. It's on Park Avenue, where businesses have converted the 1800s mansions into hip offices for lawyers and psychologists. I jump in Mom's Corolla and drive there. The consulate is on the third floor of a three-story stone mansion. I climb two flights of stairs to a reception area with a flag of South Korea on a stand in the corner. A Korean woman sits behind a glass desk. She smiles pleasantly through stylish, red-framed glasses. "May I help you?" she asks.

"I want to arrange a meeting with someone in North Korea," I say.

"I see," she says. "You need to talk with Mr. Han."

She points me to a couch and offers to get me coffee, which I decline. Then she disappears into the back while I wait. On the wall are travel posters for South Korea. It's really a beautiful country. Rolling hills, jagged granite peaks, two seacoasts, the exciting capital of Seoul where I was born.

Eventually a man in a navy blue suit, white shirt, and red tie comes to the lobby and greets me with a handshake. He has a Korean flag lapel pin. "I'm Mr. Han," he says. "I understand you want to connect with someone in the North?" He speaks English with only a slight accent. He's slender and lean. He has an intelligent face. I guess he's in his midthirties.

"Yes," I answer. "It's a long story."

"I would be glad to hear it," Mr. Han says. He tells me to follow him, and we walk down the hall into a large office that was probably once the mansion's master bedroom. Embroidered rugs cover the hardwood floors, the walls are wood paneled, and a dormered window overlooks the street. A window air conditioner hums quietly. I sit on a couch off to the side of his desk. He sits in a chair next to it.

He folds his hands in his lap and asks my name. I give it and tell him my parents adopted me when I was a baby. He asks me to tell him more about my request. I tell him about my trip to Korea and that I met my Korean grandmother. I give him a summary of her story. I'm careful not to say anything about the comb with the two-headed dragon or that Empress Myeongseong is my fourth great-grandmother. I tell him I agreed to help Mrs. Hong meet her sister.

When I'm done, Mr. Han nods. "Very interesting," he says. "How do you know your grandmother's story is true?"

I think about it for a second. "I guess I don't for sure," I admit.

He smiles. "Well, we will see what we can do."

I push myself to the edge of the couch. "So you think you can arrange a meeting?"

Mr. Han shrugs. "There are times when it can be done. But I am afraid we are not in one of those times presently."

"Why not?"

He leans forward. "You realize, of course, that North and South Korea are still officially at war. There was no formal peace treaty signed after the hostilities ended in 1953. The two sides only agreed to a cease-fire, and tensions are very high right now—especially with the North testing nuclear weapons."

"Yeah, I know. But I've read that families sometimes get to meet."

He nods. "It depends on the state of affairs between the two countries. Sometimes these meetings can shut down for years. And when they open up, it has to be done through . . . unofficial channels."

"What do you mean, 'unofficial channels'?"

He gives me a sly yet diplomatic look. "What you might call bribes, Ms. Carlson, for both sides. It costs a lot of money."

I ask, "Okay. So how much is a lot of money?"

He says an amount that's a lot more than my tuition at the U for a year. "I'm not sure I can afford that," I say.

"It doesn't matter if you can," Mr. Han replies. "As I said, the two countries are not allowing any contact right now."

"When do you think they will?"

"It is impossible to say, I'm afraid."

I nod. "Well, can you let me know? I made a promise."

"I will be glad to. Give all your information to Ja-sook at the reception desk. In the meantime, we will see what we can find out about your grandmother's sister. She might not even be alive. But if she is, and when things open up, we can help make the arrangements. That is, if you can pay the fee."

Mr. Han stands and extends his hand, and I shake it. "It was a pleasure meeting you," he says.

I give him a bow and ask for his business card. When he gives it to me, I remember to take it with both hands and examine it respectfully. I thank him and say I hope to hear from him soon.

◆　◆　◆

When I get home, I'm relieved to see that the small celadon pot I shipped from Kosney has arrived via Federal Express. I open the box and reach inside the pot beneath the packing paper where I slipped the comb with the two-headed dragon when the store clerk wasn't looking. It's still there. Somehow I knew it would be.

I take the comb to our bank and open a safe deposit box account. The ancient female clerk gives me my key and shows me to a privacy room. I close the door and take the comb out of my purse. Before putting it into the box, I unwrap it from the brown cloth and study it one more time.

Here in the quiet of the privacy room, I finally have a chance to really look at it. I marvel at how the craftsman turned such tiny pieces of ivory into the lifelike two-headed dragon. I examine the gold edge. It fits perfectly with the curve of the dark green tortoiseshell. The comb really is amazing, a thing worthy of royalty.

As I hold the comb in my hand, I think of everything it went through with my birth grandmother, and how she kept it and protected it all her life. Each of the long, delicate tines are still there. There isn't a scratch on it anywhere. Maybe the comb really is magical.

And now it has found its way to me. Now it's my responsibility. As I wrap it up and place it in the safe deposit box, I wonder—and worry—what it will mean for me.

FORTY-SEVEN

It's Thursday—pot roast day—and I go home from class in a freezing December wind. It hasn't snowed yet this winter, but the ground is frozen, and the wind is blowing from the north. The low clouds threaten our first snow of the season. The news media is practically hyperventilating, telling people to stay home to escape what might be this year's version of the "Storm of the Century." Right. Weeks earlier, I dug out my winter coat from our basement storage room, and now I wrap it tight around me. I press into the wind for the three-block walk to the parking lot.

It's a week before fall finals, and it's seriously been the most amazing college semester I've had. I decided to take a class on world history and two on political science. I'm getting all As, and I'll graduate near the top of my class. I'm also taking Korean. I'm learning it so fast that my instructor is encouraging me to take two accelerated courses next semester. I've decided to do it.

I took the law school entrance exam last month. I was nervous about it. I mean, really, some of these people have been studying for the LSAT for years. So I was shocked when I scored in the upper 5 percent. I've always been a good test-taker. But seriously, the upper 5 percent? I'm already getting letters from top schools across the country inviting me to apply. Naturally I'm making a "pros and cons" list. But I'm also trying to listen to my heart.

Before I reach my car, my phone rings. It's Mr. Han from the Korean consulate. He says he has news and wants to meet with me. Over the past several months, I called Mr. Han every few weeks or so to check in. He always gave the same answer. "We don't know anything yet," he'd say. "Please be patient. These things take time."

This is the first time he's called me, so I tell him I'll meet with him right away. I jump in my car and drive to the mansion on Park Avenue. When I go inside, Ja-sook shows me into Mr. Han's office. After a short wait, he comes in carrying a folder. He still wears the Korean flag lapel pin. He apologizes that he's taken so long to get back to me. He tells me that over the past several months, it was impossible to reach their contacts in the North because Pyongyang was testing nuclear weapons and the two countries had cut off all contact.

Now, however, relations have improved, and they've learned that Hong Soo-hee is alive and living in Pyongyang. "I must admit," he says, shaking his head, "when you told me your grandmother's story, I was skeptical. I thought you might be involved in a scam. So I inquired about your grandmother. I am pleased to tell you everything she told you is true."

I look out the window. The snow is starting to fall. So that's it. My birth grandmother's story is true. I guess in my heart I knew that it was. "Well, if that's the case," I say, "I want to set up the meeting between Mrs. Hong and her sister as soon as possible."

"Of course. It could still take months. And there is the issue of the money."

"I think I can get it."

Mr. Han frowns. "I am sorry to tell you there is a change with respect to the cost. You see, it has become more expensive."

"Oh?" I say, sagging into my chair. "How much more?"

"Well, there is a large backlog. Years' worth, I'm afraid. And that has caused the cost to double."

"Are you serious?" I reply with a gasp. I do some quick math in my head. "I can't afford that."

"Well, you could wait until there isn't a backlog. But there is no saying how long this window will stay open.

"There is one more thing," Mr. Han says. "You will have to go to Korea personally to sponsor your grandmother. It is all very complicated, and it would be difficult for an elderly woman like her to do this on her own."

"Yeah, I understand. That's another expense, I suppose. I'll have to let you know."

He smiles politely and extends a hand. I respectfully take it with both of mine and bow my head, like I've learned proper Koreans are supposed to do.

On the drive home, the streets are slick. Rush hour will be a disaster. It's just starting, so I hurry to make it home before I'm caught in it. As I drive, I think about Mrs. Hong and her sister and how they haven't seen each other for over sixty years, and I'm torn. I think about law school and the cost of tuition, books, and room and board. The only way I can pay Mr. Han's steep fee is to get a job and forgo law school for a couple of years. By then, who knows? Law school might have passed me by.

◆ ◆ ◆

When I walk inside our house, I expect to smell pot roast cooking in the oven and see the table set. But I don't smell anything, and there aren't any plates on the table.

I call out to tell Dad I'm home, and he shouts a hello from upstairs. I drop my backpack on the kitchen table and find him in his bedroom. He's facing the mirror, putting on a clean shirt.

"It's pot roast night," I say. "It's not in the oven. What gives?"

"I was thinking maybe we could go out," he says, tucking his shirt in. I almost fall down. "Seriously? On a Thursday night?"

He turns from the mirror. "I feel guilty saying this about your mother's pot roast, but I get tired of it every week. I was thinking we could go to Ho Ban instead. We haven't been there in a long time. What do you say?"

After I pick up my jaw from the floor, I agree that Korean food would be a nice change of pace. I tell him I need some time and head off to my room. As I change my clothes and brush my hair, I wonder what's gotten into my father. He hasn't been sitting in the living room in the dark as much. Twice in the past month, he came home late from work, and I had to make dinner. And just last week I was shocked to see he stopped wearing his wedding ring.

A short while later, we drive through the last of the rush hour traffic to the restaurant in a suburban strip mall. The restaurant is the only decent business in the tacky mall. It's nearly full of customers, most of them Korean. They give us a table near the kitchen. I notice they've tried to fix up the place since I was here last. There's a new greeting station at the front door, and they've painted a Korean landscape on one wall.

It doesn't help. The lighting is bad, and the tables and chairs are cheap and too close together. It's no big deal, though. People come here for the food—real Korean food, just like we had in Korea. Hot pots, rice bowls, Korean noodles, katsu, bibimbap, bulgogi, Korean monkfish. A dozen plates of banchan appetizers fill each table. And, of course, there's kimchi. The smells are amazing, just like I remember them from Korea. I wonder why it's been so long since I've been here.

We decide what we'll order, and when the waiter comes, Dad orders extra, saying we can have the leftovers tomorrow instead of our usual Friday night spaghetti. The banchan arrives, and we dive in. The kimchi is spicy and wonderful.

"This reminds me of our trip," Dad says, fumbling with his chopsticks.

"Yeah, it does," I say, picking up more kimchi.

We make small talk, and when our entrees arrive, we attack them. Dad eats like he hasn't eaten for a week. He finishes his dish and then sneaks a few bites off my plate. I notice that he's filled out a bit over the past few months. His cheekbones don't stick out, and his color is better. And he smiles more.

"I met with Mr. Han from the consulate after school," I say. "They discovered that Mrs. Hong's sister is alive and living in Pyongyang. Apparently tensions between the North and South have let up, and they can arrange a meeting now."

"Hmm, I see," Dad says. "And you made that promise."

"I'm not sure I can keep it. The cost has gone way up. It's ridiculous. I'd have to put off law school and get a job."

"No," Dad says, shaking his head. "You shouldn't put off school."

"I don't know how I'll do it any other way," I say.

Dad turns quiet as we finish our meal. When we can't eat another bite, the waiter puts all the leftovers into boxes, and we head home. Snow is falling hard as we drive north over the Minnesota River. I don't know, maybe the news was right. This is feeling like a major storm. There's not much traffic, and Dad drives slowly. We are quiet. The meal has subdued us.

Halfway home Dad says, "Anna, I want to talk to you about something."

"Oh?" I say. "What about?"

"Tell you what," he says. "Let's take a drive around the lakes. Your mother and I liked to go out in the first snow. It scares people off the roads, but I think it's beautiful."

We turn off the freeway and go to the parkway that connects the Minneapolis lakes. The snow is making everything clean and quiet. I ask Dad what he wants to talk about. He tells me that he's looked into my comb and the two-headed dragon.

"I thought I should," he says apologetically.

"What did you find out?" I ask.

"A two-headed dragon with five toes," he says. "I found out what it means. The dragon protects Korea and those who possess it so they can serve Korea." And then he says, "Five toes on a dragon. It means—"

"Yeah, I know what it means," I say. "It means it belonged to Empress Myeongseong. It means I'm a direct descendant."

"Only if Mrs. Hong's story is true," he says.

"It's true, Dad," I say. "The consulate looked into it. Her story checks out."

Dad doesn't respond to this tidbit. He keeps his eyes on the road as we turn onto the boulevard that circles Lake Harriet. The mansions surrounding the lake have their holiday lights on, which sparkle off the new snow. The pointed roofs of the Lake Harriet band shell make it look like it's straight out of a winter fairy tale. It feels like Christmas Day, and I understand why Mom and Dad liked driving in the snow.

"Sweetheart," Dad says finally, "this whole thing makes me nervous. But I've been doing a lot of thinking lately. I've been thinking about your mother and how she died. It was horrible how that damn cancer killed her. But she didn't let cancer or even death define her. She simply made them a part of her life. And it made me realize that you can die when you're still alive, holed up in your house, in your living room with the shades pulled." He shoots me a guilty look.

"And I've been thinking about you, too," he continues. "Your mother and I sensed there was something special about you when you were just a kid. You were smart, of course, but there was something in the way you carried yourself. I never figured out what it was exactly. But now you have that comb with the two-headed dragon. I don't know how you're supposed to serve Korea, but I think you need to find out. And I can help. Let me pay Mr. Han's fee."

I start to protest, but Dad cuts me off with a wave.

"I'm not just doing it for you," he says. "It won't be easy. But it might help keep me out of the dark living room."

"Thank you," I say, and Dad smiles.

"There's one condition," he says. "Promise me you'll be careful."

"I promise," I say.

"I love you, sweetheart," he says.

"I love you, too, Dad," I reply.

We come full circle around the lake, and Dad turns off the boulevard to go home. For the first time in years, I'm at peace. I can feel the two parts of me—Korean and American—coming together. Like Dad, I don't know how I'm supposed to serve Korea, but I'm not afraid anymore. As Mrs. Hong said, the courageous little seed has broken through, and someday a flower will bloom. I can't wait to see it.

FORTY-EIGHT

After Dad closes on a second mortgage on our house, I call Mr. Han and tell him I have the money for his fee. He calls me back two months later and tells me that they can arrange a meeting between the sisters anytime. All I need to do is tell him when I can go.

I make the travel arrangements for July, after finals and graduation. I tell Dad he should go with me, but he says no. He tells me he'd love to meet my birth grandmother, "but this is your thing," he says. "You should go alone." So I buy my plane ticket, and as I always do, I make out a detailed itinerary for while I'm in Korea. On the list is an entire day at Gyeongbok Palace.

Two months before I start my first year at Columbia Law School, I send a letter to Mrs. Hong telling her I'll be in Seoul and that I want to meet her. I don't tell her why. A week later, I board a 747 for Seoul to fulfill my promise to her.

After we land at Incheon Airport, I clear customs and catch a cab outside baggage claim. I give the driver the address where I'll meet the contact who has the details of the meeting. As we drive through Seoul, I look for what I remember about the city. In a strange way, it feels like a second home now. The soaring Seoul Tower on top of

Mount Namsan still dominates the city. All around, apartment buildings still stand like so many soldiers at attention. The city hums with excitement.

I'm thrilled to be back here. I want to see this country again now that I know more about its history, culture, and people. I won't be a tourist this time, but someone who shares the sorrow of this country's history and its hopes for its future. I'm beginning to understand who these people are and who I am.

I've thought a lot about the comb and its responsibility. I've decided that my responsibility to Korea is both as a descendant of Empress Myeongseong and as an American. America has helped this country, for sure. But we've been selfish, too. I mean, we're still stuck in this 1950s Cold War mentality. I'm angry that we call North Korea "evil," as if we have the right to force our values on them. How arrogant. Yet I don't want them to develop nuclear bombs, and they need to be good world citizens. Yeah, okay, I get it—it's complicated. Still, I think America can do a lot more to promote peace. And unification, too.

As a Korean, I'm willing to do what I can for the country where I was born. As an American, naturally I want to help keep my country great. I guess what I'm saying is that I want to make both of my countries proud—the one that gave me life and the one that gave me a family—because I'm proud to be a child of both.

As the cab drives through the busy streets of Itaewon, I reach inside my backpack and feel the envelopes that I've been carrying since I left home. Inside one is twenty thousand dollars cash. Inside the other is ten thousand.

I'm anxious to get to my meeting. In spite of the fourteen-hour flight, I'm not tired. I'm excited to see Mrs. Hong and tell her that I'm there to keep my promise to her. But I have to admit that all the secrecy about this meeting has me more than a little nervous.

The cab pulls up to a glass building. I see the open space above the Han River a few blocks away. I pay the cab driver and roll my suitcase into the lobby. I give the young receptionist the name of the man I'm supposed to meet. She tells me to wait. I take a seat in one of the lobby's Le Corbusier chairs. I watch as people walk by carrying briefcases and with determined looks on their faces. What they call the "Miracle on the Han River" is on full display—the rise from a dirt-poor nation to one of the world's most modern in a short forty years. I marvel at these industrious, intelligent people. I'm proud to be one of them.

Soon, a short man in a dark suit with eyes to match greets me. "I am Mr. Choi," he says with a slight bow. He doesn't extend his hand.

I bow respectfully and in Korean introduce myself.

Mr. Choi stays with Korean. "Shall we go for a walk?" he asks.

I assumed we'd meet in Mr. Choi's office. Then I remember Mr. Han saying that meetings between people from the North and South are done off the record. So I give my suitcase to the receptionist and follow Mr. Choi out to the street. He walks with his hands behind his back as if he's out for a midday stroll. I start to talk, but he quickly cuts me off with a wave.

"Let us walk a little before we talk," he says.

We walk toward the Han River. White clouds roll across the sky. The humidity is low, and the temperature is comfortably warm. We reach a small park and sit on a bench facing the river. Mr. Choi folds his hands in front of him and lifts an eyebrow. "This is a generous thing you are doing for Mrs. Hong," he says.

"She's my grandmother. I made a promise to her."

"Yes, we know about Mrs. Hong. She was an ianfu for the Japanese, and she was sympathetic to the communists. She even worked for them. She also worked in a kijichon after the Korean War. She has a thick file. She has had—how should I say?—a questionable past."

Excuse me? *Questionable past?* I turn toward Mr. Choi, ready to tell him what my Korean grandmother did for her country. I catch myself before I do. Perhaps he knows. But, like a typical Korean, he's more concerned about his country's honor than the rights of an individual.

I look at the river and nod. "Yes, Mr. Choi, I know all that about Mrs. Hong. She's had a tough life."

"Why, Ms. Carlson? Why would you spend so much of your money to do this thing?"

I meet his eyes. "Because she's my grandmother," I say, speaking Korean again. "I have a duty to her."

Mr. Choi half smiles. "You speak Korean well. Korean-American adoptees rarely learn our language. So do you have the money?"

I reach in my pocket and give him the envelope with twenty thousand dollars in it. He thumbs through the bills and is satisfied that it's all there.

"It is arranged for tomorrow," he says, tucking the envelope inside his suit coat. "You will need another ten thousand dollars for the North Koreans."

"I have it," I say. "So what's next?"

He gives me a slip of paper with the address of a bus station in the Sinchon area of Seoul. He tells me I should take Mrs. Hong there tomorrow morning before 8:30 a.m. He says we have to find the bus to Munsan. It's not an official bus, he says, so I won't need a ticket. There, we'll meet a man named Mr. Ryu, who'll collect the fee for the North Koreans. The bus will take us to the American military base outside the Demilitarized Zone. The Americans will do an inspection. Then they'll take us to Panmunjom, where our meeting will take place.

Mr. Choi puts on a serious look. "Ms. Carlson, do exactly as you are told. Panmunjom is not a place to be taken lightly."

"I understand," I say.

Mr. Choi pushes himself off the bench and heads back to the government building as if I'm not there. I walk behind him in silence. When we get there, he goes to his office without saying good-bye. I grab my suitcase, go outside, and hail a cab. I give the driver the address for Mrs. Hong's apartment.

◆ ◆ ◆

It's late afternoon when we pull up to the eight-story apartment building. It looks exactly like it did a year earlier, as if it couldn't possibly get any more run-down. I take my backpack and suitcase and climb out of the cab. As I walk up to Mrs. Hong's building, I'm surprised at how nervous I am.

I press the number 627 on the intercom and wait. There's no answer. I press it again. Finally a voice comes over the intercom and says something in Korean. I can't tell if it's Mrs. Hong.

"This is Anna Carlson. I'm looking for Mrs. Hong."

There's a pause. Then, "Ja-young. How nice of you to pay a visit. You may come in." I smile to myself hearing my birth grandmother's perfect English again. The security door buzzes, and I walk through. I take the elevator to the sixth floor and go to Mrs. Hong's apartment. I knock, and the door opens.

It's only been a year since I saw her last, but she looks several years older. Her hair is grayer, and the wrinkles on her face are deeper than they were before. Her head shakes slightly with what looks like the early onset of Parkinson's disease. She doesn't stand as straight as she did, but her eyes are still bright.

"*Anyohaseyo,*" I say with a proper bow.

"*Anyohaseyo,* Ja-young," she replies.

"It's very good to see you," I say in Korean.

"Your Korean is very good," she says, keeping the conversation in Korean. "You don't have much of an accent."

"I've been told I have a good ear for languages," I say.

My Korean grandmother smiles and tells me to come in. I take off my shoes and follow her to the low table in front of the window. A fresh mugunghwa blossom floats in a bowl on the sill. The frame that holds the photographs of Mrs. Hong's family and my birth mother still sits on the table. And, of course, the room smells of kimchi. I can't believe I'm back here in Mrs. Hong's apartment. It's surreal.

I take a seat at the table and put my backpack on the floor. Mrs. Hong leans in to the table. "Ja-young, do you have the comb?"

"Yes, ma'am," I answer. "It's safe at home."

"And how do you feel about having it?"

I sigh. "It's a lot of responsibility."

Mrs. Hong sits up straight. "Yes," she says, "I know."

After a moment, I say, "I brought you something." I reach inside my backpack and pull out the photo album that I made a year earlier. "I thought you'd like to have this," I say. "I made it for my birth mother. I've added pictures from my senior year in college. I didn't have a chance to tell you much about myself last year."

Mrs. Hong bites her lower lip. "I am honored," she says, taking the album as if it were a treasure. "I want you to tell me everything about each photograph."

Since Mother died and I had to move back home, I haven't had anyone to share my life with. Dad has his own issues, and anyway, he's my Dad, if you know what I mean. All my girlfriends want to talk about is men and sex. And even my adopted friends don't understand how I feel about being Korean. But now I have Mrs. Hong, my Korean grandmother, who's been through so much. I know I can talk to her about anything.

So I pull my chair next to her and open the photo album. We go through it together, page by page, like best friends catching up after a long time apart. We talk in both English and Korean, switching between the two as easily as changing stations on a radio. She listens carefully as I tell the story behind each photo. She asks questions and nods thoughtfully at my answers. We laugh a lot.

Two hours later, we close the photo album, and I pick up Mrs. Hong's photos from the table and study them. "I'd like a copy of these, if it isn't too much to ask. I want to know more about them. And your grandparents and aunts and uncles, too."

"Of course," Mrs. Hong answers. "They are your family, too. It is important that you know."

"But not tonight," I say, setting the photos down. "I'll be in Seoul for five days. We'll have plenty of time to talk. I need to go to my hotel and rest. You should rest, too. We'll have to get going early tomorrow."

Mrs. Hong raises an eyebrow. "Tomorrow?"

I pick up the bowl with the mugunghwa and stare at the purple blossom with the yellow pistil in the center. I say, "Last year, I promised I'd help you meet your sister. I'm here to keep that promise."

Her eyes soften, and her mouth opens a bit. "Soo-hee? Do you know something about my onni?"

"Yes. She's living in Pyongyang. She never married or had any children. After the Korean War, she became a nurse."

"That sounds like her," Mrs. Hong says. "What else can you tell me?"

I set the mugunghwa blossom on the table. "Well, ma'am, you can find out for yourself. You and I are going to Panmunjom tomorrow, where you'll meet her. It won't be a long meeting—less than an hour."

She stays silent for a long time, and her head shakes a little. I can almost see the images of her sister in her mind as she takes in what I just said. Her eyes turn watery. She gazes at the photographs and says, "Ever since I learned Soo-hee was alive, I have dreamed of seeing her again. I never thought it would happen."

She looks from the photos and smiles at me. "Tonight will be a very long night."

FORTY-NINE

The next morning I get up before my alarm goes off and take a cab to Mrs. Hong's building. It's a perfect summer day, which seems fitting. The cab waits for me while I go get Mrs. Hong. Before I can press 627 on the intercom, the security door buzzes open. I take the elevator to the sixth floor to Mrs. Hong's apartment. Her door is open, and I step in.

She's standing in the middle of the room, facing me. She's wearing her yellow hanbok, with long, loose sleeves. She has braided her hair and pinned it back with a beautiful ebony binyeo. The light from her apartment window surrounds her. She looks like a queen.

I greet her with a bow. "Are you ready?" I ask.

"I am," she replies.

I pick up her travel bag, and she takes my arm. We walk out to the cab. I help her in and climb in the other side. I give the driver the bus station address. We pull onto the street and make our way across the Han River and into the Sinchon area of Seoul. The streets are steep, and all around are green hills, some topped with granite cliffs. The flat spaces between the hills are crammed with apartment buildings. Sinchon is alive with energy.

We make our way through narrow streets jammed with tiny Korean cars and arrive at a bus terminal. I pay the cab driver and then help Mrs. Hong. She holds my arm as we walk through the bus station filled with college students carrying suitcases and backpacks. The students stare at Mrs. Hong in her hanbok. She keeps her eyes forward.

We find the bus to Munsan. Before I can help Mrs. Hong aboard, a short man in a black suit comes up to us. "I am Mr. Ryu," he says from underneath twitchy eyebrows. "Who are you?"

I tell him, and he checks us off a list. "Do you have the fee?" he asks.

I give Mr. Ryu the envelope with the ten thousand dollars Dad got with a second mortgage. He does a quick count and lets us on the bus. We take seats near the front. The bus is less than half full of people waiting silently.

"Are you comfortable?" I ask Mrs. Hong.

Her head shakes a little, and I think she's saying no. Instead, she says, "I am a little nervous."

Yeah, I'm nervous, too, although for a different reason. I'm not sure if Soo-hee will be in Panmunjom when we get there. It seems like this entire arrangement was a little too easy, a little too dependent on money. I'm worried that they've scammed me.

After a few minutes, an overweight bus driver in a white shirt and black cap climbs aboard and starts the bus. We pull away, and Mr. Ryu takes a seat in the front row. The bus grinds through its gears, and we head north. Soon we're out of the city. Rice paddies in amazing geometric patterns cover the hills. The morning sun makes diamonds in the paddy water. Farmers in straw hats bend over rice stalks. A crane stands like a statue at the edge of an irrigation pond.

Mrs. Hong sits straight with her hands in her lap. She looks out the window. Her reflection doesn't show her wrinkles and scars, and she looks like a much younger woman. Her head shakes again, as if she approves of what she sees outside.

The countryside changes from fields to forest. We pass through the city of Munsan and cross the muddy Imjin River. I remember reading in my history class about the battle that took place here in 1592. The Japanese army defeated the Korean cavalry, forcing King Seonjo to seek an alliance with the Chinese. The battle of Imjin created a divided Korea. And now, over four hundred years later, it's still divided. I shake my head at the irony.

A few miles later we come to a gate and a high fence surrounded on both sides by razor wire. The sign over the gate reads "Camp Bonifas—In Front of Them All." Behind the fence are green military buildings and a huge tank with its gun facing the gate. An enormous American flag flies atop a tall flagpole. An American soldier holding some kind of assault rifle raises his hand. The bus stops, and the soldier stands in front of it with his rifle at his chest. Another soldier walks around the bus with some device that lets him see underneath.

An American sergeant with a crew cut and a Republic of Korea soldier in a white helmet come through the gate and board our bus. The American sergeant comes down the aisle, asking to see everyone's papers. He looks at my passport and says, "You're an American?"

"Yes, sir," I answer. "I'm here with my Korean grandmother. She's meeting her sister." I notice the large black pistol on his hip.

He points at Mrs. Hong. "Why's she dressed like that?"

I'm flustered and only manage a shrug. The sergeant glares at me over the top of my passport. "I don't like it," he says. "This is the most dangerous place on earth. We don't allow just anyone through here. And I don't like the way she's dressed. Both of you need to go back."

Suddenly someone inside me takes over, and I'm not flustered anymore. I stand to face the sergeant. "Sir," I say, "I'm here to help my grandmother. I won't cause any trouble, and neither will she. She's dressed like this because it's what Korean women wear on special occasions. Surely you and the American government don't want to stop a meeting between two sisters who haven't seen each other in over sixty years. Do you, Sergeant?"

I return the sergeant's stare. After a few seconds, he closes my passport and gives it back to me. "Be sure you follow the rules," he orders. He goes back to the front of the bus, and I take my seat next to Mrs. Hong. She nods at me.

The ROK soldier steps forward and talks to the passengers in Korean. He tells us the bus will take us to Panmunjom, where there will be North Korean soldiers. He tells us to stay together and not make any gestures or even make eye contact with them. He says an ROK soldier will take us inside a building where our meetings will take place.

The ROK soldier and the American sergeant get off the bus. The soldier with the rifle in front of the bus steps aside, and we drive on toward Panmunjom. The road goes past open fields and through another high fence with razor wire on top. We pass through a security gate and come to a row of pale blue, one-story barracks. Between each one is an ROK soldier at the tae kwon do ready position. At the other end of the barracks, North Korean soldiers stand holding rifles to their chests. Mr. Ryu tells us to get off the bus and go inside the building in front of us. "Do not say anything until you are inside," he says firmly.

We let the other passengers go ahead of us and then follow them outside. The sun makes me squint. As an ROK soldier hurries me to the door, I catch a glimpse of a North Korean soldier at the other end of the barracks. He looks at me with hate-filled eyes.

We enter a long, plain room with metal tables and chairs. There are windows all around and a door at the opposite end. I help Mrs. Hong into a chair and sit next to her. As we wait, the North Korean soldier I saw outside peers through a window at us. I turn away before our eyes meet again.

One by one, people come in through the door at the far end, and North Korean and South Korean loved ones meet again. They bow, hug, cry a little, and settle in to tell each other about their lives.

Mrs. Hong and I wait five minutes, then ten. I'm a basket case. There must have been a mistake. I look at Mrs. Hong. She has her hands in her lap, watching the door at the far end of the room. Her head no longer shakes.

We wait another five minutes. I'm about to ask Mr. Ryu where Soo-hee is when the door at the end of the room opens. Sunlight pours through, and an old woman steps in. Her back is bent, and she leans heavily on a cane. She's wearing cheap gray slacks and a blue sweater over a white blouse. Deep wrinkles line her face, and her left eye is white with cataract. She searches the room with her good eye.

Mrs. Hong slowly stands and steps to the middle of the room. In her hanbok, she moves with dignity and grace. Soo-hee sees her and goes to her. They stand apart, looking at each other for several seconds. Then Soo-hee raises her hand, and her sister reaches out and tenderly takes it. They clasp each other's fingers, making a single fist, and do the same with their other hands. As everyone in the room goes quiet, the sisters step close to each other, holding each other's gaze. Without a word, they turn around each other in a slow dance and nod their approval.

◆ ◆ ◆

I see Jae-hee and Soo-hee sitting in front of their home in the hills outside of Sinuiju playing yut. From the kitchen window, their mother looks on with a smile. Their father leans against the front door, arms crossed, watching his girls with obvious pride.

Jae-hee tosses the yut sticks in the air, and all four land with the flat side down. She has tossed a *mo*, the highest possible score, and has won the game. She giggles with delight. Soo-hee pretends to be upset that she has lost.

Jae-hee sidles up to her sister, and Soo-hee puts an arm around her. "You are lucky at yut, little sister," Soo-hee says. "You are lucky in everything. I think, someday, you will be an empress."

And they sit together, side by side, under the persimmon tree and watch the setting sun turn blood red.

AUTHOR'S NOTE

SAVING THE SOUL OF A NATION

"If we don't learn from history, we are doomed to repeat it."

—George Santayana

Every Wednesday at noon, a group of elderly women march on the Japanese embassy in Seoul, South Korea, demanding an apology from the government of Japan. They march in the pouring rain, bitter cold, and stifling humidity that only Seoul can dish out. They have not missed a single Wednesday in over twenty-three years. They are the last of an army of comfort women—women the Japanese military raped and tortured as sex slaves during World War II. They are all more than eighty years old now, and many are in their nineties. The Koreans call them "grandmothers," a term of great honor and respect.

Their ranks are dwindling fast.

The estimated number of women forced into sexual slavery by the Japanese varies depending on who is doing the counting. Some Japanese nationalists say there were fewer than twenty thousand and that they were former prostitutes or willing volunteers. But the evidence supports a much higher number. Today most historians agree there were more than two hundred thousand women across Asia, predominantly Korean and Chinese, believed to have been forced to work as sex slaves in Japanese military brothels. Two hundred thousand women serving an army of over seven million. That's one woman for every thirty-five soldiers. They were Filipino, Chinese, even Dutch, but the vast majority were Korean. Some were as young as thirteen.

As the women march, you can still see the pain and humiliation in their faces seventy years later. The Japanese raped these women, these grandmothers, up to forty times per day. They were repeatedly beaten and tortured. They suffered horribly from venereal disease, and the Japanese forced them to have crude abortions when they got pregnant. Many were executed. And many committed suicide.

The empire of Japan formally surrendered on September 2, 1945. Since then, it has issued a number of mostly informal apologies for its actions during the war. Many apologies were insincere at best. For example, on September 6, 1984, thirty-nine years after the war ended, a famously disingenuous "apology" delivered to Korean President Chun Doo Hwan by Emperor Hirohito was stated as follows:

> It is indeed regrettable that there was an unfortunate past between us for a period in this century, and I believe that it should not be repeated again.

In the early 1990s, after a few brave comfort women found the courage to come forward, the Japanese issued another series of informal apologies. But just like Hirohito's, most were disingenuous. They often used the word *owabi* for "apology"—a word in Japanese only slightly weightier than "excuse me." One "official" apology was the Kono statement issued by Chief Cabinet Secretary Yohei Kono in

1993, which quickly came under fire and is still debated to this day. But the outrage grew around the globe, and finally bowing to the pressure, the Japanese government set up the Asian Women's Fund in 1995. The fund was a quasi-public organization to collect donations from Japanese citizens (there were no government contributions) to distribute compensation to comfort women. Run by volunteers (not the government), the fund collected less than $5 million and distributed it to only 285 comfort women. The Japanese government closed it in March 2007.

On December 28, 2015, Korea and Japan reached a settlement on the comfort women issue where the Japanese government agreed to formally apologize and provide reparations of $8.3 million if Korea agreed to henceforth refrain from criticizing Japan over the issue. However, for the comfort women and many Koreans, the settlement falls far short of their demands. For example, Japan's apology does not admit coercion or that the imperial army was directly involved in recruiting and administering the comfort woman program, both of which are well documented. Also, Japan does not have to teach the truth about the comfort woman atrocity or revise school textbooks that whitewash the issue.

The surviving grandmothers insist their protests are not about money. So outside the Japanese embassy they march, insisting Japan meet *all* of their demands. However, it's unlikely Japan ever will, especially with nationalist Shinzo Abe in the prime minister's office. It's a shame—a tragedy, really. Meeting these simple demands before all the grandmothers die could help restore a modicum of the dignity stolen from them over seventy years ago.

But just as importantly, it would restore Japan's own honor and save its very soul.

—*William Andrews*

For more information or to donate, e-mail info@kaforumca.org or write to:

Korean American Forum of California 가주한미포럼

701 S. Kingsley Dr. Suite #301

Los Angeles, CA 90005

PHOTO GALLERY

A comfort woman liberated in China in 1945.
The author kept this photo in view as he wrote
Daughters of the Dragon: A Comfort Woman's Story.

A photo of a typical comfort station.

A former comfort woman telling her story.
Photograph by Tsukasa Yajima

The author (center) with Grandma Lee (second from left),
one of the few surviving comfort women.

ACKNOWLEDGMENTS

To my wife, Nancy, who always supported me in this and all my endeavors; to my daughter, Elizabeth, who inspires me; to all my family, friends, and colleagues who read the book and provided input; thank you.

SELECTED BIBLIOGRAPHY

This book is a work of fiction. Nevertheless, it is based on historical facts. To learn more about comfort women and Korea, see the following books:

On Comfort Women

Wallace Edwards. *Comfort Women: A History of Japanese Forced Prostitution During the Second World War*, Amazon Digital Services, 2013.

George Hicks. *The Comfort Women: Japan's Brutal Regime of Enforced Prostitution in the Second World War*, W. W. Norton & Company, 1997.

Dai Sil Kim-Gibson. *Silence Broken: Korean Comfort Women*, Mid-Prairie Books, 1999.

Korean Council for Women Drafted for Military Sexual Slavery by Japan. *True Stories of the Korean Comfort Women*, Cassell, 1996.

Peipei Qui. *Chinese Comfort Women: Testimonies from Imperial Japan's Sex Slaves*, Oxford University Press, 2014.

Jan Ruff-O'Henne. *Fifty Years of Silence: The Extraordinary Memoir of a War Rape Survivor*, Random House, 2008.

C. Sarah Soh. *The Comfort Women: Sexual Violence and Postcolonial Memory in Korea and Japan*, University of Chicago Press, 2009.
Yuki Tanaka. *Japan's Comfort Women*, Routledge, 2001.
Yuki Tanaka. *Hidden Horrors: Japanese War Crimes in World War II*, Westview Press, 1997.
Yoshimi Yoshiaki. *Comfort Women*, Columbia University Press, 2002.

On Korean History

Michael Breen. *The Koreans. Who They Are, What They Want, Where Their Future Lies*, Thomas Dunne Books, 2004.
Bruce Cummings. *Korea's Place in the Sun: A Modern History*, W. W. Norton & Company, 2005.
Don Oberdorfer. *The Two Koreas: A Contemporary History*, Basic Books, 2001.
Keith Pratt. *Everlasting Flower: A History of Korea*, Reaktion Books, 2006.
Michael J. Seth. *A Concise History of Korea*, Rowman & Littlefield, 2006.

AUTHOR Q & A

Q: What inspired you to write this book?

A: Probably the most influential thing is my daughter, who was born in Korea. Because of her, I learned about the country and thought it was fascinating. Especially considering what happened in the twentieth century.

Q: Like what?

A: The three regimes that controlled the peninsula—the Japanese, the communists, and the Americans. And the comfort women. I'm continually amazed at how few Americans know what happened to these women. I believe this story needs to be told. And if I may, I'd like to encourage readers who agree and who enjoyed the book to recommend it to others and write reviews on retailers' websites.

Q: There's a lot of history in this book. Is it accurate?

A: First, please know that I'm a storyteller, not a history expert. Still, I tried to make this book as historically accurate as possible. I did a ton of research and got help from several history experts. So I'd have to say yes, it's accurate.

Q: Was it difficult to write some of the more brutal scenes?

A: Very difficult. I tried hard to be respectful of the reader and the comfort women. I did not want to be exploitive. But I felt I had a responsibility to show what actually happened to these women. It has to be brutal because that's what they experienced. Still, there were things I couldn't write. For example, when Colonel Matsumoto first rapes Jae-hee, I couldn't write that in real time. I had to pull it out of the narrative into the present-day frame. Even then, it was a challenge to write that chapter.

Q: You draw parallels between what the Japanese did in the comfort stations and what the Americans did in the kijichons. Were the Americans as bad as the Japanese?

A: Of course not. But what I wrote about the Americans is true. Until recently, the US military turned a blind eye to some of the illegal and unethical things our troops were doing in the kijichons; tricking girls, putting them in situations they could not possibly get out of. It wasn't anything close to what the Japanese did, however. They actually sponsored the comfort stations. But as Jae-hee says to Colonel Crawford, from the girls' perspective, what's the difference?

Q: What about the two-headed dragon with five toes?

A: I invented the two-headed dragon. However, the emperor and empress were the only ones allowed to have dragon artifacts with five toes.

Q: You talk a lot about Empress Myeongseong.

A: Yes, she's a fascinating figure in Korean history. The Koreans worship her. And please forgive a plug, but I'm working on a loose sequel to *Daughters of the Dragon: A Comfort Woman's Story* called *The Dragon Queen*. It's the story of Empress Myeongseong.

One last thing: I'd like to ask readers to please go to their online retailer and write a review of this book. Or send me an e-mail at bill@williamandrewsbooks.com. It's the only way I can get feedback from my readers!

ABOUT THE AUTHOR

William Andrews wrote at night and on weekends (and sometimes during workdays) for fifteen years leading up to his debut novel, *The Essential Truth*, a thriller that won first place in the 2008 Mayhaven Contest for fiction. He worked for more than thirty years as a copywriter and a marketing executive for several Fortune 500 companies and then as head of his own advertising agency. *Daughters of the Dragon*, a work of historical fiction inspired by Andrews's Korean-born daughter, is his third novel and follows the success of his 2014 IPPY Award–winning thriller, *The Dirty Truth*. Now retired and writing full-time, Andrews lives in Minneapolis with his wife.